THE MISTRESS
OF DARA
ISLAND

ABOUT THE AUTHOR

Averil Kenny grew up on a dairy farm and began work in the tourism industry at a young age. She studied Education at James Cook University and Journalism at the University of Queensland. Averil currently lives in Far North Queensland with her husband and four children. When not dreaming up stories, she can be found nestled in her favourite yellow wingback chair reading and sipping tea, in her library overlooking the rainforest.

Also by Averil Kenny
Those Hamilton Sisters
The Girls of Lake Evelyn

THE MISTRESS OF DARA ISLAND

AVERIL KENNY

ZAFFRE

First published in 2024 by Echo Publishing
A Bonnier Books UK company
This edition published in 2024 by
ZAFFRE
An imprint of The Zaffre Publishing Group
A Bonnier Books UK Company
4th Floor, Victoria House, Bloomsbury Square, London, England, WC1B 4DA
Owned by Bonnier Books
Sveavägen 56, Stockholm, Sweden

A CIP catalogue record for this book is
available from the British Library.

ISBN: 978-1-80418-874-3

Also available as an ebook and an audiobook

1 3 5 7 9 10 8 6 4 2

Typeset by IDSUK (Data Connection) Ltd
Printed and bound in Great Britain by Clays Ltd, Elcograf S.p.A.

MIX
Paper | Supporting
responsible forestry
FSC® C018072

Zaffre is an imprint of The Zaffre Publishing Group
A Bonnier Books UK Company
www.bonnierbooks.co.uk

For determined girls.
Especially mine.

PART ONE

And all I ask is a tall ship and a star to steer her by.
John Masefield

CHAPTER 1

PROMISED LAND

Dara Island, the Great Barrier Reef, 1957

Determination was Thalia's middle name. Or it should have been, were it not already *Blue* – so given by her ma, the proprietress of Dara Island. Named for a palette of impossible hues: the supreme turquoise of the Coral Sea encompassing their island paradise; the swarming fish shoals and shallow sea stars; the blue-glittered butterflies, fairywrens and kingfishers flashing through the jungle deep; the indigo skies of the monsoon; and the bright cyan gleam of her eyes. Thalia Blue, the heiress of Dara.

That, of course, had proved too fanciful a name for the intrepid tot growing up among the small working village of Dara's Mermaid Bay Resort, with her streaky driftwood curls perpetually wind tangled, her nose ever pink and peeling from the sun, her feet and shoulders always bare, nutbrown, salt dusted. Soon, she came to be known simply as Tally.

Eleven-year-old Tally was the whole island's daughter, not just the only child of Richard Ramsey, the most powerful man in the region. She was as beloved as he was feared.

But Ma, and Ma alone, called her Tally Ho …

'My Tally Ho – when she sets her mind on a thing, nothing can ever stand in her way.'

It was the nicest thing anyone had ever said about Tally, and no surprise it should come from Ma. There was not a kinder person, nor a gentler spirit in all the world than Nerissa Ramsey nee Forster. One day, when Dara was hers, Tally hoped to have as much wisdom and patience as Ma did – though she didn't like her chances. It was her determination that was the problem, for it always seemed to get the better of her.

This cicada-shrill summer morn had unfolded in familiar fashion: Tally had filched a fruit-platter breakfast from Anita in the resort kitchen, helped resort groundsman Frank with the coconut de-nutting, and swum with stingrays and reef sharks under the long jetty with her island playmate, Lila. Then, she had grown restless. Rebelliousness invariably followed restlessness, and so, Tally had set out to right the latest injustice in her young life.

While her father was doing his morning rounds of the resort, she determined to retrieve the red leatherette notebook he had confiscated from her weeks earlier for some forgotten misdeed and then locked away in his hallowed office – a place no Ramsey woman was permitted. She was sick of asking, and being denied. Her father, for all that he terrified her, would not stand in her way.

Had she a sibling, Tally might have engaged their help to keep watch outside the Ramseys' grand plantation house. 'Eyrie' was perched high on a rainforest rise overlooking the resort below, the panoramic sweep of bejewelled ocean and the distant mainland. With no one to whistle alarm, however, Tally tried to keep one ear turned towards the pebble path cutting up through the garden terrace. At any minute her father might return, and if Tally was caught, she'd be sorry indeed. Even Ma's intercessions wouldn't save her.

It was worth the risk. That notebook contained her 'Dara Happenings', and he had no right to steal something so private! In truth, it was only her latest Happenings book. She had ninety-nine others like it, for she was forever pilfering her father's spare account books to fill with the daily goings-on.

But this latest one was her juiciest yet, filled with more drama and intrigue than ever. She prided herself on being the first to know anything that happened here, spending inestimable hours trailing around behind the live-in staff of Dara's Mermaid Bay Resort, gathering their news and views and funny titbits. While running and hiding from her father over the years, she'd spent much time concealed in nooks and crannies across the resort, from guest wardrobes, to the groundskeepers' shed and underneath the chef's bench in the brasserie. In this manner, she'd gleaned so many interesting things from the people who made the beds, or served the drinks, scrubbed the toilets and tended the grounds. Things no staff member of Dara wanted their boss to know, much less hold against them.

And he would, oh he would.

Tally had to get her Dara Happenings book back as much for all their sakes as her own. The thought had occurred to her that she might stop recording such flammable information in future, but only briefly. As the heiress, she was learning on the job the best way she knew how: by listening well, and seeking to understand how things really worked on this island, not how Richard Ramsey decreed they should be.

In the gloom of dark wood and unlit lamps, the humid air heavier still with the scent of leather, whisky and cigars, Tally kneeled in front of Father's safe. The combination had been easy to guess, knowing Father – the longitude and latitude of Dara Island. Tally would have used the very same combination.

There was a pile of notebooks upon her lap. Her own was indistinguishable from the ones Father used for business and accounts, so that she had to check each one in turn. She knew it had to be in here – this was his favourite place for confiscated items – but she was nearly at the bottom of the safe without yet turning it up. Her heart had begun to sink – at least, that was, before she found the treasure map.

There was no better way to describe it.

In the middle of Father's accounts book for nineteen forty-six – the year of her parents' marriage and her birth – was a leaf of paper. On it, a hand-drawn map with landmarks familiar to her young eye, the sprawling shape of Dara unmistakable. X marked a spot on the opposite side of Dara, on the staggering, jungled peak of Mount Teasdale. But what sort of treasure could possibly be buried all the way over *there*? It was at least twenty miles across wilderness and mountain ranges to reach Mount Teasdale, on the steep southern side. The map marked a route mostly following meandering creeks, but to Tally's knowledge, her father never explored the remote reaches of the island – no one ever did. So, why should he keep such a map hidden in here?

A ripple of heat up the nape of her neck told Tally: *This is important.* An innate sense she'd learned to trust, second only to her mother's love and just as unfailing. Her Happenings book momentarily forgotten, she turned the map towards the light seeping around the edges of the plantation shutters so that she might snaffle its every detail.

A second ripple of instinct warned Tally that time was up, moments before she heard the heavy crunch of footsteps on pebble. Soon those footsteps would ring out on the marble staircase, stride tall across the verandah, then rap down the hallway to this room.

Father.

Tally swore under her breath, shoving notebooks helter-skelter back into the safe. It was too late to restore his proper order. For one last moment, she gripped that map close to her face, committing it to her bright mind, before returning it to the ledger book and the safe's keeping. She leaped to her feet and skidded across the polished wood to the door.

Hurry, hurry, hurry!

He was on the stairs by the time she'd cleared the office door and hustled for the staircase. She hastened up those stairs two at a time, but her legs were not yet long enough and those stairs far too many.

Almost at the turn, where she would be blessedly out of sight, he had her.

'Thalia Ramsey!' Father's deep voice sounded like a pipe organ in the high-ceilinged hallway.

She lurched to a stop, small hand gripping the balustrade. Her eyes went on up the staircase to the first landing, where a small, sprite-like version of herself seemed to peer back at her, tongue poked out.

'*Come* here.'

Tally sighed, turned and descended the stairs to stand before her father. She lifted her face to his with an angle he knew all too well: *intransigent*.

'Where have you been this afternoon?' A mild tone, all the more ominous for its restraint.

'Out.'

'Out where?'

She crossed her arms. 'Out*side*.'

'The door to my office is wide open.'

'Maybe you left it that way.'

'Were you in my study just now, after your book?'

Tally's answer was light and quick. 'Nup.'

'In that case,' he said at last, 'you won't be concerned that I'm going to check if the notebook is right where I left it.'

Fear had hollowed out her knees, but her chin angled higher still. 'And then I can have it back.'

There was a creak of floorboards as Father went into his study, the sound of the safe being opened, and then those last dreadful seconds of hope in which it always seemed possible he might find some leniency in his soul ...

'Bloody impossible child!' The safe smashed closed with a reverberation Tally felt in her bones. 'Flaming wilful brat, I can't be rid of her soon enough!'

Tally began the slow inch backwards, aiming for the staff entrance. She could be out and free in sixty seconds!

Even that was not enough time.

'Thalia,' her father called now, 'go and pick a switch!' As though punishment was just another task he could delegate to someone with less power than he.

Tally already knew: she'd pick the limpest stick she could find.

At twilight, sporting fresh welts on the back of her legs, Tally tiptoed out of the rear staff entrance of Eyrie into the sultry air. She avoided the well-lit hill drive used by the service buggies, sliding instead into the winding rainforest paths of the resort. The fabled treehouses of Mermaid Bay Resort were set on a deep, forested ravine, separated from the resort amenities by a seventy-foot suspension bridge. Tally had spent many an idyllic hour with her friend Lila playing among the treehouses and on the bridge, pretending they were dryads.

But there was no whimsy in her heart this evening as she hurried over the bridge and down the hill to the main lodge and facilities on the bay below.

The beach was covered with millions of sun-bleached staghorn coral pieces. With every gentle wave kissing the shore, myriad coral rolled and tinkled. Tally thought it the sweetest sound in all the world, *especially* when her ears continued to ring from her father's latest tirade.

Dara's long jetty jutted out front of the main lodge. Tally went all the way to the end of it and plonked down, legs dangling high over the sea, to await the stars. She was not very well hidden, but there was only one person in the world who would come for her here.

This was one of Tally's favourite places. During the daytime, island and sea were an astonishing juxtaposition of emerald and aquamarine, and the jetty hummed with happy holidaymakers. But in the evening, once all the guests had returned to their treehouses, the blue-black infinity of the sea and the starry sky above were hers and hers alone.

On the end of the jetty was Dara's newly built underwater observatory – one of the first in the world and a feat of structural engineering. An upper gallery entered from the jetty, with a set of narrow stairs descending into a theatre hidden beneath the sea. It had been Ma's long-cherished dream for island visitors to experience the rainbow-hued underwater realm – from parrotfish to brain coral – as only sea divers once could. So proud was Ma of her observatory, that she spent most days manning her little store of island trinkets on the gallery level. This way, she never missed a guest's awe upon emerging from her grotto beneath.

It was one of the things Tally loved most about her mother: how she delighted in her guests' enchantment.

Close to the east side of Dara, out beyond a volcanic rock spill, lay a smaller isle. Officially known as Little Dara, it was colloquially called 'the Hat' for its resemblance to a wide-brimmed Akubra. In this sense, Dara was not just one island, but two; the bigger shielding the smaller from the mainland. Tally might be too old for such notions, but she still sometimes thought of the closely set islands as symbolic of Ma and herself.

Tally did not have to wait long before Ma arrived. She *felt* Ma even before hearing her footsteps creak down the jetty. Her shoulders drew towards her ears, tension and longing bunching up at the back of her neck. Ma's cool, slim hand slid under her hair to that very place, squeezing gently.

Release.

Tally's whole form softened against the lean arm abutting her own. Ma's favourite fragrance, L'heure Bleue, enveloped her with its romantic melancholy: *the blue hour*. They sat pressed against one another as the ocean lapped languidly on, tinkling coral.

Why couldn't they just stay like this, shoulder to shoulder, for always?

There were many things Ma might have said, things any other mother might have said: *Why must you goad him perpetually to rage? Why can't you just* behave, *Tally?* But she only kicked her legs in time with Tally's. With Ma breathing slow and evenly, Tally's heart and breath had no choice but to fall in sync. That was the wonder of a mother, wasn't it? Her heart guarded over the one she'd made long after it no longer nestled beneath her own.

'Tell me again,' Tally said, 'about when I was born.'

She felt her mother's smile in the softening of her body.

'Ah, my *ocean girl*. Before you were even born, you loved Dara so much, you were determined to take your first breath upon it. Your father wanted you to be delivered on the mainland, and he'd found the best doctors that money could buy in Brisbane. But you were having none of that! The very morning before we were due to leave, my waters broke – a whole six weeks early. Right from the get-go the contractions were too close together, too intense for me to make the journey. You were coming with the same ferocity you've always lived life, my darling.

'Your father sped to the mainland to bring back help. He was never going to make it, but he insisted on trying all the same. I was waiting for him on the shore, and before I knew it, you were crowning. I delivered you myself, with only Irene at my side. Three furious pushes on the edge of the Coral Sea, and here you were.'

'And then …' Tally's eyes were wide and shining. 'What did Irene say when she saw my feet …?'

Ma tucked a long curl behind Tally's ear. 'She said, *you hold onto that little mermaid, she might swim away!*'

Tally sighed, gazing down at her feet, at the special sign of her belonging to this island and the sea: webbed toes – second and third – on both feet.

Ducky! cried the children of Bellen Beach's tiny local school, and *Inbred Island Girl!* But try as they might, they could never turn something so unique and precious to Tally into a weapon against her. She had been marked out for her destiny as heiress of Dara.

'And your father's *face* when he returned to Eyrie later that morning, and there I was, with a babe in arms!' Ma looked up at the stars. '*Send the doctor away*, I told him, *I've delivered her myself!* And then he didn't know whether to kiss me for making so little fuss of childbirth, or scold me for putting out the doctor and ferryman. I think he scolded first and kissed later.'

This was a departure from Ma's usual story, and Tally did not care for it. 'I *hate* him,' she blurted, the path between thought and mouth once again short-circuiting. She looked quickly to her mother, shame suffusing her cheeks.

Ma's delicate profile did not so much as flinch. Tally studied her pointed chin and small nose, the elegance of her long neck below a low chignon of warm, honey hair. Tally knew she had the most beautiful mother in all the world.

Her loathing now voiced, Tally decided she might as well go one further. 'I wish we had Dara all to *ourselves*!'

'But you *love* our visitors.'

It was pretty clear whom she wished to live without, but if Ma wasn't going to bite, Tally would say it outright: 'I wish it was like you and Grandpapa – just the *two* of us here. One day, I hope Mermaid Bay blows away in a cyclone, and Father along with it, then we can make Dara the way *we* want it!'

Ma did not respond. Tally frowned; they had talked of their shared dreams for Dara many a time – from a turtle hospital, to a clam garden, and even a marine-education hub.

Tally pressed in closer. 'I want to hear again about those days before Mermaid Bay – and *Father*.'

Ma lifted her arm, drawing Tally beneath. 'Well, it was a very different time and place then. Your grandpapa and I lived together in the old cottage, with our own orchard and chickens and goats, and all the fish in the sea. We didn't have any of this luxury and infrastructure back then, not Eyrie, nor Mermaid Bay Resort – you can thank your father for all of it.'

Tally would do no such thing! She nudged her mother on, impatiently. She'd heard the story of *Ma's* Dara a thousand times, and she'd ask for it countless more. Tally had never known her maternal grandfather, the genius who had planted them on this island – the most beautiful jewel in an archipelago of scattered emeralds. Ma's story was the closest she would ever come …

'Papa brought us here from Sydney in nineteen thirty-two, after my mother died. I was only six when Papa purchased Dara – for less than forty pounds. He suffered so terribly from his nerves, had a breakdown after my mother died, and he wanted to spend his later years in seclusion and self-sufficiency, far from his newspaper career and the city stress. Where better, he thought, than a remote tropical island in the Coral Sea?'

'*Nowhere* better,' Tally breathed dreamily. This evening, however, Ma seemed to stiffen at it, her voice laced with gentle caution.

'In many ways, it *was* an idyllic life – a simple paradise. But it was also a terribly lonely childhood for me, Tally. Apart from the Artists' Colony

12

over on the Hat, we hardly saw a soul.' She paused. 'You know, I didn't get to go away for an education, nor have *any* friends …'

'Why would you want to go *away* for school?' It was bad enough that Tally had to travel across to the mainland during term time to the small local school, where she had made far more enemies than friends. Determination *was* her middle name, and other children only stood in her way.

'An education is very important for a young woman's prospects,' Ma chided.

Tally tipped her head. 'But *why* should it be? You had your very own island! Just like one day, *I* will.' She was in a hurry to end Ma's unnerving new talk of education. There was heat prickling at the back of her neck – her instincts, which never lied.

'Tell me again about how Grandpapa made you the mistress of Dara,' Tally urged, even though she had this part committed to memory. Anything to push away the trepidation, ever intensifying, of what Ma was concealing. It was something bad, she knew it …

'Your grandpapa wrote it down in his last will and testament: *I entail my island, Dara, to my daughter, Nerissa, and to my first grandchild.*' Tally mouthed this along with her mother, smiling big and wide in the darkness.

'And one day, you'll write the same for me and my daughter,' Tally insisted.

'Which is *why*,' Ma pushed on, 'it's important that you receive a proper education – one befitting the heiress of a world-renowned resort island.'

Tally's hand grew clammy inside her mother's grip. 'What more is there to learn than what *you* teach me?'

Ma let silence reign, and in it Tally found her answer.

'No,' she said quietly. '*No …*'

Ma gently cupped her face. 'My Tally Ho,' she entreated.

Tally shook her head, vehemently at first, then turned her face to be cradled by her mother's hand. 'Please don't send me away, Ma. *Please!*'

Ma's voice quavered with empathy, but there was resolve in it, too. 'I'm not sending you away, my darling. I'm letting you go –'

'It's the same thing!'

'If you let me finish, it's very different. I have to let you go so that you might gain the education I was never permitted. So that you can make the *friends* I never had –'

'I have Lila! She's like a sister to me.'

'She's *not* your sister,' Ma said, so sharply that Tally flinched. Then Ma sighed, reverting to familiar gentleness. 'You've had a nice playmate in Lila, but you mustn't forget you're different to the rest of the island brats who come and go with our staff.'

'I *am* an island brat.'

'You need to understand the world outside your own.'

'Why? I'm never going to leave Dara! I'm going to live here all my life – like you. I only need to know how to take care of my island.'

Ma's voice grew firmer still. 'Yes, and that's why your father and I are giving you a world-class education at the very best girls' college in Brisbane.'

'*Brisbane!* But that's half a country away! I'll never *see* you!'

'You can come back every summer to be with us again.'

'A whole *year* away from Dara?!' It was worse than she had ever imagined possible.

'It will go quickly, you'll see! You'll be so busy making friends, perhaps you won't even want to come back at Christmas time.'

'Won't want to?! I'd be miserable every second away from Dara, and from you. I shall *die* of homesickness!'

There was a strength in her mother's voice to match Tally's rising panic. 'Your father says you'll mature beautifully away from home. Grow into an accomplished young woman, capable of running an international, five-star resort one day.'

Tally scowled. 'This was all *his* idea, wasn't it? He just wants to get rid of me! Since he can't beat it out of me, he's banishing me, instead.'

'You mustn't say such things about your father. He loves you.'

'He has a funny way of showing it.'

'Your father has always wanted the best for you, and *from* you. You're lucky to have a father who takes such an interest in proper discipline and formation of character. Your grandpapa ... found the same beyond him. I never want you to idolise my upbringing, Tally. I was quite the wild thing by the end of my girlhood. Without your father, I don't know what might have become of Dara – or me.'

'When are you sending me away?' What a *thing* to hear herself say!

'We've secured you a place for the new school year.'

Tally calculated quickly in her head. They were two weeks past Christmas, already. 'How long?' she whispered, full of dread.

Ma sighed. Even in the moon wash and starshine, there was no place for her mother's sorrow to hide. 'You'll leave on the *Sunlander* train from Bellen Beach next Sunday.'

Tally leaped to her feet. 'I will not! You can't make me go! I'll take my dory and row over to the Hat and I'll live there! If you don't want me here anymore, then I'll make my *own* island!'

With a howl, she hurtled down the jetty.

CHAPTER 2

KICKING AND SCREAMING

January 1957

Long before the morning glow infiltrated the mosquito netting around her bed, Tally's eyes flew open. The terrible day had arrived, despite all her fervent pleas and refusals.

She lay in stunned silence for a moment, before pitching out of bed.

After Ma had kissed her goodnight the previous evening, she had changed straightaway out of her pyjamas and into her escape outfit: camouflaging colours to blend into the shrubbery, shorts to make running, climbing, rowing, indeed whatever might be necessary, easier. She unhooked her knapsack from the wall and slid out of her bedroom, moving cautiously down the hallway. Reaching the double doors of her father's grand suite, she made herself statue-still, eyes straining on his doorknob, at any moment fearing the turn. Anxiety made her limbs quiver, her teeth chatter.

Not up yet. Fate was on her side today. She was meant *to stay . . .*

Stealthily, she descended the staircase on the bare balls of her feet, darting double quick past Father's office, then out across the wide verandah, pausing only to throw a shushing finger at the large cage housing his guard birds: a pair of black cockatoos. They looked balefully back at her, before exchanging vexed screeches. Even anticipating their treachery, she jumped.

Demons!

She hurried down the marble stairs, neck prickling hotly at the thought of him now watching her from his bedroom window, flinging open his white shutters to holler after her. Tucking her head low, she melded from hedged garden into the shadowed, winding paths of the resort, headed for the hill.

Just before the lookout, she passed the unmarked turn-off, which led deeper uphill into the jungle, through a bamboo-forested path to Grandpapa Forster's humble grave. Tally was never able to dash by without vigilant breath holding. The alternative? Possession through mere breathing.

It was hair-raising to *know* your grandpapa's bones lay just beyond an eerie, talking corridor of bamboo. A thicket filled with sepulchral gloom, choked with vine snakes and creeping tentacles and climbing ferns that seemed to burgeon out of his grave as if he was taking back the island by primordial force. Tally didn't want Grandpapa to capture her, too. Ma had always said she would be buried by her papa's side, and just the thought of that dark grove waiting to claim her mother made her sick with fear.

He wasn't taking Tally's soul, that's for damn sure!

Tally's cheeks popped as she emerged onto a stone terrace jutting above a vertiginous cliff, taking in sweeping 180-degree views. The first embers of daybreak were flaring on the east horizon. But it was to the mainland she looked: a steep, heaving topography of green, with estuarine channels opening out like a network of capillaries, the neighbouring town of Bellen Beach hidden around the headland.

Her eyes drilled into that distant olivine, searching for the first glimpse of the ferry, a speck glinting in the sunshine, island bound.

Logically, she knew it was an hour too early, but she could not help the rush of terror.

No sign of her kidnappers, yet.

Away now she flew, taking the unmarked rock staircase down through the dim jungle to the staff village. This back shortcut circumvented Mermaid Bay Resort and was used only by the longest-term island staff, who remembered the old route to Lookout Point.

The plan, once she managed to slip inside the staff village, was to hide out in her friend Lila's house until she'd properly missed the ferry – giving her mother and father plenty of time to change their minds about this whole shipping-her-away thing. Lila, she trusted, would keep her out of sight until they'd reconsidered. Just to be *sure* they couldn't send her away, Tally had unpacked her trunk after lights out, and dispersed everything Ma had so neatly folded in. It hurt her heart to undo all Ma's hard work, especially after she found the loving note hidden in the trunk for when she unpacked at boarding school.

The sea, beginning to glimmer with morning fire, could be glimpsed through tree breaks as she pounded down the staircase. Her bare feet, toughened by a lifetime of walking Coral Beach, did not give her a moment's pause. Brush turkeys and scrub fowl ditched comically from her pathway as she went, panting hard.

Don't stop, don't stop, don't stop.

She entered the village at the rear, slipping past the amenities and laundry block, weaving her way quickly through clothes lines and outhouses, the communal kitchen, and then the well-trod, narrow lanes between the staff cabins. The subdued camp atmosphere of the servants' village – woodsmoke, low rattle and hum – was a familiar comfort. How *could* she be sent away on a day beginning as ordinarily as this?

The accommodation Lila shared with her mother, Irene Threadwell, head housekeeper of Mermaid Bay, was by far the largest in the staff village, owing to Irene's seniority and loyalty. Not a cabin like the rest, but a proper, two-bedroom house. Irene had been a stalwart fixture on Dara all Tally's life; legend said she was originally from the old Artists' Colony on the Hat. And though she was an employee, Irene was also Nerissa Ramsey's oldest, perhaps *only* friend. They made an odd pair; peppery Irene, and Tally's gentle mother.

Tally knew Irene would already be at her station for the day, making this the perfect hide-out while the storm blew over – or the ferry *blew up*.

Commending herself on having reached Lila's house without being seen, Tally crept onto the front porch and knocked quietly at the glass sliding door. After a moment, there was a rustling of curtains. Lila's feline-pretty face appeared in a halo of sleep-mussed, golden-brown hair.

Tally motioned frantically, answering Lila's alarm with a threatening look.

Lila unlatched the door and stood back as Tally crashed in. 'Good *grief*, Tally – you're supposed to be getting ready for the ferry.'

This was not *quite* the spirit of camaraderie Tally had hoped for.

Lila motioned her to their dining table and hurried to bring water for the panting Tally. While she gulped at her drink, Lila's face was a silent picture of unquiet concern.

Only now, sitting here before her childhood playmate, did Tally realise how much the last few years had insinuated themselves between them. Just over three years separated the pair, but only one of them could still be called a girl. It was abundantly apparent, in Lila's small nightie, that *she* had become a young woman.

How had Tally missed this critical widening of their differences? Admittedly, they spent little time together now that Lila was working full-time as a housemaid, but Lila had still been *Lila*: older and wiser friend, always steadfast and calm. But now look at her, sitting there all grown up and disapproving.

Tally plonked down her glass. 'I just need somewhere to hide out until the ferry's gone. Is that too much to ask?'

Lila's green eyes were wide with pity. 'You can't hide *here* of all places ...'

'Why not? I thought you'd be *happy* to see me.'

Lila shifted uncomfortably, glancing behind her. She leaned forward, quite earnest. 'You must know they'll hold the ferry until you're on it?'

Tally's face heated. She'd thought of no such thing. 'Father would never let the ferry fall behind schedule!'

'He *will* to save face. Everyone knows that you're leaving today. There's going to be a big line of honour to farewell you at the jetty. Do you think Mr Ramsey will let you embarrass him in front of everyone?'

Tally blinked disbelievingly. *Embarrass him?* These were the words of the friend normally so sympathetic to Tally? 'But I *can't* leave Dara!'

'Seems to me you don't have a choice.'

'That's why I'm here,' Tally whispered, throat aching. 'I'll stay with you. I can bunk in here, help you with your job.' *Anything* to be allowed to stay.

'You can't live with *me*. We're from different *worlds*, Tally.'

'Are not! We've always played in the same waters, eaten from the same orchard and fishing hauls, gone across to Bellen Beach School each day together ...'

'And now you're going off to get a fine secondary education, while I'm staying here to make beds and scrub toilets.' This was said matter-of-factly, with nothing bitter in it.

'I'll swap you, then!' cried Tally.

Lila sighed. 'You just don't know how lucky you are. You take it all for granted – Dara, your whole future – and you don't know what it's like, being raised to serve rather than *be* served. How *good* it must feel to live up there on the top instead of down here.' Lila had never spoken to Tally of such things, but she didn't look to regret a word of it.

'You can leave Dara anytime you want,' Tally said. 'Nobody is keeping you here. Go make a life for yourself off the island, if you hate it so much.'

'That's not what I mean,' Lila said with soft patience. 'I'll never get to have what you do. Your very own *island*. You'll be owner of Dara one day – and you're not even willing to go away for a little while and earn it.'

'But I don't *have* to earn it. It's already mine.'

Behind Lila, the bathroom door banged sharply open. Tally yelped in surprise. Irene Threadwell strode forth, her small eyes fixed sternly on Tally.

Irene hadn't left yet for work? It was unheard of. Foreboding brushed Tally's neck.

'You're ready to go,' Irene said. 'Good. I suggest you keep up this punctuality for the rest of our journey south.'

Our journey? Tally stared at her, flummoxed.

'Oh, Tally,' Lila soothed, 'my mum is chaperoning you down to Brisbane. Didn't they tell you?'

'*Irene* is taking me away?' Tally looked at her, aghast. She had run straight to her kidnapper! Tally had always suspected Lila's mother didn't like her, and now, reading the satisfaction in Irene's face, she was *sure* of it.

Lila's eyes filled with tears. 'I'll miss you, Tally. Dara just won't be the same without you.'

Tally trudged back up the garden pathway to Eyrie, her spirits at their lowest ebb. Irene trailed her every step, with no less command than a frogmarching guard. Tally did not raise her head until she stood at the foot of the marble staircase.

Ma was sitting on the verandah in her treasured Bentwood rocking chair, waiting. Tally's large trunk, repacked and belted, sat alongside her. Ma stood, without a word, and held out her slim arms.

Tally climbed the stairs, tears falling.

Dara was a receding iceberg of luxuriant green amid the ferry's relentless white wake. Tally stood at the rear, face firmly set on her island. She would watch until it had disappeared entirely from view around the headland, and then she would go on looking still. And when her *chaperone* came to prise her fingers from the railing and drag her to the train, Tally would know: Dara was safely imprinted on her mind's eye. She would let no more tears fall, lest they wash away her last glimpse of home. If she had to spend the whole journey south with her eyes closed, so be it.

She did not wonder if Ma still stood on the jetty, watching her only child sail away, becoming a distant speck, for she'd promised she would be.

'It's only a year,' Ma had whispered in Tally's ear. 'Then you'll be home again. I'll be waiting, *right here*, until you come back.'

Only a year, then ...

CHAPTER 3

OUT TO DRY

Bellen Beach, 1963

On a quiet beachfront avenue awash with moonlight, a lithe silhouette with a sequinned mermaid gown tucked high into her underpants was shimmying up the drainpipe to the second storey of the Bellen Beach Guesthouse.

Tally swore as a splinter shot up under a close-chewed nail, reeling back from the side of the house. She couldn't even let go of the drainpipe to suck her damned finger! Halfway up now, she was having serious second thoughts about this plan. In fact, they might prove to be her last thoughts. Shimmying was much harder than she remembered it being; the girl who'd clambered up palms to throw down coconuts apparently was long gone.

Gone but *not* forgotten! And there was no way she was being carried home on a stretcher. She gritted her teeth, locked her limbs and abdominals into higher gear and grunted on. Or tried to. It was her brain reeling now; she was too drunk by far for this. She should give up and go lie under a bush until their hostess, Mrs Pynchon, opened up in the morning.

Imagine when *that* got back to the old bastard: *We found your daughter as pissed as a parrot in a mermaid's frock.*

She did imagine it, and the picture of her father's rage-contorted face gave her the last bolt of determination she needed. With a guttural groan, Tally scaled the balustrade of the shared first-floor verandah, tossed over her handbag and swung herself up after it. She collapsed in exhaustion, not unlike a legless, beached creature, and lay for a moment half panting, half chuckling at her escapade.

Carried on a sultry breeze from the far end of the beach – the dodgy end – came the carousing of the Bellen Beach tavern, from whence Tally Ramsey had staggered home at the end – the very tail end, mind – of the annual Coral Sea Festival.

'Why didn't you just take the fire escape?' A male voice, in the darkness.

Tally jerked up with a cry, eyes straining against the blackness. There was a winking amber light at the opposite end of the verandah and the scent of tobacco. Evidently another guest, with every right to be in this shared space. It was impossible to tell how old the man was, much less what he looked like.

She made her voice as haughty as it would go. 'And just where would the thrill be in that?'

'From where I'm sitting, it didn't sound like you were having much fun at all.'

'How would you know how I sound when I get my thrills?'

There was a shot of laughter, covered by coughing.

Tally smiled into the darkness. 'For your information, I've been dancing on tables down at the Bell.'

'That explains both your cancan costume and the raucous tavern chant this evening.'

Though he couldn't see her, Tally wrenched her sinuous gown out of her underpants. He likely had glimpsed her earlier under the porch light readying to climb, that's all.

'I'll have you know, this "costume" belongs to the reigning Coral Sea Queen.'

'I take it you left the poor girl lying naked in some alley.'

Tally choked on the laugh rushing up. She pushed onto her haunches, taking a minute to let her head stop spinning, then wobbled to her feet. 'Got a spare ciggy?'

'So, a beggar as well as the least stealthy cat-burglar in Bellen Beach.' But he did light a second cigarette. A young man's face was briefly illuminated in the flare of the match. Not quite long enough for her to recognise him, though.

Tally went forward to claim her cigarette, knocking rattan chairs. She swore noisily as pain shot up her shin.

'You're going to get us both kicked out in a moment.'

Tally took the cigarette, inhaling deeply. 'They can't kick *me* out. My father owns this place ... and half the beach now, too.'

There was an audible intake of breath from the man.

She recognised the reaction. Though he couldn't see it, Tally shrugged – a defence mechanism, more than anything.

'You're *Richard Ramsey's* daughter.' And there it was, the trepidation she always detested. He might as well have called him the *Bullshark of Bellen Beach* like everyone else did – AKA the most ruthless sonofabitch in Far North Queensland.

'Yep, I'm the Dara Island brat, home from boarding school. One-night stopover in Bellen Beach.'

One night of freedom, before she would take up the reins of island manager, under her father's instruction. She dreaded the fraught years and locked horns ahead, but what else was she to do while waiting for her island?

Tally's return on the *Sunlander* train had been fortuitously timed with the Coral Sea Festival. *Fortuitously* sounded much better than *deliberately*. Easier to seek forgiveness than ask permission, that was Tally's motto. Luck was on her side, too, Tally having been assigned a newer, younger chaperone in her old friend Lila Threadwell. Unlike her perpetually irritated mother, Irene, Lila would prove no real impediment. Tally had sold her festival idea to Lila as a fitting and harmless celebration to mark the end of her schooling years. Good old-fashioned fun, that's all. She hadn't mentioned the eye-catching mermaid dress in her bag.

And caught eyes she had. Shimmering Tally Ramsey had been plucked from the crowd, and Lila's side, by the rowdy lifesavers of the Bellen Beach surf club, and crowned as the Coral Sea Queen to ride the grand parade float. She'd got an actual shell-covered crown!

The night probably should have ended with Lila hauling her off that float at the end of her triumphant parade and marching her home to bed. But Lila had fallen asleep playing chaperone, like the amateur she was. Tally had left her sentry dreaming away and rendezvoused with her lifesavers within the hour.

Her father would have her hide for such behaviour, but her impending punishment was, as ever, worth it.

All this duplicity and disgrace, however, were more than a disembodied voice in the dark had a right to know. A voice that had gone oddly quiet. She frowned. 'And you would be?'

'Drew.'

'Drew *who*?'

'Is that important?'

'Round here, you bet.'

'Drew of no-important-name-from-round-here. I'm just passing through.'

'To where?'

From Tally's guestroom erupted a loud sleep-moan, followed by a stream of nonsensical words. She felt Drew startle beside her.

'That's just my chaperone,' Tally muttered. 'I should be glad to hear the sleeping draught I slipped her wasn't too strong.'

There was an awkward silence – was it the mention of her chaperone, or her joke about the draught? – then a screech of rattan chair on wooden decking. 'Well, I'm heading off to sleep. I'm up early tomorrow.'

So was Tally, but such details rarely impinged on her choices. She shrugged again, the last of the evening's high spirits deflating.

He was turning the knob to his guestroom. 'Don't forget to drink some water before bed.'

'Night,' Tally muttered, her only company now the squeak of a shutter in the sea breeze. She turned away to her own room, dragging despondently on the cigarette, shins re-encountering all the same furniture.

At the door, she extinguished the cigarette, then quietly turned the knob she'd left unlocked.

The guestroom interior was blacker than night. Tally stood a moment, trying to let her eyes adjust. Blindly, she moved in the direction of her bed, arms outstretched. Her hands encountered a rollaway cot: Lila's.

Tally swayed for a sickening moment. She steadied herself by grasping at a thin ankle, which flicked her off. 'It's three o'clock in the *morning*,' came a voice.

I really should *have slipped her a sleeper, drat it!*

'Had to go to the dunny. Got a bit lost coming back.'

Lila groaned. 'You promised me you weren't sneaking out again. All you had to do was stay in bed for one night.'

'What are you, my mother?'

'You certainly are being brattish, expecting me to cover for your misbehaviour.'

'I don't expect anything of the sort!'

'In fact, you'll be relying on it tomorrow. Or should I say *today*.'

'I much preferred you as a playmate than a ... killjoy!'

'Oh *grow up*, Thalia.'

Tally felt there were a hundred rejoinders she might have made. At this instant, her brain failed her.

Lila's voice, when it came again, was too earnest to be borne. 'You've put my job at risk tonight. Can't you understand how anxious I've been, picturing you lying in a ditch somewhere?'

Tally's brain snagged on this turn of phrase, so similar to the one offered in jest by the stranger on the verandah. Why was everyone fixated on the idea of Tally dying by misadventure? The world seemed to be spinning ever faster on its axis. Tally burbled out an apology, ending on a groan.

'Now you're talking nonsense. *And* you reek of grog. Just go to sleep!' Then, after a moment, the kindness she couldn't help: 'I'll let you lie in a bit later. I'll bring something out of the breakfast room for you.'

Little Miss Perfect Chaperone – it was enough to make Tally *sick*.

Nope, that was the booze.

Whoa there, Tal, steady on!

Tally swallowed back sour regurgitation. She just needed to lie very still until the hideous whirling stopped. Teeth unbrushed, face unwashed, hem of her dress still wet and coated with sand, she buried herself under the duvet, to moan at her own stupidity.

Wait until her father heard what she'd been up to. There would be hell to pay, she knew it.

Tally did not so much fall asleep, as hurtle into oblivion.

CHAPTER 4
THE MANAGER

Dara Island

Nerissa Ramsey had gone to her bedroom at nearly midnight, after scrubbing her house from top to bottom. She was awake again with the birds in the pre-dawn darkness, trilling her own triumph …

Tally's coming home today. Today, today, today!

She rose now to splash her wan face at the wash stand. There were tired blue smudges beneath her eyes, but joy undiminished within. She pulled a floaty white cotton dress over sun-browned limbs, coiled her honey hair up at the nape of her neck and slipped leather sandals on sand-polished feet. The only jewellery she ever wore was a simple bracelet she had made herself, of tiny shells strung upon a red thread.

Not another long, aching night to wait! Her heart contracted as though the ferry already had docked, as though her girl was now disembarking, feet pounding down the jetty towards her.

But would this finally be the year Thalia no longer ran to throw herself into her arms? She was almost eighteen, only a couple of years younger than Nerissa was when she married and became a mother. Impossible to think of that funny, plucky little girl with those blazing blue eyes being so near to the end of girlhood – or at least, the end as Nerissa had known it.

A spritz of fragrance and her dressing ritual was complete. Nerissa moved very quietly down the hall towards the stairs, with a hitch of her shoulders as she passed Richard's suite. She stepped into Tally's room to satisfy herself that today really was the day. Tally's bed was made up with the softest cotton sheets, freshly pressed, with every flounce on every edge sitting just so. Nerissa had placed a small gold chocolate heart on Tally's pillow. She recentred the chocolate a tiny jot to the right, smoothed the quilt cover one more time, then went downstairs.

She had no appetite for breakfast, not even her customary grapefruit. A black coffee would only provoke her dyspepsia, ratcheting up her heart rate beyond what she thought she could endure today. Without turning on the kitchen lamp, she made do with a bite of a banana, then regretted even that; the fruit sticking to the top of her dry mouth. She spat it into her hand and buried it in the bin, where Eyrie's cook, Mrs Simons, would not see. Just water this morning, then.

After one last glance around the house, Nerissa took the service exit to Mermaid Bay. She could not be seen by Richard, lest he find some way of precluding her presence on the jetty this morning. He'd tried it before. Besides, she wanted to have her admin work done down at the lodge, and the observatory already opened, so that she might spend the whole day with Tally, unencumbered.

With Richard's new resort manager arriving today, her husband – *God willing* – would be kept too busy beating his big chest to care overly much about his wife and daughter. At least for a few precious hours.

If Nerissa had been allowed, she should have liked to go herself to meet her beautiful girl off that train yesterday afternoon. Then they might have had that first night together, catching up.

All was placid and pink-tipped at Coral Beach when Nerissa arrived at the lodge. She stood, looking down the long jetty, allowing her heart to climb into her throat for one pining moment. The sea was silky smooth and could not keep her daughter from her.

Heartened, Nerissa turned and slipped her key in the door.

Right, let's get this done quickly, then my girl is all mine!

Only, Nerissa wasn't going to be allowed to meet the ferry, after all. She'd let herself want it too much. Hadn't she learned this lesson a thousand times before?

With impeccable timing, Richard's runabout man, Pat, arrived to summon her up to Eyrie. At least Pat had the decency to look apologetic as he passed on this command.

'Can it not wait?' Nerissa said, unable to keep the tremble from her voice. 'She's nearly here.'

'I do apologise, Mrs Ramsey. He was … insistent.' Nerissa watched Pat's hard swallow.

And if I refuse, you'll pay for it.

Her eyes flickered from his face to the wall behind his head, and the large, green turtle shells mounted upon it. Richard's kills. Sometimes, Nerissa didn't think it was possible to hate her husband more than she already did, but then, somehow, she found more secret venom to imbibe.

'Okay, Pat,' she sighed. 'Be right with you.'

Outside, she found a small circle of long-time staff members; an impromptu welcoming party growing. Someone industrious had even made a sign: *Welcome home, Miss Tally!*

Nerissa carried a picture of this entourage with her on the steep walk up to Eyrie. If she didn't make it back down in time to meet Tally, at least she would know there was a warm welcome for her. It wasn't the same as having her mother waiting there, but it was better than nothing.

Better than nothing should have been in her wedding vows.

Approaching Eyrie, she could already hear Richard's voice from his office, at full boom. Based on that volume, he had someone in there with him who presented a perceived threat – to ego, or clout, usually both. Hopefully not the new manager, because that wouldn't bode well at all.

Nerissa went up the stairs with a sigh. By the time she reached the closed office door, her face was a picture of tranquil indifference.

She knocked, three precise taps, neither irritation nor concession apparent in this action. 'It's only me.'

'Come in.'

Nerissa quickly smoothed the corners of her lips, then entered, eyes downcast to conceal her loathing.

Richard was at his desk, presiding over a one-on-one meeting. His associate was seated in the club chair opposite, with his back to Nerissa. She observed brown hair, height and broadness, and a Mermaid Bay Resort collared shirt.

Definitely Richard's new manager.

At her entrance, the manager stood, straightened, then turned to greet her, with hand held out.

'Flynn Barrett,' Richard said, 'I'd like you to meet my wife.'

Already stepping forward to take his hand, she faltered, the blood plummeting from her face, the name roaring in her ears.

Flynn.

He was tremendously tall, so that she would have to tilt back her head to look him in the eyes. She stared instead at his sternum, having no need to recall his dark-lashed grey eyes; the colour of a monsoon sky.

'I'm Nerissa Ramsey,' she told the manager's chest. 'It's nice to meet you.' There was a hot spasm in her solar plexus as she awaited his reply.

She watched his large hand ease carefully back to his side. 'Very pleased to meet you, Mrs Ramsey.'

The lie accomplished, she looked past Mr Barrett to meet her husband's scrutiny, feeling her skull too soft to conceal all that lay hidden within; to say nothing of her ribs, clamped so feebly around the thudding of her heart. 'You asked for me?'

'Have a seat.' He motioned to the club chair beside Flynn.

She perched on the chair, blinking at her husband like a vinyl doll.

'Flynn here is our new manager,' Richard said.

'Very good,' she replied flatly.

Richard tipped his head, his scrutiny bordering now on dissection. 'You look worried. What's the matter? You're not happy about Flynn.'

She felt, rather than saw, Flynn straighten uncomfortably beside her. *Holy, holy God.*

'Oh no, I'm only … surprised. You had mentioned the new manager was a local. Perhaps I was just expecting someone I already knew.'

'Flynn is originally from Bellen Beach,' Richard said peevishly.

'Only briefly,' Flynn added. 'I haven't been around this way for many years. Nearly two decades.'

'I see,' Nerissa said. 'And what brings you back to this part of the world?' A question posed to the front of Richard's desk.

'Fond memories of the area,' he said. 'I was very young and only passing through the first time, but it left its mark on me.'

Nerissa nodded politely. 'And where have you come from most recently?'

'Western Australia.'

'Indeed, that far?'

'Even further,' Richard cut in. 'Our new manager has seen half the world in his old sailboat.'

'Fancy that,' Nerissa said with a tight smile for her husband. 'You did say you wanted a "worldly manager for a world-class resort", and so it seems you've found him.'

Richard leaned back in his chair, linking hands behind his head, his smile triumphant. 'And *you* said I'd never find someone to satisfy me!'

'It seems I was wrong.' She folded her hands on her lap. 'Pat said you required me?'

'Yes, I wanted you to meet Flynn.'

'Well, thank you,' she said, shifting forward on her seat to leave. 'Was there anything else?' She dared not even the briefest glance at the ship's-wheel clock above Richard's head. Maybe she still had time to meet Tally on the jetty?

Richard smiled knowingly at Nerissa, reaching for his cigarette case. 'Sit back, sit back. I want you to hear some of his plans for Mermaid Bay. Go on, Flynn, why don't you tell her your ideas.'

She sat back into her chair with all the ease of a coiled spring.

Nerissa loitered in Eyrie for five, full-counted minutes after she and Flynn had been dismissed from their meeting with Richard, before daring to follow him out the front door.

The garden was empty when she emerged. At the top of the stairs, she breathed out slowly, then went down at a clip.

Tally! I'm coming, I'm coming!

Beyond the hedged terraces, in the shelter of giant bismarckia palms, she came to a standstill with a sharp hiss of dismay. Flynn was returning along the path, directly towards her. She looked helplessly left and right, then half spun to fly back the way she'd come. But what would Richard say to spy his wife running out of a shaded grove, with his island manager on her tail?

She turned and stood very still, waiting.

He stopped in front of her, and this time she tipped her eyes from sternum to face, and then to those grey eyes.

'Mrs Ramsey,' he said.

'Yes.'

'I wanted to apologise.'

In a serene face, only her constricting brows betrayed her.

'When I accepted this role, I was given to understand Dara had been sold to Richard Ramsey quite some years ago.'

'No, Dara is still mine.'

'And Mermaid Bay?'

'Is Richard's business. I try to have very little to do with the resort and its operations. You'll be working almost exclusively with my husband.'

After a beat, he nodded. 'Your father, if memory serves me, was very much against the sale of Dara before he passed.'

'Yes.'

'And that you were resolved to hold onto Dara – come what may.'

Come what may.

She thought her legs might fail her, and was astonished those trembling bones managed to hold the sinking weight of her aloft. She opened her mouth, with no answer forthcoming.

Flynn studied her quietly. Unable to bear it, she lowered her eyes to careful examination of the ground between them, and his Sperry topsiders, well worn.

'That was all such a long time ago,' she managed finally.

'It was,' he agreed. 'The resort is spectacular. You must be proud of all you've achieved here in the years since.'

Without expression, she raised her shoulders and let them drop. 'And how do you find the island?' she asked. 'Very much changed, I think.'

He passed a hand across his jaw, which had once sported a beard. She watched his index finger brush his philtrum.

'Dara is more beautiful than I remember.'

There was a commotion coming from the jungled path behind him. Nerissa almost expected a train from the amount of huffing going on.

But it was Irene Threadwell who emerged into the grove of bismarckia, red-faced with exertion and urgency. She jerked with the shock of stumbling here upon them, her eyes flying between the pair.

'Irene,' Nerissa said calmly. 'Have you met Richard's new island manager? This is Mr Barrett. We've just been showing him around this morning.'

Irene stared at him, her small eyes more penetrating than ever. 'Yes, I remember you, Flynn.'

There was a careful pause before he answered. 'Your recollection must be better than mine, then. I do apologise.'

Irene harrumphed. 'I need to speak to Nerissa alone.'

Flynn accepted this dismissal, readily.

After he had gone, Irene swung her piercing glare on Nerissa. 'We've got a huge problem on our hands, and when Richard finds out, there's going to be hell to pay!'

Nerissa's stomach roiled. She wanted to clutch Irene's hands in desperate appeal. *Help me, tell me what to do …*

But Irene had a different catastrophe in mind. 'The *girls* didn't arrive! No one knows where they are. The last time your bloody useless daughter was seen, she was dancing on a bar table with her skirt up around her waist. How many times have I *warned* you about that girl? You're not going to be able to cover for her this time, Nerissa. He's going to have *both* your hides!'

CHAPTER 5
HOMECOMING QUEEN

Bellen Beach

A stream of water arced across the bed. Tally screeched and shot upright, mouth agape. It took her a minute to comprehend why she was lying in bed in a shimmering teal gown covered in sand, and now water.

'All right, I'm awake,' she warbled, reeling out of bed to stand before her friend-turned-chaperone.

Lila was dressed already in her Dara Island uniform of tropical print shirt and safari skirt, woven straw hat pinned on. Her unruffled uniform belied the stark distress of her expression. 'Oh, thank *God*! I almost thought you were in a coma, Tally. I feared I'd have to *carry* you home!' She held out a wash cloth. 'Here, dry yourself.'

'You must be pleased to have got your revenge so soon,' Tally griped, dabbing at her face and arms.

'You have to hurry,' Lila said. 'Please!'

Tally stooped to peer at Lila's watch. 'Half past *six*!' she cried, scrabbling around for clothes and finding not a stitch to wear. Was she supposed to go home still dressed as a mermaid?

'Here,' Lila said, motioning at her side: Tally's trunk, already packed, a sensible travelling outfit laid out. A plate of cold toast sat alongside.

Tally's face slackened with relief. 'Was I really so hard to wake?'

'You've been an immovable slug. I don't think we'll make it to the ferry on time now. I should call down to Brian at the kiosk and let him know. Your father may have to send a special boat for us.'

Tally gripped Lila's hands. 'Oh, please don't, he'll *kill* me!'

'But it'll be even worse if we miss the boat without explanation.'

'We'll just *have* to make it!' Tally started struggling out of her gown. 'Come on, we'll run!'

At least, they *tried* to run – though they were sorely hampered by Tally's heavy trunk and the fierce, wilting heat of the summer's morn. The jetty was on the opposite end of Bellen Beach, and never had the beach seemed so long. They loped through the sleepy residential stretch of cottages, aching arms and legs reducing them to a lumbering pace as they entered the touristy expanse of the beachfront, passing the tin beach kiosk, Tropicana picture theatre, the kitschy Palace of Shells and the Bellen Beach Lifesavers clubhouse. At last, they crossed the broad, coconut-lined sweep of the beach, onto the jetty.

The Dara Island ferry was gone. They could just see the wooden vessel sailing towards the blazing sphere aloft the horizon.

Lila stared after the ferry as though trying to turn it back by sheer force of will. She put her head in her hands. 'We're *done for*! I'll never work in Bellen Beach again. I'm out on my tush. Mum and I will starve to death!'

Frankly, Tally just wished Lila would pipe down for one second so her poor, pickled brain could think of a way out of this predicament. She leaned over her knees, fighting back nausea.

They were definitely dead. But so too was the ferry skipper when he arrived back on Dara without them. She straightened and cast about the marina, searching for a bell to ring, a horn to toot, anything she might use to avert disaster. But what about *that*? A red motorboat, about to power off.

'Lila,' she hissed. '*Stop* that boat!'

Lila hurried to the boat's owner, a young man with a deep golden tan and sandy-blond curls tufting untidily under a straw hat.

'Excuse me,' she called. '*Excuse* me!'

He turned, perplexed. 'May I help you?'

'We're meant to be on the Dara Island ferry,' Lila said. 'We simply *cannot* miss it!'

The man looked towards the boat sailing off into the sunrise, then slowly back to her. 'Well, then, I don't know how to tell you this …'

Tally wanted to laugh, despite the rising misery of her stomach – and it was rising. She twisted away and evacuated its contents onto the sand, followed by a miserable groan.

The man nodded at Tally. 'Is he okay?'

He?!

She considered her state briefly: sweat-matted hair rolled up under a worn jockey cap, figure hidden under Lila's chosen outfit of slacks and loose T-shirt. No, fair enough: Tally bore no resemblance to a girl, much less the crowned beauty of evening last.

'My friend,' Lila said, 'is just a bit under the weather. I do need to get *her* across to Dara, though, as quickly as possible. If only I could find a gentleman chivalrous enough to offer his assistance …'

He chuckled. 'I'll take you. Happen to be going that way, anyway.'

'Excellent,' said Lila, then whipped around to Tally. 'Come on, quick-smart.'

He looked dubious. 'She's going to make a mess of my boat, though.'

Tally was now heaving and retching onto the sand.

'Oh, for Pete's sake,' Lila muttered, digging in her pocket for a handkerchief. 'Do I have to take care of *everything*?'

She certainly had to lug the trunk to the man's waiting arms. Tally managed only her own knapsack; carrying her head alone was contribution enough. Trunk aboard, Lila ushered Tally to climb ahead of her.

She took an inelegant step onto the boat, as their new skipper waited with a hand on offer, should she need it.

Lurching wildly as the boat rocked beneath her, Tally accepted this offer most readily. She looked up under the brim of her hat, observing deep-brown eyes in a sun-tanned countenance, fine features at odds with his rugged appearance.

'Thank you,' she said genuinely.

'Most welcome,' he replied.

Balance regained, Tally sat at the stern, her face turned to the wind. Lila, finding no other place to perch around the trunk, moved to sit up front beside their skipper.

Only once they were burring safely across the sea towards the headland – frothy contrail streaming, wind tossing Tally's driftwood curls into wild, salty knots – did Lila ask their skipper's name.

'Drew Huxley,' he said easily.

Tally, till now occupied with the stitching inside her make-do spew-cap and her supreme self-control not to use it, whipped up her head to study the gold-stubbled sheen of his cheek. His hands were supple and relaxed on the wheel. *Huxley* definitely wasn't an important name around here.

'Nice to meet you, Mr Huxley,' Lila said. 'And if I may be so bold, I'd ask that you wouldn't discuss your kindness here today with anyone else. We have a need for privacy ...'

Tally's quiet groan was whipped away on the wind.

Drew shrugged. 'I have no intention of telling anyone that I offered a lift to Richard Ramsey's daughter and chaperone.'

Lila was crestfallen. 'How did you guess who we are?'

'Apart from the fact that we're chasing down the Dara Island ferry and her trunk is marked *Ramsey*? As it happens, I have business with Richard.'

'You're not from Bellen Beach, though.'

'Nope. Adelaide.'

'What kind of business do you have with Mr Ramsey?'

Hearing the fear in Lila's voice, Tally groaned again, this one definitely not siphoned off on the wind.

Drew nodded in Tally's direction. 'I've got ginger beer in that thermos back there – if either of you is thirsty.'

'Yes, please,' Tally blurted, just as Lila said, 'No, thank you.'

Tally eagerly took up the thermos and poured herself a cup, ignoring Lila's scandalised face. The ginger beer was dry and spicy and cooling, all at once. She drank it down greedily, making no attempt to cover the series of belches that followed.

'No one ever accused me of being a lady,' she muttered.

He chuckled, returning to the topic. 'Richard is selling me a boat.'

'*What* boat?' Tally interjected. Even straining forward between their seats to enter the conversation, she still had to shout over the engine going full throttle.

Drew smiled back at Tally. 'Yacht. Forty-five-footer.'

'The *Polaris*! You must be joking.' Her father hadn't said a word about selling his beloved boat. 'Must be quite a sudden sale.'

'On the contrary, we've been in discussions for months.'

'What are you paying?' Translation: how could a man skippering a red runabout afford the *Polaris*?

His answer drove a wave of heat up her face. *Daylight robbery!* Was her father in some kind of trouble that he should need to sell it so cheaply? How fascinating. She would try to steal a look at the ledger once she was at Eyrie …

'You'll be paying more than that, though.'

'Why should I?' Drew's smile was wide. 'It's quite settled.'

'You mustn't be properly acquainted with my father. Now that he's got you here, he'll price it higher and watch you beg for it.'

'We've already made the deal.'

'Perhaps you'd *like* to think so, but ruthlessness runs in the Ramsey blood.'

Drew threw back his head to laugh. 'Yes, that was my first thought when I saw the Ramsey girl stranded on the Bellen Beach jetty as her own boat steamed away without her … she's ruthless!'

Tally's answering laughter was a spray as warm as that misting off the ocean. 'The Bullshark of Bellen Beach *always* gets what he wants. Even the sea conspires with him.'

Drew cocked a brow. 'You're going to have to explain how the sea does that.'

'It's a long story.'

'We've got a way to go yet.'

'*Fine.*' She grinned. It really was too long a tale to shout into the wind, but Tally was not one to turn down a storytelling opportunity.

'My father, you see, was a property baron who came to Bellen Beach in nineteen forty-five with the object of acquiring Dara Island – the most beautiful island in the Coral Sea. In those days, it was only my ma and grandpapa on Dara, living self-sufficiently.

'My grandpapa, Bertie Forster, was a newspaperman who bought Dara after a nervous breakdown, for his own private sanatorium. I won't tell you what he paid for it, since it makes most people quite green. There was also the Artists' Colony, peopled by nomadic, bohemian types, encamped on the smaller isle we call the Hat.

'My father lost his heart to Dara – everyone does. He made Bertie a substantial offer right off the bat, but he was rebuffed. Grandpapa told him: *Go find another island to plunder!* Not at all deterred, my father went again the very next day to make an even better offer and faced his second refusal from Bertie over the barrel of a shotgun. *Come back here again*, he told my father, *and you'll be croc bait!* Should have been the end of it, but not with my father. While the world was just getting over a war, my father and grandpapa were starting one of their own. Grandpapa would never have surrendered Dara, but it was the *sea* that settled it, in my father's favour …'

She waggled her dark brows, expressively. 'Here it comes, are you ready?'

Drew's eyes were bright and keen.

'One fine day, when the wind had changed to a northerly, Grandpapa waded into the ocean with his cast net, as he must have done a thousand times before, only for the sea to give him the kiss of death: a sting by an invisible jellyfish, tinier than your nail. It was called a sea wasp back then, but now we know them as Irukandji.

'Grandpapa only had time to stagger out of the water, before he collapsed in front of my ma and convulsed on the sand. There was no one to help her, no way to save him. In less than ten minutes, he was gone – leaving my mother all alone in the world, and now the *mistress* of Dara. She wasn't quite twenty.

'And here my father comes, swooping in. Sailed over to make her an offer she couldn't refuse, but they fell in love, instead. They were married soon after. He got his island in the end, without paying a cent for it.

'Then, he quickly set to work developing it: cleared out the Artists' Colony, designed Ma a big old house with an eagle-eye view of the sea, built his Mermaid Bay Resort and established *himself* as the Bullshark that everyone's so afraid of.'

Tally looked expectantly at Drew. It had been one of her best retellings, even hungover and hollering into the wind.

'You spin quite a story,' he said. 'And does your father still use these invisible sea wasps to close deals?'

She shrugged. 'You can poke fun, but I'm giving you fair warning: my father gets what *he* wants.'

'Should I turn around right now and go home?'

'Not before you drop us off! But listen, I'll see what I can do from my end. I'm going to be the resort manager.'

Lila turned her head to stare at Tally. 'You're *what*?'

'Now that I've graduated, I'm returning to take up the role. Since I'll inherit Dara one day, I should be more involved.'

Lila went on staring, but Tally's eyes flew beyond her. They were rounding the headland, and on the horizon was Dara. Tally drew a deep breath, feeling she might soon be able to exhale again.

She allowed herself to enjoy the pleasurable thrum of the engine bringing her home for several minutes, before leaning forward once more to grip the front seats.

'What *do* you do for a living, Mr Huxley, that you should need such a prestigious vessel?'

'Marine archaeology.' He gave a self-deprecating nod. 'Shipwrecks, mostly.'

'A treasure hunter?' Her tongue was firmly in cheek, but his reply was surprisingly earnest.

'The stories these wrecks tell are worth more than any gold bullion. I spend a lot of time desk-bound in Adelaide, so I'm stoked to be out in the field again for an extended period.'

'Reckon you'll have much luck here?'

'No doubt. The Great Barrier Reef is a veritable graveyard of undiscovered wrecks, not to mention the many wartime relics.'

'Do you think there might be a wreck on Dara?'

'Do *you*?'

Tally saw again her 'treasure map' of long ago, glimpsed only once, imprinted on her imagination ever since. 'Every island has her secrets . . .'

'An island this large is bound to.' There was awe in his voice.

Dara Island rose steeply from the turquoise sea, as an ancient volcano lushly overrun with jungle. If blue and green were never to be seen, Tally wondered why the effect of rainforest meeting the reef was so sublime. A sweeping white beach comprised of sun-bleached coral, and hemmed in each side by volcanic rocks, dominated the north side of the island – the site of Mermaid Bay Resort. Beyond lay more than twenty miles of jungled mountains, the highest southern peak of the island, Mount Teasdale, aspiring for the billowing cumulous clouds of the monsoon. Hidden on the island's west side was the tiny Akubra-shaped isle of Little Dara.

Tally was leaning so far forward now that she was almost crouched between chaperone and skipper. Throat, heart and lungs sharing an ache of quenched longing, she smiled dopily.

Drew turned his head to look at her – *really* look at her – and nodded. '*What?*'

'Just wanted to see what it must feel like, coming home to your very own island.'

Tally coloured, as much from pride as embarrassment. Her throat was a touch hoarse from shouting over the engine, but her blood pumped with excitement. She felt herself rightly charged.

The motorboat was slowing. With every yard closer now, landmarks separated out from the verdant jungle and white sands. The coconut trees lining the bay took shape against the mountainous backdrop, casting chandelier shadows. Red-and-white umbrellas flowered along the beach. The resort treehouses could be glimpsed in the tangled rainforest climbing the first rise. The Ramseys' private sand cove, tucked around the corner from the resort, was just visible.

Stretching out long from the resort was the island jetty, with the underwater observatory upon it, several private yachts moored, along with the Dara Island ferry, its passengers disembarked. The first glass-bottom boat was just setting off, with passengers' heads bowed close together as they stared down at the viewing section.

Tally looked to Drew, and was pleased by his evident admiration. Dara always *had* shown her best and most glamorous side to new arrivals.

The motor ceased and finally Tally could hear the tinkling lap of the waves against the shore.

I'm home.

Drew was anchoring them in sand – as close as possible to shore, but careful to avoid damaging the coral bed.

Lila was beginning to look very pale, despite the flushing heat. Tally swallowed guiltily. She wasn't the only one who had to pay for last night's revelry, much less having to also account for arriving late, and stinking of seasickness.

Drew was already out of the motorboat, waist deep in water, motioning for the women to hand him their possessions. Lila waved away Drew's offer of assistance, swinging herself over into the water, then deftly stepping in front of him to help Tally down in his stead.

The sea was crystalline, and as warm as a bath as they waded towards Coral Beach. Lila and Drew had kept their sandshoes on to protect their feet against coral scratches, but Tally already had slung her own, laces tied, around her neck. It was time for her feet to acclimatise, once more.

The trio crunched up onto the beach, eyes narrowed to slits against the blinding glare. They came to a standstill in a semicircle.

'Well, then, Mr Huxley,' Lila said. 'We can't thank you enough for your assistance in getting home, and your discretion. All the best with your negotiations.'

Tally shook hands with Drew. 'Tried to puke over the back, but didn't quite manage to clear the stern. I owe you.'

Lila hoisted up Tally's trunk and made an abrupt departure.

Drew, releasing Tally's hand from his warm, callused grip, nodded at her feet. 'You've got mermaid toes.'

'*Pardon* me?' She'd heard him the first time, but she wasn't exactly going to stand there blushing wordlessly.

'I see a lot of bare feet, but none like that. What a marvel.'

Tally dug her toes under the coral.

'Oh, that reminds me.' Drew's voice dropped low. 'I have something of yours.' From his bag, he pulled a wreath of shells and held it out to Tally. 'Think you dropped this last night at the bottom of your drain pipe.'

The Coral Sea Queen's crown.

Tally swept it from his hands, glancing around quickly for witnesses, before tucking it into her knapsack. 'Looks like I owe you double, then.'

He smiled. 'Next time, don't forget to drink some water.'

Tally joined Lila in three hurried strides, and they walked on together under the giant resort entrance arch: *Welcome to Mermaid Bay*. The line of floral-shirted porters that met the morning ferry each day on the leafy promenade, tipping their hats of woven palm fronds, had long since disbanded.

They followed the ixora-hedged pathway that ran along the large resort pool with its central blue butterfly motif. Here, the resort's fitness director was leading a group of swim-suited women in a movement class. They had just begun their cheek-reducer exercises.

Tally and Lila ducked behind this group, heads low, quickening their pace past the main lodge, containing the brasserie and Monsoon's cabaret nightclub. If Tally were sighted here, they would lose even more time greeting familiar faces.

'There's been such excitement for your return,' Lila said. 'There was even a welcoming party organised.'

And Tally had let them all down.

Slipping by the tennis courts and cinema, they came to a path marked 'strictly private', which wound through beach scrub to the 'servants' village'. Tally had long petitioned for an official change of name to 'staff village', but her father had refused point-blank. Once Tally became manager, it would be one of her first acts of business.

As they passed this staff turn-off, Lila's jiggling nerves became impossible to ignore. Tally shot her a sidelong glance. *Look on the bright side*, she wanted to say, *you'll never be asked to chaperone me again!*

The women were climbing into the resort proper, where Dara's upmarket guests sojourned in private treehouses, tucked away on the jungle-shrouded rise of a deep creek ravine. Presiding over all of it was Eyrie, situated in a nest of private, manicured gardens.

They bypassed the swinging rope bridge, prettily fairy-lit in the sunless jungle, taking instead the thoroughly unromantic service driveway, straight up the hill.

The closer they got, the more anxious Lila became – it was in her breathing, which snagged on the intake and shuddered on the outbreath.

'I won't let him blame you,' Tally said. 'It's not *your* fault.'

'Please tell him how I *tried* to convince you to stay in.'

'There's no reasoning with an exuberant drunk.' Especially one in a crown, with every lifesaver in Bellen Beach begging her to come play.

I'm out of lifesavers here, though ...

They emerged through the large-leafed foliage of the garden to stand, panting heavily, before the grand white house, regal and imposing against its jungle backdrop. One needed to always arrive at Eyrie in a sweat, already flustered and discomposed. Tally thought that had to be the whole point.

Ma was waiting on the verandah, seated in her Bentwood rocking chair, countenance shaded by a wide-brimmed hat. Her graceful posture belied the evident tension in the small hands folded on her lap.

Sighting Tally, Ma stood, smoothing down her white bohemian dress, before raising her arms in invitation. 'Tally,' she pronounced, overloud, as for an unseen audience. 'You finally made it out of June's clutches!'

Tally's eyes flicked past Ma to her father's office window. The lamps were on – the Bullshark was in.

Ma confirmed this with a tiny nod. 'I should've warned you to avoid the lodge once you got off the ferry. Everyone's been so looking forward to seeing you again, I suspected you'd get caught up there. I almost went down to rescue you, but your father says I mustn't baby you in front of staff anymore. *Was* it June who wouldn't let you go?'

'June,' Tally answered loudly, enjoying her mother's subterfuge. 'Blabbermouthing as usual.'

Lila tsked quiet disapproval at her side, but Tally rushed on to embrace her mother for the first time in nearly a year.

'Oh, *thank God*,' Ma whispered as Tally's arms wrapped around her. 'I've been worried sick.'

Tally had outstripped her petite mother by a foot, and she felt like an overgrown child as she cleaved to her. But it was more than height; there was something new and particularly fragile in her mother's figure. Tally drew back to study Ma, whose face had turned pink with pleasure. 'You've *shrunk*! What's wrong?'

Ma waved this away. 'Not eating well, that's all. Terrible dyspepsia.' She looked down at the watermarks left by Tally's embrace. 'But you're soaking wet,' she hissed. 'Did you *swim* here?'

'Just had to help some fellow who'd run his motorboat up on coral.'

'You can't go dripping on my floor. I'll ring for Hildy to bring some towels, then let's get you out of the way quickly, before your father's meeting finishes.'

Ma acknowledged the young woman waiting patiently at the bottom of the stairs, a hand on the balustrade. 'Thank you, Lila,' Ma said evenly, 'you can go now.' Then she turned and walked inside Eyrie.

Tally cringed. No invitation for Lila to join them for morning tea? No gratitude for her service expressed loudly enough for her father's benefit? It was unlike Ma to be ungracious.

Lila's cheeks were a hot colour. Tally thought asking her chaperone in for tea would rectify this injustice, and was the very least she should do. Instead, feeling thoroughly ashamed, she watched Lila go back down the garden pathway.

She was alone on the verandah now, sodden in the steamy air, trunk at her side. Within the office, her father's sonorous tone rolled on and on; a storm tide beating against the rocks.

She opened her knapsack, peering in for a glimpse of her glinting crown.

Should I put this on now, or save it for dinner?

CHAPTER 6

USURPER

Eyrie

With only minutes until her father rang his infernal gong, Tally headed directly to the kitchen, where she intended to spoil her dinner before her father did it for her.

She hadn't yet seen him, much less faced the reckoning. By now, he might have received word of her exploits. He had been occupied all day in meetings, and after morning tea with a strangely quiet Ma, Tally had gone promptly to bed to sleep off her night's misadventure. At least now, she would meet her father freshly rested and with a full belly.

Despite the ire of Cook, Mrs Simons, Tally was stooped over the large central bench, availing herself directly of the pineapple bundt cake left over from morning tea. Tally knew, the very instant she stopped scoffing, her hangover-induced nausea would return – along with her nerves.

The evening meal was always a formal occasion at Eyrie, with VIP resort guests frequently invited. In this manner, Tally had been 'seen but not heard' by a prime minister with a penchant for spearfishing, a Hollywood star moonlighting as a marlin fisherman, mining magnates with their many mistresses, and countless businessmen closing the deal – rarely the one they'd come to make. Tally often had thought of herself as an aquarium fish at these meals: prettily displayed, fed a few flakes of attention, and mind-numbingly bored.

She had her fingers crossed that this evening it would only be their immediate family. Her profound hope: that Mermaid Bay's staff had closed ranks, refusing to report her antics.

While Mrs Simons' back was turned, Eyrie's pretty housemaid, Phoebe, was fussing about near the range, adding last spices to the first course: tomato soup. Phoebe had served more than a few spicy words to their kitchen interloper, too. But the hide of her, when Tally knew exactly what *she* was! Before leaving for senior year, Tally had been unfortunate enough to glimpse Phoebe serving Richard Ramsey private favours, at this very bench.

Remembering it, Tally's appetite evaporated.

No doubt this latest girl harboured *aspirations*; they always did. But Phoebe eventually would go the way of all her father's young things: on the boat home, without a reference from the mistress. How did Ma abide such humiliations?

Hearing her father's office door bang open, Tally shoved the last of the cake back in the refrigerator and skedaddled. Since she planned to arrive three resistant minutes after her father's bidding, she needed to first get out of sight.

When Tally sauntered up to the formal, second-floor dining room in a svelte buttercup sundress that made her skin and hair glow, she was taken aback to find an unfamiliar male figure approaching the door ahead of her. Her feet were beginning already to back-pedal when he turned.

'We meet again, Thalia.'

Thalia? She whirled rapidly through her recollection. *Ah*, Angus Harmon – it was that overlarge chin cleft that did it. She'd hated the sight of that pugnacious chin when he had been the toughest-talking kid at Bellen Beach School. She hadn't seen Angus since she'd left for boarding school, but she'd grant that he'd mostly grown into his looks. However, there was no growing into that chin.

'Angus,' he supplied, as if she were daft.

'Not ringing a bell for me,' she said, smiling as though he were dafter.

'It'll come back to you.' His smile became wider than hers. It helped that his jaw was so bloody big.

Angus Harmon, the boy who'd taunted her relentlessly about her webbed toes – tried to get the name 'Ducky' going through grades four to six. Worse, who'd refilled her school milk bottle with heat-curdled milk prepared a day earlier. She'd been violently ill and hadn't been able to properly stomach dairy since.

Surely, he hadn't been invited to dinner? What dealings could the son of a Bellen Beach boat mechanic have with Richard Ramsey?

Tally swished through the door ahead of Angus.

The dining room, with its sweeping view of the sun liquefying into the mainland, was all quiet. Her ma and father were already in their usual places, at opposite ends of the long table. She was dismayed to see two more men seated. The first, Tally recognised as Angus's father, Joe. If the Harmons were both over from the mainland, it had to be for something boat related. Perhaps they'd been involved in the sale of *Polaris*?

Her father rose as they entered, and Tally deposited a perfunctory kiss on his cheek, sliding quickly past to her seat at his left. She watched her father clap Angus warmly on the back, frowning as he assumed the seat opposite her.

There was a bowl of tomato soup set, steaming, before her. Tally busied herself with laying her napkin on her lap, stealing a glance at her mother. To Tally's shrewd eye, Ma was seated with all the stiffness of a wooden plank. It was a wonder she didn't topple off her seat. Ma briefly met her eyes, before darting away. This, a plea: *Be good. Please. For my sake.*

Tally turned her attention now to the third man in the room, on her mother's right. He was taller even than her father, with a thoughtful mien and chiselled jaw. One of her favourite childhood games to play at these formal dinners was 'guess the guest'. Although this man had the suave looks of a film star, possibly foreign, it was at odds with both the outdoorsy, capable air of a sailor and a scholar's solemnity. She was unusually stumped, but settled on her first instinct: something to do with movies; he had too much *presence*.

'You're *late*,' her father pronounced, without even looking at her.

'Nice to see you, too,' Tally muttered. If the old coot was going to fire the first shot, she'd waste no time, either.

Now his head jerked towards her. 'What did you say?'

At this, Ma's eyes flicked once heavenward, before settling on the hands folded in her lap.

'I said, it's nice to *see* you, Father.' She picked up her spoon, filled it with a loud tapping on the rim and lifted it to her lips. Ma, too, swallowed hard, though she had not yet picked up her spoon.

Her father turned to Joe and Angus Harmon with a charming attentiveness intended to slight her. Ma, and the newcomer to whom Tally was yet to be introduced, listened in silence.

Tally watched her father command this table with magisterial aplomb. He had always possessed the most commanding looks in any room, but she saw his cheeks and jowls had thickened noticeably over the last year, along with his midsection. Too well fed on his own power and prestige, like an overstuffed lion. This was perversely pleasing – perhaps time would diminish him, if nothing else could. Her father was swallowing the soup efficiently between conversation, evidently impatient to be done with it.

When he twisted back to Tally, her stomach emitted a brief, acidic gurgle.

'I've been in meetings most of today,' he said, clattering his spoon into an empty bowl. 'I regret I wasn't there to meet you off the ferry this morning, Thalia. I understand you had quite the crowd waiting.'

Tally's heart gave a quick double beat to remind her it was ready to fight or flee – whatever she chose. She looked her father straight in the eye. 'Yes, it was quite touching.'

'Was it? How many would you say turned out?'

In her periphery, she saw Ma issue a single headshake.

'Oh, I don't know,' Tally replied. 'Must have been ten or more.'

'Well, then, I'll have to dock the wages of all those who continued to stand around on the jetty long after the ferry had failed to deliver you.'

The sprung trap snapped closed.

Tally bemoaned her liquor-blunted wits. Her father always knew how to use Tally's greatest strength – her determination – against her. 'I can actually explain that –'

He swatted this away. 'Don't bother. I fired Martin.'

'It wasn't the skipper's fault. *I* was the one who slept in!'

'Come off it, Thalia. You really think I'd entrust my guests to a ferry that may or may *not* be waiting in future, much less a skipper who can't check a simple manifest? He's an imbecile and he'll never work for me again, nor in Bellen Beach itself. I've given the job to young Angus here.'

Angus the doofus. She shot a dart of fury across the table at the new skipper watching this exchange most animatedly.

'I've also been informed,' her father went on, 'that you managed to get yourselves a lift across with some local yokel in a dinghy.'

'He wasn't a local. In fact, he's here to dive for –' Tally truncated this sentence. She would not implicate the man who'd given her back her crown.

Her father caught this. 'Why wouldn't you just say it was young Huxley who gave you a lift? Stop your silly games!'

'But you can't seriously be thinking of selling your *Polaris*?'

'Already sold it to the boy. He's merely here to collect it. He paid too much for it, but I threw a weekend's accommodation into the deal – only in the servants' village. The kid's got some notion of discovering shipwrecks in the region. Offered *me* an investment opportunity to sponsor future jaunts, the insolent chit.' There was something vaguely admiring in her father's voice, despite the sentiment.

'I'm surprised you're letting go of the *Polaris*.'

'I want a bigger, better boat.' He indicated the stranger further down the table. 'Mr Barrett here is going to help me find exactly what I want. His first job as my new manager.'

This announcement seemed to land on her plate like a whale. Tally reared back, collapsing on herself with the posture of one winded. 'Your *what*?' She flung a look Ma's way, but her mother's eyes were fixed on her bowl.

'But I want the role. Now that I'm finished school, I can take it up.'

'I told you, I have just the right manager. Flynn's going to be a real strength for Mermaid Bay going forward.'

'But who could ever know this island better than *me*? I've been preparing for this my whole life!' She ought to stop right now, she knew it. It was inappropriate. Not to mention, she was bound to lose in front of all these men, and badly. 'I'm the best person to manage the resort. One day I'll inherit Dara, and my chief focus *is* the island's proper management. I thought it was a … given.'

But had her father ever once promised a position for her at his resort? *Never*. Her naivety was starkly apparent; she'd come home expecting to waltz straight into a paid role of influence. Had thought it her due.

Her father smiled at Phoebe as she entered and swept around the table, removing bowls, her aproned bosom brushing too near his shoulder. Tally scowled. How could Ma bear to just *sit* there while he carried on the way he did? If it were Tally, she'd throw the soup tureen at his head!

His eyes stayed on Phoebe, though he did answer Tally. 'A woman isn't suited to managerial work, much less the running of Dara.'

'What rot! I *will* run Dara one day – the whole island!'

'We'll see.'

'Tell him, Ma,' she appealed to the silent figure at the table's end.

Beside Ma, Tally's usurper – this Mr Barrett fellow – was waiting, equally, on Nerissa's reply.

Her father cut in. 'Your mother has nothing to do with this.'

Tally watched Joe and Angus exchange a smirk.

'It's Ma's island!'

'My resort, my business operations, my employee to hire.'

'None of which you'd even *have* on Dara, if you hadn't married Ma.'

'And if Dara had been left to your mother alone, you'd have nothing to manage but the chickens scratching your dirt floors, or maybe a goat lost in that *leper* colony they called *Artists'*.'

'*Ma!*' Tally cried, affronted on her gentle mother's account.

'Tally,' Ma said with an entreating look, 'one day you'll be the stewardess of Dara, but you're still very young, with so many wonderful things to do first with your life.'

Tally sat in stunned silence. She had a bone stuck in her throat, although the second course of Spanish mackerel had yet to arrive. The conversation had moved on, the whole table seeming to breathe a sigh of relief with it.

But Tally wasn't done. The moment Joe Harmon left open a gap in his endless stream of inanities, she dived in. 'So, you've hired *this* new fellow to force me out.'

'*Enough,*' her father hissed, the warning edge glinting like a blade.

Tally crossed her arms, a pose of resistance as old as she. 'What am I supposed to do *now*?'

Her father settled back in his seat, positively smug. Tally *knew* then. He planned to send her away again – only this time, there would be no end in sight.

'Enjoy your Christmas break on Dara before you head off.'

'Head off *where*?'

Ma spoke up here. 'Grandmother Pauline needs companionship. Your father has booked your departure for after Boxing Day.'

Granny-sit that controlling old hag in stodgy, cold Armidale? Like hell! She might have anticipated her father's cunning, but not Ma's complicity. Why didn't she argue how she needed Tally to stay for company? Why didn't she say she had missed too many years with her daughter to give up a single one more?

'Nope. I'm not going anywhere.'

'You'll go where I send you.'

'You can't *make* me.'

'You're not lounging around here wasting my time and money.'

'I've never wasted a day in my life! I can do *any* job on Dara. Give me the lowest position you have going – dishwasher, I don't care – and I'll work my way up to the top.'

'I have nothing suitable for you, Thalia.'

She fixed him with a contemptuous look. 'Perhaps Ma would prefer me as housemaid in Eyrie – probably a vacancy *here* soon.' She was being indelicate and heedless of Ma's feelings, but desperation had turned her into a flailing swimmer – she'd take the lot of them down to save herself.

Nerissa was all mottled mortification. Her father looked ready to deliver a backhander: nostrils flaring widely, lips pinching. Tally felt her determination blaze big and bright, knew the goading insolence of her own expression …

Go on, then, do it. Do it! *Ruin your power play with a temper tantrum. You're the one who'll make yourself appear* weak *in front of your new manager and skipper …*

Angus seemed to read her mind, and just in time. He swooped in with a diversionary tone. 'But I think the newly crowned Coral Sea Queen will have more than enough work ahead on the pageant circuit, won't she?'

Tally swivelled to stare at him. Now *here* was a power play she had not seen coming. Angus smiled with all the munificence of a favour bestower.

Her father's voice boomed between the pair. '*What* are you talking about?'

Angus turned his winning smile on the boss. 'Thalia's appointment at the festival last night. As far as I know, it comes with quite a few commitments – ribbon cuttings and such.' He nodded at Tally. 'You'll be kept busy in your swimsuit in the year ahead …'

There was that curdled milk, served up anew.

Phoebe was swishing back through the service door, bearing the main course, but Tally was fed up already. She observed her father's purpling rage, her mother's silent, quelling plea, then stood and dumped her napkin on the table.

'None for me. I'm done here.'

The livid roar that blasted after her was only wind in her sails.

CHAPTER 7

NIGHT SWIM

The lounge area around Mermaid Bay's pool lay in full darkness, deserted; even the nightclub now was closed. The gentle slap and rushing tinkle of the tide could be heard from here, but did not reach Nerissa's submerged ears as she floated dead-centre of the inky water, above the butterfly motif. She was a starfish, enclosed by white noise and the sound of her own bubbling movements. Above her, stars shone between palm fronds stirring in the balmy breeze, and Nerissa knew it would take her longer yet to rouse herself out.

Here, she could be alone; unseen and unhindered. No longer the heiress of Dara, not the boss's wife, nor a mother; least of all the Bullshark's bride. Just a woman, weightless and free, suspended in space. The game was to lie so still she might imagine herself floating away among the stars themselves.

This quietude ruptured all at once in an explosion of sound and movement that knocked her from her celestial hammock on a wave, water rushing up her nose and mouth. She felt the intruder shoot like a missile beneath her, as she spluttered and coughed to the surface with a cry of astonishment.

She heard the diver surface at the other end of the pool, as she paddled for the edge, still coughing hard.

There was a shocked curse from the far shadows. 'I'm sorry, I didn't realise there was anyone in here!'

Nerissa hauled herself up onto her elbows at the edge, snorting water from her nose, the indignity of this incursion overtaken now by acute awareness. She would recognise that voice anywhere, even in darkness after a shockwave.

Flynn.

Who else would come lobbing into her solitude with no care for how he might drown her?

'It's me,' Nerissa said.

Flynn stroked towards her.

Get out, pull yourself out, now! You cannot be caught alone in a dark pool with Richard's man.

'I apologise,' he said. 'You must have been invisible there.'

'I was trying to be,' she said, turning so that only one elbow held the edge.

'You still like a night swim, then.'

'I still like peace and quiet. The pool hours suit my habits.'

'I almost went down to the beach. In future, I'll know this is your swimming time.'

'I don't like to broadcast my routine,' she hurried to say. What if he were to mention Mrs Ramsey's late-night forays to Richard? *'Nobody knows I swim here –'*

'It's no problem, Nerissa.'

How would you *know what will be a problem for me?*

From the pathway, a pair of thongs squeaked by on cobblestones, a coil of smoke wafting after. Neither Flynn nor Nerissa spoke again until the staff member – or guest – had gone.

'I'm actually glad I caught you,' he said, in a voice much lower than before. 'I wanted to make an offer.'

Her arm tired of hanging, Nerissa slid into the water, submerging to her chin. Was it her imagination, or did the star-dusted water ripple in time to her quickening heartbeat? *Careful…*

'I don't usually discuss business. That's Richard's domain.'

'It's about your daughter.'

'And I definitely don't discuss my daughter with employees.'

'Naturally. Though I feel my employment itself has spoiled her homecoming, to say nothing of her ambitions.'

'I'm sorry you had to be involved in our personal family matters this evening. It won't happen again, I assure you. Tally's been away a year. I think she's simply … forgotten her manners.'

Swim away, get out – run back to Eyrie!

'I hope I'm not crossing the line in saying this, but I do think she was treated unfairly. If she had her heart set on managing Mermaid Bay, I don't see a reason why she can't be of some assistance while learning the ropes. She seems like a clever girl, and she was right to argue her knowledge and experience. I'd be more than happy to mentor, as you both see fit.'

'Absolutely not.' A hard whisper. 'Tally has a bright future ahead of her – *away* from Mermaid Bay. I'll thank you to *never* suggest to my husband what you just said to me.'

'Even if she were interested in working alongside me?'

'*Especially* if she shows interest. My daughter has the world to conquer for herself. She must be given no choice to stay on Dara. Not an inkling of an opportunity here.' Nerissa's agitated movements had sent a series of waves towards Flynn. The water rippled around his still figure, his eyes unreadable in the darkness.

She tightened her voice. 'You say *nothing* to my daughter. Do you understand me?'

A beat of silence, and then: 'Perfectly well. I won't interfere in family matters again.'

She wanted to cross the liquid space between them, take hold of his arms and shake him: *What were you* thinking *coming back here, after all these years?*

'I'm surprised,' she said, 'that you would've accepted a permanent position on Dara.'

'Why so?'

'If I remember correctly, you don't like to stay in any one place more than a few months at best. An *ocean wanderer*, I think you called yourself.'

'I was a young man then.'

'And I suppose you haven't told Richard you're only here until the sea calls you away again.'

His silence was her answer.

'If I were you,' she said, beginning to stroke gently backwards, 'I wouldn't talk to Richard too much of your wanderings. He's funny about pasts – and futures. He'd like to think none of us ever existed at all, except for him, right here.'

Flynn was vaulting up out of the pool now, shaking water out of his hair. In his dim silhouette, she saw he wore only bed shorts, unsuitable for swimming – everything was outlined. She had been within feet of him just now, wearing less, and only water between them. If Richard had walked down tonight, looking for her …

She floated, gaze hoisted again onto the firmament. The stars had disappeared, covered over by fast-moving cloud wisps.

'Goodnight, Mrs Ramsey,' Flynn said. The gate screeched open and closed.

She went on staring at the sky, knowing her game was up. Everything weighed too heavily now, and she could no more float away than ever be free.

A hot tear rolled down her cheek into the warm water.

She knew what she had to do, for Tally's sake, and it would be a long time before any of it ever made sense to that determined girl.

CHAPTER 8

IMPOSSIBLE BOTTLE

A ship in harbor is safe, but that is not what ships are built for.
John A. Shedd

A full night's sleep might have cured Tally of her hangover, but it had done nothing for the shame and fury still hanging on.

She slunk out of Eyrie, without breakfast, and went to console her hurting heart in the company of the staff. Her father might have no use for her, but she hoped she would still have the love and loyalty of their employees.

It was her tried-and-true strategy, but it wasn't working today. Instead, every familiar face brought the salty sting of fresh humiliation to her wounded pride.

It started with June at reception – her round face glowing not with the rightful joy of Tally's return, but the swooning excitement of her usurper. 'Have you met our new manager, Tally dear? He's an absolute dreamboat. Worldly and clever, well travelled to boot. He's already causing quite a stir with the girls down at Monsoon's. We've got a full staff meeting this afternoon for his official introduction, and …'

It just went on and on from there, getting worse at every turn.

Frank, the groundskeeper and the nearest she had known to a real grandfather, called him a 'good bloke' with 'fresh ideas'. Anita in the brasserie, dependable feeder of runaway girls, thought he would bring a certain 'pizzazz' that had been sorely missing. The coterie of long-legged dancers from Monsoon's cabaret nightclub, sharing a late breakfast poolside, were all aflutter over the most eligible bachelor on the island.

The staff were enamoured of a man they didn't know from Adam, and not one of them seemed to care that the girl they'd known all her life had been betrayed by her own father. Far from providing solace, her long-time friends and neighbours only magnified her fury.

Tally found only one ally, and he was too young to count. Cook's son, Shep, peeling potatoes at his mother's side in Eyrie's kitchen, was indignant as only a teen could be.

'*You* were supposed to be our manager one day,' Shep said with the incisiveness, Tally thought, of the peeler at hand. 'You'd be better than the new guy, anyway. He doesn't know any of us like you do.'

'*Exactly*,' Tally said. 'The new emperor *has* no clothes.'

Good God, she wasn't far wrong…

Tally had stormed off to swim at Sandy Beach, Eyrie's private access beach, a narrow, secluded cove. The staff's colloquial term for this was 'Nude Beach', by virtue of its being strictly out of bounds to them and thus tantalising. Tally had long suspected Sandy Beach was the site of secret staff hazing rituals – the naked swim on the boss's personal beach – *now*, she was convinced of it.

Her father's new man was swimming alone in the cove, and those were definitely all his clothes draped over a driftwood log under the shade of beach almonds.

Comfortably concealed by the trees, Tally stood and watched his head bobbing around in the sea for a while, sending drowning thoughts.

She wondered if the new manager had remained at the Ramsey table last night as her father went into a paroxysm, exchanging smirks with the Harmons, or if he had excused himself. Possibly he was accustomed already to the Bullshark's ire, though few people were quite prepared for Tally's uniquely provoking effect on her father. Fewer still could sit coldly by.

She bet this guy could, though.

I'll fix him!

Without another thought, Tally collected Mr Barrett's clothing, balled up the lot and high-tailed it out of the cove.

Good luck getting to your first staff meeting now.

She did leave him his shoes.

In the last hour of the day, Tally was helping Frank gather golden cane fronds from around the treehouses. They grew like weeds, and their discarded fronds were the bane of Frank's stoop-backed existence. Since *her* father refused to let Frank replace the lot of them with something less labour intensive, Tally felt it her duty to help Frank. It was hard and heavy work carrying piles of fronds down the cobblestone resort paths.

Tally certainly hadn't missed this task while she was away, but she had missed Frank's taciturn presence at her side in the lush gardens of Mermaid Bay.

Like the best kind of pseudo-grandfather, Frank had let 'Young Tally' do most of the talking again this afternoon. In truth, it was mostly ranting, but at least he knew Tally well enough to understand she was really hurting under all the hatred. Today, they had been joined by 'Young Shep' – Frank's prefixes related to favouritism rather than age – and he too had been a patient listener. Tally might have liked to have a younger brother, if brothers were all like Shep.

It was Shep who alerted a still-ranting Tally to the manager's arrival in their midst. Shep's eyes boggled, his head tipping comically to the side. Tally trailed slowly off, turning to glare at the very tall man standing behind her.

Mr Barrett found himself some clothes, huh? Good for him.

Shep and Frank suddenly found their arms incapable of holding a single frond more, and they went off together to dispose of their loads.

Tally stood her ground. '*Yes?*'

'I was hoping you'd be at our meeting this afternoon.' He sounded sincere.

'Why?'

Even in the muted rainforest light, his grey eyes *looked* sincere. 'I think you must be one of the most valuable, untapped assets on Dara, and I'd love to help you find a role that fulfils your talents as much as it benefits the resort.'

What kind of managerial gobbledegook is this?

She crossed her arms. '*Manager* is the role I want.'

The corners of his mouth showed patient amusement. 'I admire your ambition – even if it frightens me a little. I don't know how much sabotage I can take before I'll be forced to hand in my notice to Mr Ramsey.'

'If you could advise what *kind* of sabotage would prove adequate, that will save us both some time.'

'A week of parading my bare backside through the resort ought to be enough.'

She rolled a 'sorry' around on her tongue, then swallowed it whole. 'That serves you right,' she said. 'You're not allowed to swim in Sandy Beach. It's our private cove. The area is out of bounds.' She sounded, and felt, every bit like the boss's brat daughter. Guilt prickled up her neck.

'The error is all mine, then,' Mr Barrett said. 'When I first knew Dara, she had no such zones.' He nodded around at the treehouses. 'Or indeed, any of this.'

'When did *you* come to Dara?' she blurted, her natural curiosity getting the better of her.

'Almost twenty years ago. Mermaid Bay wasn't even thought of back then.'

She hated that he had so long a connection to Dara, because it entrenched his suitability. Never over *her*, though. 'No one here cares about the old Dara. You've got a lot to learn about the way things are done now.'

'Tally,' he said, using her nickname quite easily, as though he had any right to it. 'I think neither of us would want to see Mermaid Bay suffer because of any conflict between us. How about this? You have a ponder about the responsibilities you might like to take on here and then come and see me. My door will always be open to you.'

Tally did not care for the grudging respect – *very* grudging – that this statement left her with. She did not want to *like* the man who had stolen her role.

'Don't get too comfortable in that office,' she said, hoisting up her pile of fronds to go. 'Better not forget that this is my *mother's* island, not his.'

'I hardly think she remembers it herself.'

Wasn't *that* the truth …

Tally had been too incensed to seek out her mother and apologise for winding up her father in front of guests. She knew it hurt Ma more than anything when her husband and daughter were at loggerheads, and she'd publicly humiliated Ma just to score points against him.

Anger had thus far sustained her, but something in her encounter with Mr Barrett softened her resolve. By day's end, she was ready for repentance.

At ten o'clock, well after the dinner Tally had skipped out on, she heard her mother's footsteps come quietly down the hall. Her breath shortened, expecting Ma's circumspect knock at any moment. But though Tally straightened up, face set with remorseful expectation, her mother's footfalls did not so much as pause outside her bedroom.

Was it possible Ma was not *ready* to absolve her? After all, she had agreed to send Tally away to Armidale, even before the dinner-table blow-up.

Tally would have to go and get forgiveness for herself, then.

Ma was reclined gracefully among silk pillows in her mosquito-netted bed as Tally slid into her suite, but there was nothing restful in her pose. She took in her mother's wet hair, slumber-netted, and the smell of chlorine on her. Ma had been for a *swim* instead of coming to forgive her?

She toppled onto the bed to lie prostrate, face buried in Ma's lap. 'I *hate* him! I won't live under his control one more day!'

Ma's hand threaded soothingly through the whorls of her hair. 'But you don't have to, that's why going to stay a while with Grandmother Pauline is the best solution ...' Tally thought Ma had just caught herself from saying *for everyone*.

'How many more times will you send me away from my island?'

'Because it always *is* your island, Tally, no matter where you are.'

'Then make him leave! Let *me* run this place. How can you bear to live here with him, anyway? You can't possibly love him anymore after everything – every *girl* he's done here.'

'*Tally!*' Ma's lap dunked her neatly aside. 'I don't want to hear you say such things.'

Tally sat up, scowling. 'He's the biggest womaniser in the Far North. And there you are abiding it, for – what? He's a bigger detriment to our island than he is an asset.'

'That's not true, or fair. Think of everything he's created here for us.'

'So, he built some resort for toffy, rich VIPs. You and I could make so much more of this place together. We could finally start our turtle hospital, save the green sea turtles caught up in fishing nets and litter. We could make this place an inclusive haven for artists, open it up to nature lovers and families and school children wanting to learn about the reef.'

'All those things are still possible in time, you'll see. Your father even says –'

'I don't care what he says! He's an inveterate liar and you'd have to be *stupid* to believe a word that comes out of his mouth.'

'*Tally!*' Ma's face was crimson.

'I'm not sorry. He's a manipulative, controlling sonofabitch, and I'm sick to death of him running all our lives. He's got everyone on this island toeing the line – especially you. But I'm not putting up with it for one more day. And while ever you allow *him* to stay on Dara, *I* can't be here!'

Ma had gone quiet. Sometimes, that worked on Tally; Ma's calm and softness like a veil of heavy rain falling over the seething jungle. But not this time, not when her silence hurt so much.

Tally slammed a fist into the downy bed. 'You're just going to let me go, are you? You're going to stay here under his big, dirty thumb and let your only daughter sail away?'

Ma blinked slowly, big tears at the corners of her green eyes, so different from the stormy aquamarine of her daughter's. Why should Tally even try to muster tears, when Ma could do it so easily, so prettily? She hadn't cried for many years, and she wasn't starting now. 'All right, fine, if that's what you want, I'll *leave*!'

'You'll stay a while with Grandmother Pauline. It's not forever.'

'Like hell I'm trotting off to live with his cunning mother, to be ruled by proxy. He'll have just as much power over me there.'

'Out of sight, out of mind –'

'Nursing a vindictive old bag who's never shown the slightest care for me, but now wants to tie me up in unpaid servitude.'

'Free of your father.'

'No, I want *real* freedom and achievement,' Tally cried, suddenly possessed.

A *valuable, untapped asset*, Mr Barrett had called her. The notion that had been fulminating in her subconscious for hours burst now into flaming, impetuous light …

'No more being the boss's brat daughter! I want to go and make a success of *myself* – earn my own money and respect!'

'I want that for you, too, my darling, I've always wanted that.'

That's right, Ma has been trying to push me off the island for years.

Tally's face hardened. 'If I go, I won't come back until you've found the guts to kick him off our island!'

'You're very young, Thalia,' Ma said. 'You've lived a sheltered life, between island and boarding school, and you have a lot to learn about the way things work. Perhaps it *is* best if you were to experience the real world for yourself.'

It was the *Thalia* that hurt most. 'But hear this – no matter how far away I go, I'm never giving up my island.'

'Of course you won't, it's just not your *time*, yet.' But Ma's tone was too placating for Tally's liking.

She swooped forward to grip her mother's hand. '*Promise* me that grandpapa's will is still safe and sound, where *no one* can find it or interfere with it!' Her intensity was crushing.

Swear you'd never be so weak or witless to let it fall into my father's hands.

'You're hurting me,' cried Ma. 'I've promised you a thousand times: no one will ever know where it is. Only you and I. It's *safe*.'

Tally stared hard at her mother, searching for the truth and courage in her. Ma blinked widely back, pain and pleading in her eyes.

Reluctantly, Tally released her mother's hand.

Ma drew her fingers to her chest. 'If not Armidale, where else would you go?'

'The one decent thing that came of your sending me away to school, is the connection I've forged with my very good friend Maisie, who I'm quite sure will put me up in Cairns until I can find work.'

'What kind of work might you find?'

'I had thought to try my hand at journalism.'

'Like Papa,' Nerissa breathed, a glow in her eyes and tone.

'Writing is about the only thing I'm any good at.' Despite the money heaped upon private tutors, and her father's lavish donations to the school at assessment time, Tally's educational career had been far from illustrious. Her teachers consistently bemoaned her inability to sit still or stay focused on anything outside her own, particular interests. *A bright and curious girl*, was the common refrain, *but with no self-discipline, a poor aptitude for learning.*

Ma seemed to recall this anew, her face losing its brief lustre. 'I'm not sure if you'd stick it out in a newsroom, Tally. Surely, there are other ways to do your writing? Grandmother Pauline has promised you'd have Sunday afternoons off after church, to do exactly as you please. You could write *then*. You'll be taken care of, have the security of family and money, while still enjoying your hobbies.'

Unlike you, *I don't need to be taken care of.*

Tally's cheeks burned. 'I think I'd do quite well as a reporter. You must remember my Happenings books? And what about the "Island Times" newsletter I used to write? Can't you imagine the scintillating stories I'd ferret out in a city?'

'No,' Ma sighed. 'I'm afraid he won't give you permission to go off and do something as shocking as that. His plans for you are set.'

'I'm going where I please, doing what I want, and he can't stop me. I'll leave on the ferry tomorrow.'

'You really *can't*. He's issued a memorandum to staff, to call for him if you try to board the ferry or supply boat. They'd all know about Martin's sacking. You won't find allies this time.'

That just about summed up her father: didn't want her on Dara, wouldn't let her go of her own free will. And who would dare to go against the Bullshark?

'Then I'll *swim* to shore!'

'It's seventeen miles. It's never been swum before.'

'I'll be the first!'

Ma's look was pitying, and Tally despised the way it made her feel: small and petulant.

But no more …

Tally pushed up off the bed, charged with determination. 'I *love* you, Ma,' she said fiercely. 'But I have to go and make a life of my own. It's up to you now. When you're ready to be brave, I'll come back for you, and Dara.'

So, the Bullshark was trying to stop Tally from leaving on her own terms. *Fat chance, buster.* She would have to work fast; he had outmanoeuvred her many a time before.

Her objective now was twofold, and equally urgent: find a way off this island before her father blocked her, and secure her inheritance before her mother could be manipulated out of it. She only had her mother's promise – and how good was that against her father's power?

It occurred to Tally, while jamming essentials into a knapsack, that she had not even unpacked her school trunk. Even in her worst imaginings, she couldn't have anticipated a transition as brutal as this.

She had not forgotten how to run and hide – in fact, she'd only honed her skills in the intervening years. It was well past closing time at the lodge when Tally had clambered from window frame to melaleuca branch, trunk to ground, and into the safety of the jungled resort paths. The lobby had long since emptied of guests, a bell had replaced June at the reception desk, and only Monsoon's cabaret bar kicked on to a raucous cheer, which conveniently covered the sound of a jimmied lock in the admin office.

Inside, it was all too easy to locate the keys to the staff cabins and access the accommodation manifest to determine which ones were empty. At this time of year, heading into the Christmas break: not many. But she was in luck, pinpointing one vacant cabin on the far edge of the village. That would do nicely for Tally, while she figured out her next step.

After amending the manifest to fill the empty cabin with one 'T. Ho' and filching the key, Tally levered her way into various nooks and crannies to take these additional things: one empty cash tin, a torch, letter opener, paper and pen. She already had pocketed the key to the underwater observatory from Ma's hiding place: a concealed pouch inside her hat-pin box, where Ma kept her private copies of important keys.

Tally hurried down the jetty to the observatory with her supplies, impatient – in truth, even excited – to have this betrayal of Ma's trust over and done with.

She was admitted into the briny air of the silent observatory and stood a moment, listening for … what? An alarm? Footsteps pounding down the jetty? There was only the gulp and burble of water around the structure, the tinkle of the pastel-dyed shell chandelier above Ma's desk.

Emboldened by the familiar comfort of both, she went on her way, torch zigzagging around the gift shop towards her mother's art desk at the back. Ma had been busy, lately. The shop was filled with handmade souvenirs: shell-encrusted jewellery boxes; crocheted coral; sketched postcards of Dara; cowrie shell turtles topped with tiny rattan hats; and the souvenirs most coveted by guests, Ma's mermaids-in-bottles – tiny yarn maids with fine silk hair, shimmering felt tails and delicately embroidered faces. Looking at Ma's mermaids again brought an ache to Tally's throat.

While at school, she would often soothe herself by imagining Ma, tucked away here in her overwater office, crafting mermaids to her heart's content. Tally sighed, wishing her tight throat might be relieved by even one single tear. Life on the mainland had sucked her dry – could she really endure yet more time away from home?

It's not forever. And when I come back, it will be to claim my island!

She moved on, her torch illuminating the disarray of Ma's desk, her magnifying glass stand still hovering over her current project. Tally saw that Ma was working on a new line of shell bracelets – tiny white shells knotted on a red silk string. She nabbed one for herself, settling it around her wrist next to her leather watchband.

Travelling on, her torch picked up the dusty shape of a large, corked apothecary jar mounted upon a wood stand. *Here it is.* Within, the intricate shape of a wooden sailboat. An impossible bottle, originally Grandpapa Forster's.

For as long as she could remember, Ma had kept this ship-in-a-bottle at the forefront of her workspace. Tally was only eight when Ma had first revealed the bottle's true significance ...

'Hidden inside the ship,' Ma had whispered, setting all Tally's senses a-tingle, *'is your grandpapa's will.'*

Handwritten, Ma had described it, signed and dated, and protected from moisture and humidity in the bowels of that wooden ship.

Tally had never sighted the will herself, Ma not wanting to open the wax-sealed cork of the bottle, but she already knew the words off by heart ...

'I entail my island, Dara, to my daughter, Nerissa, and to my first grandchild.'

The greatest gift Tally would ever receive, and she'd never met the man who would bestow it upon her, Grandpapa having made up his will the year before Tally's birth. It had to have been shortly before his death, when Richard Ramsey was circling near, threatening their halcyon peace and paradise. Had some eerie prescience prompted Bertie Forster to make this will? Tally would be forever grateful.

Ma had been wise to preserve it out of sight all these years, but as the heir, Tally needed now to go one step further. Her plan was self-preservation – nay, island preservation. She would take the will with her – safe and dry in a cash box – to keep far away from her father, until such time as it was necessary to produce it. It would pain her to break Grandpapa Forster's sealing wax tonight, but she thought she understood enough about the man who'd first loved this island to be sure he would want her to protect it from Richard Ramsey at all costs ...

The problem was, Grandpapa's seal was already broken.

Tally looked at the seal's remnants in dismay, the tendons in her neck tightening with a spasm. The cork had been tampered with, and removed at least once – the mark of a sharp implement visible.

Breathless with fear, she propped her torch on the wooden stand, drew the magnifying glass over the bottle and set to work. It did not take much effort to remove the cork with her letter opener. But she saw it wasn't the only thing interfered with; the ship had been too. Bending close, she spied a new slit in the hull, running full length. The lines of the wooden planks no longer precisely matched. An aberration, perhaps invisible to any normal eye, but not to Tally – she who had spent so many hours dreaming over this bottle, trying to discern the secret compartment.

Tally worked hastily now, taking Ma's long-handled tools and beginning to prise open the hull at the newly exposed line. At first, the wood seemed to resist, peeling with such reluctance she thought it might splinter in two. Finally, the top layer lifted wide enough to expose a hidden chamber.

There it was: a single scroll, safely encased.

She exhaled, inserting the second set of long tweezers. Ever so slowly, she drew forth the scroll to drop upon Ma's work mat.

Tally stared at it, dumbstruck.

It was one thing to have *believed* in this all her life, but another entirely to see it before her eyes.

She untied the string with infinite tenderness, fearful it might disintegrate after being so long interred. The string fell away, and the scroll unfurled cleanly.

This, her incredulous eyes beheld, written in her mother's small, neat hand:

> Tally Ho,
> It's here, I promise, safe and sound.
> Please trust me.
> Ma x

'Oh no,' Tally whimpered. 'Oh, Ma – *no!*'

She turned the scroll over and over, desperate to find some other words on it, any other words than these.

Ma had known that Tally – her determined, snooping *Tally Ho* – would come one day to breach the ship, and she'd been one step ahead of her. It was absurd, really, that Tally *hadn't* thought to come for the proof sooner. Ma probably hadn't been able to fathom Tally's incuriosity before now.

But what did she mean it's *here*? Where?

She turned her attention back to the ship now, heedless of the damage she might inflict, as she dug her tweezers into the empty compartment searching for a second note, a deeper panel, a secret string.

Why promise it was here when it certainly was not? Why carry on the game, once Tally's curiosity inevitably had exposed her?

Horror clawed at her chest: what if there never was a will at all?

Tally plonked the ship back down on its base, withdrew her tweezers and jammed the cork back in – done with the whole futile exercise. Who would hide a will in a *ship* anyway? It was likely Grandpapa Forster had done no such thing. Probably hadn't dreamed of making a will before the sea wasp's fateful sting. The whole story had been a fanciful fairytale for a girl who, with her natural cynicism, ought to have known better.

She looked now at the bottle and was perversely pleased by the schooner's dishevelled shape as she placed it back on its stand.

She stood up, pocketing her mother's note.

I'll make my own way in the world, and when it's time, I'll return for my island …

CHAPTER 9

STEALING TENDER

Tally slid into the back pathway circling the staff village, face hot with shame. Not only for the destruction she'd caused to Ma's schooner, but the dread of what she might do next. She imagined herself as a canon cut loose, smashing around the island.

She went directly to the Threadwells' place, needing commiseration or absolution, preferably both.

Irene and Lila's home was freshly painted and spruced up, with a fenced veggie garden, potted plants crowding the front verandah and even a herb garden constructed vertically against the house. The evident pride these women took in their allotment made Tally hanker for something she'd never known: some small place of her very own.

She knocked on the door, and prayed for Lila to be the one to open it.

No such luck. It was Irene, and she looked in no mood to absolve anything. Behind her, Tally caught a glimpse of Lila hastening into her bedroom. Her friend did not wish to see her this evening.

'So, you've brawled with your father again,' declared Irene.

'I've really done it this time,' Tally agreed, letting her voice wobble a touch. If there was ever any sympathy to be found in Irene, now was the time to reach for it.

But Irene was as impassive as stone. She went on blocking the doorway. 'Don't think that you can come down here and involve *my* daughter any further in your harebrained rebellion. You nearly cost Lila her livelihood.'

'I am sorry,' Tally said. 'I would never want to jeopardise Lila's position.'

'It's too late for that,' Irene said darkly.

'I'll never put her in danger again.'

'Going to turn over a whole new leaf, are you?'

'Probably not,' Tally admitted. 'But I won't compromise Lila in future, I promise.'

Irene stepped out onto the porch, closing the door firmly behind her. She looked at Tally very coldly. 'The fact of the matter,' she said, 'is that your conflict with your father puts *all* of us at risk. It can't go on. You're playing a losing game against him, Thalia, and we're pawns *in* it. We won't have any peace with you back here.'

Tally's head slumped low. 'I see.'

Her last knot of hope unravelled. There really was no way for her to stay on Dara, not with her father at the helm, and everyone she cared for at his mercy. She needed to leave her island behind.

Tally found she could no longer breathe for sadness. Without another word, she turned and fled back down the way she had come.

She found one T. Ho's cabin situated on the bushy outskirts of the village, furthermost from the busy common area and kitchen. It was clear why this cabin remained vacant – it was the worst of the lot, in need of structural repair; there was even a gaping rot hole in the front verandah.

Never mind, it would do for T. Ho, who felt herself deserving of nothing more right now. All she needed was some brief shut-eye, then she would see about bribing or stowing her way off Dara.

Tally sighed, slid open the door and stepped into the dark cabin.

She stopped in her tracks. Inside, just visible through the barest crack of the bedroom door, was a glowing hurricane lamp.

What the devil?

Easing her bag down and slipping out of her plimsolls, Tally tiptoed closer. There was definitely someone sleeping here. She could just make out the curved arch of a large foot dangling over the edge of the bed. But *who*? They weren't on the manifest – had they sneaked in here, too?

Curiosity led her forward, but the wooden floor betrayed her with an abrupt and telling *creaaaaak*.

Tally froze, watching that foot, which jerked and then withdrew beneath the hibiscus-print linen ubiquitous throughout the staff village. When there proved no further movement, she resumed her creep, nudging open the door. The lump in the centre of the bed, concealed by a mountain of pillows and the pooling shadows, stayed still. Confident that her squatter was soundly asleep, she edged brazenly along the side, curiosity at a pitch.

There was a sudden, rolling flash of movement. Tally had the momentary impression of a great marlin surfacing, before she was swept off her feet and onto the mattress, to lie face down, trapped under a bare, muscled arm. She opened her eyes after this dizzying shock, to stare at a man's armpit hair.

Keeping her pinned, he stretched and fumbled for the lamp. Now bathed in closer light, she heard him swear, then she was dropped like a coal. The bed jerked as he withdrew to some safe corner of the room.

Tally rolled up with a grimace, for she had recognised the voice. Were they ever to meet in any other way than *indignity*?

Drew stood, back firmly against the wall, looking tousled and wary. 'If it isn't the cat-burglar.'

'Housekeeping,' Tally said, straightening herself. 'Turn-down service.'

'Seems more like turn-up-uninvited service.' If she was not mistaken, there was something like *hurt* in his brown eyes; she'd put him in a difficult situation. It was apparently what Tally did best: compromise others.

She shrugged. 'Some guests appreciate the personal touch, but I'll leave you be.' She stood and made to leave.

He held up a hand to delay her. 'Would this happen to be the famous Ramsey ruthlessness at work?'

'What's that supposed to mean?'

'First your father rips me off on the sale of his boat, then you're sent to steal it back in the dead of night?'

She almost laughed, but something in the depths of her consciousness had stirred at his preposterous suggestion.

She found herself offering an honest answer. 'I'm not the kind of daughter you send to do your nefarious bidding. I'm the sort you send far *away*.' Perhaps an answer too honest; there was understanding, even empathy in his eyes, and she didn't care for it. 'Look,' she said. 'I was after a place to lay my head tonight, and this cabin was supposed to be the only one vacant. Innocent mistake, didn't mean to disturb you.'

'Hey, no harm done.' He seemed to second-guess this pronouncement and motioned towards the bed. 'Unless I hurt you, just now?'

The recollection of having been so recently wrestled onto this bare-chested man's bed made her cheeks heat. 'No harm done,' she agreed brusquely.

There was a stretched silence.

'All right,' Tally said, 'I'd best keep moving, then.'

'Yes, I suspect you've got a busy night of breaking and entering ahead.'

Tally scowled. 'I know what you think of me.'

'Do you?' There was unchecked amusement in his voice.

'That I'm a rich brat, privileged, entitled and ... ridiculous!'

He smiled. 'Now you sound sorry for yourself, and that doesn't really seem your style, Tally.'

'No, it isn't,' she agreed. 'Nevertheless, I *am* sorry for myself. He's trying to steal my island right out from under me!' She sounded brattish, she knew it, but he didn't seem to mind. In fact, he relaxed more fully against the wall, arms folded, as though he had all the time in the world to talk to morose, possibly crazed intruders.

'Tell me how he plans to do that.'

She did tell him her story, as best as one might summarise to a stranger. He had such a nice, listening face, one that waited and encouraged but did not react. Her whole tale of promise and longing, punishment and defiance came pouring out. She did not spare her part in any of it, either. Why should she? Tally owned her transgressions as much as her ambitions.

Coming towards the zenith of it all – Ma's beloved ship-in-a-bottle – she sensed Drew was quite on her side, despite the unflattering light in which she had painted herself. She decided she'd come far enough, and she needn't go into the desecration of the ship. He was still a stranger, no matter how nice his listening face. 'So here I am, trying to hide out in this cabin until I figure out my next step.'

'You have to bust off your own island?'

'It isn't exactly Alcatraz, but yes.'

He studied her for a moment. 'Might I offer you a *lift* to shore?'

'On Father's *Polaris*? Wouldn't that be the kicker!'

'*My* boat,' he said dryly.

She grinned. 'Would you have time?'

'Plenty of time, as it happens. I'm staying in Bellen Beach for at least another week while I finish up prep.'

Oh pooh, that wouldn't work. He'd be left here to face *her* consequences, like everyone else who got caught up in her drag net.

She couldn't implicate Drew – of no important surname, but such a nice, listening face – in her schemes.

'No, that wouldn't be fair,' Tally sighed. 'If my father ever caught wind of your having smuggled me out, you'll be *ruined* in Bellen Beach!'

'Or thrown to the invisible sea wasps,' he remarked.

'Believe me, my father can destroy your life in far more real ways.'

'I'm inclined to believe you.'

'But never mind,' she said. 'It turns out, another solution has presented itself.'

It had too, this very second. With almost divine providence, she'd caught sight of her answer, sitting on his bedside table not five feet away. She did wish her solution didn't have to take sly advantage of Drew's kindness, but at least this plan absolved him of any guilt or involvement. She thought he would be a good sport about it, in the end.

'You're sure you won't accept my lift?'

'No, I need to take matters into my own hands,' she replied.

Drew had straightened, taking the first polite step towards the door to escort her out.

Her new plan did hinge on one final duplicity. She feigned a yawn, not moving from her seated position on the bed. 'I did wonder if I might ask one last favour of you, though.'

There was a brief pause, then he asked, all courtesy, 'How may I help?'

'Would you mind, terribly, if I crashed on your couch tonight? It's just that your being here has rather foiled my hide-out, and it's very late.'

His nice, listening face had changed to something more … she didn't want to claim *shrewd* because she hardly knew the man, so how could she even guess how he might look when seeing right through her? Still, she had to blink extra hard to appear innocent. 'I don't want to be a bother.'

After a deliberation, Drew gave in. 'You're welcome to my couch. I'm starting to begrudge reception allocating me your hide-out, though.' There was a definite twinkle in his eyes now. 'I think I can trust you, kid. But I'll shut my bedroom door – for my reputation's sake.'

'Thank you.' Tally grinned. 'You do that.'

She knew: his doorhandle had no lock, and would prove no match for her …

All was dark and hushed on the shores of Dara Island in the last hour before dawn. The birds had not yet even begun to sing. No light reached the lapping, tinkling tides as Tally stood in the warm shallows, preparing to wade out to her escape boat.

Only it wasn't hers at all. Tally was going to steal a motorboat. She opened her palm to stare at the ignition key in its centre. Drew Huxley's motorboat, to be precise.

She had left a note on his bedside table in place of his key. His slumbering breath rate had not changed as she placed the torn corner of notepaper, inscribed thus:

Never trust a cat-burglar! I'll leave it at the Bellen Beach jetty. Tell my father I stole it, he'll compensate you to keep you quiet. x

Tally did feel guilty for taking advantage of his kindness. But what else had he really expected from her, other than more outrageousness?

She hoisted her knapsack higher, well out of the water's reach. Its shape was distended beyond recognition, essentials jostling for position with keepsakes like her Dara Happenings books of old. If she couldn't take her ma and friends with her, she would at least have her memories as comfort. Topping her possessions, just protruding from the knapsack's engorged mouth, was the shell crown that had proved the last straw.

Perhaps it was for the best that her beloved Dara loomed in shadow and the mainland waited still in darkness. She could not bear to see what she was leaving behind, nor what lay ahead.

She thought of her goodbye letter: two hurriedly scrawled lines slid under her mother's observatory door. Her lips moved, reciting those bitter words …

Forgive me, Ma.
'For the mighty wind arises, roaring seaward, and I go.'

PART TWO

For whatsoever from one place doth fall,
Is with the tide unto an other brought:
For there is nothing lost, that may be found, if sought.

Edmund Spenser, *The Faerie Queene*

CHAPTER 10

SEA MAIDEN

Dara Island, September 1967

In the sun-glittered brilliance of a spring morning, Nerissa was beneath the barnacled jetty in a snorkel and mask, cleaning the outside of her underwater observatory windows. A weekly task for which she closed the place; Richard refusing to let her make a spectacle of herself in front of their guests.

Only her daughter had ever been allowed to watch her cleaning from inside the observatory. She knew very well that young Tally had imagined her mother was a mermaid in her blue-lit marine world, honey-warm hair streaming softly in aquatic light. Nerissa had always hammed up the game for Tally – in fact, once she'd even surprised her daughter by donning a cocktail dress of aquamarine sequins. Oh, Tally's absolute delight that day! Nerissa knew her daughter had kept that silly dress ever after.

What a funny little girl …

Nerissa bubbled up to the surface, treading water. Remembering those golden years, before Tally ever went away for school or work, was too painful. Four years after Tally had moved to Cairns, Nerissa still missed her more than she'd even thought possible. And though she tried to visit Tally at least twice a year, it would never again be the same as the old days.

True to her word, Tally had not returned to Dara once since she'd left – pride and *Richard* keeping her far from the island's tinkling shores. Nerissa understood how much it had to hurt Tally to stay away, though she seemed to have carved out a life of genuine fulfilment and success for herself in the city.

Nerissa counted down the days, even the hours, to her monthly letter from Tally. To hear her voice again – even in writing – was like rocketing up from the sea bottom for breath. Tally's latest epistle had been expected days ago, and had not arrived with the mail at Eyrie. As soon as Nerissa was finished here, she would dash into the lodge to double-check it hadn't been caught up with the resort mail.

She duck-dived again, with new urgency. The last two windows almost cleaned themselves. As much as she could spend all day drifting with turtles over iridescent blue-lipped clams and intricate brain coral, there were small flashes of wonder to glimpse above the surface, too.

A look, skimming too long; her name on his lips when no one else might hear it; a corridor encounter, in front of her husband's closed door.

Even underwater, Nerissa's face burned.

Close now to lunchtime, Nerissa padded up the jetty, swinging her bucket of supplies. Her hair, normally rolled each day into a low chignon, hung to her lower back, streaming with water. Her face, she knew, would remain imprinted for another hour by her face mask. She glowed with the pleasure of a sea swim: skin scrubbed and tight, salt caught in creases; lungs warmed up; heart filled by the beauty that existed for her more underwater than anywhere else.

There was the brief freedom, too, of walking right through the resort in only her cream swimsuit with a sarong tied around her waist, high split revealing her shapely legs. Richard didn't like it – the boss's wife making such a display of herself. It was true, however, that Nerissa washed her observatory windows and then took the long, meandering path home a little more frequently than was necessary.

She went, with a smile playing behind her lips, into the lodge to check with June for her letter.

No letter was caught in reception's in-tray. Now she was crossing the swaying suspension bridge and climbing the winding, rainforest paths between treehouses, towards Eyrie. Fan palms touched over the path to form an elegant ceilinged tunnel, lit only by tiny sun glints.

Ahead, Nerissa heard the rattle of a housekeeping trolley coming out of a treehouse onto the main cobblestone path. She saw the trolley emerge, and the pretty young maid pushing behind it. She drew back into a grove of lipstick palms, some heightened sense of warning freezing her legs.

Sure enough, an unmistakable laugh came, deep and gruff and self-satisfied. A second later, she watched her husband emerge from the treehouse, hot on the tail of the maid. He hadn't even tucked his shirt back into his slacks. She saw him tweak the young woman's waist then send her giggling off ahead with a derrière pat. Waiting to the count of three after the maid had gone, he walked up the path after her.

The old rage stinging her cheeks, Nerissa tore off in the opposite direction.

She pulled up short.

Flynn was standing silently on the pathway behind her, and from the look on his face she understood that he, once again, had seen it all.

'Mrs Ramsey,' he said. 'Good morning.'

He wore the chambray shirt she loved best, sleeves rolled to his elbows. It turned his eyes to steely sky.

'Morning.' Nerissa lifted her chin in an effort to counteract the great dragging weight on her body created by his proximity. If she wasn't careful, she might roll down the hill like a stone, taking him tumbling with her, into the sea.

Now they had entered the familiar stand-off – one of silence and restraint, a long gaze that had to contain everything unspoken …

I found the nautilus shell you left down at the observatory. It's the most beautiful piece you've ever found for me. But how was your date on the mainland, Saturday evening? I wept myself to sleep thinking of you with her. *When you stayed all Sunday over there, I was so angry that I threw your shell right back into the sea. It took me a whole hour to find it again, and the whole time I feared I'd cursed you forever.*

The memory seared. She cut the gaze short, lashes falling over her eyes as she twisted the string bracelet on her wrist. Now that Flynn was standing mere feet from her, she wondered how soon it would be until she had the excruciating relief of his next business trip abroad, or another long fishing jaunt away with clients.

I can't even think *with you here, yet I can't* breathe *when you're gone.*

He moved closer to her, something he was usually at great pains to avoid. Her heart hitched in agony, but he was merely taking something out of his pocket. 'This is *yours*,' he said, placing it in her hand.

She looked down to find Tally's latest letter.

'But where did you *get* this? June said they hadn't seen a letter all week at reception.'

Flynn set his serious eyes on hers. 'It wasn't at reception. I took it from Mr Ramsey's desk. I apologise, but it was opened already.'

Nerissa blinked back tears of fury. So now, he was stealing her letters *before* she'd opened them? She pressed the envelope against her chest, lashes still lowered to conceal her despair. Nothing made her so ashamed as Flynn knowing what kind of man she'd married. Not even Tally's lecturing could stir her regret the way Flynn's mere gaze did.

'I guess *I* must have put it there and forgotten –'

'*Don't*,' he hissed. 'Don't make excuses for him. Not to me.'

'I'm only making excuses for myself, though, aren't I?' She tried to smile, but there was a new and most unbecoming quiver in her bottom lip.

She never lost control in front of Flynn – *never*.

He stared at her, a deep furrow forming between his brows. She pressed her lips closed, trying to constrain the wobble.

'I'm not asking you to explain yourself,' he said.

She swallowed, or tried to, looking him full in the face. 'I do wish you would …' she was stunned by her own daring, and stupidity '… ask more of me.'

Flynn's eyes searched hers. 'Ask *what* of you, Nerissa?'

Forget the boulder rolling them both into the sea. If she were to collide with him right now, she thought they wouldn't make it past the cobblestones at their feet.

There was a shuddering rattle on the path behind them. Nerissa jerked: Richard's housemaid, still weaving her way around the treehouses. She saw the noise register as starkly with Flynn as it did her, his whole manner changing in a millisecond. He cleared his throat, lifting his arm to consult his watch.

'I was on my way up to a meeting just now,' he said in a clipped tone. 'I'd better get a move on.'

She did not step aside, so that as he went by her, his covered arm brushed her bare one, raising every hair upon it.

After he had gone, she stared down at Tally's letter, fear turning its familiar crushing vice. 'I shouldn't have done that,' she told Tally's handwriting in a miserable whisper. 'I'll ruin everything.'

Nerissa had taken Tally's letter to her observatory to read in relative privacy, only having to glance up now and then from her desk to welcome visitors. All her windows were pushed open to the sea breeze: teasing tendrils from her hair and stirring her shell chandelier overhead.

As she drew Tally's letter from its envelope, resentment gripped again. *How dare he steal her letter?* Richard hadn't once deigned to add so much as a line to Nerissa's letters to Tally, though she always invited him to do so. Neither did he own to wanting any of Tally's wonderful news – and it was *all* wonderful. Their daughter had made a shining success of herself, without help from either of them, much less a penny or drip of kindness from Richard. Nerissa regularly passed on snippets about Tally's life and career in Cairns – it was the decent thing to do – and in return, he did nothing but mock and belittle.

Was that why he took this letter, looking for some weapon to use against Tally? The blood drained from her face. Or had he taken it hoping to find ammunition against *her*?

Her eyes went to the impossible bottle on her desk. The ship, decimated by Tally during her last night on Dara, had long since been repaired. Tally and Nerissa had never once spoken about that evening. Nerissa had beaten her daughter to Papa's will by mere hours. She had waited every day since for Tally to confront her over it, to demand the explanation due her.

Shame and betrayal, on both sides, had formed an unbridged chasm between them …

I'll ask you when I'm ready.
I'll tell you when it's time.

What if Tally finally had decided, in this letter of all letters, to ask her mother about the ship and Papa's will?

Her hand trembled as she unfolded the thick wad of pages. Tally's epistolatory flair was as rambling as her journalistic style was succinct. Enclosed in the letter was a fresh pile of newspaper clippings. Tally had mailed home every story she'd ever had published, and Nerissa had pasted the lot into hardcover journals, charting the steep trajectory of her daughter's career. The earlier journals were full of Tally's stories as a junior cadet, the regurgitation of homemaking tips and fashion advice that had so infuriated her. In short order, the clippings had become longer and more exciting as Tally turned her nose to sniffing out local controversary; not even the most banal ribbon cuttings or Show Association spats were safe from her instincts. The island girl who'd honed her listening skills hiding in cupboards had become the *Cairns Ledger*'s not-so-secret weapon, known around town as Girl Reporter. Nerissa's latest scrapbook was teeming with Tally's scintillating feature articles and investigative pieces, with her very own by-line …

Tally Forster.

Nerissa knew she'd adopted this name as much to hurt her father as please her mother. The latter, she certainly had achieved – though Nerissa would never own to it. It was fitting that the fine Forster name had returned to newspapers. She thought Papa would have given his raspy chuckle to know it.

Nerissa turned her attention to Tally's letter. Her first read-through was a frantic skim, dreading at every line the potential mention of Papa's will. But she came to the effusive valediction with a great sigh of relief. Nothing mentioned of Tally's inheritance, nor her ambition for Dara. A smile stole onto Nerissa's face. So, Richard had suffered through eight pages of Tally's happy independence and success, with naught to use against her and not a single word for him.

See, dear? She doesn't need you for anything.
Maybe she never did.

It was with this spirit of subversive pleasure that she took out her paste and scrapbook and began to put in Tally's stories.

Nerissa's swimsuit and hair had dried completely by the time she returned to Eyrie. Ascending the marble stairs to the cockatoos' tattletale screeching, she saw the back of Richard's head through his office window, still at his desk. His resounding voice filled the verandah as if there was no wall between them. There was the briefest pause in his conversation, to let her know her return had been duly noted.

Was *Flynn* in there?

She opened the screen door just wide enough to squeeze through – any further, and it would squeal. Then she stood for a moment in front of the hat stand, though she had nothing to hang up.

When she heard Flynn's voice interrupt her husband's long stream, warmth filled her chest. How wrong it was that another man's presence should make her feel happier in her own husband's home.

Compared to Richard's bullying loudness, his manager's subdued tone was one of patience and restrained power. Indeed, the louder Richard seemed to go, the lower Flynn's voice would drop. Flynn, in his role of the last few years, had learned to manage the Bullshark as much as the resort. It was a dynamic she knew well now, but though she had lingered at this stand many times before to hear it, there was something different in today's exchange. Perhaps a little less restraint than their manager would normally show, and even less control to her husband's booming.

They were arguing, she realised, and not just the usual conflict between Mermaid Bay's owner and its manager. There was ripping spite to her husband's words today, and an immovable strength to his manager's.

Whatever Flynn had said or done to provoke Richard's infamous vindictiveness, he would not come out of this interaction unscathed.

She could not help her paranoia: was this something to do with earlier today?

When she heard *Mrs Ramsey* from Flynn's lips, followed by the young housemaid's name, ice coursed through her veins.

Oh God – it is *to do with this morning!*

But why would Flynn be taking Richard to task over so commonplace a misdeed? Flynn knew what her husband was, they all did. Had she instigated this with her foolish lack of caution?

Heart hammering, she took a small step towards the office door, inclining her ear. She heard Flynn take another steady jab, and Richard's boisterous deflection.

Stop, she mouthed, *please, stop*!

Didn't Flynn realise there was no possible way for him to win? Richard would fire him on the spot for such insolence, *especially* since he had such respect for Flynn's cleverness and instinct for business. He would be sent away from her island, and then she would never see him again. Had he suddenly forgotten how precarious and extraordinary their position was? Every stolen glance and small kindness depended on Flynn carrying on, in patience and restraint, just as he had been.

Terror looped around her heart, yanking tight. Perhaps he knew very well what he was doing and simply had nothing left to lose.

Was he off to wander the seas, once more?

She could not bear it. She would not survive it this time.

The dinner gong roused Nerissa from a sullen stupor at her dressing table. She had been ready for hours, having come straight here from Richard's door to await her fate.

With her face pressed against the window, she had watched Flynn go down the terrace gardens a long time ago. He had not returned. Even still, she dressed in pale lavender muslin to compliment her honey tones. One never knew when Flynn would be invited to their table, directed to sit on her right-hand side. Perhaps owner and manager miraculously had made up after she'd slipped away from Richard's door, maybe they had shared a bottle of cognac to toast the solidifying of their working relationship. There was always hope. There'd only ever been hope...

When she entered the dining room, however, she found a wholly unwelcome guest. Angus Harmon, ferry skipper, smug and suited in the seat adjacent hers.

'Good evening, Mrs Ramsey,' he said, as she sat in front of the meal and folded her napkin over her lap. She had long known Angus liked her about as much as she did him – not one bit.

Richard's eyes had been on her since she entered, but only now did she look across the table at her husband. 'Evening, dear,' she managed through the fear-parched folds of her throat.

'You look unwell,' he said. 'Is something the matter?'

'Too much sun,' she said. 'I might have overdone it cleaning my windows today.'

Richard turned promptly to Angus. 'There you go. That can be one of your first tasks in the role. I don't want Mrs Ramsey cleaning those windows herself anymore – it's an unnecessary exhibition. Send a servant down there to do it. Monthly is frequent enough.'

Nerissa, watching Angus accept this command with obsequious zeal, turned her head very slowly to her husband. 'Why should Mr Harmon try to interfere in my habits?'

Richard smiled at her. That once-winning smile – the large, straight teeth of a man raised in money and prestige – now very much yellowed by tobacco, coffee, liquor. 'Nerissa, I'd like you to meet my newly appointed manager.'

'Pardon me?'

His smile curled back to expose his gums. 'I promoted Angus here to manager today.'

'But he's only a … skipper.'

'He's a born and raised Bellen boy, with respect and a good work ethic, not like some other managers I've tried to whittle into shape.'

'What happened to –' *FlynnFlynnFlynn* '– your last man?'

Did she imagine it, or did Richard's left eye twitch accusingly? 'He's already gone.'

'Oh?' she squeaked, taking up her bread knife to butter the roll she knew would pass through her gullet no more easily than a brick.

'I fired him this afternoon. He's been *stealing* from me.'

You lying sonofabitch.

'Stealing,' she repeated, fumbling with her butter. 'Gracious. Who would have thought.'

'I had his number a while back. Thought he was so clever, didn't he? But I was on to him. He's a thief, and he's done here on Dara.'

'So, you put him on the afternoon ferry home and pulled this gentleman off it?' *Listen to herself! Transparent as the shallowest lagoon.* Her heart accelerated wildly, waiting for his bellowed accusation of adultery.

Richard was breaking large pieces off his bread roll and tossing them into his soup. She had the absurd image of a shark feeding. 'He'll be gone by morning,' he said. 'He pleaded time to pack up his sailboat – I must have been in a merciful mood to allow it.'

The thought of Flynn's boat no longer bobbing just past her observatory, where she could always mark his comings and goings, filled her with an unholy desolation. She did not know how she would make it through the rest of this meal sitting across from her husband, much less one more day trapped on this island without Flynn *or* Tally.

She had picked up her fork and now sat staring sightlessly through the prongs at her salad. Richard's eyes were heavy on her, insisting she meet his gaze. Finally, she looked up with a smile that only filled her cheeks.

'That sun really did a number on you today,' he said. 'You look terrible.' She did not imagine the exultation in his voice, she knew she did not. 'Eat up, my dear.'

It was well past midnight by the time Nerissa was satisfied that her husband's jackhammering snores, heard all the way up the hallway, were authentic and not simply a snare for a wayward wife.

Leaving her bedroom suite deadlocked, she went to the window and considered the verandah awning beneath. If she were brave enough to climb out onto it, she could cross to Tally's bedroom window and take the arching melaleuca branch that she knew her daughter had always used to escape Eyrie.

Flynn. Flynn. Flynn.

Tucking her dress into her underpants, she pushed open her window and eased one leg out onto the awning, followed by the other. Then she clambered gingerly across to Tally's windowsill, there to cling. She could no longer hear Richard's snores. He might have woken already, might even now be demanding admittance at her door. It had been many years since last came that dreaded knock, though she knew the waning of conjugal visits had not lessened in any way his sense of entitlement. She had the sickened feeling he was in just the sort of mood tonight to want to revisit nostalgia.

Go! Go now!

Desperation surging up once more, she scooted down the awning on her bottom towards the branch.

She had taken the old rear pathway, from Lookout Point down to the village, nearly toppling down several stone staircases in her haste and the pressing night. Insect song was a maddening neon buzz around her. Nerissa emerged at the back of a staff village that was nearly fully dark. Only a single kerosene lamp glowed in front of the amenities block. She tiptoed over the low seasonal creek bridge and through the back laneways towards the senior cabins, where she knew Flynn had lived these last few years.

Nerissa located it next to Irene Threadwell's house – though she had never once set foot near his bachelor abode – seeing immediately that his front door was wide open. She went up onto the porch and through the sliding door into the one-bedroom cabin.

Empty. Though not yet cleaned by housekeeping. She could still smell his hair cream and aftershave, the peppermint toothpaste always on his breath.

Had he packed up and sailed away so quickly? He had once before, when she wasn't even another man's wife. Why should he delay one more minute this time?

She walked out onto the porch, nursing an internal scream. *Not again, not again, not again.*

To her right, she saw a lamp lit and curtains shuffling in the Threadwells' house. She knew she was exposed here, but couldn't seem to draw herself away into the interior.

A moment later, the front door rolled open and Irene stepped out onto her own porch. 'Nerissa,' she hissed. 'Get over here.'

Nerissa moved across to stand in front of Irene's balcony. 'Where *is* he?'

'Just go home.'

'Please, tell me.'

'Go home *now*,' Irene ordered. 'Don't make a fool of yourself! You'll put all we've worked for here in danger, every one of us at risk. How can you still be so selfish after what I've done for you, after *everything* I've borne? Go back to your home and your husband, and forget about him.'

Nerissa glared at the backlit outline of her old friend, so much wider and squarer than in those lean, hard years together on Dara. 'How can you say that? You should understand better than anyone the mistake I made the first time, and what it has cost me.'

'I know better than anyone how *stupidly* you will act, how rarely you think of anyone else but yourself. I know you would sacrifice us in a heartbeat to have your own way … and I won't *let* you! Do you hear me? A promise is a promise. Go home *now*!'

Nerissa lifted her chin, a tremble in it. 'Forget you ever saw me here,' she said, and went on fleet feet through the village towards Coral Beach.

She'd been given a second chance, and she could not squander it.

The Milky Way moved over the dark jetty, a tall ship nodding leisurely at its end, ready to fly into that cloud of multitudinous stars.

Nerissa streaked over the jetty planks, certain this was the most urgent moment of her life.

Flynn, loading crates onto the boat, gave a cry of shock. She felt his disbelief as viscerally as her own panic. 'Nerissa! What are you doing here?'

'Stopping you.' She could hardly speak for the pain in her middle. He put down his burden.

'From sailing off –' her voice broke '– for another two decades!'

'Nerissa, your husband fired me. Your *husband*.'

'I can change his mind if you will just *wait*.'

'I'm not waiting another day. I've tried to quit this place fifty times before. He's just given me the push I needed to go.'

'This isn't about him.'

'It's all about him. You got what you needed in Richard Ramsey – money, security, and most of all, a reason to stay put on this goddamned island. After all this time, everything you've seen in him and copped from him, you're sticking with it. That's your choice, Nerissa, but I'm sure as hell not remaining here to watch it any longer. You deserve *infinitely* better than him.' At this, his voice shook.

She stepped nearer. 'I wanted *you* back then. But you sailed away to live your own dreams. You weren't *here*!' He stood, motionless, while she advanced closer. 'And then somehow, miraculously, you were here again, and I still couldn't have you …'

She was almost under his chin, so close she could feel the heat emanating through his chambray shirt. He took a step back. 'Then come away with me – now.'

'Come with you *where*?'

'Anywhere else but this island that has you so in its thrall. I asked you once before, and I'll ask you once again: let's go, together, and make a whole new life in another sea.'

But … Tally … Papa …

'You don't understand.' She writhed with misery. 'I *can't* –'

He watched her in the moonlight as water lapped at the hull, halyards slapping on the mast. He seemed to see all the endless, circular, cowardly vacillation in her. 'Can't or won't?'

'Aren't they one and the same?'

'No, Nerissa. They're two entirely different things.'

'It's … impossible.'

'Only until you've given it a red-hot try.'

'I need more time. I'll lose everything!'

'We've already lost a lifetime.'

'I have to figure a way out of all this first …'

He extended a hand. 'Here's a way, right now.'

She turned back to look at her island, primeval in the lesser light of evening.

Tally would never forgive me. I could never forgive myself…

In her stubborn silence, he had his answer. He bent, took up another crate and moved up the gangplank.

Nerissa spun away, all emotion drawing back on the front of sorrow's vast tsunami. She fled down the jetty to her observatory, fumbling with her key in the lock, finding it stuck there, unable to wrench it free again for the desperate need to be inside. The doorbells jangled and clashed. A great breaker of emotion was cresting over her. She slapped the key in frustration and left it there in the lock, throwing herself behind the safety of the door.

No sooner had she slammed it shut, the sadness crashed over her. She heaved and gulped and choked on the outrush.

How had it been only this morning she was cleaning her windows, looking forward to whatever brief and precious glances she might share with Flynn in the day ahead? Why couldn't they just have stayed as they were? Even the agony of unrequited love was still preferable to a cold, empty horizon without him.

Love.

The only thing this island could not offer her going forward.

She stumbled downstairs into the profound darkness of the sea grotto, to press her face against cool glass.

Tally.

Flynn.

Tally.

Flynn…

Overhead, the door banged open.

There was a beat of silence, then she heard footsteps cross the floor and move heavily down the stairs, to stop at the bottom.

She turned away from the porthole, unable to make out his form in such blackness, thankful that he could not see the unassuageable anguish of her face. She did not dare speak, lest he hear it in her voice.

'*Riss*,' he said. None but he had ever called her that, and he hadn't used it once since he'd come back. 'Do you *know* how many times I've wanted to knock his lights out, sweep you up in my arms and take you off this island? Sometimes, I thought I wouldn't care if I had to carry you kicking and screaming over my shoulder, as long as I could get you away from here – from him. Can you understand how many times I've kicked *myself* for coming back here to find you so unhappy – no, for ever leaving you here in the first place. I've blamed myself for every ill word he's ever spoken to you, every wrong he's ever done you. If I hadn't left, you might never have married him – you might still be mine.'

She could not stop the guttural cry that burst from her. 'Flynn, I've always been yours. I'm yours still, I'm yours *now* –'

He crossed the room in giant strides, crashing into her in the dark cavern. She was a drowning woman reaching out, flailing with the want of him. 'Please,' she choked out, 'please!'

He swept her up against the wall, his mouth opening hers with a furious kiss, then a shared, desperate pant. Her arms cleaved at his neck, pulled at his shoulders, clawed at his back, her legs hoisting up around his waist.

He lifted her dress, tugging aside the last barrier, then pushed deeply into her, both of them groaning the full length of his sinking. They stayed like this for a trembling moment, forehead pushing against forehead.

'Oh *God* – how could I have forgotten this?'

'I've thought of nothing else these four years.'

'Only *four* …'

Then there was no more talking, the ageless rhythm sweeping them up together; his head buried in her neck, her back rocking hard against the observatory window, tiny yelps leveraged out of her.

It was over like a depth charge, their shouts intermingled. They crumpled in a shuddering, heart-hammering silence. His arms alone kept her from dissolving onto the floor.

While he was still inside her, even as the aftershocks were running through her tender warmth, a sound came from overhead. A booming voice, unmistakable.

'Nerissa? Nerissa! Where are you?'

His footsteps approached the stairwell.

CHAPTER 11
GIRL REPORTER

Cairns, March 1968

Mainland life was pretty good, all things considered.

Tally Forster thought so every morning as she rose and poured her first cup of strong, black coffee in the Freshwater cottage she rented with her housemate and old school friend, Maisie. She would stand then, sipping quietly, before the rear window overlooking their bush backdrop, where small wallabies bounded down the mountain each morning to nibble grass in the sun-dappled clearing.

Wallabies were a novelty still for the island girl. As had been their pet emu, Edgar, whom they were forced to give up after Mrs Larson next door reported them to their landlord – no doubt in revenge for their habit of sitting out on the back porch on Friday evenings with a bottle of plonk, giggling loudly until all hours. Those late-night, squealing nudie runs in torrential rain probably hadn't helped their reputation much, either. But what else were you meant to do when a cyclone cut off both your power and water for the whole weekend?

Mainland life wasn't perfect, but it came pretty close. In Cairns, she'd found freedom and frivolity, hard work and good money – not to mention *success*.

Tally did not linger after morning coffee – her adrenaline already firing for the day's adventures – and she would be out the door, with a banana from their garden tucked in her knapsack, usually before Maisie had even slapped quiet her alarm clock. Maisie was a bank clerk, and though they might have shared a ride into town in Tally's Morris Minor, Tally insisted on keeping a journalist's hours rather than a banker's.

This Monday morning, Tally gunned her little car over Freshwater bridge, smiling as she remembered the weekend's fun. The creek had been up after yet more heavy rain and the bridge, predictably, had gone under. Maisie and Tally had joined local friends for a Saturday flood-swim, hurtling out on a rope swing over the rushing creek. The best fun had been swimming underwater against the current to the air bubble beneath the middle of the bridge. A daring feat of strength, courage and lung capacity, and Tally had managed it to raucous cheers.

She didn't need a head any bigger these days, but thanks to her weekend victory, Tally entered the newsroom on the second floor of the *Cairns Ledger*'s historic building with even more oomph than usual in her step.

She already swaggered around that busy office with the air of a veteran journalist – although she was the youngest feature writer on the team, and the only female reporter on staff. *Reporter*; a title that still thrilled her, even after almost five years, and a position she had created for *herself* when she had fronted up to the *Ledger*'s temple front façade with classic white colonnade and outright demanded it.

Tally had been in luck that day. Long-time editor Jonathon Tremblay had just returned from his daily roast lunch at home with his wife, and as he would later confess, with his belly full of warm grub and his mind tender towards Mrs Tremblay, he'd been disposed in the moment to think quite highly of the opposite sex.

The slim, full-throated girl standing arms akimbo before his secretary's desk had planted her feet, refusing to move until she could speak to him.

THE MISTRESS OF DARA ISLAND

She was boldly spruiking her writing prowess before he'd agreed to grant her an interview. Jonathon liked women with pluck, he told her that straight up, and Tally had more than most.

Tally had been hired on the spot as the *Ledger*'s newest cadet, immediately dubbed 'Girl Reporter' by the all-male newsroom team. Tally hadn't minded, setting out to make that moniker her very own. She'd won the start she wanted, and she was not afraid of hard work. In fact, Tally *lived* to work. She had earned respect both for her courage and capability. Here was the reporter who could be relied upon to snap up the seemingly banal lead, sniff out a better story angle, ask audacious questions with an indomitable smile and deliver her piece to deadline – even if it took all night. More than once she'd slept at work, with her head under a desk lamp still burning.

Around town, she'd also come to be known as Girl Reporter, and the novelty of a female journalist in men's clothing opened more doors than it closed.

Girl Reporter was Jonathon's favourite, and her peers knew it. Tally, for her part, adored her editor, and had the self-awareness to recognise she was playing out some of her good-daughter fantasies through her relationship with him. He, being so unlike the old mongrel who'd tried to belt her temperament out of her. And would wonders never cease? Tally Ramsey wasn't, as it had turned out, incurably oppositional. Under Jonathon's affirmative hand, she had learned to harness her wilfulness in far more productive ways.

Using my determination for good, not evil.

She'd certainly used her determination to score one of the best desks in the newsroom, and she recalled all the reasons she loved her working environment anew as she waded across the busy space, a sea of grey tweed and olive herringbone. Her quiet corner was conducive to concentration, far from the smoke-filled tearoom, where her male peers proved they were just as capable of malicious gossip as the opposite sex. Most importantly, she was close enough to Jonathon's office that she might be the first to jump up when he emerged with an exciting job, but at enough distance to protect her autonomy.

Before the daily newsroom meeting at ten o'clock, she had a series of telephone leads to follow up. Tally settled into her seat, with her second cup of coffee steaming alongside her typewriter, and cracked her neck noisily from side to side. With her nosy neighbour, Hamish, sufficiently irked by this ritual, she opened her spiral notebook, ready to get calling. Phone-bound days were far more tiring than those out on the city streets, so she promised herself a long walk along the Cairns Esplanade during her lunch hour for a reward. A glimpse of azure sea and silver-hazed horizon would re-energise her more quickly than her fifth and final coffee ever could.

It felt like hours before she put down the handset and uncrooked ear from shoulder to loudly crack her neck, once again. Hamish wasn't there to cringe this time, and she hadn't even noticed him leave. She stretched back in her chair, shaking out her aching fingers, so that the delicate string of shells on her wrist rolled and shone. Looking down at her notebook, she smoothed her fingers over the hieroglyphics of her own competence – the Pitman's shorthand that filled the many towers of notebooks rubber-banded under her desk.

Among the shorthand today, she'd been doodling compulsively again. Always the same doodle, but of course that was how doodles went. Hers was a bird's-eye sketch of Dara. One *might* call it a map, if they were prepared to overlook Tally's lack of cartography skills. But it wasn't supposed to make sense to anyone else. She was forever doodling her Dara maps over story quotes, later having to decipher her own shorthand among island icons. Jonathon had ribbed her for those doodles many a time, calling her *Robinson Crusoe*.

With Dara on her mind, it was inevitable that her thoughts moved to Ma.

Her eyes alighted on the framed photo of her mother at the top of her desk. The only personal artefact she kept on public display, for the fewer people who knew about Tally's idyllic and unusual childhood, the better.

Tally nudged Ma's portrait to the left to better see it. Ma was sitting on her Bentwood rocking chair on the verandah of Eyrie, legs primly crossed in her sundress of seafoam green, smiling graciously. *The mistress of Dara*, Tally liked to murmur under her breath. She had taken the photo herself on her beloved Minolta one summer home from boarding school, and had cherished it ever since. Ma had seemed so much happier in those days, hadn't she? Tally hadn't seen her mother smile properly for what felt like years.

Granted, she only saw Ma the two times a year when she came to stay in Cairns, the long journey by ferry, train and bus exhausting her too much. Ma ought to have been pleased to sojourn with the two young women in Freshwater. They certainly tried to give her a good time, took her shopping at Bolands, to the Rex picture theatre, even along to garden parties with friends, plying her with their favourite plonk at every chance. Tally *knew* her mother craved the break away from Richard, so why, then, did it not seem to lighten the worried parentheses around her lips, the fault line between her brows?

Tally sometimes suspected it was her own absence from Dara that made Ma so eternally sad, and then it was hard to sympathise. Ma knew precisely what she had to do to finally bring her daughter home again.

Grimly, Tally pushed the frame out of sight. Time for the newsroom meeting, and she had a prime seat to nab.

With a short break for lunch, Tally decided to grab a sandwich at the milk bar and take that invigorating stroll along the palm-lined Esplanade.

She had not made it ten steps along Abbott Street, before she came face to face with a spectre. A young woman with golden-brown hair, her feline-pretty face so startlingly familiar that for a second, Tally's mind simply could not place her in this setting.

The woman took a step forward – calm and self-possessed, in a belted safari skirt, with a coloured blouse tucked in, bearing, of all things, the embroidered logo of Mermaid Bay Resort.

And *then* Tally had it.

'Lila? *Lila*, is it you?'

'Hello, Tally. You've changed your name – I was asking around for Tally Ramsey.'

'It's unofficial, but I prefer it.' Tally went forward quickly to kiss her cheeks, quite astonished at finding her island playmate on her city street. 'What are you doing here?'

'I'm here to see *you*.'

'*Me?*' Tally drew back to inspect Lila's face, noting with some envy the healthy colour of her skin, the sun-tinted depth of her hair. Tally's own skin had a peaky office pallor, her driftwood curls were smoothed down, sun streaks long grown out. 'Well, that's unexpected, but how lovely,' she declared. 'I was just about to grab a bite at the milk bar. Will you join me?'

'I'd really rather go somewhere private,' Lila said firmly.

Fear twitched its tail, a prehistoric creature stirring in the mire.

'All right, then,' Tally said overbrightly. 'We can go straight to the Esplanade.'

They walked the two blocks to the grassy foreshore, Tally compensating for Lila's tight-set lips with general chatter about landmarks and local happenings. Tally Forster had the presence of a local luminary, attracting greetings, nods and looks all along their route. She was pleased for Lila to witness it.

Do you see what I've accomplished? I've made a new *name for myself here. My father might be the biggest fish in Bellen Beach, but the Ramsey name means next to nothing in this city.*

The tide was out on the Esplanade, exposing the mudflats to a cluster of big, white pelicans. The salt air was heavy with mangrove tang. Locating a row of slender palms under which to sit, Tally patted a sea-facing wooden bench. 'Will here do?'

Lila sat promptly, looking very grave. Tally lowered herself slowly, hackles raised. Lila turned to face her, their knees abutting, taking Tally's ink-stained fingers between her small, work-roughened hands. 'Tally, there's no easy way for me to say this, so I just will.' Tally stared down at the hands gripping hers. 'Your mum has disappeared from Dara.'

Tally threw off Lila's hands. 'Don't be stupid!'

Lila sighed. 'Would I come all this way to say something stupid?'

'I wonder that *you* came at all. If something had happened to my mother, I'm sure my father would have telephoned me. He's a prick, but he's not a *monster ...*'

'Well, that's a whole other story you'll find out for yourself. I'm only here to relay the news about Mrs Ramsey.'

Relay the news! As though this was a thirty-second piece on a radio bulletin. The lag of shock abated. 'What do you mean Ma has *disappeared*? When? Where has she gone?'

'Okay, here are the facts. Your mother disappeared two weeks ago –'

'Two *weeks*?!'

'Will you let me finish? A fortnight ago, Mrs Ramsey vanished in the middle of the night – presumably from Eyrie, given she was last seen at dinner before retiring to bed at her usual time. The next morning, when she didn't come down to breakfast, and couldn't be roused through her locked bedroom door, Mr Ramsey broke it down. She wasn't in there. Her bed wasn't even slept in. It's quite a mystery how she vanished from behind a locked door.'

Tally was up and off the bench, hollering, 'What are the *cops* doing about this? Why haven't they come to see me in their missing-person investigation?'

'As far as I'm aware, your father hasn't made a missing-person's report.'

'For crying out loud – the first twenty-four hours are crucial after a person goes missing! We've already lost two *weeks*! Why wouldn't he go to the police? Why hasn't anyone else?'

'There was a *note*, you see. Left on her bed.'

Tally whimpered. 'What kind of note?' *I know she was unhappy lately, miserable even, but please don't let it be … that.*

'A goodbye letter.'

God, no – no, no, no!

Seeing her face, Lila rushed to cushion the blow. 'Oh please, don't panic, it was only a goodbye *for now*. It was also a plea for privacy. She begged him not to send a search party for her.'

'She ought to have been reported missing straightaway!'

'Your father has informed the staff that she's gone on a "restorative holiday". Only those present at Eyrie on the morning she was discovered missing know the truth – that Mrs Ramsey has deserted him.'

But … Ma desert Dara? *She would never!*

'How can he possibly think he can keep it hidden? That sly bastard, what the devil is he up to? I should've been told immediately!'

'I wrongly assumed you had been – sorry. It was only when you didn't arrive, guns blazing, on the very next ferry, that I realised he must be keeping it from you. So, here I am to bring you home.'

'You've come again as a chaperone, have you?'

'If you'll come home with me …' The plea, even in Lila's soft voice, was unmistakable.

Tally walked rapidly around the bench, trying to think clearly.

'But I can't just up and quit Cairns at the drop of a hat. I've got my job – I love my job! And I have my dear little house with Maisie – I can't leave Maisie in the lurch! And what about our wallabies …' Horror was making her babble, for there was this realisation: if Ma had disappeared of her own free will, why on earth hadn't she told *Tally*? There was no way she would just trot off without alerting her only child. Something terrible might have befallen her.

And who else in the world might have something to gain from Ma's disappearance? That greedy, duplicitous man who sat up in Eyrie this very minute, presiding over Tally's bloody island.

She stopped prowling and spun around. Lila sat watching her, bottom lip tucked between her teeth.

'I have to go home,' Tally cried. 'If Ma is gone, then I have to protect Dara until she gets back. I don't have any time to waste!'

Tally marched directly from her meeting with Lila to see Jonathon in his office. Lila, having nowhere else to be, went for a wander around the city blocks.

Jonathon was at his desk, behind a closed door, with a semicircle of dark-suited subeditors and higher-ups visible in the large internal window, through which he liked to survey his newsroom. Tally motioned urgently at the window. Jonathon looked up, and seeing Tally, raised a hand to the subeditor speaking to his left, then indicated for her to enter.

Tally closed the door firmly behind her and launched without preamble: 'Jonathon, I need some time off, starting right now, for a family emergency.'

The interrupted subeditor now hooked an index finger over his lip to cover a grunt of laughter. 'In the family way,' he muttered.

Tally rounded on him. 'Unlike you, Mr Eight-mouths-to-feed, I know how to use contraception.'

Laughter shot around the circle.

Jonathon adjusted his glasses with sausage fingers, heavily print-stained. 'All right, we'll just have Tally in here, thank you.'

Papers were shuffled and chairs scraped aside. Tally set her back against the large window, hopeful of concealing her face from the many watching eyes now trained upon the two of them. As the last man loped out, Jonathon motioned to a chair. 'You've truncated a meeting I wasn't very much enjoying, so you've got my full attention. What's *wrong*, Tally?'

'My mother is missing. I've got to go home – right now.'

She saw the newspaper man's expertly honed interest pique first. *A missing woman?* To his credit, however, he responded with immediate and emphatic concern. 'Okay, then. How long do you need?'

'I ... frankly, I'm not sure, Jonathon. Can you give me a week?' She considered the travel there and back, which was two full days alone. 'On second thoughts, can I have *two* weeks?'

'You haven't taken a decent block of time off in years, yes of course you can access your leave. I'm not going to like losing you for so long, though.'

Pleasure pinked the apples of her cheeks. Neither would she enjoy being away from the *Ledger*, much less Jonathon. She'd landed on her own isle of plenty here.

She jerked her head towards the newsroom. 'You'd better not let any of those duds out there muscle in on my column.'

'Your work will be right where you left it. You're irreplaceable.'

'Thank you,' she said, with firm sincerity.

He rubbed two frankfurters along his chin, watchful now. 'Your family still have that island off Bellen Beach? Is that where she's gone missing from?'

'Yes,' she answered shortly.

'Uh-huh.' He tilted his head with a judicious look. 'And what do you plan on doing about your mother when you get there?'

What *plan*? There was no plan. Tally just needed to get back home as soon as possible to find Ma's trail. And if it came to it … protect her future.

'I'm going to help with the search, and … find out what my father has done.'

Jonathon's silver-bushed brows shot up. 'You think it's like *that*, Tally?'

'No!' She frowned. 'I don't know. I hope not. I'll get to the bottom of it all.'

'Your poor family won't know what hit them. You're a bulldog with an idea, you tear in hard and fast, and you don't let go until you've got the meat of it.'

Fine words! Tally might have beamed with the delight of them if she didn't also see an unflattering picture of herself tearing up the hill to Eyrie, a ravening wolf baying for her father's blood.

Jonathon came around now to kneel in front of her, where he might not be seen by craning heads. She wanted to reach out and pat his head. *Thank you for everything you've been to me, for restoring some small faith in mankind.*

'You're my hardest-working reporter,' he said, 'and you've moved extraordinarily fast up the ranks. Quicker than most men I've mentored. It's admirable, but it must have come at a cost to you, especially being so far away from your family and all.'

Tally fixed Jonathon with the expression he called her *Bunsen-burner look* – eyes of flaming, furious blue. 'I'm not bloody well making up a missing mother to get out of work!'

'I'm suggesting some rest and island tonic might do you the world of good. So, if you need longer than two weeks back home – maybe even a month – that's all right. Whatever you require …' Briefly, he massaged his temples. 'But you just make sure to *come back*, okay?'

'Without question,' Tally said, overemphasising the second word. She didn't think she'd outright lied to Jonathon before; he was always so fond of her irreverent truth-telling. But what else should she say in this moment? *I don't know if I'm going home to discover my mother disposed of, and my father trying to steal my inheritance, in which case, I can never leave Dara again until he's gone.*

'In my experience,' Jonathon sighed, reading her more clearly than she cared to admit. 'Home is always home. And when home comes calling … it can be hard to say no.'

CHAPTER 12

HOMEWARD BOUND

I must go down to the seas again, for the call of the running tide
Is a wild call and a clear call that may not be denied

John Masefield

A bolt from the blue was sleeping on Tally's couch, in Tally's little
cottage – and the sense of displacement was dizzying.

Maisie had been every bit as supportive as Tally had known she would
be, when she'd arrived home to find a strange woman needing a place to
crash and Tally packing to flee. Maisie barely had laid down her handbag
before she was rustling up a hearty meal for the trio, and helping to dig
Tally's clothing out of their mountainous shared pile.

In her bedroom now, with her suitcase packed by the door, Tally
sat at her lamp-lit desk, in a room burgeoning with shadows and dark
angst.

*Where are you, Ma? Why would you run away from him without
coming to* me? *What has he* done *to you?*

She should have been asleep hours ago in preparation for their
pre-dawn departure, but she was deep in the throes of rereading Ma's
monthly letters. Four and a half years of them. She was scouring those
words now with the benefit of hindsight, on the hunt for a clue to Ma's
mental state and whereabouts.

A niggling doubt: if Ma had left a clue, why wouldn't Tally have spotted it before now? She knew her busy career had made her self-absorbed, and homesickness had given her a rather large blind spot when it came to certain, painful topics in Ma's letters – chiefly, any mention of her father. But *surely*, her instincts would have alerted her long before now if Ma had been in real danger?

Tally had begun by first holding those beribboned piles to her nose, desperate for the salty scent of home and the blue longing of Ma's perfume. Then she'd started rereading her letters from the beginning. She was now approaching Ma's very last lot. One thing was abundantly clear: the longer Tally had stayed away from Dara, the less she seemed to recognise Ma.

Nerissa Forster had evolved steadily over the last four and a half years in a manner barely noticeable from letter to letter, but which was screamingly bloody obvious when read altogether. Ma of the first two years after Tally's departure was full of hope for her daughter's future, and insistence that she stay to pursue her dreams on the mainland. Even if Tally had wanted to throw in the towel and go home, she didn't think that version of Ma would have ever allowed it. In retrospect, it was almost as though Nerissa didn't *want* her daughter back on Dara.

As the years and letters had gone by, Ma's pride in Tally's success had remained undimmed, but her focus had turned to herself. She spent far too long recounting the mundanities of her existence – what she might have worn and the way it complimented her figure or colour, how her skin or hair was responding to some new beauty treatment or other, what clever thing she'd said to make those around her laugh. Was it some kind of midlife crisis? Surely women of Ma's age, stodgily married for two decades, were past such things. She apparently spent an inordinate amount of time beachcombing, for she was forever including drawings of new shells in her possession.

And then there was this letter, dating from about six months ago, dramatically shorter than the rest. It had come with a warning of something Tally had long suspected on her own:

Your father reads our mail. Be careful.

Tally sat very still, considering this letter. Had she ever given anything away she shouldn't have? No, nothing – Tally was sure of it. Both wife and daughter already had been careful to write one another as though some wartime censor would trawl through their communication.

Why had Ma suddenly become so paranoid about Tally's letters?

She set this letter aside and continued reading. Quickly, she divined that the letter was indeed a watershed. Ma's correspondence had never been the same again after the warning. They were only short notes, dull, filled with the inconsequential happenings of Mermaid Bay – for heaven's sake, what colour hibiscus flowers they were using lately for the brasserie's table decorations! There was no more of Ma's self-care and shell-love that had predominated, indeed *nothing* of herself.

Guilt oozed in Tally's throat: Ma might be missing from Dara now, but she had been slowly vanishing for months.

How could she have overlooked this? Tally's workload certainly had picked up once she'd been promoted to her very own column, but that was no excuse for such egotism. Ma had been putting out a giant, strobing, blaring signal of her unhappiness, and Tally's letters back were all self-centred posturing – filled with *her* clippings, *her* adventures around the traps, not to mention the outright boasting: compliments verbatim from Jonathon. What kind of daughter was she?

Her panic was near asphyxiating. Had Ma simply walked herself into the sea, never to arise from it?

She should have gone home at least *once* in the last four years to see for herself how Ma was faring. It was one thing to have hosted Ma as a guest, but Tally ought to have squashed her pride and just *gone home*.

What if it was too *late* now?

Oh, Ma...

Sorrow tore through the thin wall still holding her together, pain rushing forth with no outlet. She was a submarine breached, a body floating dull-eyed to a sealed hatch. Not one tear streaked her pale cheek. Never from lack of trying, though.

Tally screwed up her face, tensed her belly muscles and emitted a long, squawking groan. *Dry-bawling*, she called it. About as effective as a mimed sneeze.

She dry-bawled for another second or two, then quit abruptly.

All right, enough of that. Time to be practical. Let's get home – and then I'll find Ma.

Tally's Morris Minor was hurtling through the early-morning darkness towards Bellen Beach. Lila dozed in the passenger seat, head against the window. The interior was filled with the aroma of their packed breakfast. Hearing Tally's alarm go off, Maisie had risen with them to make their egg-and-bacon sandwiches and fill a thermos with hot coffee.

Tally wished she hadn't. It was hard enough to reverse away from that darling cottage, without Maisie standing at the top of the driveway in her nightie, waving like a mother sending off her children to a Girl Guides camp.

'See you in a fortnight,' Tally had promised, throwing her arms around Maisie. An hour on, the vow still lingered in her throat like acid.

Dawn was breaking on the east horizon, a crimson demarcation between charcoal sky and fields of cane flashing by. Tally pressed her foot down harder; they had to be at the Bellen Beach jetty by seven for the ferry. Always chasing that damned ferry, weren't they?

Lila did not stir against her windowpane, even as the sun began to burn up, bathing her skin in bright yellow light, setting glints on her golden-brown hair. Tally stole glances away from the endless ribbon of road, panning for a glimpse of her childhood playmate. She might have picked up a hitchhiker for all she felt she knew about Lila Threadwell anymore.

The sun glare might not have disturbed Lila, but Tally's probing looks seemed to. She startled awake, checking their position. 'God, my neck.'

'Better start on breakfast now,' Tally said, nudging the brown paper parcel. 'We're not going to have time before the ferry. Is that prick Angus still the skipper?'

'No,' Lila said, unwrapping her sandwich. The smell swept into Tally's nostrils, triggering a flood of saliva. 'He's the island manager now.'

'He's the *what*!' Tally swerved back into her lane, gripping the wheel. 'Shivers, sorry!'

Lila's right hand had shot out to brace against the dash. She left it there for another second, before returning it to the sandwich clutched in her lap. 'Yes, Mr Ramsey appointed him in September.'

'That useless sonofabitch managing Mermaid Bay, I can't believe it! What happened to the other fellow, the big shot?'

'Mr Barrett? Mr Ramsey sacked him for stealing. He just vanished overnight, never to be seen again. It was quite a hoo-ha.'

Tally ought to have been pleased; some payback for the man who'd stolen *her* job. But she'd grown to feel glad he'd come along and taken a role that was never really right for her. If she hadn't been thwarted, she'd still be stuck on Dara warring eternally with her father, never knowing the friendship of Maisie, the mentorship of Jonathon, the esteem of her wide readership.

I'm better off for not getting what I wanted.

Lila was tearing into her sandwich, the smell of it now close to torture.

A new thought had occurred to Tally. In the past six months, as Ma's happiness had so evidently decreased, Angus had been managing Richard's business – and by default, *Ma's home*. The resort manager could make or break spirits on the island – especially her mother's.

Tally glanced at Lila. 'How's it been going since he took over the role?'

'Angus has changed since primary school.'

'So, he's not a bully anymore?'

'No, he thinks he has *real* power and influence now, and with no teachers to check him. Mr Ramsey thinks he's the best thing since sliced bread.'

'Good, so we still hate him, then?'

'Just between you and me …?' Her voice dropped to an unnecessary whisper. 'I call him the Bullshark's Bully.'

Sweat had lined Tally's palms. She took each one off the wheel in turn to wipe on her plaid shorts.

Lila had gone on with her next hearty bite, but Tally's appetite had evaporated. Had Angus's toadying up to Richard somehow made Ma's life hell?

The left turn-off to Bellen Beach approached. From here it would be twenty more minutes to the sea, passing through dense rainforest.

Lila was balling up her paper wrapping.

'From what you observed,' Tally began, willing her voice not to break, 'how would *you* say my ma was feeling over the last few months?'

'I wouldn't want to speak for Mrs Ramsey. It's not my place. She has her own good reasons for holding her cards close to her chest. Anyway, you know she never gets personal with staff.'

Tally sighed. 'I'm just asking what you *observed*, Lila.'

'All right, then.' Lila swivelled in her seat to fully face Tally's profile. 'I'll tell you this. Eyrie might have been a locked tower for the way Mrs Ramsey stuck to it in recent months. And when we did catch sight of her, she was so pale and desolate, it was like she'd become a … ghostship, drifting around.'

What might Ma have done in such a frame of mind?

'Do you think Ma could ever have …' *Say it, you coward.* 'Done something silly?'

'Truthfully, I might have been more worried about that, if she hadn't seemed to come good in the last few weeks before she disappeared. She was almost … her old self again.'

Tally's neck prickled ominously. An abrupt change of mood after a long sadness. Was that a warning sign of self-harm? Despite the dread tumbling her heart, Tally's next question was restrained.

'How so?'

Lila took a moment before replying. 'I approached her, you see, about a … personal matter, and through it all she was so very kind and generous to me. She gave me … a great deal of help. She was the gracious mistress I remembered, all over again.'

'Okay,' Tally said stiffly. 'Thank you.'

She fixed her vision on the winding, jungled road ahead. 'We'd better watch out,' she said, indicating a large painted sign affixed to a tree. 'We're entering cassowary territory.' Both women craned for a better view of the sign: a caricature of a ten-foot-tall cassowary, with a matchbox-sized car crumpled up against it.

It would be almost humorous if she wasn't so afraid.

There was nothing – *nothing* – like that first glimpse of the turquoise sea between Bellen Beach's dense line of coconut palms.

While Lila hurried off to collect their ferry tickets from the kiosk, Tally puttered slowly along the beachfront, looking for a safe parking spot for her car. Her eyes, hungry as a tourist's, absorbed every alteration in her old town. She had been away long enough for buildings and trees to seem shrunken.

I have come up in the world.

The oddest change was the mass of lawn signs that dotted the beachfront bungalows. Hand-painted placards in all caps: 'SAVE OUR REEF!' But save which reef, and from what? Her story sense tingled. Maybe she could even pull off a column for Jonathon while she was visiting.

She wandered down onto the wide, golden expanse of sand and threw off her plimsolls to revel in the million tiny sand balls underfoot created by the sand-bubbler crabs. She breathed in the salt tang, tugging off her aviators to marvel properly at the vivid turquoise. She had worked only three blocks from the harbour in Cairns, but it hadn't been *her* sea, and never *this* colour. Her soul had been parched for the sight of it.

Stooping, Tally picked up a large sand dollar from among many. She rotated the coin between thumb and forefinger, marvelling anew at the perfect artistry. The currency of the sea, adorned with five-petalled tropical blooms: plumeria, hibiscus, pentas. *Coins lost by mermaids*, Ma always said. She used to sell gold-tipped sand dollars in her shop for a while, until too many guests complained how easily they crumbled. But that was how they were supposed to be, ephemeral. *The coins of Atlantis*, Ma would sigh, *not meant to be kept by land dwellers*.

By the time they'd rounded the headland, Tally was standing alone on the ferry foredeck, hungering for her first glimpse of faraway Dara. She'd thrown off her hair barrette so that her tresses streamed long and wild behind her, damp with sea spray. Out here, she didn't have to force more conversation with Lila, nor hide her emotions.

Tally had left her little car parked behind the tavern at Bellen Beach, and her possessive dismay was being worked off by the cool wind and cushioned bounce of their voyage. And now, the blessed sight of her island again – at first, only a wedge of blue on the silver horizon, growing steeper and greener and more real with every nautical mile. Why should it surprise her to find Dara had not been swallowed by the sea – that it still lay here, after all this time?

It loomed up now: luxuriant green peaks, with white yachts anchored around. Excitement flared in her solar plexus.

I'm like a turtle, irresistibly drawn back to the beach of my birthplace. Home is always home.

She had been away for far too long. Seeing Dara again made it seem so pointless: living in suburbia, strutting around Cairns as Girl Reporter, chasing mainland stories for mainland readers. Because *look* at this paradise sublime. How could she ever have let her father drive her off, much less *keep* her away? She'd been punishing only herself.

No man was an island, the saying went, but Tally certainly *was* Dara.

Exhilaration tore through her veins and inflated her lungs, making her heady with impatience. She'd been missing, but knew herself now to be found.

I'm nearly home, Dara. I'm nearly here, Ma.

CHAPTER 13

MAD KING OF EYRIE

Tally, first to disembark from the ferry, not even waiting for Lila, fairly flew up the gangplank, ignoring the hand offered at the top by a crew member. She took one giant leap onto the jetty, knowing exactly where to land to avoid the squeaky plank. All her vision was set on the underwater observatory, twenty yards ahead. If this was all a bad dream, then Ma was waiting just inside for her daughter's return.

Tally scampered over the last few yards, passing the salvaged anchor displayed at the front and into the giftshop.

Empty.

She halted, eyes scouring the giftshop as though she somehow had missed the sight of her mother among the displays and artefacts. She stepped closer to a shelf, picking up a garishly purple-dyed shell among many others. Ma never would have stocked something so tacky, much less priced it so high. Come to think of it, half the shop was filled with these mass-produced-looking gifts. They had to be importing cheap goods from somewhere else? Had Ma stopped making her art of her own accord, or had a 'business' decision been made on her behalf? She put the shell down and went to the glass cabinet at the back of the store, still housing Ma's lovingly handmade mermaids. There were two dozen left. Tally decided she would come back here and take the lot of them.

She walked down the steep steps into the observatory chamber.

There wasn't a soul downstairs, no one to reach a cool, pale hand to the special spot at the back of Tally's neck. Nonetheless, she stood for a moment, neck tingling under phantom fingers, *hoping*.

Gradually, her eyes adjusted to the muted blue glow of the room. Shoals of fish swarmed by, deep-indigo shadows shifted between tridents of light, seaweed swayed, but there was only stillness in this cold, briny chamber.

Tally's gaze locked on the nearest porthole, frowning. The outside of the windows needed a thorough scrubbing; it looked like it hadn't been done in months. Ma was always so fastidious about keeping them clean.

Re-emerging on the upper level, her eyes went to Ma's desk, the bottom of her stomach dropping open as though improperly hinged. Ma's ship-in-a-bottle was gone.

Had Ma taken it when she disappeared, or had *someone else*?

All these years, Tally had avoided challenging her mother about the missing will, and now it might be too late. Such an easy thing to have asked: *Hey, by the way, where'd you put my birthright?* But the words had been as impossible to get out as the ship was supposed to be from that bottle. To her great shame, Tally had never apologised for the ship's desecration, always determined Ma should be the first to break. Her pigheaded pride! Whatever Ma had done with the will, she did so because she'd not trusted Tally to be patient, much less to respect her property. On that count, she'd been exactly right.

Frustration sent Tally scuttling out of the observatory. She wanted to get the worst of today over and done with. She had to face her father.

Pulling her aviators down from her head, Tally ran smack bang into Lila, standing on the jetty outside, with Tally's suitcase waiting beside her.

Lila lifted the case. 'Are you ready to go up?' Her chaperone once again seeing her safely home.

Tally took the case from her. 'Let's do it.'

They went along the jetty, under the welcome arch, and splitting off onto the service drive to Eyrie. In her periphery, she saw only what was missing: no line of porters in their woven hats, no waiters bearing welcome drinks outside reception, no guitar player strumming an unhurried ballad. The ixora hedges around the lodge had proliferated to the height of a man, tired signs needed several licks of paint, golden cane fronds littered the garden paths, and there were bottle caps and cigarette butts left to languish on the cobblestones when they never should have been allowed to drop at all.

Where has the paradisiacal ambience gone?

Lila had no trouble reading Tally's outrage, huffing and fuming as she was. 'You'll find everything much changed,' Lila said quietly. '*People*, too.'

It was a clear warning.

The women climbed the steep drive and emerged into the terraced gardens of the Ramsey residence. Lila stopped three paces short, while Tally stood, depleted of breath and speech, at the bottom of the marble steps, peering up at her home. Within the coterie of towering melaleucas, Eyrie looked old and tired, though no less formidable.

Here, courage failed her. She tried to imagine herself as a battering ram – no door or father able to withstand her – but without Ma, she was more vulnerable in the face of this house than she'd ever felt before.

She frowned at the grand verandah.

Something's wrong.

The black cockatoos, still caged after all this time, had sent up a strident alarm, but Tally could hardly hear them for the roar of blood in her ears.

The all-wrongness of Eyrie was now shockingly apparent …

Ma's beloved rocking chair lay on the verandah in splintered pieces.

Tally went dazedly up the stairs, nerves racked by the cockatoos' shrill refrain.

He'd destroyed Ma's chair?! His wedding gift to Ma; indeed, the only thing she'd asked for, the chair in which she had rocked a restless Tally to sleep every day. Ma always said it was the closest she could give Tally to a boat bobbing on the sea.

Tally squatted in front of the ruined chair. 'What the hell has he *done*?' He hadn't just destroyed it; he'd slaughtered it, and any hope of ever putting it back together again. And then what? Left it here for anyone to see.

Tally felt Lila climb the stairs behind her, though she had not been invited. She stood with her hand resting on Tally's shoulder. 'I'm sorry,' she said.

Lila's sympathy was intolerable, it made all of this too real. Tally stood up so that Lila's hand fell away. 'Thank you for travelling with me this far,' she said.

'It was the very least I should do.'

Lila went back down the stairs. At the bottom, she turned. 'After you've seen things out here, you might come and visit me.'

As Lila disappeared into the gardens, Tally took a breath and advanced.

A thin housemaid had appeared in the doorway, wiping her hands on her apron. She was as pretty as any of the maids Richard hired, but skittish in a way they normally were not. Notably, she was wearing a frilly sundress rather than the prescribed uniform. 'You're not meant to be all the way up here. This is private property!'

Tally smiled. 'Yes, I know – it's *my* house. I'm Richard's daughter.'

She might have declared herself a door-to-door bible seller. The woman was impervious. 'He's not expecting you, sorry.'

'It'll be a nice surprise, then, won't it?' Clearly, she was going to have to push past the girl. It wouldn't be the first doorway she'd breached, having learned fast in her death-knocking days.

She worried that the maid might be stronger than she appeared, but she did, at the crucial moment, give way.

Admitted, Tally dropped her suitcase in the hallway and looked around, eyes landing on Richard's closed door. 'Where is he?'

'He can't see you right now. He's in a meeting.'

'I'll wait,' Tally said, arms folding.

The girl's lips pinched. She indicated a long wooden bench set against the wall. 'You sit here. I'll find out if he has any time for you.'

Tally sat, crossing her legs. 'You must be the latest ring-in. My mother hasn't mentioned you – what's your name?'

'Olga,' she replied with a miffed look, before making an abrupt about turn.

Tally watched Miffed Olga scurry away down the hallway, out of sight. She tipped her head, following the sound of the girl's footsteps, urgent now. Eyrie's service exit squealed open and slammed shut.

Just where was she *off to?*

Tally sat, absorbing the familiar smells of her childhood home, and the new and eerie silence. Her father's voice did not sound behind the door. Even the cockatoos had hushed. There was only her own breathing, overloud and ragged.

She had to be in shock. How else could she explain the way she simply sat and waited on that bench, in her own home?

She stared down at the wood beneath her, ran her hands along it, realising it was not a bench but one of the pews from Dara's secluded old seaside chapel. A relic of the island's bygone past, once Grandpapa's hand-built cottage and the place where Ma had grown up. Grandpapa's funeral had been held there, before they carried his coffin to his final resting place. It was sadly run-down nowadays and used only rarely for ad hoc services and guests' private reflections.

Her father had long wanted to bulldoze the chapel for further resort development, but Ma had resisted with uncharacteristic backbone. Ma and Tally had talked of one day turning it into a proper wedding chapel, for couples visiting from all over the world. Ma said an island for lovers needed a place to elope.

But looking further down the hallway, she sighted another pew. Had he finally gutted Ma's childhood home now that she wasn't here to *stop* him?

With that, the enervating spell of shock was broken. Tally jumped to her feet and turned to her father's office. She would not wait another moment.

She rapped on his door; a strident cracking, expecting a raised voice in return. When no answer came, she put her hand to the knob, drew breath and gently eased it open.

The study, with curtains drawn, was dark and stuffy. A single pedestal fan stirred the muggy air within.

He's not here.

Tally was about to turn and go when she noted the fan was set to blow directly at her father's enormous leather chair, and though it was rotated away, she saw a figure hunched within its shadowed concavity.

Tally crept closer, eyes adjusting, to stand before the desk.

Leaning over the chair, Tally swished one side of the curtains open. Sunshine rushed in. She blinked rapidly as Richard Ramsey took corpulent shape from the gloom. For a second, she thought he was dead and had been merely propped up here like a dummy. Then she saw his chest move.

Her heart thudded, a hoof kick to her own chest.

She took her time to observe him, seeing how much the last four and a half years had widened and wizened him. The smell of liquor was a noxious miasma around him, though the ship's-wheel clock above the desk showed it was only a bit past nine. She was one part gladdened to see his human mortality; the other, staggered by any such vulnerability.

She gazed quickly around his desk, taking in the clutter and disarray peppered with aging food scraps. His Siamese fighting fish, unmoving, in a murky bowl.

Her father stirred.

She instinctively smartened herself up as he rose slowly to consciousness. He stared blindly through her for a long moment, before his eyes switched focus, observing her with a bewilderment that deepened rapidly into alarm.

'It's only me.'

He seemed to see something or someone else entirely. 'Get away! Get out of here!' He scrabbled in his chair, falling back, before clawing at his desk to stand, swaying unsteadily, face rage-mottled.

Tally stepped away, hands in open entreaty. He had to be still asleep – trapped in some nightmare. 'It's me, *Thalia*!'

Her father had picked up a paperweight and held it aloft, as though to pelt it at her.

Behind her, footsteps thudded up the hallway, and the office door was flung wide. 'Step aside!' came a male command. Angus Harmon, with Olga pinch-faced behind him.

Tally backed up as far as the bookshelves while Angus went, as pacifying as a nursemaid, to settle a muttering, stinking Richard into his chair. She watched this performance – the Bullshark soothed once more into a leaden stupor by his manager – and saw most clearly: this was not the first time Angus had undertaken the task.

Her mother was missing, and something was wrong with her father. Very, very wrong indeed …

'Tea?' The pot was rattled in her direction from the serving trolley, rolled out to the verandah settee.

Tally blinked at Olga standing behind it. She could take in the girl's exasperation, but nothing more. Tally's eyes peered past her, past Angus, to the blue, blue sea beyond.

How long had her father been an alcoholic? She spun a reel of childhood highlights. The acrid scent of alcohol had been ever present on her father's breath: he had meetings most days at which he served his best whisky, he opened wine with every meal and returned to his office each evening with his decanter at his side. But this level of dissipation? She didn't think so.

'Thalia?' Angus waved a hand in front of her face. 'Do. You. Want. *Tea?*'

She shook her head. Nodded. Reached for the cup and saucer without so much as murmured gratitude. She took an indelicate slurp, then dumped the teacup on the table, her eyes once more on the ocean. With a mind so fatigued by the transformations wrought upon her island and family, only the infinite sea offered any comfort.

As Olga rattled away with the trolley, Angus cleared his throat. 'Thalia, I have things to do. We can't keep sitting here.'

Her eyes flicked back to him. 'Go away, then.'

He frowned. 'I work here.'

'Not here you don't. Go back down to Mermaid Bay and leave me alone with my father.' She didn't really mean that, though, did she? The last thing she wanted was to be left alone with that man.

'I work *here*,' Angus said, enunciating for an imbecile. 'At Eyrie. With Richard.'

137

She didn't bother to hide her distaste. 'You just stay out of my way during the day, and we'll both be happy.'

'I'll do my job. Also, it behoves me to tell you that I have a private suite here, at Eyrie.'

Tally almost laughed at *behoves*, before the latter part of his sentence caught up with her: 'You *what*?'

'I was given a suite as part of my employment package.'

'Which room?' she asked, between gritted teeth.

His smirk was answer enough.

'In that case, where are all my things?'

'You'll find your possessions boxed up in your mother's suite.'

Her father had hired this cretin and then shifted him into their family home? Poor Ma, having to live with Angus *and* her father's latest mistress. The picture forming in Tally's mind was developing more disturbing shades by the minute.

Instead of harping on about hibiscus table stylings, Ma might have mentioned she was under such an unusual form of ... it was almost a *house arrest*, wasn't it? Constant surveillance either by her husband or his manager.

Why?

She fixed her Bunsen-burner look on Angus. 'Strange, my father not contacting me to inform me of my missing mother ...'

He didn't even bother to feign surprise. 'He thought she would've told you herself that she was planning to run off.'

Behind closed lips, Tally pressed the tips of her canine teeth together; a precise rage. 'Even stranger, then, that my father didn't call to *check* whether she was with me. It should've been the first step any normal father took.' As if hers had ever been normal ...

'If you say so.' He was a model of civility. 'I apologise that calling you didn't come in higher on our list of priorities.' Tally knew she was being handled like a difficult guest. 'How may we help you now?'

Our, we – Lila was on the money with the 'Bullshark's Bully'. *Thank God* Lila had come for her. How long might they have carried on secretly here with Ma gone?

'I'll report Ma missing straightaway,' Tally said, 'and the police will make proper inquiries about her whereabouts and safety.'

Angus shrugged. 'Richard could've already gone to the police, but as you can see, he's been left devastated by her abandonment.'

'You might have made the report yourself.'

'Well, it's family business, isn't it? Mucky stuff. Not a good look for Mermaid Bay Resort. Though, I was planning to have a bit of a chat with Sarge at the Bellen Beach Charity Golf Day next week. See what he recommends under these trying circumstances.'

'The circumstances of a missing person, you mean.'

'Nerissa told your father not to follow or search for her.'

'Allegedly – where's this note?'

She'd expected him to spit out another excuse; to her surprise, he moved into her father's office and returned with a very shabby note in hand.

She whipped it from his fingers, but she refused to read it in front of him. 'I'll have my mother's suite,' Tally said, rising hurriedly. 'In fact, I'm heading up there now, to refresh.'

CHAPTER 14

HER LAST WORDS

Eyrie

Tally went up the staircase as calmly as she could manage, given the note burning a hole in her palm and the man watching her. She imagined he was feigning composure as much as she, ready to bolt into Richard's office the moment she had gone.

She had caught them off guard in Eyrie, arriving unexpectedly. Tally had the upper hand, but it was a short advantage. She'd have to work quickly to divine the truth, before they might cover up anything critical.

She passed her old bedroom with a hiss of anger. The nerve of him, camped out in there. How she'd love to march in and throw all his things out. *Later*, she swore to herself.

The first thing Tally noticed, arriving at Ma's door, at the opposite end of the long hallway, was the broken deadlock. Broken wasn't the right word – *shattered*, that was what Richard Ramsey had done with his wife's privacy lock.

She entered Ma's hot, shuttered room as though it was bound with some enchantment. She almost expected to find Ma slumber-struck in her bed, wild brambles grown up around her.

Her bed, however, was primly made and very much empty.

It wasn't only Ma missing, her scent was gone too. Her L'heure

Bleue parfum had not been misted into this air in far too long. Had Ma stopped wearing it altogether?

Tally flung open the white shuttered window to the sunshine and sea view. Much better. She leaned out of the window, surveying the roof awning beneath. If she knew anything about disappearing from behind a locked door, this was the only way down. Ma did not have so handy an escape branch as Tally's old bedroom did. She examined the long, angled expanse of awning, considering the dangerous drop in a way she'd never done when it was her own spine on the line. If Ma had escaped this way, then she was more audacious than Tally had known.

She withdrew inside, taking a moment to study the bedroom. It looked the same – neat as a pin, all white and full of grace and femininity. The only difference was the stack of Tally's boxed possessions.

What else had she expected? Signs of hasty packing with clothes tumbling out of drawers, perhaps a packing list crossed off? Or signs of a struggle, with Ma's last words scrawled out in blood …

But she *had* Ma's last words; she was holding them.

Tally sat down heavily on the bed, steeling herself, before spreading out the page. She made this assessment within seconds: Ma's handwriting, on Ma's writing paper. The illustrated border of tropical birds and plants was so very Ma, and so very naff.

Please, let her be all right.

The letter was addressed to no one in particular, for which Tally found herself, in some small way, thankful. She couldn't bear to go on thinking Ma had taken the time to write her father and not her. At least, she could pretend Ma always had intended for Tally to read *this* letter.

*I am seaweed withering on the rocks, coral
fading upon the shore.
I am brittle driftwood breaking, fish spine*

*stripped clean, the blistered burn that never finds
cool.
My sails hang limp and tattered, and there is
only one wind that ever filled them – long gone,
and faraway now, perhaps never to be found –
but I <u>must</u> try.
I chose this island once before over my own heart,
and I cannot do it again.
Do not look for me, nor set a search after me.
Allow me <u>this</u> freedom, at least.
Forgive me.*

Tally sat blinking in the bright, streaming light, her soul black with anguish. She ought to have cried – she wanted to cry! She was furious with herself for failing at it. What kind of daughter couldn't flush some drops out of her ducts for her missing mother?

Panic climbed her throat, instead. If only she'd come home earlier, more often, *at all*, before her mother apparently had lost the plot. She'd gone to find a *wind*? Oh, the bitter shock of Ma's mental state! Father always had seemed the one who would descend into a twisted reality – and maybe he was still drinking his way there, but gentle, placid *Ma*?

Tally jumped up and paced the room. Adrenaline, and the desperate urge to run after Ma, made her thighs ache.

Think, think!

If life with a cruel, drunken, philandering Richard – not to mention his live-in manager – finally had pushed Ma over the edge, where might that edge be? The end of the flat earth, by the way Ma talked about it …

Do not look for me, nor set a search after me. No doubt she was afraid of being brought promptly home again by her husband, and who could blame her? But it was more than that. Tally stopped pacing, realisation dawning.

She didn't want me *to come after her. She wanted a head start on* me.

That's why she didn't contact Tally directly to say she was leaving. She knew *Tally* would never let it go.

I chose this island once before over my own heart, and I cannot do it again.

Tally objected to the notion that she'd made her mother choose the island over anything. And as for her father, wouldn't he have gladly accepted Dara as recompense for a wife run off to find her wind?

Oh my God.

Was that what Ma had done – thrown Dara in for her freedom? She'd certainly made no promises to return. Would she sacrifice Tally's future for her own? There was a pain in Tally's chest, a driving knife with every breath. She sat and pressed a hand to her sternum, trying to pull oxygen past the piercing pain. She wondered if she'd been poisoned by Olga's tea.

The letter had fallen to the floor at her feet. Tally put her head between her knees and stared dumbly down at it, while her chest throbbed on.

No, Ma wouldn't be so cruel as to leave her daughter in the lurch. And if she'd guessed Tally inevitably would turn up here, she had to have left some additional clue for her eyes only...

Standing up, she began to walk around the room, observing everything, opening drawers and shifting possessions. In Ma's walk-in robe, she located the hat-pin tin, secret pocket still filled with keys. She counted them into the palm of her hand – all still here – smiling for the first time since entering the suite. There were *some* positives to Ma's penchant for secrecy, and Tally intended to exploit them.

But there was something extra in the pocket now, tucked in the very bottom, out of sight. She could only feel it – made of paper and fabric.

Her fingers were too large, her nails too short; she couldn't seem to get a grip. She went back out into the main room, searching now for some tool. Set alone on the middle of Ma's dressing table, as though expressly laid out for her purpose, was a pair of tweezers.

The material pried loose first. Out of the pocket, she drew one of Ma's tiny, handwoven mermaids – unbottled.

Tally spun the mermaid in her fingers, considering it. She saw immediately that it was made to look like Ma and couldn't help but smile: honey hair, green eyes, and the shimmering blue mermaid gown Tally long ago had stolen for herself. A miniature Ma. She slid the figurine into her shorts pocket – it would be a fabric talisman until she found her ma of warm flesh and blood.

She returned to the pocket, delving deeper and more firmly with her tweezers. At last, the wedged paper began to shift. She fished out a tiny scroll and unwrapped it with trembling fingers. There was only a single line:

Tally Ho, the answer lies in 1946.

X

Astonished, she sat back and took the mermaid from her pocket to stare at both together. So, Ma had always known that Tally was using her keys. Indeed, she'd *counted* upon it.

Once again, Ma had hidden a riddle for her.

How to make sense of it, though?

The year nineteen forty-six had been a big one on Dara. The date of her parents' wedding, Tally's birth and the birth of Mermaid Bay Resort, too. What did Ma want her to discover in this date?

Tally exhaled in frustration. *Would it have killed you to just speak plainly, for once?*

144

She pocketed both clues and stood up. Ma had to flee with little time or willingness to warn Tally. What else did she take, then?

She walked around the room with renewed purpose.

Gradually, she began to compile a mental inventory: Ma's travelling suit and trunk; her button tin, which Tally knew concealed surplus kitchen money and shop savings; her favourite sun hat and sandals. Equally, she noted what was left behind: Tally's newspaper articles, every one of them pasted into Ma's journals; Ma's beloved portrait of her young self with Grandpapa on pristine Coral Beach, still on her bedside; her shell-covered jewellery box, full to the brim, her wedding band among it all.

Wherever Ma thought she was going, she wanted to be unencumbered of her life as a wife and mother.

Tally was on her way down to Mermaid Bay's happy hour, looking decidedly morose. It wasn't that she thought she might find her mother at the bottom of a gin cocktail, but where tipples were poured, tongues wagged.

Besides which, she could not sleep in that nest of vipers called Eyrie tonight until she was sure she wouldn't be murdered in her sleep and dropped into the sea. Someone on staff had to be made to talk.

As she was just coming around the back of the tennis courts, another thought occurred to her: Ma had to get off this island somehow, and that required a boat, stolen or otherwise.

Tally bypassed the lodge, going out to Coral Beach. The sky was a graduated wash of pastels – pink and peach, yellow and lavender. On the bone-white shoreline, a ruddy-haired young man was hauling canoes back into the Beach Hire Shed.

He looked up in wonder as Tally barrelled over.

'Shep,' she cried, stunned to find not only a familiar face, but a welcome one, too, the son of Eyrie's long-time cook, Mrs Simons, apparently forced into premature retirement. Shep had only been a schoolkid when Tally left, surely? Now he was a foot taller than her, gangly and blemished.

He doffed his hat. 'It really is you.'

She grinned. 'Really me.'

'Someone just said you were back, but I didn't believe it. Been plenty of Tally sightings over the years.'

'It's good to be home again.' The words were brave, and hollow. 'But Eyrie isn't the same without your mum. I couldn't *believe* it when I heard she'd moved away.'

Shep shrugged. 'She likes being back on the mainland.'

Tally frowned, discerning otherwise.

'Is it true you're gonna run the island now?' Oh, the *hope* in his voice!

'I'm just here to keep an eye on things while my ma's away. She'll be back very soon. She wouldn't want to be away from Dara for long.'

Shep had grown a prominent Adam's apple, and she watched it bob up and down, uneasily.

'Why do you look like that, Shep?'

He fiddled with his cap. 'Before she left, Mum said Mrs Ramsey was the saddest woman she had ever seen in her life. Said she wasn't eating a thing, even though Mum was making all her favourite dishes. That she must have been existing on air, because she was fading away into nothing. Mum thought it was Dara doing it, she said Mrs Ramsey needed to get off Dara before it actually killed her.'

'It does seem Ma was quite unhappy,' Tally said, as neutrally as she could manage. 'But I'm sure a short break will do her the world of good. She'll be back, you'll see.' False, false confidence.

Tally watched Shep's throat bob harder. He put his hat back on, shielding downcast eyes. 'I'm sorry,' he said.

Her neck prickled at the *guilt* she read in him. She stepped closer, voice rising. 'Why should *you* be sorry?'

'Nothing,' he baulked.

'*What* are you sorry about?' she cried, aware she was nearly stepping on the poor boy's shoes.

'I don't know – *please* forget I said anything!'

Tally stared at him, exasperated. *Remember your manners*, she checked herself, *you are not in a newsroom anymore*. He was just a flustered kid, not a source she could drill into confession.

She forced her lips to smile. More a grimace of patience. 'Shep, I need your help.'

'*My* help?'

'I'll need a lift to the mainland, probably tomorrow, on important business. And I don't want to take the ferry. Would you be able to help me with that?' To be very clear, she nodded at the motorboat languishing nearby, bearing Dara's insignia.

'I'm not allowed to pilot the new runabout – Mr Harmon said.'

'He doesn't let a capable young man like you handle a simple motorboat?' She hammed up indignation. 'I'll be having something to say about *that*. I think you're just the sort of fellow we need taking on more responsibility, maybe even skippering the ferry one day...' She saw the pinking of his cheeks and knew she had him. 'But look, I understand you don't want to go against Mr Harmon. Can I save you the trouble and just borrow the boat for myself now and then?'

Loyalty and fear twisted against one another on his young face. Loyalty won out. 'Sure, Miss Tally. Only, would you mind signing the boat out on my register?'

'Yes, if you show me where it is and how to use it?'

Shep led her into the shed, and over to a clipboard hanging from the wall. On it, was a tabulated list of beach equipment. While he was pointing out the runabout's column and how to tick it under the hire date, Tally's eyes already had alighted on another runabout's column – ruled out with black liner after its last use three weeks earlier.

'Out of curiosity,' she said, tapping the cancelled boat. 'What happened to this one?'

Shep's face jerked up, eyes wide, face flaming. 'Mr Harmon sold it.'

'To whom?'

'I don't know. It was a Sunday. I don't work Sundays.'

'Who does?'

'We don't open the shed.'

Tally watched Shep very carefully as she posed her next question. 'So, on the one day you weren't working, Mr Harmon took one of your boats and sold it?'

'Yes,' he said, very quickly.

She went on watching, her scrutiny making him squirm and twist his neck.

'That's right about the time my ma disappeared too, isn't it?'

Shep flicked the pages back down on his clipboard and rehung it. 'S'pose so.' He was moving her towards the door.

'What a coincidence,' Tally mused aloud, following him out. 'Well, thank you, Shep, you're an absolute treasure. If you think of anything else, anything at all, please come find me.'

The plea made, she headed back up Coral Beach.

So, she might have found the means by which Ma escaped Dara. The question begged: was it of her own free will with a young man's collusion, or was she *taken away* in the dead of night?

CHAPTER 15

ISLAND HOSTESS

Mermaid Bay Resort

News of her return had run ahead of her to the lodge, and as she strode through the ixora hedges towards the pool, a small crowd of employees were gasbagging at reception. She hardly recognised a face, though, the rate of turnover in the last four and a half years seeming astronomical. Where was dear Frank, and bubbly Anita, and round-faced June? Anyone to embrace her warmly, once more.

What she most needed, in lieu of a soft mother, was a stiff drink.

She moseyed on into the pool area, to find happy hour in full swing, balmy and festive against the pink ombré sky.

Before entering the fray, Tally considered herself: still in the same daggy singlet and shorts, hair wind-knotted, and her nose and shoulders, as she was beginning now to feel, quite sunburnt. It would have to do.

The crowd was strung out between the palms like the necklace of fairy lights above. A ukulele, strummed by a porter, competed with convivial laughter and clinking glasses. At the thatched-roof bar, on the other side of the pool, she was startled to see Lila seated elegantly on a bamboo stool. She hardly recognised the sensible girl who'd chaperoned her home only this morning.

Gone was the cargo skirt and uniform blouse, even the ponytail and practical shoes. Now she looked impossibly fresh and pretty in a cinch-waisted pink sundress, golden-brown bouffant styled just so, gaily laughing with guests. Behind her ear, a pink hibiscus; in her hand, a coconut shell topped with a paper parasol.

The whole effect made Tally think of Ma in much happier times. And it hurt.

She pushed through the mingling crowd, all her anger of the last twenty-four hours boiling up. She was ready to vent, at anyone, and Lila had made herself an easy target by sitting there, as happy as the hour demanded. How *dare* she drag Tally back to Dara?

Lila, seeming to sense the approaching tempest, pivoted on her seat. Her eyes went wide at Tally's thunder, but she smiled, taking a sip. 'Tally, hello. I was about to send up a rescue party. You've saved me the effort.' Lila, Tally saw, had sprouted doll-like lashes of blackest black, her green eyes made coquettish.

'Are you wearing *false lashes*?' Tally demanded. *Who puts on false lashes when Ma is missing?*

'It's part of my new uniform here.'

'You call that a uniform?'

'Angus recently appointed me island hostess,' Lila said dryly. 'My job is to mingle with our VIPs at happy hour, serving drinks and compliments, and generally spreading island cheer.'

'What's your job – sleep all day, flirt all night?'

'I'm expected to *clean* all day and then polish male egos at day's end. Probably not much difference between me and your garden-variety housewife.'

'I think you're both going out of fashion,' Tally quipped.

Lila laughed; the sound of a mellifluous songbird lifting off. Tally could smell rum and pineapple on Lila's breath. Her stomach clenched. She hadn't eaten all day, and that drink smelled like exactly the kind of thing she would imbibe before dancing on tavern tables in a mermaid's dress. The desire to rain all over happy hour had dissolved; she felt nothing now but misery.

She looked around, seeing that the ratio of men to women at this gathering was skewed heavily to the less fair sex. This was supposed to be a honeymoon isle, so why were there so many single men?

She frowned at Lila. 'Angus is changing Dara's clientele into a bunch of sleazebags. You can't possibly be paid enough for this job.'

'I'd rather be homeless on the mainland than carry on much longer doing this. But the way I've been looking at it, with Mrs Ramsey away, *someone*'s got to keep an eye on Mermaid Bay.'

Tally tipped her head, wonderingly. 'You've taken it upon yourself to watch this place for my ma?'

Lila's eyes were sage and searching. 'Tell me, how was your first day back?'

'My father is a drunk, my mother really has disappeared into thin air, and my old bully Angus is camped out in my bedroom ... probably sniffing my underwear.'

Lila let loose that laugh again; a vivid parrot in a dim clearing.

'On top of all that,' Tally added, 'I'm getting the sense that there's something very *wrong* happening in this place.'

'Thank goodness you came home, then, just in time.' Lila was deadpan.

'You didn't just haul me back here for Ma's sake, did you?'

'No, Tally, for all of us in Mermaid Bay.'

'What good will *I* be? I can hardly think straight with Ma missing and I can never stay rational with my father. I've only been back five minutes and I can already feel this place bringing out the worst in me again.'

Lila motioned to the barman, pointing at her drink. 'What you need is an island hostess.'

'How can *you* help me?'

'It's the name of the cocktail,' Lila said with a wise look – one so much like the kind she'd make in girlhood, that something long forgotten stirred in Tally's heart. A yearning for her first and oldest friend.

All the energy went out of Tally at once. She slumped on the bamboo stool opposite Lila's. 'How am I supposed to just ... *carry on* here without her? Not even knowing if she's alive or dead.'

With impeccable timing, the barman produced a second drink. Lila took the coconut shell, sliding it in front of Tally. 'Right now, you let our guests see you having a lovely time. They've paid good money to enjoy their island fantasy.' She sounded like the cool and steady Ma of old days, always obsessed with her damned ambience.

'What *difference* does it make if I'm nice to these blokes or not?'

Lila lifted her striped straw to a pasted-on smile. 'Because, my dear girl, how else do you plan to find out what's rotten on the island of Dara?'

Angus arrived a half-hour later, wading through the throng of happy swillers. He was not alone.

Swaggering along behind him was a broad-nosed man at least two decades older – sun-desecrated in a way that stood out, even among the weathered faces of this Far North Queensland clime.

'Thalia, I'd like you to meet Mack,' Angus said.

Mack the knife, Tally told herself as a mnemonic. The song had been one of her favourite swing dance numbers. She observed Lila's hostess smile stretch wider. They were meant to be nice to *this* guy? What would *he* know of her island's secrets?

She extended her smooth, young hand to his, the colour and texture of rotisserie chicken.

'Well, well, look here: it's Thalia Ramsey, all grown up,' Mack declared, drawing her hand towards his face as though en route to his chapped lips.

Tally whipped her hand back and gave it occupation in swizzle stick-stirring. She was on her second rum-and-pineapple concoction and already had pledged herself to a third.

While Lila procured drinks for the men, Mack looked Tally up and down quite openly. Her backside clenched on the barstool.

'And you're a reporter,' he said. 'Such a waste of a pretty face. You might have gone into your mother's profession, instead.'

'I *will* take over from my mother, when the time is right.'

'Don't leave it too long. They might call it the "oldest profession", but that's a misnomer.'

At her expression, Mack hooted. 'Don't tell me you're a grim little prig like Mrs Ramsey, too.'

Tally blazed her coldest blue look upon him. 'You're just not funny.'

'Can this be the harpy I've heard so much about?' Mack nudged Dara's manager. 'You oversold it.'

Tally glared. 'I intimidate some more than others.'

At this, Lila swept off her seat and came to be kissed on both rouged cheeks. 'What a surprise to see you around these parts again, Mack. It's been such a long time.'

'You were only a tiny tacker last time I saw you, and haven't *you* grown in all the right places. How's your mother? She and I have a lot to catch up on.'

'She's very well, thank you.' Lila stepped back then to stand directly beside Tally, her soft arm brushing firmly against Tally's. *Careful*, it seemed to say.

It was impossible to ignore the way Mack's eyes dwelled on Tally, feeding some private enjoyment. It wasn't lasciviousness, she comprehended, something much unkinder. Her jaw set hard. Forget being *nice*. She was a journalist, not a hostess.

'And where do you live, when you're not a guest on my island?'

His smile was a slow menace unfolding.

'Mack was born and raised on Bellen Beach,' Lila supplied smoothly. 'He was instrumental in the development of Mermaid Bay. A very old friend of Mr Ramsey's.'

'Not *so* old, am I?' He squeezed Lila's shoulder. Pressed so close as they were, Tally felt the touch through her.

'A *long-time* friend, I should say.'

On Mack's left arm, just visible at the bottom of his shirtsleeve, Tally glimpsed three long, snaking scars, a furious red, as though whipped by a cat-o'-nine-tails. He had survived a box-jellyfish sting. She'd never heard of a soul who'd tangled with a box and *lived*.

Somehow, the very existence of this man made Tally's throat run dry. 'And are you . . . just visiting Bellen Beach?'

'We'll see. I'll be around.'

Tally was regretting the rum haze tempering her instincts. There was something vitally important about Mack; she *felt* it. Her hand sought to pat the mermaid in her shorts pocket.

Come on, Tally, get your wits together!

But Lila was taking matters, and Mack, into her own hands. At her invitation to dance, they went off together under the swaying palms, drinks held high, and were swallowed up by the crowd of poolside dancers.

Tally was marooned with Angus. She wondered which one of them would eat the other first.

The ukulele player had launched into a breezy rendition of 'Fly Me to the Moon', and Tally watched Mack twirling a laughing Lila around the dance floor.

'She's in *quite* the celebratory mood this evening,' Angus said stroppily, not taking his eyes off Lila.

Tally side-eyed him. Lila had better watch out; Angus wanted to make her his private hostess.

'And what have *you* been up to all day, Angus?' She removed the paper parasol from her cup to toss back the last of her drink.

'Getting rid of evidence for Richard, obviously. Like a good manager should.'

Tally choked on an uprush of outrage, her nose and eyes burning. She saw she had given him exactly the reaction he wanted; he was smirking hard.

'I do find it odd,' she said, 'that my father would replace Mr Barrett with someone so young and inexperienced.'

'My dad and Richard go way back.'

'So, nepotism, then.'

Angus nodded, this insult apparently sailing right over him. 'Should have heard how proud my dad was to boast: from living in the Artists' Colony himself, to his own son managing the island.'

'You only manage the *resort*,' Tally said. 'When did your father live on the Hat?'

'Before the war.'

'What kind of artist was he?'

'He was no artist, only ended up there for somewhere to live. They were taking in all sorts back in those days. As long as you could contribute in some way, you were welcome to stay. It was a good, free life, Dad said. He only left 'cause there was a falling out among the folks there. A hostile takeover, if you ask Dad, not in keeping with the original spirit of the colony.' Angus kept looking in the direction of the dance floor. Tally narrowed her eyes, following his gaze.

'Your father must have been on the Hat around the same time as Lila's mum.'

'Yeah, Irene tried to run that island like she tries to control this one.'

What? Irene was a godsend for Mermaid Bay. They had no other employee so long serving or dedicated. Tally couldn't imagine their staunch Irene getting embroiled in some kind of coup.

But who cared about the politics of a long-lost commune? She already knew the ending. Richard Ramsey had married Nerissa Forster, gained Dara and promptly set about disbanding the Artists' Colony. Sent them all away, citing development needs. Out of the colony, only Irene had been given a place on Dara – saved by her friendship with Ma. There were to be no freeloaders in Richard Ramsey's grand vision for Dara, though nothing ever had been built on the smaller island. The abandoned shanty village was left to rot.

She wondered what relics were still there, after all this time, and made a mental note to visit the Hat again.

In her distraction, she'd left herself unguarded. Angus was leaning forward with an intense stare. 'Thalia … why do you dislike me?'

'I despise a bully.'

'You think *I'm* a bully? You gave as good as you got – the great and mighty daughter of Richard Ramsey.'

'Does *Ducky* ring a bell? Or how about *Inbred Island Girl*? And remember that time you exchanged my school milk for one that had curdled in the hot sun days earlier?'

His jaw slackened, memory properly jogged. 'That was a long time ago. You can't hold onto a childhood grudge forever.'

'Can't I?'

'No use crying over spoiled milk.'

Tally pushed her cocktail onto the bar, regarding Angus with a cold, regal wrath. 'I *don't* cry.'

She went to find Lila. They should stick together tonight.

It was Tally who chaperoned a very unsteady Lila home, after ten. The island hostess was well and truly in her cups, and Tally did not envy her having to be up again with the seagulls to scrub all day. One of Tally's hands was supporting her friend's elbow, the other carried Lila's shoes, handbag and the flower from behind her ear, already much trodden on by dancers. Lila had refused to leave the pool area without it.

Tally was exhausted by the long evening at her old friend's side, watching the island hostess's flawless verve. She was even more wrung out from keeping an eye peeled for Angus or Mack, both of them always in her peripheral vision, shadows half glimpsed in underwater gloom. The pair eventually vanished together, but her unease did not let up.

At one point during the soiree, Tally thought she was about to be relieved of her Lila-minding duties. Irene made an abrupt appearance on the opposite side of the dance floor, evidently checking on Lila now that she was back under Tally's bad influence. No one could say so much without any words as Irene could with that *glower* of hers. She looked like she wanted to drag her daughter home. Tally had seen that done before, when they were children.

To her surprise, Irene came no further into the gathering, and Lila, whirling her skirts and paper parasols alike, remained blissfully unaware of her mother's censorious glare. Even after Irene passed from view, Tally was acutely self-conscious. *I won't compromise Lila in future*, she once had promised Irene.

That promise rang in her ears anew as Tally guided Lila now through the lantern-lit pathways of the village, most cabins already dark. Her heart was heavy, as one leaving a large wake; the loss hers as much as Dara's. In the last few hours, she had queried and grieved the departure of so many dear friends from Mermaid Bay: Anita had married herself off the island; June had left to run a caravan park in Townsville; saddest of all, 'Grandfather' Frank had gone to live with his equally aging sister in Mackay.

Dara was a sinking ship deserted by its best sailors. In the end, she thought only the rats might remain.

'Oh *blast* –' Lila cried, wobbling to a stop under an umbrella tree. 'I think that last cocktail did me in.'

'Or the half-dozen before it.' Tally tugged at Lila's elbow. 'Come on, just a bit further to go.'

'*Now* who's the chaperone? We've traded places. How about *you* go and live with my mother for a change.' Her head lolled back on a grimace. 'Nooo, she won't take *that*. She doesn't like you, Tally. She says you can't ever be trusted with Dara.'

Tally snorted. 'I think you deserve a raise. You're a one-hostess show.'

'It's not a *show*,' Lila cried, clutching at Tally's arm with a drunk's sudden urgency. 'I'm trying to keep you *safe* – don't you see?'

Tally's smile faded. Lila's eyes were heavy-hooded and bloodshot, but there was wild conviction to her; the sense of a floodgate straining.

'Safe from what?'

Lila was shushing so hard she nearly blew herself over. She hunched closer. 'You just … trust *me* … orright?'

'All right,' Tally repeated. 'And thank you for keeping me safe.'

'You're welcome,' Lila said, agreeing now to go on down the last lane, to the Threadwells' cottage. Still the largest and best-cared-for home on the island, after Eyrie.

The lights were out. Nonetheless, Tally nervously eyed the curtained windows for movement. She hoped to God she would not have to answer to the irascible Irene Threadwell tonight.

Stay asleep, stay asleep, stay asleep …

'*Oh*,' Lila said, at the bottom of the porch. 'You brought me back *here?'* She staggered on upstairs, looking like she might topple over the balustrade.

At her door, just when Tally thought she had been forgotten, Lila turned again. *'Hey,'* she hissed, comically loud in this row of quiet cabins. *'Psst,* hey, Tally!'

Yes, Tally mouthed. *I'm here, be quiet!*

Lila nodded obediently, but her volume only rose. 'I had such fun with you tonight. Just like old times. I'm awfully glad you came back.'

Old times, Tally echoed bemusedly as she weaved through the village lanes. These were like no times Tally ever remembered.

Tally had beaten Angus to Eyrie. The great, white house was silent and dark, the front door yawning open.

Where was their housemaid, and what was she doing leaving the place unlocked? More worryingly, where had her father gone now? She was yet to face him sober, and was impatient to get it out of the way.

On the first floor, Tally went directly to her father's suite. His door was locked, but she could hear something or someone inside. Before raising her hand to knock, she pressed her ear against the door, straining to distinguish the sounds.

She shot back, holding her ear as though her cartilage was burned. So that's where Olga was.

Some things were better left unheard …

CHAPTER 16

MANTA RAY

Tally had crawled into her mother's bed many a time over the years, but she'd never slept in it alone. Ma's queen-sized bed, that first long night, was smaller and lonelier than any single bed she'd been assigned at boarding school. Tally did not so much sleep as suffer the night.

She arose in the pre-dawn darkness, grateful to have survived with only a chair wedged under the doorknob to protect her from whatever Ma had needed a deadbolt against.

She was determined to investigate her father's office before dawn busted in, or anyone else for that matter. Taking her knapsack and Ma's secret key, Tally slid silently out into the hallway. She was barefoot and breathless; the thrill of an early-morning escapade undiminished, even as a grown woman.

She had two doors to get past this morning, her father's and Angus's, but she managed it without a squeak. She eased down the stairs and along the ground floor hallway, remembering each precise foothold to avoid a single creak.

Her father's office was locked, as she'd expected, but Ma's key turned. Tally slipped inside, pressing back against the door as she fumbled for her trusty torch. The smell of spilled spirits was cloyingly thick. She could not help the sense of being watched from her father's desk, and her neck bristled hotly.

A quick skim of the torch around the room showed all the chairs were empty. No one stood in the corner, though her light beam lingered on the coat stand, just in case. The ship's-wheel clock above her father's desk read half past four. She did not have long before the arrival of whichever cook had replaced Mrs Simons.

Now what? she asked herself, with genuine curiosity. There was no one who could surprise Tally as much as herself. *What*, exactly, *do I want to find?*

Proof of *rottenness*, she decided, recalling Lila's words. If Lila too suspected there was something wrong on Dara, then it wasn't just Tally's bitter distrust of her father.

But what rottenness might she discover here? Ma's ship-in-a-bottle broken open and Grandpapa's will altered? Or, God forbid, some evidence of her mother's death covered up?

There was one place she knew to look for Richard Ramsey's secrets. She crossed the room to her father's safe. Would his combination lock sequence have changed in the many years since she'd last breached it?

It had not.

Tally's teeth, holding the torch, trembled with the urge to smile. *Fortune favours the brave.*

The safe was in disarray, so much paper and so many account books shoved in, she hardly knew what she was looking at, much less where to start. She swore silently as a pile of papers tumbled into her lap. There was no time to sort through this chaos. At least, she didn't have to return the contents to any particular position.

She closed her eyes, exhaling long and hard, to centre her thoughts. *Picture what you want to find*, she told herself, *see it clearly.*

Her mind's eye, however, was not cooperating. Instead of some dossier of dark secrets, all she saw was her Dara map doodle. *Oh, come on!* She exhaled again with some force, trying to erase it.

Her eyes popped open.

The map.

The one she had glimpsed in her father's accounts book as an eleven-year-old – and had been doodling ever since. And what accounts book had she found it in? The ledger of nineteen forty-six. The same year Ma had left as a clue.

Find nineteen forty-six!

Tally gritted her teeth around the torch, swallowing back the saliva threatening to overspill, and set to work. She rifled at speed, hunting for the older-style account books among the newer editions. Her curiosity burned; what she would give to sit down with a coffee and go through it all, properly. But there was no time to waste!

In fact, no time left at all …

Overhead, there was the sound of a door scraping open, then a creaking progress down the long hallway, past the bedroom suites. She'd been expecting noises from the servants' entrance first. Who could be up at *this* hour? The footsteps weren't heavy enough for her father, but they were heading directly for the stairs. Was it Angus on his way down *here*?

'Shit,' Tally hissed, shuffling faster. *Where the hell is nineteen forty-six?*

The footsteps were almost at the staircase.

There – there it is!

Tally shoved the book deep in her knapsack, throwing papers and books back into the safe. Whoever it was sneaking about, they were now on the stairs. The balustrade gave its telltale groan.

Having secured the safe, Tally streaked across the office. Her panic was strangulating. It was imperative no one knew she had access to

Richard's inner sanctum – or indeed, any keys at all. There were many doors left to open on this island.

She was through her father's office door seconds before the footsteps had made the staircase turn. She couldn't get out of the front door unheard, nor would she make it back down the servants' passage.

Her hands flapped desperately in the dark.

The hall cupboard! Go, go!

Tally threw herself into the cupboard, a space only wide enough for a broom and stepladder, sucking in her stomach as she tugged the door closed.

She pressed her face against it, heart thudding, as the footsteps arrived at the study. She'd escaped by the skin of her teeth.

Now that she was safely hidden, however, her mind counted all the evidence of invasion she surely had left behind.

Father – Angus – whoever it was, had reached the door.

She waited for the sound of a turning key, realising with a bolt of dismay what she had forgotten: to *relock* the door. Her teeth skewered her lower lip, a painful buttress against obscenities.

She tensed, awaiting this discovery. Sure enough, there was a mutter of surprise, truncated. Then, a long silence. Already holding her breath, Tally began to purple.

This is stupid, she told herself, *I'm a grown woman, in my* own *house*.

Finally, the office door clunked open and closed. The quality of hall silence changed, becoming benign. She waited, counting to an arbitrary number, before daring to ease open the cupboard. A thin bar of light showed at the bottom of Richard's door.

Now or never …

She squeezed out, scurrying up the hall towards the back staff entrance. Only once she was outside and hidden in the jungled path did Tally's heart stop thundering in her ears.

She skated along the edge of Eyrie, staying in darkness, until she was just below the front verandah. Dodging the rectangle of light, she eased in close, peering towards the office window. From this neck-straining vantage point, she could just make out the back of a man's head, seated at her father's desk.

Angus.

What the *hell* was he up to at this hour?

Tally fled the terraced garden, incensed. The sooner she got herself somewhere safe to study the book of nineteen forty-six, the better!

There was no sound but her breath and the gentle slap of an oar, as Tally slid through the water in her kayak – signed out for Shep's sake. She was paddling east towards the Hat, already out beyond Coral Beach and the volcanic rock spill, as a coralline dawn suffused the horizon.

Tally rowed faster, setting herself the challenge of reaching her destination by the time the sun scorched out of the ocean. Around her lonely kayak, luminescent orange sky merged with silvered sea in a boundless, glowing sphere. Her lungs sucked hungrily at the ocean breeze and salt tang, her soul basking in the infinitude of space and air and colour.

Sky above, reef below – nothing better.

The old Artists' Colony was situated on the east side of the Hat, the isle's west side a sheer rock face, to match the steep, inhospitable topography of Dara's east. Tally had the sudden thought that it was like the two islands were not on speaking terms, their backs turned against one another.

She paddled around on a wave of exultation. Her shoulders burned with long-forgotten effort, but her heart was light. Even her chest felt wider, as though it had shrunk while she'd been away. For the first time, she felt herself to have come properly home.

A brief movement astern – something like the fin of a shark breaching the surface – startled her. She paused, manoeuvring the kayak for a better view, rocking gently as she waited for the fin to emerge again.

Moments later it reappeared; a flash of wedge-shaped grey, quickly submerging. She drew delighted breath. That was no shark fin, but something far more magical; *lucky*, even. A third time the wide, flat, triangular shape darted from the water, rolling just below the gold-lit waves.

A majestic, gentle manta ray frolicking in the golden sheen of dawn. One of Ma's favourite sea creatures, second only to the turtle. And what did she say the manta ray represented? Tally opened Ma's whimsical almanac of sea lore: *grace, strength, determination*.

Tally floated here, hands loose on her oar, as the sun lipped the horizon and sparkled a glorious path towards her. Only when the manta ray had glided out of sight did she move.

It was a short paddle to the small beach, which was hidden from view of Dara. She dragged her kayak up onto the sand and stood a moment admiring her old haunt.

The smaller island possessed a unique vantage point on the untouched wilderness of Dara's east side, with its plummeting cliffs, tumbled granite headlands and the jungled steepness of Mount Teasdale. Dara might show her best angle to luxury guests, but freeloaders knew her darker side.

The Hat always had been one of Tally's favourite hideaways as a child, the romance of an abandoned village so captivating. She could not recall the last time she'd paddled over. But she knew why she'd come this time: some trace of Ma, who had loved this place more than anyone.

When Ma was a young woman, the old Artists' Colony had been the only community she'd known. Indeed, the only *people* she saw beside her father. Since settling in Cairns, it had struck Tally how truly strange an upbringing her ma had had; insular and isolated. *Lonely*.

Ma no doubt had lamented the loss of their sister settlement after Richard had evicted the colony. It was probably why she'd kept Irene on.

Passing the casuarinas and pandanus palms fringing the beach, she moved into the isle's rainforest heart, hiding the overgrown ruins of the Artists' Colony. The skeleton structures remained in evidence, but after over two decades exposed to the elements, they were dilapidated.

It was still possible to discern the community's old shape: here was the communal living-area shed, there the kitchen hut and laundry shack, and dotting around the grove were the decimated huts that once had provided housing.

Ma had long dreamed of offering Little Dara as private accommodation for single couples. She wanted to call it *Honeymoon Island* – an idyllic castaway for lovebirds. *'Every couple deserves their very own deserted isle,'* she said.

She wondered where Ma got all her romantic ideas. She could summon up no believable image of a lovesick Nerissa Forster swooning over Richard Ramsey. Oh, the irony of being raised in a honeymooner's paradise by two people who hardly even seemed to like each other.

She sighed, continuing on with her inspection. The place was deserted, but not entirely forgotten; there were signs here and there that someone had visited recently. Remnants of coal in a campfire, the stone ring neatly intact, a stack of firewood kept dry by a hanging boulder. One hut stood out among the others for a roof patched with palm leaves.

Probably just kids from the mainland. Locals often tried to sneak onto Dara with their own dinghies, to make holiday camps. For years, Richard had waged war on 'illegal' beach huts set up by mainlanders and on 'trespassing' picnickers who made their own way across.

She prodded at the sandy floor with a toe, as though hoping to kick out a clue. Maybe a broken shell bracelet, or better yet, a long strand of honey hair. Some proof that Ma had hidden out *here* after fleeing Dara.

It was a long shot. If Ma had resolved to finally leave Richard, there was no way she was hiding close by, sending up smoke signals for her husband to discover.

She turned abruptly and left the hut.

Back on the beach, Tally sat and opened her knapsack. Already, the sun was elevated above the sea, the day fully lit and sparkling. She tugged out her father's account book and touched the hand-scrawled title: *Dara, forty-six*.

Whatever Ma wanted her to know about nineteen forty-six, Tally hoped this book would answer it.

Beginning to turn pages, she wondered if her memory of the map would prove accurate, or if she'd simply dreamed up the whole, mysterious X-marked spot.

Like hell she had! There it was, pressed into the book like a centrefold; an illustrated oasis in a dry book of figures. She saw her memory had been almost photographic: all the same landmarks and symbols were there, including that X at the very peak of Mount Teasdale.

Tally tapped her lip, then stood and returned to the jungled heart of the Hat. She passed the village, pushing through an overgrown path to reach the steps cut roughly into the steep western rise of the isle. Climbing and sweating and swearing, she emerged to stand atop the hill.

She couldn't help but smile to behold this three hundred and sixty degree view, once more, feeling herself an ocean bird over the wrinkled sea.

The dark side of Dara loomed large, a verdant brontosaurus rising from the deep, Mount Teasdale as much a dinosaur's jagged maw as ever. Some childhood images you just never outgrew.

She held out her father's drawing, eyes flicking between map and island.

And saw … *nothing*.

Whatever Father had marked on that mount, it was hidden high in the jungle, on the wild, uncharted side of Dara, many days' trek from Mermaid Bay. She would never be able to find it by herself.

But might this X have been seen by passing boats, or artists encamped here on the Hat? Someone else had to know about it. Tally made a mental note: *hunt up some locals who were around in nineteen forty-six.*

Irene was the obvious source to start with, but Tally was loath to approach her first thing this morning after the way she'd been looking last night.

Maybe I'll give her a wide berth, just until Lila placates her properly. Lila had better tell her mother that I had nothing to do with her intoxication, and everything to do with getting her home safely.

Probably wasn't going to be enough, though. She heard Lila's voice again. *'She doesn't like you, Tally. She says you can't ever be trusted with Dara.'*

It was years too late for Tally to win Irene's trust and esteem. She'd have to appeal to Irene's long history and bond with her mother, instead.

In the meantime, Tally would pop over to Bellen Beach to see if she could find some other locals willing to talk – ideally, a disgruntled ex-artist.

For now, it was time to face her father and get some answers about Ma.

How drunk could he *be* at breakfast time?

CHAPTER 17

LION'S DEN

*S*winging drunk, as Tally quickly deduced, coming up the path to Eyrie at half past eight. Her father was carousing inside his office, loud bangs and yodels flying out the window. A dissipated Richard would be as useful as a snowplough in the tropics. How the devil had he managed that so quickly?

At the top of the stairs, she was astonished to find Olga at the settee, calmly enjoying tea and jam crumpets, not three feet from Ma's shattered chair.

Tally threw up her hands. 'What do you think you're *doing*?'

Olga shrugged. 'What does it look like?'

'A paid employee presuming to sit at our family table when she should be working.'

Olga stood, picking up her plate. '*I will* be family, soon enough.' She flounced away, still chewing.

Tally did not pause to knock on the office door. She was charged and ready to confront the father so transfigured he'd come to resemble a shambolic monster. She closed the door behind her and turned the lock.

Her father lurched in shock at her entrance. He had a golf club in one hand, a whisky glass in the other, and a sea of golf balls surrounding

169

him. He had been driving balls across his office, into the void beneath his prized Tasmanian oak bureau. The raucous cheering had to have been for his own skills, or lack thereof, given the damage to his bureau, the wall, his lamp, even the ceiling.

Richard stared at her – his bleary eyes wide but otherwise unreadable – before turning back to his game in progress. He smacked the golf ball with a swing that had lost none of its power in the intervening years. His shot went comically wide, the ball clanging right into the front of his safe.

Tally flinched. It *felt* like a rebuke.

'Hello –' Tally didn't know how to address this man anymore. *Father* was always too formal in her younger years; *Dickhead* was more fitting, but probably not constructive right now; *Dipsomaniac* seemed the most accurate.

'Thalia.' He took two steps towards her – alarmingly, as though he meant to embrace her – before pitching widely to the left, failing to right himself and staggering into the sideboard beneath his window. A spinning globe and a tray of highball glasses slid off the table, crashing onto the floor.

At the sound of this havoc, rapping came at the door. 'What's going on in there? Are you okay, Richard?' Olga, lurking outside like a good little spy.

'Go away, Olga,' Tally hollered back, as she went to help her father. *Run and get Angus.*

He made no protest as she pulled his large arm over her shoulder and with a herculean effort eased him off the sideboard. He weighed a ton, and was as cooperative as an overturned dinghy. She had a fleeting mental image of the giant marlins strung up by the big game fishermen down on Bellen Beach's jetty. Half the town would turn out to see those magnificent fish displayed and weighed.

Richard sank into the wide cavern of his chair with a groan. Tally stared at her father, making no effort to check her repulsion.

He grew red under her look. 'What are *you* doing here?'

Impulse seized her. *If you want the truth, then lie …*

'I came back as soon as I received Ma's letter.'

She watched the shock hit his face, rolling out in waves of confusion, disbelief and then finally – fear. 'You're not welcome here.'

'Ma's instructions were explicit. In her absence, I'm to act on her behalf, safeguarding her estate – and mine.'

He looked belligerently at her. 'Where's the letter, then? Show it to me!'

'No,' Tally said, taking a seat on a club chair. 'Ma was very clear that I should withhold her letter from you. But you would've expected Ma to be so careful, wouldn't you?' She crossed her legs, knapsack nursed brazenly on her lap.

'You're bluffing.'

'You wish. I'm here to assume control of my island. Your business operations on Dara will shortly be coming to an end. But we'll get to all that in due course, won't we?'

Richard answered this with a look of desolation.

Tally hated the ache it gave her, in the pit of her belly. She reached for the jug of water sweating on his desk and poured two large glasses, pushing one in front of him.

He threw back the water in a torrent, the finishing belch a blast of dog's breath. She waved a hand in front of her wrinkling nose. 'God, you stink! How long have you been doing this for?'

'Had a bloody Mary with breakfast, that's all.'

'Had several by the smell of you, then chased it down with a whole bloody decanter of whisky.' She motioned a hand around his ball-dented office. 'When did you start drinking yourself into a daily stupor?'

'What do *you* care?'

I don't. I want to know if you hurt my mother in your fool drunkenness.
She shrugged. 'Your resort's being run into the ground by a
nincompoop – losing stars by the day – but if whisky and housemaids
make you feel better about it, who am I to question your debauchery?'

'You keep your nose out of my business.'

'I'll be getting to the bottom of everything on my island.'

'You just listen here – Nerissa took herself away. She abandoned
Dara!'

'Is that so? Where'd she go?'

'I don't know, okay? I don't know, I don't know, I don't *know*!' He'd
purpled in this repeating of self.

'Fancy that, the Bullshark of Bellen Beach has no idea where his own
wife went.'

She had braced for a roar of fury, but the arm lashing out, knocking
pens and folios off his desk, still made her leap in her chair.

'You can threaten me, but I'm still going to ask the questions Ma
wanted asked.'

At this, Richard reached for the whisky decanter. Tally was faster,
but in the hand scrimmage that ensued, she discovered he was still the
stronger and was soon the victor.

She sat back, watching him take a large swallow. Did Angus also
wrestle with him every day for the liquor bottle? Far from it. He allowed
this decanter to sit on Richard's desk, probably refilled it each morning.

She knew what she had to ask. She stared at her hands, trying to
summon up the courage of her profession. Tally Forster had interviewed
all manner of person, never shying away from questions considered
indecent for a woman. Why, then, did it feel so impossible to ask this
most important question of the man who'd sired her?

Say it.

She was too old to be cowed by this man, too wise to be tricked by him. For Ma's sake, she had to press this.

'Did you *hurt* her?'

His ready answer crackled through the air. 'I didn't raise a hand to that woman, even when she flaming well deserved it.'

'Aren't you the big, tough man,' she fired back. 'Took it all out on your daughter, instead, didn't you?'

'I disciplined you the way any father would've. Spare the rod and –'

'Just answer me: did you *hurt* my ma?'

'Did I *kill* my own wife?' Richard was on his feet, roaring. 'That's what you're accusing me of, isn't it?!'

Footsteps pounded down the hallway. There were keys tossed around a ring, a fumbling at the doorknob. She didn't have a second to waste.

'Yes, that's what I'm damned well asking you!'

He could barely get out his words for rage. 'Like … *hell* I murdered my own wife, you insolent brat! I *loved* her. Gave her … everything she ever asked for! And what does she do? Leaves me here to … rot away … while she's whoring down in that –'

'Richard!' Angus barrelled through the door. 'That's enough.'

Sauntering in on his heels, was the implacable Mack.

Angus hastened to her father's side, muttering directives to calm and cool, to sit and take a breath. But Tally's attention had drawn back to the third man in their midst.

Mack stopped close beside her, too close, resting a hand on her chair. She could smell his unwashed clothing, a cigarette, just extinguished, on his breath, the sour fruit of his armpits. The box jellyfish's scarlet whiplash on his arm was mere inches from her face. Her throat thickened and dried, all the nerve endings of her cheek afire.

Mack's coarse voice cut across her head.

'Your slut wife has really done a number on you, Dick, hasn't she? But we're here for you, ay? Don't you worry about this little bitch, either. We're going to look after you, *and* Mermaid Bay...'

CHAPTER 18
SHELL PALACE

Tally was powering the Mermaid Bay runabout towards the mainland in searing midday sunshine, navy cloud shadows moving over the sea. Behind her, staggering cumulonimbus mountains built on the horizon. Into the drone and spray she seethed aloud: 'Just get in your car and screech back to Cairns. Never look back – never come back! To hell with saving the island for Ma, to hell with fixing Mermaid Bay, and especially to hell with Father!'

She'd go straight to the police and report her mother missing. Why should she have to handle it alone? Let *those* guys sort out her father and Mack!

Do not look for me, Ma's voice begged over the burring engine, *nor set a search after me*. Tally bared her teeth against the wind. *Dammit, Ma! How could you ask that of me?*

After mooring at the jetty, Tally hurried to her car, still parked at the back of the tavern. Her Morris Minor, a dear friend among the dilapidated shacks and disembowelled cars of the Dodgy End. Though she sat in the driver's seat and clenched the wheel, she did not start the engine. Her resolve to flee had kited off on the sea breeze. Now at a safe distance from her father, his cronies and the high emotions of their confrontation, Tally felt her determination billow out, once more.

She hopped out of her car and gave the bonnet a reassuring pat. 'You'll be right here for a little bit longer, won't you?'

She went in search of a public telephone. The tavern, with the benefit of daylight and sobriety, was much weathered and shrunken. There was a jukebox playing, but no lifesavers ready to hoist her up onto the tables. She waved g'day to a gnarly-looking Mr Hillman behind the bar, and moved quickly to the red telephone at the back, digging out her wallet for coins.

Tally wanted to hear a comforting voice from her past – *future*, she meant to say.

Jonathon's voice down the line was exactly the balm she needed, as was his dispassionate interest. 'How's it going there? Turned your mother up yet?' Only he could say it like that and make her smile.

'Nope, still missing.'

'Might her disappearance hold any news value to *me*?'

'*No*,' she said dryly.

'What are you calling me for, then? Shouldn't you be laid out on the sand in something small and yellow polkadotted?'

'It's not a holiday.'

'Well, it should be. Because I'm putting you to work the moment you're back. We miss you here, Forster.'

She winced. 'Just be quiet for a second, will you,' she ordered. 'And hold out the telephone towards the newsroom.'

He shushed and let her listen to the clattering typewriters and rumble of male voices, like a far, distant sea in a shell.

When she'd had her fill, she cleared her throat, loudly. 'All right, that's enough.'

Jonathon resumed the line. 'Anything else I can do for you?'

'As a matter of fact,' she said, just now hitting on the idea, 'I was wondering if you might look up a fellow for me?'

'I might remember how to do that.'

'It is going to put your skills to the test, though – I don't even have his last name.'

'What's this bloke to you?'

'No, it's definitely not like that. Old man of the sea, and I rather think he *would* eat me, given half the chance. Somewhat of a local legend, from what I can gather. Has some long history with my father – allegedly – but I've never heard of him. Goes by the name of Mack.'

'Short for Macheath?'

'Ha! I thought of the *Threepenny Opera* too. Must be Mc-something. But listen, he's got some terrible scars on his arm from a tussle with a box jellyfish.'

'A *box*? You don't say!'

'I do say, and unless he's hauled himself up from some sea grave, the man survived it. I think a thing like that might have landed him in the paper. Would you mind?'

'Not at all, kid.'

'All right, ta.'

'And now you can do something for me?'

'What's that, then?'

'Stop looking for stories –'

'Can't. I live and breathe intrigue.'

'– and go do something decadently tropical, instead, won't you? Get yourself a proper tan and a habit for sundowners, have a holiday fling.'

'No one here to romance.'

'Pah, you're wasted as an island girl. Better get back home soon.'

Outside the tavern, she considered the sleepy settlement of Bellen Beach curving out before her.

While we're here, she told herself, *let's get some background information on the happenings of nineteen forty-six*. And who in Bellen Beach liked the sound of their own voice more than the most unflagging broadcast journalists? *Ginger Lowry*, that's who.

Tally set off at a trot, brainstorming questions aloud. By the time she'd passed the beach kiosk and crossed the road to stand before Ginger's old shop, she was humming with readiness.

Ginger's Palace of Shells stared back at her in all its glitzy glory; the flashing, bulb-lit marquee above, the plastic-strip-curtained entrance and the wide windows filled with shell creations in gaudy hues. There were not one but three 'SAVE OUR REEF!' signs planted out the front of Ginger's.

She pushed through the strip curtains into the shop, which still smelled, peculiarly, of briny candies and plastic-doll heads.

The Palace took its name from a huge castle sculpture, made entirely of shells, which was set centrestage. It had been one of the beach's favourite attractions for a generation now. She wondered if youngsters still swarmed around it after school trying to spot the tiny figurines moved regularly by Ginger. When Tally was young, some claimed to have counted all ten thousand shells comprising the sculpture. Tourists too adored the kitsch and novelty of the shop. It was a wonder Ma sold so many of her own bespoke trinkets, given the popularity of the Palace of Shells.

Aha. That was where Ma got her money to run away with. She'd been slowly collecting her observatory giftshop takings. A mere pittance in Richard's eyes, so she'd never been asked to hand it over, but it would have been enough for a decent head start.

Ma had financed her freedom selling her bottled mermaids.

'My *oath*, is that Thalia Ramsey I see?'

Tally spun to see Ginger coming in from his attached flat. He had the same madcap air; bald head with a wizard-length goatee; chicken legs under a bear's gut; skin mottled with the barnacles of old age.

'That's me,' she said, with a habitual swipe under her thighs to check her skirt was down, though she was wearing shorts. Too well she remembered his penchant for schoolgirls' legs.

'Lookin' as good as ever,' he said. 'Always a shame to see a pretty girl grow up and become as ugly as her mother. But not you, still a peach, just like Nerissa Forster.' He sucked his teeth, crassly.

'I've got a few questions for you,' Girl Reporter said.

She watched the barricade clunk down over his face, and kicked herself for misjudging her approach. Island Daughter swept dryly in front of Girl Reporter; *let me . . .*

'I'm putting together a souvenir booklet for Mermaid Bay – with stories and photographs of the district – and I wondered if you'd like to contribute.'

'You want me to help *you* make souvenirs? Your flamin' gift shop's been undermining my business for years.'

'Thought you might want your name in print, but that's fine – I'll ask someone else.' She turned to leave.

'Now, cool your heels. Just thought you should know your mother's store has been hurting me for a long time.'

'Duly noted. Do you want in on my booklet, or not?'

Did he *ever . . .*

In his adjoining flat, Ginger had been yammering on for an hour about his beachcombing prowess, without coming close yet to the colony on the Hat. The photo album he'd promised to show her sat unopened beneath his bowlful of belly. Apparently, he intended to catalogue every shell he'd ever picked up, including the ones that got away.

'So, then, Thalia,' he said, stroking his long goatee, 'it's quiz time. What do you reckon the most dangerous creature in the Coral Sea is?'

'That'd be jellyfish,' Tally replied, grateful to use her voice instead of enduring his. 'Everyone knows a box-jellyfish sting is basically a death sentence. And then you've got the sea wasps – or the Irukandji, as they're calling them now.'

'That's where you're wrong!' he cried, rattling the basket of shells he was using for demonstration purposes.

'I know I'm right. Grandpapa Forster was killed by an Irukandji. Walked into the sea, and a half-hour later, he was gone.'

'Probably had a weak heart. Swimming kills old fellas all the time. Nope, the most dangerous creature in the Coral Sea is the cone shell.'

She laughed. 'A *shell*?'

'You bet.' He'd pulled a beautiful cone-shaped specimen, brown patterned on violaceous white, and pointed it at her like a dart. 'If you're holding onto this shell when the snail inside shoots its little harpoon at you … you've got ten minutes, tops, till you're a goner.' He clicked the fingers of his other hand. 'Dead, like *that*.'

Tally swallowed. 'Guess you learn something new every day.'

'Don't know much for an island girl, do you? Really think you're gonna run Richard's island one day?'

'It's my *mother's* island.'

'Your mother nearly gave that island clean away after old man Forster carked it. Had the papers ready to sign and all.'

'She did no such thing.'

'Better believe it.'

'Who was she selling it to, then?'

'Folks from the Hat.'

Tally laughed, but a big sea cucumber had slid down her throat. 'Who were these prospective owners from a destitute colony that came so close to getting my island?' She nodded at his photo album. 'Give me some proof.'

Ginger slapped the cover. 'You think I'm pullin' your chain? Mad Ginger spruiking his bull crap again? I've got them right here. Used to buy shells off that *artiste* colony on regular trips there.'

He bent over his album, goatee brushing the flipping pages. 'Here!'

Tally leaned to look at monochrome images, turning the page with a tiny hiss of triumph: two group pictures of the Artists' Colony members, a dozen or so men and women. Unhelpfully, there was no date pencilled in either of the corners.

'When did you take these?'

'Sometime before the war. The colony moved back to the mainland during it – most of 'em, anyway. Didn't want to be sitting ducks if the Japs came. Only the *crazies* stayed out there.'

Tally bristled. 'My mother and grandpapa stayed on Dara.' Unlike other, well-settled islands in the Coral Sea, Dara had remained untouched: never annexed by the RAAF, hosting no radar station or fortifications.

'Yeah, and ask yourself: what kind of useless, selfish father keeps his daughter out there in wartime, when most of the women and children on the coast were being evacuated south by train?'

Tally knew: *a father who would never let his daughter be sent away.*

Why hadn't Ma talked more about this time? They would have been hard, lonely years after the colony decamped to the mainland. There was a hole in Tally's knowledge, that mostly wartime gap between her mother's girlhood and the death of her beloved father in nineteen forty-five. What kind of *young woman* had Nerissa been before she became a wife and mother in short order? It was a feature of Tally's self-absorption – and she'd own it – that Dara's history prior to that year was about as useful to her as the Old Testament: mostly mythological, really just setting the scene for *her* momentous birth.

'If you ask me,' Tally said, 'it was pretty brave of my ma and grandpapa to stay out there all alone.'

'Wouldn't say they were all alone in the archipelago. There were people sneaking around out there, up to things they should'na been. Folks who couldn't account for their whereabouts during the war, and their winnings in the years after.'

An electric feather stroked the back of her neck. 'What do you mean by *winnings*?'

'I've asked myself many a time over the last twenty-odd years, how *did* so many American greenbacks come to be floatin' around this town? Why'd some folks do so well after the war?'

'Are you referring to folks from the Hat?'

'Can't say.'

'Sure you can.'

'Not going to.'

She stared him down, but he wasn't shifting on this.

Her eyes snapped back to the Artists' Colony portrait, seeing the greyscale peak of Mount Teasdale behind the group. What if her father's treasure map, the Hat's wartime residents and the wealth floating around after the war were all related?

Her father didn't take control of Dara until nineteen forty-six; surely his map would have been drawn up after that?

'May I?' Without waiting for permission, Tally pulled his album onto her own lap. Straightaway, her eyes lit on the petite form of an adolescent girl – no more than sixteen, perhaps – standing among the group. Her heart contracted.

Ma.

Her eyes tried several times to move on past Ma, but it was near impossible. She was more carefree than Tally had ever seen her, fresh-faced and unworldly.

'Can you tell me who the rest of the folks in the colony were?' How sad to think that these were the only friends young Nerissa had ever known ...

'Most of them were roaming gypsies, long gone now. I can't be expected to remember all their names.' Ginger tapped a short young man standing close to Ma. 'That urchin beside your mother is Walter Isaac. He was sweet on her. The bloke there next to Walter is Joe Harmon.' Angus's father. Tally thought she would hardly recognise this thin man as the heavy-set mechanic he had become. The next stream of names meant nothing to her. 'And *that* one –' Ginger stabbed a thumb at an unsmiling, middle-aged woman '– is Irene Threadwell. Ring a bell for you?'

Tally smiled to see Irene look so irascible, even then. 'Irene is our longest-serving and most loyal employee at Mermaid Bay.' *More important*, she didn't add, *than even our island manager*.

Ginger chortled. 'Of course she's *loyal*. Richard Ramsey paid Irene off with that job and house when he took the island your mother was just about to *give away* to her.'

'Ma would never have *dreamed* of selling Dara. It was all she had left of my grandpapa. He's buried on our island!'

Ginger shrugged. 'Irene was getting that island until Richard intervened. I'm tellin' you what I remember, but if you don't want to hear it ...'

'How was Irene going to afford Dara, then?' She made no effort to hide her scepticism. Irene, a single mother, deserted by a scoundrel husband, with no home or fixed employment – the idea was *preposterous*.

'Maybe you should ask your mother what the devil she wanted to throw it all away for, and why to that woman.'

A grid of consternation was stamped on Tally's forehead. He had to have misunderstood the situation. Irene and Nerissa had known each other for years before Ma married Richard – Ma probably offered her old friend a permanent home on Dara, not the whole island! It was odd, though, that Tally knew so little about a woman who'd played such a big part in Ma's life – present even at Tally's birth.

Restless impatience made her limbs twitch. Why was she sitting here listening to Ginger, when she could be seeking answers from Irene?

'And who's *that*?' Her finger hovered above the man's lean, shirtless chest. She already knew; it was why she couldn't even bring herself to touch his image.

'Murphy McLeod.'

Mack. So, that was his name.

'Is he still around these parts?' Her face was a pantomime of nonchalance; she almost expected Ginger to laugh at her bad acting.

'Can't say,' Ginger replied gruffly. 'Heard he might be.'

How interesting – Ginger doesn't want to touch Mack any more than I do.

She considered Ginger's photo anew: so many key players, all still connected to Dara. She was going to need *this* photo.

'Ginger, you've got some real gems in this album. Would you let me borrow them for my booklet?'

'No way. If anyone's puttin' out a history booklet, I've decided it's me.'

Crafty old bugger. 'Perhaps we could join forces on it, then?'

'What do I need *you* for? *I've* got the photos.'

Tally pretended to mull this over. 'On second thoughts, I was looking at some of your picture postcards in the shop, and my ma has been selling ones *just* like them. Seems to me, we must already have copies of our own ...'

Ginger pushed up to stand. '*Which* pictures?' he huffed. 'Show me!'

'No, don't trouble yourself,' Tally said, making no effort to stand with him. 'I'm probably mistaken, and anyway I should be going now ...'

'You stay right there,' he barked. 'We'll sort *this* out.' He puffed into the next room. Tally's heart rate rocketed up.

Easier to seek forgiveness than ask permission.

With her eyes locked on the doorway, her hand slid into the album. She eased a nail under the photograph and leveraged it off its mounting, then slipped it into the pocket of her shorts.

Just in time.

Ginger steamed back into the room with a pile of postcards.

Tally reached for them eagerly, sliding the photo album off onto the side table. Thus ensued a verbal tussle over the postcards. Hamming up envy, Tally admitted that no, she did not think Dara Island was selling the same picture postcards, after all. She had been mistaken, what a shame, Ginger was very lucky to have them, she bet they sold well, et cetera. His attention sufficiently diverted from the photo album, Tally thought to make her escape.

She stood, trying not to look at the discarded album, nor touch the pocket on her hip. She bade him adieu and beat a path to the front door.

'Hey!' he called out. 'Not so *fast*, Miss!'

She turned, brows hoisted innocently. 'Yes?'

'Don't think I'm gonna let you get away with it!'

'With what?'

'I made your crown, I'll have you know!'

'My *what*?'

'That crown you got when you were made Coral Sea Queen!'

'*Oh*,' Tally said, breathing out. 'Right.' She'd never once considered where the tiara had come from. 'It's a lovely crown, I'm very fond of it.'

'You weren't meant to *keep* it! You were supposed to give it back, for the next girl. I had to make a whole other one to replace it!' He was wheezing with vexation. 'You give it back to me or pay me what you owe!'

'I didn't bring it with me from Cairns, but I'm happy to compensate you at a fair price.'

'You can't pay for something that beautiful. It was a work of flamin' art!'

'Then I do apologise. It was teenage wilfulness on my part. Thank goodness we grow out of it ...'

This sanguine tone apparently had hit the wrong nerve. His goatee was white against a reddening neck and face.

'Your mother didn't, though, did she? Always was a stealthy little floozy. She's still up to her old tricks.'

Tally's mouth opened on a rush of shocked air. '*Pardon* me?'

'Nah, you heard me. Your mother was a *hussy*, sneakin' over to the Hat at night when her father's back was turned, sleepin' with that dopey Walter Isaac. Everyone out there knew it, even Bertie in the end. Walter's just lucky he got himself safely off to war, before Bertie made croc bait out of him.'

Croc bait. That was a phrase that rang true for Grandpapa. He'd threatened Richard Ramsey with the very same, hadn't he? When it came to Dara and his daughter, Grandpapa had been prepared to do *anything* to protect his property.

'Nerissa hasn't changed a bit,' Ginger sneered. 'Runnin' off on the man who saved her island for her. Ask yourself: who's she shacking up with this time? That's where you'll find her.'

Mad, Mad Ginger, Tally told herself as she wrenched the door open and charged through to safety.

His taunt followed her out onto the footpath. 'I feel sorry for your father, that's who, gettin' caught in that honey trap! Looks like Nerissa Forster wasn't worth that island, after all!'

CHAPTER 19

MRS THREADWELL

The afternoon storm brewing in the east seemed to suck the runabout towards it. The horizon was a heavy-handed charcoal rendering, the sea glowing an eerie, iridescent aqua. Every bounce, over every wave, seemed to punctuate Tally's internal diatribe.

That crude, rude, sonofabitch!

She passed the afternoon ferry, mainland bound, and imagined how she looked to its sun-sated guests: a wild-eyed Valkyrie braced over the wheel, driftwood hair streaming cape-like behind her.

Rage drove her on into the steep green bowl of Dara's embrace. Puttering to a stop, in the warm shallows, she patted the photograph in her pocket.

What am I to do now?

Her determination was a lit match burning fast towards her fingers, with nothing but herself to ignite. Well, there was always her *father* to scorch …

But at Eyrie, she discovered he was one step ahead of her. Splattered open on the garden bed in front of the verandah, as though tossed from Ma's bedroom window above, was her suitcase. Thrown out of home – again. Frankly, she was surprised it had taken him a whole day without Ma here to intercede.

Beginning to gather up her belongings, she comprehended that they were strewn in too wide a fashion, even for a suitcase exploding from a second-storey drop. He – *they* – had searched her belongings first. She gave the knapsack on her shoulder a grateful pat, for it contained everything important, from secret keys to stolen map.

Through the screen door, in the shadowy recesses of the hallway, Tally saw Olga skitter away.

Do run and tell the master I'm back …

Beneath her discarded belongings, she discovered the real indignity: the bones of Ma's broken chair. He wasn't just throwing her out, but sending her a message.

She straightened tall, lifting her suitcase.

'No,' she told the heckling cockatoos, strutting in their cage above her. '*I'm* the lucky one.'

She went back down the garden terrace and into the rainforest paths, there to join her own cackle to the electric screech of insects rejoicing in the storm.

Tally had taken the scrub track around to the private cove of Sandy Beach. By the time she'd moved through the large boulders to the cove, the storm had beaten her. Torrential rain pelted the hot sand like stones, pockmarking the grey sea. Here, she hid her bags from the rain and thieves in a rock cave she knew all too well. In fact, there was still an old bottle of Hanush's sarsaparilla, her childhood running-away-drink-of-choice, sand-filled in the rocks.

The roaring rainstorm had swallowed the world whole – mainland and sea blotted out before her, island obliterated behind her, sand inundated beneath her. She shed her clothes now, even her bra and underpants, and ran to the sea, rain driving into her bare skin like needles. The water was warmer than the air as she crashed in. The rage she'd sustained over so many hours had emancipated something of the old child in her. She lay back, face to the heavens, mouth open laughingly, and let the rain blind her.

Ma always said there was therapeutic benefit to a rainstorm over the sea – some invisible charge that elevated the life force. Tally had done her own research since leaving the island, and thought perhaps Ma was onto something, after all: negative ions, scientists called them. The more Tally learned, the wiser Ma seemed to get.

She rose at leisure and waded back to shore. As she shucked off water under an overhanging rock, she considered her next step.

You might come and visit me, Lila had offered that first afternoon.

All right, then, she would.

Lila, however, was not yet home from work. It was the formidable Irene Threadwell who met her at the door of the house, the gutters running like a waterfall at Tally's back. Irene did not look pleased to see her, but neither did she seem surprised.

'Lila isn't here,' she said, sans a *welcome home to Dara*.

Tally smiled. 'I actually wanted to catch up with *you*, Irene.'

Irene folded her thick forearms. 'I see.'

'I've interrupted your cooking – can I keep you company?'

Irene grunted, hardly agreement, but she did stand aside.

Inside, the rain was thunderous upon the tin roof, making inquisitions difficult, if not impossible. Tally let Irene relax back into her meal preparations, hoping to warm her up with small talk. But shouted over such a din, it engendered no such warmth.

Giving up, Tally sat silently on her stool and watched Irene work, eyes darting around for a stickybeak.

Two things were apparent: Irene's home was still as beautifully maintained as ever, and Lila remained the centre of her mother's existence. The Threadwells' residence stood in stark contrast to the dilapidated state of Mermaid Bay Resort. If Tally wasn't mistaken, the interior had even been renovated, with new furniture and curtains.

The main decorating theme was Lila herself; every wall and surface boasting framed photographs, from toddlerhood to womanhood. Tally had thought Irene Threadwell took pride in nothing as much as her position, and yet here was Lila, displayed like a trophy. It had to be hard for Lila, still living with her mother at her age.

But hang on . . .

It wasn't only Lila in some of those images.

Tally slipped off her stool to peruse the wall gallery between the two bedrooms.

Ma!

The picture: Nerissa Forster, still in the bloom of adolescence, standing with Irene on an unspoiled Coral Beach. They had arms slung about one another, as though they were dear friends, or even, given their age difference, mother and daughter. Ma's hair was long, light and windblown, and Irene's face had not yet grown so grim with perpetual disapproval. Even in monochrome, the image was paradisiacal, their contentment clear.

Tally's ribs ached to see such happiness in Ma's face again.

'When was *this*?' she asked, her voice failing to carry over the rain. But no matter, Irene was watching her closely from behind the kitchen bench, wooden spoon hovering.

Tally's gaze went to the next picture alongside, heart sinking with dismay: it was Ma, embracing a tiny Lila on Dara's old dock, built by Grandpapa. She could not help the flare of jealously – her ma with arms around another small girl, and Tally not in the picture at all.

She turned back to Irene, who had laid down her spoon and covered the frypan with a lid, waiting for Tally's next question.

'Who took these pictures?'

Irene came to stand beside Tally. 'Bertie.'

'I didn't know Grandpapa took any photographs,' Tally said, voice smaller than the storm might be blamed for.

'He had a Kodak thirty-five,' said Irene. 'He was quite devoted to his photography. Used to send his film cassettes away to Brisbane for development. Even after leaving the newspaper behind, he retained something of the newsman's interest in people.'

Tally turned her head to stare at Irene. Why had she never known this woman might be a font of stories about her grandpapa?

She frowned, returning to the first image. There was no denying Irene had aged less than gracefully. There were heavy, sagging pockets under her eyes now, a greying crop of hair where once had hung almost girlish lengths.

She tapped the picture. 'When was this?'

'Mid-forties, I should think.'

'During the war?' Tally asked, lightly as you please.

'Perhaps,' Irene said. 'Yes, I think so.'

'So, you were on Dara with Ma and Grandpapa during the war – when the rest of the colony moved back to the mainland?'

'Yes, I was here.'

'You *and* Lila?'

'Yes.'

'And Mr Threadwell?'

'No. He wasn't here.'

Lila is just over three years older than me, Tally mused, *which means she was born in nineteen forty-three ...*

'Was Lila *born* on Dara during the war?'

There was a silence, drawn out. Tally thought Irene might decline to answer; something in the shift of her body, the nose sigh. She

192

understood that she had walked Irene into a snare she could take no credit for setting.

'She was,' Irene allowed finally.

Fancy that. No Mr Threadwell, only a Lila.

Tally studied the image of Irene again and her not-quite-faded blush of youth. She'd still been an attractive woman for one entering, what, her forties? Old enough to interest a world-weary man like Bertie Forster, young enough to befriend his daughter. No societal restrictions to impede passion in *this* beguiling paradise.

Alarm beat beneath Tally's breastbone as the hypothesis formed: the rest of the world at war, and one man tucked away on a secret island with a beloved daughter … and his *mistress*.

Tally swallowed saliva into a mouth gone dry. 'That was very kind of Grandpapa to offer you a home here, when Lila's father ran off on you at such a delicate time.'

It was a challenge laid down, and she was determined to have it answered.

'Bertie Forster was the epitome of kindness,' Irene said, turning now to stare at Tally. Her blue eyes were piercing above soft pouches. 'He always intended for Lila and me to be properly taken care of, for the rest of our lives.'

Tally absorbed this declaration with a thudding pulse. Irene had been Grandpapa Forster's late-in-life lover, and Lila his illegitimate daughter.

Oh, Ma, why didn't you ever tell me? What good could come of trying to hide such a thing?

Realisation was a cold slap: *It threatened the future she had promised me!*

She could no longer meet Irene's penetrating look. Tally turned back to the photograph of Ma embracing tiny Lila, interpreting this pose in a whole new way. Despite the monochrome tones, she saw their similar eyes and pert noses, the shared lightness of their hair …

Sisters.

But why would Bertie Forster have drawn up and concealed his will, specifying that his *only* daughter should inherit Dara – knowing he had another, illegitimate child?

'Were you *here*,' she ventured carefully, 'the day that Grandpapa died?'

'Swimming right beside him.'

'I thought he was cast-net fishing.'

'No, swimming.'

Tally blinked rapidly; a well-developed moving picture reverting to storyboard.

'You saw him stung?'

'I watched him die not fifteen minutes later.'

'Ma always said she was *alone* with Grandpapa when he died – that there was no one here to help her.'

'In fact, your mother was lazing around on Sandy Beach that morning, nowhere to be seen. Lucky for her that she didn't have to witness such a terrible death.'

Why would Ma lie about such a thing? Shame, perhaps.

Tally pushed by Irene. 'I need a drink,' she said. What she *needed* was a moment to sieve facts from fear.

Irene took out the water jug and poured her a glass.

Tally dumped her bottom back on the stool, sipping shakily. A new and most alarming question was forming …

What might Irene Threadwell stand to gain from Grandpapa's death, and now Ma's absence?

With fear tight in her throat, Tally placed her glass down on the bench, where it clinked against a decorative tray of shells. She turned her gaze to this tray, picking one up at random. A cone shell, striped bronze and white. In fact, the tray was *filled* with cone shells. Large and small, with differing patterns, but all cone shells.

The most dangerous creature in the Coral Sea, according to the lore of Mad Ginger. *Ten minutes, tops . . .*

Tally dropped the shell back in the tray, a rash of goosepimples spreading along her arms.

She looked up to find Irene's eyes fixed coldly upon her.

What if the most dangerous creature on Dara has been hiding all this time in a tightly guarded lie?

She swallowed hard. 'Irene, do *you* know where my ma is?'

Her small eyes didn't even flicker. 'I do not.'

Tally stared back. 'It's completely unlike Ma to suddenly up and leave us all.'

'Your mother has always acted for her own selfish reasons, without respect for the rest of us. Why would this time be any different?'

Shock punched the air out of Tally. Was there no end to the terrible things she would hear spoken of her mother today? And from Irene now, of all people – Ma's oldest friend. She gaped at Irene disbelievingly, blood rushing to her face.

Irene regarded Tally with the disdain of one explaining how the world was not flat. 'Everything is always about *Nerissa's* feelings and what *Nerissa* wants and needs, and to hell with everybody else.'

'What baloney,' Tally choked out. 'My mother has done nothing but put her needs second to my father's lust for power and control.'

'Richard would do anything for your mother, if only it would finally make her happy.'

'I haven't seen my father concerned with my mother's happiness a day in my life!'

'You don't have a clue. There never was a man so besotted as

Richard Ramsey when he came to Dara to woo Nerissa Forster.'

'Came to woo her out of her island, you mean.'

'You think he married your mother for land? You sulky child. It would've been far easier for him to have made her an exorbitant offer we could never refuse.'

We? Tally's eyes narrowed. 'Ma would never have sold Dara.'

'No, she kept her island and still made herself a very wealthy woman in the process. She's been putting on airs ever since.'

Tally's voice wobbled. 'Ma didn't need to marry for money, not when she had Dara. Ma's a romantic at heart, that's why Father's philandering has always hurt her so much.'

Irene's eyes were hard, pale stones. 'Nerissa had been trifling with Richard's feelings from their very first meeting. He was a goner the instant he laid eyes on her, and she *knew* it.'

Tally looked again at the photo of her mother, seeing her as her father had: standing under sultry palm trees in a white cotton slip, with a hibiscus tucked behind her ear; a scantily clad siren. Nothing like the respectably buttoned wife of Richard Ramsey she'd become.

Her throat ached. 'I'm sure she did look beautiful … standing on prime real estate.'

'Richard came to buy Dara from Bertie, but he was sent away desiring Bertie's daughter more than he ever wanted this island. He was obsessed. She could have asked for *anything*, and she knew it!'

'That's rich coming from the head housekeeper who replaced at least a dozen housemaids due to my father's womanising.' *Like a dealer of girls.*

'He turned to that nonsense much later on. It isn't easy for a man to love a woman like Nerissa, to be rejected over and over again.'

'Of course, it should be *her* fault that *he* couldn't keep it in his pants around his own employees.'

'Don't you dare patronise me! I understand that marriage better than you ever will! I'd always known this day would come, your mother running off on her promise to us, just to please her own dumb lust! Now it's up to *us* to counteract her reckless stupidity!'

'Is that why you sent Lila to get me in Cairns? To safeguard Ma's island?'

'I didn't send Lila. That *fool* girl went to drag you into this of her own accord. *You're* nothing but a liability. You always were! None of us want you back here. Lila should've listened to me and left you where you were!'

This outburst done, Irene threw her pointer finger at the door.

'*Get out!*' she ordered. 'I don't have anything more to say to you.'

Tally stood, more in shock than acquiescence, and walked to the door.

Outside, the rain finally had stopped, and in the sodden silence, Tally's brain rang in alarm …

Irene, secret mistress of Bertie Forster.

Lila, his illegitimate daughter.

Ma, with a past Tally did not understand.

Whom and *what* could she trust now? She was homeless on her own island, motherless and rudderless, too. And where could she go next?

CHAPTER 20

DESK-BOUND

There was no room at the inn. With torch scything, Tally had let herself into the darkened lodge and Angus's locked office to check the accommodation roster, finding no free beds in the resort. Nothing in the staff village, either – even T. Ho's cabin was filled.

As she saw it, there were two places left to her: Ma's observatory and Grandpapa's tiny beachside chapel, tucked away in its private grove beyond the staff village.

The former was closer, lockable, familiar. The latter she hadn't seen in many years – it might be dilapidated now, certainly had been gutted of furniture; she'd seen the pews for herself in Eyrie. It was safest to stay in the observatory tonight and scope out the chapel on the morrow.

She slid the roster back in Angus's top drawer. While she was in it, she rifled through his things a bit, mostly out of curiosity. The roll of mints she pilfered was definitely out of spite. There was nothing else interesting here, not even a fob of keys to borrow indefinitely. She eased the drawer closed, ready to sneak back out.

At a distance, Monsoon's nightclub could be heard, heaving earlier than normal. They would have moved happy hour undercover this evening. Tally did not want to think of Lila being in that dark and smoky lounge with the likes of Mack or Angus – or her father.

Did anyone else on this island know who Lila was and what claim she might have on the place?

Outside Angus's office, Tally heard the lodge door whack open to admit a group of male voices. Someone with a key – Angus and associates?

Indeed. They were coming straight towards reception and the offices beyond. Tally flicked off her torch, leaping up.

Where to hide?

Her eyes flew around the dark room. Should she slide into the hallway, and if they saw her just play lost – and dumb? No, they were at reception now, and she'd never make it, much less be believed.

The rowdy party had entered the hall behind reception.

Ah, shit!

She gripped Angus's desk with a hand, considering it. Deep, wide and door facing; she could fit underneath and not be seen. There was nothing else for it …

Tally bundled herself under the desk, pulling the chair in after her. She curled up hard in the corner, hugging her knapsack, as a key scraped in the lock.

A hand smacked at the light switch, and the room burst into brightness. Tally felt more starkly exposed now than when she had swum in the sea in her birthday suit earlier. She flattened her spine against the desk front, daring to exhale only in tiny puffs.

They had brought the smell of liquor and cigars into the small office with them. She recognised two individuals: Angus and Mack.

Can't a journo even sneak into an office in peace?

Angus came to stand behind his desk. Tally crooked her index finger and put it firmly between her teeth as she waited for him to draw back his chair and shove his long legs, or worse – *far worse* – in her face.

But he apparently wasn't here to stay – thank God. He was stooped over the top of his desk, shuffling items.

'Your organisation leaves a lot to be desired.' Mack's coarse voice. 'Does Dick know you leave his money just lying around?'

'Gimme a break, I've been busy!' Tally wanted to grab his leg and pinch. *Don't piss him off – not with me in here!*

'Your time management is lacking, too, boy.'

'Here,' Angus crowed, and not a minute too soon. 'Right where I left it.' Angus's legs shifted closer to Tally as he handed the prize to Mack.

There was the sound of an envelope torn open, then the rapid shuffling of bills. Tally tried in vain to count those sliding notes. It was a *lot* of money.

'All there?' Angus said.

Mack finished with a grunt, then the envelope was crinkled into his pocket. 'Yeah, all right.'

'Okay, then,' Angus said. 'Now I'd like to go over the job.'

Mack hawked spit, the mucus projectile hitting the steel bin beside Tally's hiding place with a resounding ding. She grimaced.

'I don't need you explaining nothin' to me! I know exactly what I have to do. You were still in your nappies when we found the lady – so don't come at *me* with your fake competence. You're Dick's useful idiot, nothing more.'

Tally might have cheered agreement to that last part, if she didn't feel like throwing up. What *lady*?

'Idiot or not,' Angus fired back, 'Richard gave *me* instructions to pass on with the payment. But if you don't want them, just say so.' Only Tally saw the tremor in Angus's knees.

'All right,' Mack drawled. 'Go.'

'Okay.' Angus leaned forward, shuffling through papers again. Tally cursed herself for not having looked at those documents, earlier. There had been a secret sitting right in front of her, and she'd been concerned with accommodation?

'I've drawn up a mud map, based on Richard's description. If you look here –'

Rough laughter sprayed across him. 'I don't need your pathetic excuse for a map. I could find the way myself, blindfolded. Dick was telling *you* how to get there, or are you *that* thick? You shouldn't be drawing things like this – ever heard of the concept of evidence? Destroy it now or I'll destroy *you*.'

Tally's hand, on her knapsack – and her father's stolen map within – had begun a fast quiver.

She heard the click of a lighter, followed by the whiff of paper burning, then a second missile tossed into the metal bin. Smoke coiled up under the desk. Tally waved a hand in front of her nose, begging herself not to cough or asphyxiate.

'Right, then,' Angus said. 'Directions aside, what provisions do you need from me? Digging equipment?'

'Holy shit,' Mack expostulated to his unseen audience. 'I'm supposed to take *this* moron with me? How're you going to get your Bobcat up Mount Teasdale?'

'Obviously, I didn't mean a –'

'Look, mate, I've decided it's better if I do this with my own people.'

'You heard Richard, he's adamant no one else is to be involved or consulted. Skeleton crew only. That's why we're paying you the big bucks.'

'He owes me more than he could possibly repay.'

'Richard said to remind you that it's in your interests as much as his to make sure she disappears for good.'

'He can stick his interest up his arse. If I'm not satisfied that she's properly covered, I'll have to take the rest of her off Dara in pieces. We need this monsoon to shift so we can get moving.'

'We're already running out of time.'

'If he'd let me dispose of her properly when *I* wanted to, we wouldn't be under this time pressure now, would we? Be ready to head off by week's end and get a brain in your head, or I leave without you – do you copy?'

'What about Thalia?'

Tally's neck spasmed painfully.

'What about her?'

'Richard thinks she's going to be a problem. She's always nosing into things, he said, can't keep her mouth shut. And now she's got a whole bloody newspaper for her bullhorn.'

'I thought he took care of that stupid git.'

'He threw her out … but she's still on the island.'

'*You* get rid of her, then. It's not hard!' This was followed by some miming action her imagination made gruesome pictures of. She wondered at her mettle to endure such eavesdropping.

Angus was muttering something in response – not quite assent, perhaps appeasement.

'Do you need me to hold your hand through anything else?'

Angus seemingly declined, for there was another loud hawking into the still-smoking bin, then the door whacked open and closed.

Mack had gone.

Angus's legs remained a mere yard from her face as the older man sauntered away; a jovial, tuneless whistle in his wake.

Left behind, Angus discharged a flurry of curses. The wooden chair before her pushed in further as he took hold of it to shake it violently. '*Sonofabitch!*'

Tally closed her eyes against the tumult, expecting at any moment to lose an eye to the seat edge or the chair leg.

She waited God knew how long after Angus finally departed. Fear had iced up her limbs and will to leave.

Outside the lodge, the frogs were a noisy, invisible legion. *Werk, werk, werk*, from drooping leaf to drumming drainpipe. *Brawk, brawk, brawk.* The cacophony covered an internal horror reel – *going to have to take the rest of her off Dara in pieces, dispose of her properly* – as she hurried through the paths to the jetty.

Tally locked herself in the observatory, then walked slowly around, shining her torch into every nook and cranny until she was sure she was alone. She avoided the stairs, not wanting to think about the dark, cavernous void below.

Rain rolled over the observatory roof, seeming to shake the structure itself. Moisture swept in through the window gaps, tinkling the shell chandelier above Ma's desk.

Don't think about it anymore tonight, she told herself sternly, *just get through until the morning*.

Wrung out, she settled herself down to sleep behind Ma's desk, hidden from view of that blackly gaping void. The rain pounded on, damp air sliding around her curled body, the chandelier of shells stirring a discordant spell.

She'd never been so lonely or afraid in all her life.

CHAPTER 21

THE SHATTERING

Tally was woken by the sound of the morning ferry disembarking, a procession of laughter and footfalls past the observatory door. Her eyes opened to a world fully lit and already steamy, finding herself nose to nose with Ma's chair leg.

She dragged herself off the floor, and staggered blearily out from behind Ma's desk, wiping at her mouth and eyes. Her first impression was of a blinding glare, and the polished gleam of the tropics after a deluge. Her second, confused thought was that she was somehow bleeding.

She stared down at her stinging foot for an uncomprehending moment.

What on earth ...?

She sat in Ma's chair, lifting the sole of her foot for inspection. There was glass in it – how the devil had she managed *that* while sleeping?

Tally scrounged through Ma's top desk drawer for the first-aid tin kept on hand for nasty coral cuts. She and Lila had come through their island childhood together with limbs almost permanently iodine stained, Ma being always so anxious to prevent coral-cut infections.

After quickly tweezering out the glass and bandaging up the laceration, Tally turned her attention to the cause of it ...

Lying broken on the floor, was one of Ma's bottled mermaids. Her eyes slid to the cane hutch behind Ma's desk. At some point during her fitful night's sleep, Tally had kicked the hutch, jettisoning the bottle.

She kneeled on the floor, gingerly picking up each glass piece, and the mermaid she had trampled underfoot. Guilt pricked her conscience. She could not help but think of Ma's broken rocking chair.

Between us, my father and I might destroy everything she treasured.

Glass shards collected, she sat back against the desk, holding the mermaid in her hand, twirling it this way and that. Stroking the delicate stitching of the face, smoothing down the soft dress, combing through the long silky hair; fingers freezing, suddenly still.

What on earth?

Something was concealed under the mermaid's long hair, with just a stitch holding it against her back.

Tally's eyes were stark wide as she lifted the doll's hair and took hold of the small paper roll beneath, excising it from the doll with a quick snap. A tiny scroll – just like the one she had discovered in Ma's hat-pin box – now lay in her palm.

Hands shaking, Tally turned quickly to the task of unravelling the scroll. It was her mother's penmanship, but made so tiny she almost needed a magnifying glass to make it out. Squinting close, she read,

> *A mermaid's futile plea,*
> *aching to be free,*
> *Flotsam on the tide,*
> *without you at my side.*
> *Not a bird on my horizon,*
> *no sign of your return.*
> *For distant realms now,*
> *forever I will yearn.*

Ma's most secret anguish, hidden with her bottled-up mermaids.

And I might never have known it ...

Tally set to work smashing every bottled mermaid free.

One after another, they sailed across the observatory to crash against the wall, and lay beached in a lagoon of glass. The sound was cataclysmic.

From the corner of her eye, she saw Shep peer in, pale and aghast. She shooed him off and continued throwing until two-dozen maids lay on the observatory floor. Only then did she sit and stare dumbly at the destruction she had wrought. It was too late to ask permission, but she would surely need to beg Ma for forgiveness.

She pulled on her plimsolls and crunched over shards to retrieve the mermaids, gathering them up together in an armful. Glass-dusted as they were, tiny splinters pierced her arms. She dumped the pile on Ma's desk and turned the first, flaxen-tressed maid over, to wrench up the seed-pearl-encrusted plait of her hair.

Delicately pinned to the underside, was another scroll. Tally unfurled it between thumb and forefinger, leaving an imprint of blood. She pressed her throbbing digit to her lips and sucked away the metallic taste.

It began in much the same way – a songless mermaid's tears – and carried on with more of Ma's suffering: dried up like seaweed, longing for her ship to come in, waiting for her tide to turn, and so on and so forth. The excessive metaphors might have made the journalist in Tally smile if she wasn't so desolate for Ma.

But here was the thing: Tally remembered when Ma had made this particular flaxen-haired mermaid, for it was one of her girlhood favourites. It was a decade old, at least. Had Ma been hiding these scrolls in her mermaids all this time?

Tally took another mermaid and unravelled the scroll: once again, the glassed-up sea maiden and her wasted siren's song. Ma had been *so* deeply unhappy and no one had known it, though she'd hidden her secret in plain sight.

Tally went on with the task, finding scrolls hidden on every mermaid. She finished up with a small, neat bundle of lamentations, and sat staring at this evidence of her mother's great, unrequited longing for … what?

No, not what – *whom*?

For it was clear that Ma's far, distant horizon, her sailor sung no closer to shore, was a long-lost lover.

And it was *not* Richard Ramsey …

Shep had returned with a dustpan and broom, insisting on being allowed to help.

Tally looked at him, ashamed. 'Don't be silly, I made this –' She couldn't bring herself to say *mess*; it was worse than that, for she'd destroyed years of Ma's precious work.

They cleaned up the destruction together in blessed silence. She thought Shep was as embarrassed for her as she was for herself. But as the minutes and glass swept by, she began to understand that he wanted to talk even less than she. He was afraid of being asked questions about the missing Mrs Ramsey, wasn't he? In any other mood, she'd have questioned him anyway.

It would have to wait until they were both ready.

When the last shard had been swept away, Tally stood and covered her face with her hands. A silent dry-bawling.

She felt Shep's hand on her shoulder, a brief squeeze, then it was gone. Opening her eyes, she saw him making a hasty exit, heading for the door. 'Thank you, Shep,' she called after him.

He paused at the entrance, looking out to sea, and in his posture, she saw wavering resolve.

Tally took a chance. 'My ma owes you so much. I don't know how she would have done without you.'

He did not turn back to her. 'I just wanted to help.'

Tally hurried into the staff village to change for an urgent trip to the mainland. After showering, she stopped to check herself at the single mirror in the amenities block. Even with blue smudges under her eyes, and a dart of worry between, she looked surprisingly well in her halterneck navy swimsuit with high-waisted white shorts belted over it. Strong and healthy. How quickly the island had brought her back to life: fresh colour in her skin, new highlights in her salt-tangled whorls; even her feet were hardening up again to hot sand and coral beaches.

It was with renewed confidence in gait and heart that she took out the runabout from Shep's shed.

CHAPTER 22

POLARIS RETURNS

Tally was returning from the mainland, thwarted. Her visit to the tavern to make, if not a private phone call, at least one that might not be overheard by any on Dara, had been for naught. Jonathon was out, and his secretary, Daisy, hadn't the slightest clue where he'd gone, nor when he might come back. *(What the hell did he pay the woman for?)*

'But did he leave any messages for me?' Tally had asked, panic rising. 'He's following up something for me of utmost importance.'

'He didn't say a thing about you. Anyway, I thought you were supposed to be on holidays …' She could feel the dull sag of Daisy's disinterest. She pulled the handset away from her ear to mouth curses at it.

Shoving it back against her ear again, she snapped, 'Please let Jonathon know I'm definitely onto something here – something *critical* – and I need that information. I'll try to call again tomorrow if I get a chance. No, I *will* call, tell him not to go *anywhere …*'

After hassling Daisy, she might have taken her concerns straight to the beachfront Queenslander housing Bellen Beach's solitary police presence. But not this Girl Reporter, no sir. She'd hurried past with eyes averted, as though the sergeant himself might come barrelling out demanding to have her account of all that ailed her tropical isle.

It was still *her* island to protect, and she was determined to do so.

Reaching the Dara Island runabout, Tally beheld an ominous vista on the horizon: a rough slate and wrought-iron sky, the sea a luminous aquamarine. More storms coming this afternoon, then. She tipped her head to consider the beach almond above, stirring restlessly. Not much birdsong here, either. She lifted her knapsack higher. Better get a move on!

Nearing Dara, her gaze was drawn to the Hat, viridescent against the grey horizon. If she wasn't mistaken, there was a sailing craft out there, beyond the smaller island.

She raised a hand above squinting eyes: in fact, a a forty-five-footer. Father's! But what was *he* up to over there?

The runabout bounced over the sea. She was certain now that was definitely her father's yacht, anchored off the east side of the isle.

There was no sign of Richard as Tally stopped alongside the *Polaris*; white magnificence against a dark backdrop. She cupped her hands around her mouth and hollered out her father's name, raising no answer on board. The only movement was a lone sooty tern reeling in the sea breeze. Where was he?

She spied the *Polaris*'s tender, pulled up onto the sand. From the rainforest heart, hidden in the Artists' Colony, rose a single plume of smoke.

Was he burning something in there? *Evidence?*

Splashing ashore, Tally went to the tender for a stickybeak. Shoes and a Panama straw hat lay discarded within it, but there were no bottles lolling on the bottom boards, nor signs of additional passengers.

She turned to the bordering belt of casuarinas, and nearly fell backwards in yelping shock. A man had crept up on her from within the dense vegetation, and stood now in the sand, eight feet away, staring hard.

Only the tender had prevented her tumble, and Tally gripped thankfully at the gunwale, exhaling relief.

'Cat-burglar?' he said disbelievingly.

Drew Huxley!

'What are *you* doing here?'

Drew looked from Tally to the tender she was gripping, and shook his head in a slow lament. 'Oh no ... not again.'

'What's *that* supposed to mean?'

'A man never expects to lose so many boats to one woman ...'

The laugh cannonballed out of Tally. 'I'm not stealing *this* one.'

'Yet, your mitts are all over it.'

She straightened, arms crossing over her chest. 'If I wanted it, I'd already be sailing off into the sunset with it.'

'Yes, I learned that the hard way.'

Tally grimaced. 'Sorry.'

'Are you?'

'Not very. That boat was a lifeline when I needed one.'

'In that case, you're welcome.'

'You were far too trusting, anyway, letting a *stranger* stay the night.'

'Didn't seem like I had a choice. I figured you weren't sneaking into my cabin for my company.'

'Be thankful the boat was *all* I took advantage of. There were worse things I could have implicated you in.'

'For a second or two, when you sidled up beside my bed, I did wonder ...'

'You were awake? Your eyes were closed, you looked completely out to it!'

'I hoped I was dreaming.'

Tally grinned, a curious heat climbing her chest: exhilaration, on slow burn.

Drew smiled back, brown eyes curving.

With no words now forthcoming, she went on grinning at him. He still had his nice, listening face, and his arms were so much stronger, tanned in a green polo shirt. The breeze was picking up, and almost simultaneously they raised a hand to wipe hair back from their eyes. She decided she liked sandy curls on a man more than any other type of hair. She thought she might like this man even without any hair at all.

Tally turned back to look at the yacht bobbing uneasily on the sea, a dense, silver curtain of rain rolling towards it. 'So, you kept the name, then.'

'Too right. It's in the Ledger of the Deep.'

'You're as superstitious as the rest of them.'

'I'd just rather stay on Poseidon's scroll, thanks.'

Tally thought of Ma's scrolls again with an internal wince. 'What brings you and *Polaris* back this way? Last I heard, you were sailing the Queensland coast looking for treasure.'

'Sailed it, found it.'

'You *must* have some stories.'

'I was about to enjoy my pancakes with a campfire coffee. Are you hungry?'

'Famished.'

'Shall we?' Drew grabbed her knapsack off the sand and onto his own shoulder. The glow in her belly kicked up a notch.

They walked together into the Artists' Colony. Tally looked with interest at the swept-out common area, the pancake-filled skillet by the fire and roll of bedding in the roofed hut.

It clicked: *Drew* was the mysterious visitor to this crumbling colony. 'This isn't your first stay here, is it?'

He looked abashed. 'If I make you a hearty enough breakfast, I was hoping you might waive any outstanding accommodation fees.'

'They'd better be bloody good pancakes, then.'

Drew set to work making her a generous pile, honey drizzled on top.

'How long have you been here?'

'I only blew in last night. But I'll admit to having stayed here occasionally between jaunts. I like the peace and quiet.'

As if in reproof, the first splatters of rain cut through the jungle canopy, fat and warm. Behind it, a barrage, drumming up over the sand.

'That's us,' Drew cried, 'quick!' He grabbed the skillet and basket, Tally took the camp kettle, and the pair scampered across the common area and into the hut. An obliterating roar pressed down upon the island.

Tally and Drew squatted in the hut, wide eyes upon one another in the gusting darkness.

'I never get tired of it,' he shouted with a goofy grin.

She laughed. 'What, *rain*?' His excitement made her feel quite giddy.

'This isn't rain – it's something else!'

You're something else.

Tally held her plate as he made his own and poured two mugs of coffee.

'Here, sit.' He rolled out his sleeping bag and patted a place alongside him.

She shuffled close, the water on her arms making her shiver a little in the sudden cool. Seeing this, Drew took a folded towel and flapped it around her shoulders.

'Thank you,' she said, her plate of pancakes suddenly all too fascinating.

'Don't think me a heathen,' he said, 'but I left the cutlery on the boat.'

She picked up a pancake, rolled it inelegantly and took a bite.

They ate and listened to the rain. Tally licked her fingers clean, then settled with her back against the wall of the hut, nursing her tin mug. 'So, you stay at the Hat for these run-down facilities.'

'I like my accommodation rustic.'

'You don't ever moor off Dara?'

'Your father banned me from Mermaid Bay after I aided and abetted a fugitive.'

'Again, I'm sorry.'

Drew only laughed. 'So, what *is* the famous Tally Forster doing back in her father's kingdom?'

She looked at him in shock. 'How do *you* know my pen name?'

He put his hand over his heart. 'Ms Forster, I'm a huge fan of your column.' His smile was roguish.

Why should the idea of this one particular reader be more incredible to her than knowing her wide circulation? In her blushing pleasure, she fumbled her reply: 'I wouldn't have thought ... I'm surprised you've read my work.'

'I read the *Ledger* whenever I'm back in the area – your articles hold up well, despite the fish-and-chips grease. And even when you're delivering three-month-old news to me, you still manage to retain your piquant voice.'

She was too flattered for words. *Piquant!* If she were a sailor, she'd have it tattooed on her arm.

He grew quite sincere. 'You're very good at your job.'

Even the tips of her ears were now burning. 'I *know* I'm good at it, so please don't suspect me of false modesty here.'

'I don't suspect you of any modesty at all.'

She laughed like she was choking.

He looked quite pleased with her reaction. 'And are you back down this way for a story?'

'I feel like I've *become* the story ...'

'Beauty Queen Returns for Old Swimsuit?'

Reminded of how well she did look today in her navy-striped halter neck, Tally grinned. 'Girl Reporter Returns to Vanquish Bullshark and Find Missing Mother.'

His smile dropped off a cliff. 'How long has she been missing?'

'Couple of weeks,' she said. 'No real leads. Unless you're counting my father's descent into drunkenness, and his henchmen holding secret late-night meetings discussing the bit-by-bit removal of an unidentified *lady* ...'

She'd set out to be funny, but finished this summary clawing at her throat for air. 'I can't ... *breathe*.' She heaved and shuddered as the panic attack took constricting hold.

Drew pressed a hand against the middle of her back. '*Hey*,' he said. 'You're breathing just fine.' A gentle, unhurried murmur. 'You've got all the oxygen you need – just in and out, in and out. You're okay.'

She was okay, but only because the firm, heated pressure of his hand anchored Tally to her own breathing.

He maintained his touch as she resurfaced slowly to herself.

'Sorry,' she muttered quietly.

'You should be,' he quipped.

Tally smiled, albeit wonkily. Only then did he let go.

She saw she had spilled her coffee on his sleeping bag. 'Shit, and this, too – sorry!' She dabbed hurriedly at the material.

He waved her away. 'I've got a spare. You have to stop apologising to me, though. It's not like the Tally I remember.'

'It isn't like the me I remember, either.' The last few days had made her vulnerable in a way she hadn't known before. Her determination had not wavered, but her heart was in all kinds of pieces. 'I'm a bit of a … wreck at the moment.'

Drew turned that nice, listening face on her again. 'I'm not sure if you used *wreck* deliberately, but I will. If I've learned anything in my work, it's that wrecks tell the best stories.'

She did give up her story. For the second time, she found herself pouring out her whole tale to this man – every last development in her search for her mother, from map to Mack, not even omitting the pilfered photograph, under-desk spying or shattered bottles. And though he didn't ask a single question, she felt, coming to the end of her exposition, that he was a better interviewer than she'd ever been. How effective a nice, listening face was! Tally wondered if Drew dived down to his wrecks and simply *looked* at them until they gave up their stories.

Drew refilled both of their mugs, then settled back beside her.

She wasn't waiting any longer for a reply. 'I'll grant you, it does sound like a soap opera.'

'No, Tally, it doesn't. You and I both surely have learned in our line of work that life is stranger and inherently more dangerous than fiction.' He combed rain-tightened curls away from his forehead. 'You've got me intrigued about some things.'

'What things?'

'McLeod being back in these waters, for a start. I'd like to know what the devil he's after.'

Mack. Her pulse quickened.

'Last I saw of the bloke, he was working near Straddie – North Stradbroke Island, I should say. That's off Brisbane.'

She nodded impatiently.

He smiled. 'I keep forgetting, it's a big state but a small world. McLeod does marine salvage – a lot of it *off the books*, let's just say. We've come in contact a few times.'

'What, worked together?'

'No,' he said dryly. 'My life's work is in preserving wrecks and their histories, his is in plundering them.'

'A modern-day pirate.' She slapped her thigh. 'I *knew* it! So, what's he after on Dara, then?'

'You mentioned something about a map,' Drew said.

Tally scrambled for her knapsack. She was immensely pleased by the respect he gave her map, drying his hands thoroughly on a towel before taking it carefully by the corners. There was a great, expectant balloon in her chest as she watched him study it.

Finally, he looked up at her. 'You've got something here.'

The burner in her chest puffed her hopes sky-high. 'Tell me why *you* think so.'

'No one draws, much less conceals, a map to the most inaccessible heights of Mount Teasdale, unless there's *something* important up there. But then to bring a man like McLeod into the picture? He's not a man you trust lightly.'

'From what I heard under that desk, this wasn't the first time my father had called Mack in on it. In fact, he claimed to have been involved from the very beginning.'

'Dates fit,' Drew mused. 'I believe he's originally from Bellen Beach.'

'He spent time here during the war.' She dug out her stolen photograph of the Artists' Colony.

He inspected the monochrome image, unlike her, having no problem putting his finger on Mack's face. 'I agree that he's likely connected to whatever your father is guarding on Dara. Something they first dealt with around nineteen forty-six.'

'Mack was "instrumental" in Mermaid Bay's development, according to Lila, so he was definitely onsite at the time. I wonder if it was something they discovered during the course of surveying the island?'

217

Drew caught at this line of thinking. 'If I know McLeod, it's something valuable.'

Tally started. *Money*. Any journalist worth her salt knew to look where the money went, and where it came from.

She could hardly get her words out quickly enough. 'Mad Ginger was talking about American greenbacks floating around Bellen Beach after the war. He said something snarky, too, about people not being able to account for their whereabouts during the war and their wealth after it.'

Drew stood. 'Come on, you and I need to walk up the hill to look at something.'

'It's pouring rain.'

'It stopped five minutes ago.' He extended a hand to pull her to her feet.

Tally looked around in wonderment. She had not even noticed. She put her hand in his and allowed herself to be lifted.

They were wetter from exertion than rain by the time they'd climbed the stair-cut hill to the lookout. The rainstorm had moved over them completely now, to white-out the mainland. Dara floated once more in dazzling sunshine and turquoise, her jungled drapery freshly washed. Tally paused with an aching sigh.

Drew, leading the way, turned back to consider her expression and nodded. 'Yep, that's what I thought.'

'*What?*' she said, remembering this game.

'How it must feel to be *owned* by a place.'

'Am not,' she said, moving by him to take the lead.

Atop the hill, they stood with arms on hips and elbows bumping to behold the island. A waterfall had sprung from the sheer face of Mount Teasdale, plummeting hundreds of feet to the sea. It was so Edenic a scene, it might have been a director's technicolour dream.

Drew nudged her elbow, and she turned to meet his pointed look. 'Fair enough,' she agreed. 'I am. But don't tell anyone. They all think I'm a big-city girl now.'

Drew laughed.

'But it's not always so pretty,' she said. 'When the peak is covered by a monsoon trough, Mount Teasdale puts me in mind of a volcano of doom, belching ash over the world.'

'Amazing how much of Dara's highest mountain is often hidden by heavy clouds, isn't it?' There was a distinctly leading quality to his voice.

She looked between Drew and the mountain, trying to interpret his meaning.

'So high a peak,' he went on, 'obscured in the monsoon season, might be quite dangerous for air traffic ...'

'Well, we really don't get that much air traffic ...' Her heart was thumping. 'We used to, of course, during the war.'

He was fully facing her. 'May I have the map again?'

But she wasn't letting *him* plant the flag. She delved into her knapsack, fumbling with the map in her haste. She shook it out, eyes flicking rapidly between map and mountain. Drew came close to survey the diagram over her shoulder.

I've got it!

She felt, in the jolt of his body behind her, that he had seen it, too, but he waited for her to triumphantly declare it.

'That's not an X marking some buried treasure – it's a plane! My father and his cronies are trying to keep a *plane crash* hidden on Mount Teasdale!'

She thrust the map back to Drew, desperate for him to confirm it. He took it without stepping away and studied it quietly for a long time, while she luxuriated as much in the glow of discovery as his proximity.

'I disagree,' he said.

'*What?*' She turned indignantly. 'You don't think it's a plane?'

At so close an angle, she could not miss the wicked light in his eyes. 'It *is* a plane. In fact, I'm surprised you ever mistook that obviously plane-shaped symbol for an X –' She snapped the map out of his hands to smack him with.

He grew more earnest. 'But I disagree that it doesn't mark a treasure.'

She was no longer sure whether her heart slammed against her ribs from the excitement of their shared sleuthing, or the sudden impulse to plant a big, fat smacker on those lips so close to hers.

'Enlighten me. You're hogging the epiphanies now.'

'Well,' he said, 'when you were telling me about the conversation you overheard between Mack and the other fellow – what's his name?'

'Whatshisname is fine.'

His cheek showed a dimple of amusement. 'You said they talked about "the lady", and I understand you worried they meant your mother –'

'I didn't say that!'

He ignored this. 'But I've had another notion.'

'Go on …' *Say* anything *other than my mother's body has been hidden somewhere on Dara …*

He licked his lips; quick, efficient. 'There was a plane that disappeared in this region during the war in nineteen forty-two, presumed crashed in the Coral Sea. In fact, there were many planes lost, but this one in particular has remained an enduring mystery. Her name was the *Lady Lily*.'

'The *lady*,' she breathed.

'An American plane,' Drew went on. 'A B-twenty-four Liberator, carrying US soldiers …' He paused significantly. 'As well as a hefty payroll bound for American troops in New Guinea.'

Her throat was like parchment paper. She swallowed convulsively. 'How hefty are we talking?'

'As I recall, hundreds of thousands of US dollars.'

'*Holy smoke.*'

'Indeed.'

'And the plane just *vanished* over the sea?'

'It was monsoon season and on the evening in question, the plane flew directly into a ferocious storm somewhere past Ingham, never to be seen or heard of again. Not a clue has ever turned up, even after more than two decades.'

Tally had chills. '*You've* been looking for this plane wreck, haven't you?'

'Not specifically. I have a whole list of wartime wrecks I hope to find one day. I'll admit, I was expecting to find this one underwater, certainly not on a mountaintop on a popular resort island.'

'It *wasn't* popular then, nor was there any resort. It was all but deserted, only my ma and grandpapa here.' *And Irene and Lila.* 'They knew nothing of a plane crash. Ma never would have concealed such a thing. It must have gone down unseen and unheard in the storm. Besides that, at his age, Grandpapa was in no condition to mount a week-long expedition twenty miles across the island and up to Mount Teasdale. How would he ever have found it? More critically, how did my *father* come to know about it?'

The pair looked at each other. '*Mack,*' they said in unison.

Tally drove home the conclusion: 'He might have sighted the wreck when they were surveying the island for development. They should have alerted the authorities, but instead they raided a wartime graveyard for cold, hard cash …'

Soldiers' stolen wages, plucked from among their burnt bones on Dara's unreachable heights.

But Mount Teasdale wasn't really unreachable. Given adequate time, correct equipment and favourable weather, not to mention good health and fitness, and most of all, a *map*, any intrepid adventurer might make it across the large island in two or three days.

I could. I could find it and report it.

I could be the one to expose Richard Ramsey and Murphy McLeod – on the front page of the Cairns Ledger – *no, make that every paper in this country! Island playground of the rich and famous hiding a dark crime with international significance.*

'I'm going after it,' she said.

'Thought you might,' he said.

'I need to get there as fast as possible, before they destroy any more evidence. Something has got them worried about exposure. My mother's disappearance must have put a bomb under them.'

'Or,' said Drew, carefully, 'your appearance has been the bomb.'

She smiled. 'You know all the right things to say.' She rubbed her chin in mock thoughtfulness. 'And what are the chances I should randomly run into the very expert who can help me with this?'

He cocked his head, sunrays slanting into his eyes, liquefying them caramel. '*May* I help you with this?'

'Frankly, I'm touched you haven't already thrown me off this cliff face to scoop the exclusive – anyone in *my* industry would have.'

'My line of work is slightly more collaborative.' He smiled. 'Unless you're stripping my wreck, that is …'

'I promise not to plunder your wreck.' Her tone was wry.

He laughed, but she already had turned serious. 'I really would appreciate your help, Drew. I've intuited that I'm in some danger on Dara.' Seeing his alarm, she tried to backpaddle. 'But maybe I'm just sleep-deprived, not seeing sense.'

'How are your instincts usually, Tally?'

She fixed him with big, clear eyes. 'Spot on. I trust my hunches even when I don't – if you understand?'

'Yes, I've got you. All right, then, when do we leave?'

'We strike while the iron's hot. First thing tomorrow morning.'

'Excellent. I'll make a dash to the mainland for essentials. Leave it to me. Shall we reconvene this evening at Mermaid Bay – at say, happy hour?' He was smiling, lips thoroughly kissable in a sprinkling of sun-glistened, fair stubble.

She smiled back. 'We're going to make quite a team, Mr Huxley.'

CHAPTER 23

SUNDOWNER

Tally could not separate the elation of discovery from the excitement of pending adventure with Drew, and the nerves of detection. Her hands were shaking as she scurried around the back rooms and sheds of the resort and lodge, pilfering what she could to fulfil her part of Drew's packing list.

Beginning with the lost property cupboard behind reception, she'd dug out a large backpack, shaken off the cobwebs and set to work filling it. So far, she had torches and insect repellent, gardening gloves for dealing with barbed jungle vines, a waterproof staff jacket, first-aid kit, Swiss army knife, and a large water bottle for refills along the island's creeks and pools. To all this, she hoped Drew would add more sophisticated camping equipment, such as a tent to share.

Several days' hiking would require fast and easy sustenance, light to carry. With Drew in charge of main meals and tinned food, Tally only had to infiltrate the brasserie's storeroom for high-energy snacks: nuts and beef jerky, fresh fruit and honey.

During her scavenging, she saw neither hide nor hair of the island manager, nor her father, and thank Christ, not Mack. But there was this nagging thought: what if they already had left for the site of the *Lady Lily*?

The sun was burning low over the mainland as Tally finished her preparations and headed for Grandpapa's old cottage to stake out her night's accommodation.

Though the chapel lay beyond the staff village, Tally took the longer and more scenic guest route along the shore. The chapel was nestled in a grove of tall coconut trees, ponderously hung and long overdue for de-nutting. She stood, admiring the small cottage in the full-frontal glow of lowering sunshine: a simple rectangular timber structure perched on low stumps, with verandahs to all four sides and hibiscus flowering bountifully around it. A small seasonal creek babbled cheerfully alongside. That Ma should have come from so humble a cottage to something as ostentatious as the white palace of Eyrie still surprised her.

Tally ascended the low stoop, Ma's key in hand, feeling chipper. She would have quiet and privacy here this evening to prepare for what lay ahead. She'd already deduced the chapel had been stripped of pews and purpose, she just hoped that her father hadn't taken his bloody axe to the inside of it with the same vindictive might he'd swung upon Ma's rocking chair …

Far from it. To her shock, the chapel was not only unvandalised, but fully furnished and elegantly decorated in the style of a woman's abode.

The woman in question was standing with her back to the door, before a small hanging mirror, applying the last dash of red lipstick to rosebud lips. She was wearing a blush-pink tea dress, with a hibiscus pinned behind one ear. She met Tally's gaze in the mirror with a cat's wide, vague shock.

'Lila,' Tally cried. 'What are you *doing* here?'

Lila turned, lipstick trembling in hand. 'How did you get in?'

'I have Ma's key,' Tally blustered. 'How did *you* get in?'

'With *my* key, silly.'

Tally's eyes flew around the chapel, taking in the details of a lived-in home. The flowers on the small table, the line of lacy underwear pegged up to dry, new curtains fluttering gently in the salted breeze. 'You're *living* here?' She did not mean to sound aghast.

Lila's face showed her apprehension, plainly. 'Do you mind?'

'Maybe.' Tally frowned. 'No, I suppose I don't mind. I just don't understand. You're going to have to explain what's going on.'

'I was given the chapel for a home, by Ner— Mrs Ramsey. I had approached her for my own accommodation in the staff village. I have well and truly outgrown living with my mother. I'm twenty-five years old, Tally. She and I don't...' Lila flushed '... see eye to eye anymore.'

Tally could sympathise entirely. Irene would be no easy woman to live with, especially for a daughter. But why would Ma have given Lila this cottage for her own instead of just reshuffling cabins or bunks in the staff village?

Because she's Ma's secret sister.

'Why, then, did you let me walk you back to Irene's house the other night?'

Lila's petite face coloured up. 'Honestly, I was quite drunk that night and feet do tend to follow familiar paths. I only moved in a few weeks ago.'

Only a few *weeks*? So, Ma had handed over Grandpapa's chapel to his secret daughter before disappearing herself. She was settling accounts. What *else* had she handed over?

In prompt answer, Tally's seeking eyes fell upon the side table, next to Lila's single bed. Sitting atop it, in a pool of barrettes and bobby pins, was Ma's ship-in-a-bottle.

Tally's eyes veered sharply away, not wanting to flag her interest in it.

Her mind, however, was fixed on that bottle and its implications. Not only had Ma given Grandpapa's home to Lila, she had entrusted her with his will, too.

She allowed herself one more skirting glance, seeing the ship had been repaired and put to right. Ma had fixed the damage Tally had done, without ever mentioning it.

Is the will back inside the ship?

She knew what she needed to do. 'This *is* a predicament,' she said. 'Since my father has thrown me out, I have nowhere else to stay on Dara.'

Lila smiled. 'What's the predicament? You'll stay here with me as long as you need. I have a rollaway cot you can use, if you don't mind sleeping a little close to the ground?'

'I slept on the floor of the observatory last night.'

'You goose, you should have come here earlier! Well, you're *my* guest now. Chuck your stuff in the corner and we'll sort out your side of the cottage later.'

Tally glanced guiltily at her bag of purloined trek supplies. *Tell her you won't be staying more than one night – tell her you're off to expose the dark, rotten secret of Dara!*

'Thank you,' Tally said. 'That will be lovely.'

'Okey-doke.' Lila clipped her lipstick closed and turned back to the mirror to puff up the bouncy curls at her shoulders and pat the tightly cinched belt of her tea dress. 'I'm late for hostessing. Will you come with me to happy hour?'

'Better clean up first, I've been out boating. Shall I see you down there?'

Lila went off on her way with more spring in her step than Tally would have expected, given her sudden intrusion.

She's lonely, isn't she? She thinks of me as a friend come home, rather than a muckraking journalist. But does she *know what else I am to her?*

Tally waited until Lila had gone towards the staff village, before she turned abruptly and picked up the ship-in-a-bottle.

The afternoon sun was a floodlight at Tally's back, pouring into the cottage, filling the bottle. She turned it around in her hand, smarting hard. Ma had gone to such care. The ship looked as good as new, not a sign of Tally's desecration. The hull slit was invisible once more, the cork sealed. Ma had reglazed the wood, too, the gloss only highlighting the delicate hand carving, every knot and imperfection.

What a shame it would be to ruin it for a second time, and yet she had to. Too bad she didn't have the appropriate tools here. She had a poke around Lila's tray of cosmetics, searching in vain for a pair of tweezers. Did she not need to pluck *anything*? While Lila was sleeping tonight, Tally would have to slip out and get Ma's long-nosed tweezers from her observatory.

She returned the ship-in-a-bottle to its stand, then roamed around the room, wondering what more she might find in Lila's possession.

But what else could she expect to find? Lila had freely invited her to stay, then left her unattended, so it was unlikely she had secrets just lying around.

This detail did not impede a nosy Tally. Fifteen minutes of digging and prying turned up nothing of interest, until she got to Lila's small writing desk, under the west window. Here, her nimble fingers paused on a pad of writing paper buried in the single drawer below. She took it out, eyes narrowing to a squint. It was Ma's writing pad, unmistakably so, with its kitschy border of bright parrots in broad-leafed foliage. The goodbye letter she'd been carting around for days, in her knapsack, was torn from this very pad.

But now, the writing pad appeared to be in use as a brainstorming notebook. A *shared* brainstorming notebook – for there, in starkly contrasting handwriting, side by side, were Lila's contributions with her mother's.

The secret sisters were in cahoots of some kind or other.

Tally flipped rapidly through the pad, observing pages of collaborative ideas for the future of Dara: the turtle hospital Ma had long talked about; a marine education park, to be designed in consultation with Indigenous knowledge; the magical clam garden Tally had dreamed of, with an array of colourful sketches accompanying the plans.

It appeared they had discussed brand-new ideas, too. A range of accommodation to suit all guests' budgets, from camp grounds and school dormitories, to family cabins and even sole hire of a refurbished Little Dara. There were notes jotted about the potential for a biological research laboratory onsite. They even had a proposal to cater to cruise ships. *Cruise ships!* Richard had put his foot down on the notion many a time.

But Lila and Ma were planning Dara's future without Richard's involvement, weren't they? Without Tally, too.

Mixed emotions churned through her: envy of their evident bond and shared ideals, awe at their clear-eyed concepts and creativity pooled, and even a trembling elation …

Ma hasn't given up on life or the future. She still dreams and hopes for Dara. And while she's gone, she trusts Lila to hold her vision for her.

In a daze of wonder, Tally took out her Minolta and photographed a few of the best pages, before sliding the pad reluctantly back into the drawer.

Enough prying. Time to change and get over to Mermaid Bay.

Tally hadn't brought anything worthy of a breezy sundowner at candy-floss sunset, though. She turned to stare at Lila's small wardrobe. Would she mind terribly if Tally borrowed something of hers?

Make yourself at home, she had called back over her shoulder as she skipped out the door. In Cairns, Tally and Maisie shared wardrobes as freely as they did cutlery. Was that what a secret aunt and niece might do also?

Tally flicked through the hanging dresses. They were organised by colour, a rainbow rack of prettiness, all ladylike vacation dresses and flowy gypsy numbers, eerily similar to what Ma wore. Lila was a little Nerissa-wannabe, almost as though her wardrobe was comprised entirely of hand-me-downs...

Actually, that was *exactly* what this wardrobe was, Tally realised, fingering a frothy mint-green dress she recognised. Ma had given Lila her cast-offs as well as her home, plans and most treasured possession.

And why shouldn't Ma have taken Lila under her wing? Her own daughter had never deigned to set foot back here again. And unlike Tally, Lila seemed to *want* to emulate Nerissa – her grace and femininity, her simple contentment with island life...

Except, *content* was the very last thing Nerissa Ramsey had ever been on Dara. In fact, she had been entombed alive by yearning and regret.

For *whom*?

Tally's fingers stilled as they reached the blue and indigo numbers at the end of the rail. There was one item here that Tally could imagine herself wearing, because she'd loved her mother in it – a dusty-blue dress with a boat neck, slim waist and skimming skirt. It would go perfectly with Lila's stringy leather sandals. Tally smiled.

She pulled on the dress, sucking in as she wrangled awkwardly with the back. The zip tugged to its zenith. She breathed cautiously out and considered herself in the mirror.

The dress was doing her all kinds of favours. The colour set her sun-browned skin aglow, made the windblown whorls of her hair shine and accentuated the depth of her aquamarine eyes. *Now* she was ready for a happy hour with Drew.

About to close the cupboard, Tally's gaze snagged on a straw sunhat, hung up against the side of the wardrobe. Inside it, in delicate white hand stitching, was a name ...

Delila.

There was no sign of Drew as she cut through the chirruping crowd milling around the pool. Perhaps he'd been held up in Bellen Beach?

He *will* come, she promised herself, making for the Tiki Bar and the golden-brown head just visible above the crowd. First a drink, to settle her nerves. Though, she thought Lila might be the calming influence she was really after ...

Lila spun on her seat at Tally's approach, thick-lashed eyes popping wide with surprise – and clear and evident joy.

A smile rounded out Tally's cheeks in response, and she gave a tiny spin to let Lila admire her. 'Hope you don't mind I borrowed it ...'

'*Mind?* I'm smitten with you in that. And you're wearing a flower like *me.*'

Tally tapped the cerise hibiscus behind her ear with a smile. 'Stole it from your front garden. That's what they're there for, right?'

She realised that Lila had been entertaining a guest – a pugnacious-looking man with his hand resting on the bar, dangerously close to Lila's bust.

'This is Chase,' Lila said dryly. 'He's here with a stag party. The rest of them are just out tying the groom to the bow of his yacht. Chase has been trying to convince me of the party's need for hostessing of the less-clothed variety ...'

Seeing Tally's face, Lila winked.

'Well, don't let us keep you,' Tally told him, indicating he should give up his barstool. 'You've got some poor woman's unfortunate choice to celebrate.'

Chase vacated his stool as though it, or he, had fewer legs than normal. 'You don't have to be so bloody rude! The lady and I were having a good time before *you* showed up.'

'She was having nothing of the sort,' Tally said. 'Off you go now. This resort doesn't offer babysitting.'

Lila took her red-striped straw to red-lined lips. 'Whatever you call the opposite of hostessing, that was it.'

'And you're welcome,' Tally said, waving to the barman for the same drink as Lila.

'Should have heard how much he was offering for his little stag-party gig.'

'Just because they're rich, doesn't make them classy.'

Lila swirled her straw with a noisy clinking of ice. 'You might have just coined our resort's new tagline.'

'Speaking of coining new things,' Tally said, swinging herself onto the stool to accept her drink. 'Have you changed your name, *Delila*?'

She might have said Aunty Delila, for the shock writ large on Lila's face. 'Pardon me?'

Tally explained the sunhat discovery.

'Oh,' Lila exhaled. 'Just wishful thinking, I suppose.' She gave a little laugh. 'Do I look like I could make a Delila?'

Tally answered her playful tone with a serious one. 'I think you could make *much* more of yourself on this island than *they've* let you.'

Lila smiled, cheeks crimsoning to match the flower at her ear.

Tally went on studying Lila's features over the rim of her coconut, hunting for a glimpse of her own mother, and finding it. The colouring was slightly different – Lila's golden brown to Nerissa's honey hues –

but they shared the petite height, pointed chins, *God*, even the same kitten-green eyes.

Did Tally's father see it?

Here was her chance to find out, for he was coming directly towards them, strutting by the lounging guests like a lion through his pride. Tally's heart gave a double-quick beat.

Be calm, she told herself, *he hasn't any idea what you know.*

She saw immediately that he was sober, and straightened on her stool. 'Hello, old man.'

He did not reply until he was towering over her. 'I threw you off Dara yesterday.'

'No, you had a tantrum and threw my suitcase outside.' He wouldn't dare backhand her here in front of his own guests, would he?

Lila didn't look so sure. She leaned smoothly between father and daughter. 'May I get you a drink, Mr Ramsey?'

Tally did not miss how her father's eyes swept down over Lila's body. To him, she was no more or less an object than any other young woman on this island.

Her father declined the drink with an irritable wave. Well, this *was* a surprise. Just what was he up to?

The answer came a moment later, with the arrival of Mack and Angus. Father had no such qualms ordering on behalf of his associates, and the two men took up their drinks. Her father, she understood, was trying to keep *his* wits about him.

Mack looked mockingly between Richard and Tally. 'Having a wee family reunion, are we?'

Tally lifted her chin. 'Reunions are only for my mother, when she returns.'

Mack shrugged. 'Nah, you'll never see that slut back here again.'

Tally scowled at her father and his whatever-the-hell-Mack-was.

Don't take the bait, do not give him the satisfaction ...

'Spoken,' she rejoined, 'like a man who never got a look-in.' From the editorial quarter of her brain, came a groan.

Tally turned a hard look on her father. 'Where *did* you find this creep?' She watched his left eye give a micro twitch. His tell, even as he dialled up the arrogance.

'Watch your *mouth*. Mack has been a friend to me longer than you've been alive.'

The semicircle shifted in an uncomfortable silence, into which Angus now blundered. 'These blokes used to go spearfishing together round the archipelago back in the forties. They used to call the passage between Dara and the mainland *Shark Alley*. This one time, a three-metre-long bull shark rams into Richard, readying to bite. Mack comes up from behind, shoves his spear right into the back of that shark's head, and *bam*! You pretty much owe your father's life, in fact this whole place, to Mack.'

Based on the group's reaction, Angus might have been lumbering around a minefield in flippers. Tally alone was smiling. Good backstory. *Useful* idiot, indeed.

Mack issued a curt command for the men to convene in the lodge. Angus followed Mack, shoulders hitched high, while Richard hung back, presumably to address his daughter. Lila excused herself, weaving away into the gathering.

Tally was at a distinct disadvantage beneath her standing father; lifting her head to look at him made her feel like a girl again. Her lower jaw jutted in automatic resistance.

'I want to speak to you, Thalia.'

'You already are.'

'No, not here. You're to come up to Eyrie tomorrow morning.'

'Why *should* I?'

234

His nostrils flared. 'Can't you just do one thing you're told without acting like a petulant brat?'

'Then ask me, instead of ordering.'

His lips tightened. 'Would you be at Eyrie by nine tomorrow?'

No, I'll already be well on my way to exposing your great lie ...

She shrugged. 'I'd prefer to know first what you need to discuss.'

'*Dara*,' he snapped.

Her heart lurched.

He nodded. 'Yes, that got your attention, didn't it? Bloody *Dara* – the only thing that you and your damned mother *ever* cared about.'

'You're the one who married Ma just to get this place.'

'I married the woman I loved, and I would've loved Nerissa, island or not.'

Tally laughed, too late registering something strangely like candour in her father's eyes. 'I guess we'll never know,' she said, 'since she came with an island.'

Richard brought his darkest frown to bear upon her. She tried not to quail beneath it, focusing instead on the myriad silver threads in his dark hair, glinting in the last, flaring light.

He seemed about to strike back for a tremendously long moment, before he muttered simply, 'Be at my office at nine sharp tomorrow.'

Drew arrived just as smoky, blood-red ribbons were rippling across the sky. A red sky was no reliable indicator of fine weather in the tropics, especially not in the monsoon season, but Tally took it for herself, and their pending adventure, as a good omen.

She was seated on the edge of the pool, legs kicking in the water. She had given up on drinking this evening, wanting to remain sharp for the morrow. Lila, this moment being whirled around the dance floor, was taking enough cocktails, and dance partners, for the team.

Drew strode towards her with a roguishly lopsided grin. She noted the effort he too had put into his appearance: a button-down linen shirt and long slacks; his blond curls brushed back wetly, perhaps with hair tonic.

As Drew passed the dance floor, Lila broke from her partner with a cry of pleased recognition, taking his arm with both her hands. Drew allowed himself to be thus waylaid, his smile and conversation now all for Lila.

Tally's legs in the pool had taken on an agitated tempo, water sloshing up onto the hem of her skirt.

At length, she saw Lila nod in her direction, and then at last Drew was en route, once more – arm in arm with Lila.

'Look who I found,' Lila cried as they reached her. 'Do you remember Mr Huxley? He saved us long ago – when I was your chaperone home from school.'

Tally pulled herself to her feet. 'I vaguely remember our knight in shining waters – how are you, Mr Huxley? I'm Miss Forster.' She extended a hand to shake and watched Drew's eyes light up with amusement as he took it.

'Not *the* Tally Forster?'

'The very one.'

'I've got to tell you, I'm a huge fan of your writing.'

'You don't say!'

Lila, looking between the pair, narrowed her eyes. 'Oh, I see – joke's on me. You two have already reconnected recently.' She clucked. 'I'm beginning to understand why Tally *bothered* to come dressed this evening.'

Drew considered Tally. 'She normally comes undressed?'

Lila shook her head. 'Wearing little more than a Ramsey scowl, anyway.'

Drew nodded in Tally's direction. 'Like that one, you mean?'

Lila joined her nod to his. 'Yes, that's it. *Brace*, she's about to lose her temper...'

Tally turned to Lila. 'Shouldn't you be dancing with something lecherous?'

Lila's pretty, parrot laugh lifted into the air between them. 'I think I've done more than my fair share this evening. What brings you back to Mermaid Bay, Mr Huxley?'

'Just Drew, please,' he said. 'And as it happens, I dropped in to see Tally...'

'We're working on a story together,' Tally finished smoothly.

Lila's levity vanished. 'Oh? What story might that be?'

Lie first, explain later. Tally saw a flashing image of the placards picketing Bellen Beach. 'The grassroots campaign to save the reef,' she answered. *Don't ask me what from, I've been too self-involved to investigate.*

Drew nodded, taking up this angle, seamlessly. 'If they allow some cane farmer to start mining Bellen Reef for lime, what's next? The future of the Great Barrier Reef is at stake.'

Tally turned to Drew with an aghast cry. 'They want to *what*? Ruin our reef for some cheap fertiliser...?'

'Yes, exactly,' Drew said.

'Holy *smoke*,' Tally huffed. 'But that's an *excellent* story! You'd better give me everything you've got on it.'

'That's what I'm here for,' Drew said, lips pressing back a smile.

Lila looked between the pair with a slow headshake, then settled on Drew. 'I don't know what scheme Tally has got you wrapped up in this time, but I can assure you, they typically end with some form of banishment.'

Drew laughed. 'I usually lose a boat in the process, too.'

Lila took in Tally's wicked look and rolled her eyes. 'Well, heaven help you, Drew. Now, may I get you both a drink?'

'No, let me,' Drew replied, patting his pocket for a wallet.

Lila reached out a slim hand to touch his arm. 'It's my job,' she said. 'Please, let me give you two a moment to get your story straight …'

As Lila went to the Tiki Bar, Drew regarded Tally with a mischievous twinkle. 'Are we obliged to cart your chaperone along with us on our trek, too?'

The sun had set, and in the dusky light, his deeply tanned skin was velvet smooth. She wanted to run her fingertips up his arm to the loosely rolled sleeve at his elbows, stroke a finger down his cheek.

'She isn't my chaperone anymore. As it turns out, we're secretly related. I'm not sure if she knows yet, but then, there are so many secrets on Dara, I'm surprised the island hasn't sunk under the weight of them.'

He rubbed his freshly shaved chin in contemplation. 'If I had to guess, based on the constant sparring, sisters?'

Tally laughed. 'As widely as my father tries to sow his wild oats, she's actually my *grandpapa's* illegitimate daughter.'

'Your aunt, then.'

'Secret aunt,' Tally said with a lip-zipping, lock-turning motion.

'We all set for tomorrow?'

Tally laid out her preparations, then listened to Drew do the same, exhilaration zinging beneath her skin. 'I think we should make an early start, well before dawn, to avoid being seen. How does half past four sound to you?'

'Sounds nice and early. And where will I meet you?'

'Staff village turn-off. We can take the established paths as far up as my grandpapa's grave, but it's all wilderness after that.'

'I've brought a decent machete.'

'An indecent one would never cut it. Now, I don't think you should leave the *Polaris* anchored off Dara. It's too obvious, my father's old boat bobbing out there.'

'Way ahead of you. I've put her in at the Bellen Beach Yacht Club for the rest of the week. I'll sleep out under the stars tonight, so my name isn't on any rosters.'

'Very good. No one should know where we've gone or what we're up to. Unless you're planning on double-crossing me?'

'I'd be too scared to even single-cross you.'

She smiled. 'All right, then.' Over his shoulder, she saw Lila returning, coconuts in hand. Above them, the fairy-light-strung palms stirred restlessly, the sea breeze bringing the first whiff of a rainstorm. 'Listen,' she said, instincts suddenly afire. 'I don't think we should be seen talking too much tonight. My father is just inside the lodge and he could be back out at any moment. If – *when* – they notice me missing over the coming days, I don't want them associating us together. As soon as Lila returns, I think you should ask her to dance and give me a chance to slip away.'

Drew nodded his agreement, brown eyes molten in the soft light. 'Frankly, I'd hoped to dance with you, but I see the point. Tomorrow, then?'

'Tomorrow.'

Lila arrived on a heady cloud of laughter and fragrance that smelled suspiciously like L'heure Bleue.

Tally smiled benignly as Drew asked Lila to dance. They went, arm in arm, through the crowd to the dance floor. Her neck elongated enchantingly as she lifted the perfect cupid's bow of her smile to his.

Tally slid her coconut onto a nearby table, heavy with rum and cream, and made for the dark garden path out of the pool area.

Just because she'd suggested their dance, didn't mean she could bear to stay and watch it.

CHAPTER 24

DARKEST BEFORE DAWN

Tally had set her wristwatch alarm for four o'clock, but as was her custom, she jerked awake less than a minute before the alarm was due to go off. Ask an efficient brain to wake you at a precise time and it'll do it.

Tally eased herself off her rollaway cot with barely a squeak, and tiptoed to her backpack, waiting near the front door. About to swing it up onto her shoulder, she had a second thought.

She'd forgotten last night to get the tools for Ma's ship-in-a-bottle. By the time she had remembered, Lila was coming back in, flushed and rain-spangled after a cloudburst put an early end to happy hour. She'd hoped she might have another chance once Lila finally drifted off, but lying side by side in the humid darkness, rain drumming on the tin roof, Lila's soft, confessional tone had put Tally to sleep first.

She could not bring herself to leave without that ship. After Lila's revelations in the darkness, Tally thought she understood why Ma had entrusted the bottle to her. But it was Tally's ship to keep safe.

She returned to Lila's bedside table; soft, slumberous breath coming from the pillow alongside. Tally lifted the bottle gingerly from its stand, lest it should clang against the pair of water cups Lila had laid out. In its place, she dropped the brief goodbye note she'd scrawled earlier for Lila. She couldn't leave her without some explanation …

Delila,

Drew and I have gone after our story, it couldn't wait. If anyone asks, just tell them I've gone to the mainland for a few days. Don't mention we are together.

We'll be back down in a week. If we're not, call in the cavalry.

Thank you for your kindness,

Tally x

She did not turn on her torch until she was well beyond the chapel grove. Here, she paused to remove the bottle from under her arm. Once it was hidden deep in her backpack, she shook out her fingers vigorously, trying to relieve tension.

She stuck close to Coral Beach, staying out of the moon's cloud-bedraggled light, weaving her way under the leaning cover of beach almonds and coconut palms.

The tide clinked restlessly against the shore, white breakers running behind it. A bedevilling breeze tossed hair tendrils into her face and mouth, making her eyes water and sting. She would be glad to be hidden in the jungle, away from the windblown grit and the eerie sense of being watched, even followed. She stopped several times, drawing up against a tree, to look back the way she had come. At any moment, she expected a figure to appear. The sooner she got away from Mermaid Bay, the safer she would feel.

Touch wood. She tapped the nearest tree trunk and pressed on.

Lila's confiding chatter from the evening past was a worm in her ear as she went, burrowing deep. There were moments last night where Tally had wanted to stand up and cover Lila's face with her pillow, just to quieten her down for a bit …

Lila was apparently Ma's new best friend, if Tally was to believe that voice in the dark. She thought she did believe her, too; Lila could no more fake how enamoured she was of Nerissa, than she could the things she knew about Ma's life and history on Dara. She sounded for all the world like a besotted fan. One inviting Tally to share in this praise and affection, rather than trying to incite jealousy or resentment.

When Tally finally managed to swallow down the seed of envy, she conceded Lila might have some valid insights.

'You mustn't forget,' Lila said, 'Nerissa is a *woman*, just like you or me. She wasn't born your mother, Tally, or even the heiress of this island. She was *Nerissa* first, with her own heart and mind and desires. She's not a placeholder for your inheritance, nor a handmaiden to her husband's ambitions. She gets to go after the future *she* wants, whatever and wherever that might be …'

Had they another few nights together, Tally thought she might have learned more about Ma from Lila than she had ever sought to know.

As she was passing the Beach Shack, she glimpsed movement in her peripheral vision. Most definitely *not* a gale-tossed tree this time. She was being trailed down the beach, in the tree line. She flattened her back against the shed, heart hammering as footsteps crunched over the coral shore.

'Miss Tally?'

She jumped in the same instant as she recognised the voice. '*Shep*,' she hissed, 'you *scared* me! Have you been following me all this way?'

'I didn't mean to. Wind woke me an hour ago, so I got up to check I'd bolted the shed door, properly. Then I saw you out here.'

So easily spotted, and she'd only just set off. Who else might have seen her?

'Are you okay, Miss Tally? What are *you* doing down here so early?'

She didn't have the time or patience for any more evasions. 'If I told you I had come down here to steal a runabout and use it to escape this island and Mr Ramsey, what would you say to that, Shep?'

At first only silence, with wind blustering in it. Then an answer as clear and heartening as a rising sun. 'I wouldn't say anything. I'd help you drag the runabout to the shore, push you out to sea, then black its column out of my ledger. If anyone asked about that runabout, I'd just tell them Mr Harmon sold it.'

'And did Mr Ramsey ask?'

'No. Mr Harmon did though, and I told him Mr Ramsey sold it. And that was that.' It was impossible to see Shep's face, but she imagined that he smiled.

There was one more thing she had to ask before she could go on. 'Was she frightened, Shep? You can tell me the truth.'

'No, she was … resolute. She called me her lifesaver, and then she hugged me.'

After embracing the young man herself, Tally crunched over the coral and onto the dark paths of Mermaid Bay, singing a silent mantra …

She's alive, she's alive, she's alive, she's alive.

And now it was time to *take back* Ma's island from Richard Ramsey.

At the turn-off to the staff village, Tally extinguished her torch and waited. Her brain was beginning to clang about, demanding coffee. She recalled the comfort of Lila's warm cot with regret as she stood in the dark rainforest, waiting for the sound of Drew's footfalls up the rain-slicked, cobblestone pathway.

For a long time, she heard nothing but the brush turkey's early-morning scratch through the underbrush, a jarring flap of wings shooting through the canopy. She wondered if she should go over to Sandy Beach and make sure he was awake.

And then suddenly, there were footsteps advancing upon her down the back pathway from Eyrie.

Instinct made Tally draw warily into the forest, well off the path. She crouched low, hugging her backpack to her chest, eyes painfully large in such darkness. Who could it be? Someone who knew the old ways.

Not Drew, then.

Two sets of footsteps, sharing a low murmur: a procession of Not-Drews coming down from Eyrie. They were near enough now for her to catch the first line of low conversation and a brume of cigarette smoke.

'– Dick says we wait until he's made his final offer to her, then it's go time.'

Mack.

'We all know what she's going to say. He must know it, too – what's he really waiting for?'

Angus, the bloody idiot, thinking he's playing with the big boys.

Mack hawked a spit. She imagined it hurtling through the underbrush, like a Tally-seeking missile.

'He's a damned fool. We're not going to be rid of that bitch, easily. It's too bad he's always been so piss weak when it comes to women –'

Am I the 'bitch' that won't go away easily? Of course I am.

They were so close, she could smell Mack's body odour, his smoke-stained, salt-steeped clothing. She was sure she was well concealed, but hoped they wouldn't smell the fragrance she had so vainly spritzed on before bed in preparation for meeting Drew.

Drew!

At any moment, he would come jauntily up the path in the opposite direction, with his torch swinging and a big, telltale backpack.

She closed her eyes against whatever might happen next.

Stay back, Drew, please stay back …

By some mercy, she heard no startled encounter on the path beyond. The men's voices simply moved down the path to the lodge, leaving behind only the stench of cigarettes.

The forest took back its dripping, rustling quietude.

Tally waited ten full minutes, with her ears nearly straining off her head for the sound of Mack's return or Drew's approach. The path lay empty. Where the heck was *her* partner in crime?

Eventually, it was boredom and burning thighs, rather than bravery, that forced her to move from her squatting position. She slid onto the path like a shadow and stood still, considering her options.

Drew was very late. Twenty minutes late.

Just go. He'll catch you up.

Tally hoisted up her backpack, and went on up the hillside, towards the dark, forested labyrinth of treehouses.

She was halfway across the swinging rope bridge, with only the soft glow of the fairy-lit ropes to guide her, before she sensed that she was being followed again. She stopped, dead-centre, listening keenly. She was a sitting duck in the middle of this bridge, her figure illuminated in the dark void of the ravine. There was a scuffing footstep at the end of the suspension bridge from where she'd come, then the bridge swayed beneath her feet as a second person stepped heavily upon it.

What now? She could hardly run on a rope bridge in full swing, even without this blasted backpack weighing her down. She gripped at the damp ropes as the dark shape advanced wordlessly upon her.

To behold Drew slowly emerge from the gloom, to grow brighter and more real with every closing step, was a crushing relief. She sagged gratefully as his eyes, shining with the thrill of adventure, found hers.

'Sorry I'm late,' he whispered. 'Just got a bit caught up.'

'Doing *what*?' She was indignant.

'As it happens, hiding behind a groundskeeper's shed while your mate Mack tried to smoke me out.'

'*Your* mate Mack,' she said, with a smiling frown. 'Look, if you're just going to slow me down, it's probably best if I cut this bridge right now and go on alone.'

'Save yourself,' he agreed. 'I'll hold them off as long as I can.'

In the warm radiance of the fairy lights, she looked him over openly from top to toe, taking in his backpack – twice the size of hers – his sturdy walking boots and bunched-up hiking socks, his legionnaire's hat and hanging water canteen, the machete and compass at his belt.

Should a guardian angel look like such a nerd?

'Are you sure you've got everything?' she said tartly.

She watched his gaze not leave her face at all. 'Now I have.' He smiled.

A laugh burst from her – and not a quiet one, either. She hoisted up her backpack awkwardly; a diversion from her goofy grin. 'All right, then, let's get this show on the road.'

Drew reached for her. 'Hang on, first let me fix your backpack.'

She stood still as he stepped in very, very close to adjust both straps. Firm, efficient tugs that made the soft shelf of her breasts lift and jiggle.

His face, so close to hers, all his attention focused at the level of her chest, was too serious to be believed. She smiled dryly and watched his lips, within an easily kissable distance, move with an answering wryness.

Their eyes met, lingered and skirted away.

'All right, Miss Forster, lead on …'

They were now well past the treehouses, beyond even Lookout Point, and heading up through the bamboo forest towards Grandpapa's grave. It was still pitch black, with only their low lights to guide their journey, and under the wind's duress, the bamboo forest was singing a discordant lamentation to their progress.

'I *hate* this place,' she muttered. Her very bones seemed to quake in time with the clanking bamboo.

They entered the grove of her grandpapa's final resting place. Tally's torch beam glanced around the clearing, illuminating the lone headstone and the undisturbed ground below it. Drew's torch beam joined hers, darting away then to illuminate the bamboo stirring restlessly around them. The graveyard, in greyscale, was frightening even with Drew by her side.

'Meet my grandpapa.' Her dry tone was undermined by the shiver that followed. She could not to this day account for her childhood terror of Bertie Forster possessing her.

'The trick,' she said, 'is to hold your breath as you run past, so as not to breathe in his soul.'

'You might have warned me earlier, now I'll have to lug him all the way up Mount Teasdale.'

Tally laughed, discharging a rush of adrenaline. 'You're good value, Mr Huxley. And to think I only brought you along to carry my purse.'

'Wait until you hear the other jokes I've been rehearsing.'

CHAPTER 25

THE CLIMB

Here's where it gets tough, she might have told Drew as they left Grandpapa's grave. But that would have been stating the obvious. Almost immediately, any semblance of a pathway ended. Now, they were moving uphill through the bush, still in darkness. They would not rejoin a seasonal creek bed – providing a natural uphill trail – until after they'd topped this first rise.

'Tell me we were right to set off so early,' Tally muttered to Drew's back, swearing under her breath as yet another branch, in a long line of sneaky branches, thwacked her cheek. She had the growing suspicion he was taking far more than his fair share of sneaky face branches up front there to spare her.

'We were right to get a head start on any other parties making the trek,' he said. 'Right to avoid being seen departing, too.' He did not credit the darkness.

'Let me go in front for a while and take some of those bastard branches,' she said. 'This is *my* dumb island, after all.'

'No, thanks,' he said. 'I'm safer in front. Monsters come from behind.'

She dispensed a droll laugh, nevertheless shortening the gap between

248

them. She did not care to think about other parties – much less *skeleton crews* – coming from behind. Surely, they had at least a few days' head start on Mack? He did say they were waiting until after the monsoon. *God, please!* She needed time to document the wreck before the clean-up crew came in.

'*I* happen to think,' she said accusingly, 'that you were secretly raised to be a gentleman.'

He chuckled. 'Not secretly, no. My mother has five boys and no daughters, and her gentleman-raising was outright declared.'

Tally felt a smile fill her cheeks. There were people in the world who loved this man; he did not merely exist in the vacuum of her island and the cogs of her schemes. Somehow, being reminded of this made him even more real.

'Wait,' she mused. 'There are *four more* Drews out there? What am I doing right now wasting my time with this one?'

'I'm the youngest, and the only unmarried one, if that changes your day's plans.'

'I'll keep you round for the jokes.'

'You only get those from a youngest son of five.'

'Where are the rest of the humourless Drews, then?'

'All still in Adelaide. Bankers and accountants, the lot of them.'

'You're the sole adventurer of the litter? Your father must be proud.'

'I'm sure he is, though his main occupation is resting in peace.'

Tally lurched to a stop. 'I'm sorry, I didn't mean to be glib.'

He turned back, though she couldn't read his face in the darkness. 'You weren't glib, and no need to apologise. I never even met my father. He was a prisoner of war on the Japanese *Montevideo Maru*, torpedoed by the USS *Sturgeon* near the Philippine coast. A thousand prisoners died with him. It was Australia's worst maritime disaster, though the shipwreck has never been found.'

In the darkness, her face burned. 'Oh, *Drew*.' No wonder he'd spent his life searching for wrecks, telling their stories to the world.

Her hands, on her backpack straps, clenched with the urge to touch him. It would be too easy for such a touch to be misconstrued as mere pity, instead of admiration.

'So,' he said lightly, 'you get it now.'

'Yes,' she said, emotion making her voice thick. 'You don't want any wrecks to lie forgotten, do you? If only you could find every one …'

'You catch on pretty quick for a reporter.'

'Though, it doesn't fully explain why a man who hardly knows a woman would join her wilderness search for an airplane wreck that may be nothing more than a figment of her imagination.'

There was a long beat of silence. 'Not fully, no.'

She smiled, hoping he could see it.

'And is your ultimate hope to find the *Montevideo* one day?'

'I'm in the wrong sea entirely, and even if I wasn't, the wreck is miles down. I just hope I'm still alive when they finally find it.' This stated, he pushed on.

Tally fell back a step or two, allowing this knowledge to sink deep into her marrow.

The wind had dropped away and the forest was singing a glad song before they reached the top of the first rise. Breakfast stop, according to their handwritten plan, rolled up in Tally's pocket. But they'd made excellent timing, beating the sunrise. Tally declared she'd be happy to go on, putting off the stop, but Drew was having none of that. 'We can't burn ourselves out on the first day.'

'I suppose not,' Tally grumbled, firing on all cylinders and feeling she could have sprinted to the peak of Mount Teasdale.

'We're clear of Mermaid Bay without being seen,' Drew said. 'It's important to take our planned rests. The hardest days are still ahead of us.'

Tally went on grumbling, as Drew disappeared into a thicket of trees for a toilet break.

His cry minutes later brought her running after him – heedless of respect for his privacy.

He was halfway up an enormous rock, wider than a truck, a storey higher than the trees around.

'Come up,' he beckoned. 'There's an incredible view on top.'

Tally began her own clamber, smiling at his chivalrous hand held down, but not taking it. '*This* doesn't feel like rest,' she said with a laugh.

She emerged onto the flat surface of the rock, an isle of its own above the treetops. She'd lost her breath, not from exertion, but wonder. The sky wrapped around them in a swirling stir of lilac and rose gold. The sea was a glimmering teal, every island of the archipelago lying velvety purple upon it, bronzed by first light. She turned in a slow circle, east to west, absorbing the staggering sense of expansiveness.

'I wouldn't call this incredible,' she said. 'More like … superlative.'

'That's why you write and I discover.'

'You did pick a good spot,' she agreed. 'Though, I discovered it first.' She had her bearings now.

'You've been up this far?'

'Never. I marked this rock from the sea when I was a girl. I always thought of it as "Table Rock". It's smaller up close than I imagined it to be.'

They sat in a companionable silence, sharing a thermos of coffee, as the pastel hues faded and the sun blazed up in gold-shafted clouds and long, glowing ribbons, gilding the channels of the archipelago.

'Are you worried for Dara?' Drew asked. *Not quite out of nowhere*, Tally thought.

'Why should I be worried?'

She watched him construct his question with care. 'If you're right about *Lady Lily* being up there on Mount Teasdale, that your father and his associates really did interfere with a war grave to steal US government funds ... and if you expose them, in your usual style, such an outrageous story could even be picked up internationally. Have you considered the public relations disaster this might prove for Mermaid Bay?'

'I don't care one bit about that.' A breezy lie.

Drew's brown eyes were fixed on her face. 'Translation: you care very much. I'd wager you *hope* it damages the resort's fine standing.'

'I think my father and his idiot manager have been running Mermaid's reputation into the ground themselves for some time now, turning it from a honeymooner's dream into a philanderer's playground. I think Mermaid Bay is already dead in the water, and Dara needs to be revitalised for a new generation of holidaymakers.' She felt the defensive thrust of her own chin.

'So, yes, you're quite happy for your investigative piece to be the death knell of your father's operations. Sounds suspiciously to me like you've thrown your journalistic impartiality to the wind.'

She allowed herself a second to enjoy his metaphor, imagining her prized objectivity flapping away over the sea.

'*Look*,' she sighed then, needing to be very clear. 'If we *are* right about the *Lady Lily*, and if my father did rob it and launder all that money, then he's looking at federal charges, isn't he? Jail time. It'll be the end of him here.'

'I'd say that makes you one seriously dangerous woman right now.'

'Indeed. I intend to *write* Richard Ramsey off my island.'

Drew was squinting with a new thought. 'Puts our expedition in quite a perilous category. Wouldn't want to be caught out here trying to expose your father ...'

Tally stood, keen now to be moving. She slotted her thermos away in the side of her backpack, delving deeper into the bag to reassure herself that Ma's will-in-a-bottle was safe. No need to mention to Drew that she carried something this valuable on so risky a mission.

She swung on her backpack. 'Shall we go?'

When she wrote the story of this island-crossing expedition, Tally decided she would not bore her readers with a long exposition on the arduous trek itself. Travelling up the creek beds was saving them from having to cut a path through deep scrub and thick jungle, though it was still slow, wet, rock-hopping progress. The machete was in constant use, hacking back the long, looping vines that sought to trip, choke and snag.

As far as she could tell, six hours into their first nine-hour day, this journey was one never-ending ascent into hell. Because hell, as it turned out, was near the clouds. The requisite demons – mosquitoes, sandflies and leeches – were all there, it certainly was taking an eternity, and the burning was in her limbs and admittedly under her collar, too.

Must this mountain range be so damned mountainy?

Poor Drew, she told herself, *putting up with a far-from-glamorous, far-from-sanguine trekking companion.* He'd be glad to get back to his lonely life on the sea after this. She herself planned to kiss the linoleum floor of her newsroom, once she returned to work.

To pass the last hour, she had been describing for Drew in great detail and real time all the tedious parts she'd decided to omit from her investigative piece. Given his grim, forbearing silence, he appreciated this commentary.

She was just winding up a long rant about the unstable rocks of the creek bed underfoot, and had decided to take a break in her commentating. A very brief break, she told him – best not to get his hopes up.

'I think you'll change your tune,' he said, 'once we reach Mount Teasdale.'

'Sure, as if we're ever reaching the end of this interminable climb...'

'Your complaining is interminable.'

'How many times in the last hour,' she mused cheerfully, 'have you thought about hanging me with the straps of my own bag?'

'Not once,' he replied.

'Not *once*?'

'I've come up with much quicker methods.'

'What a waste all this wilderness is anyway,' she said. 'You wouldn't make a paid tour out of this trek.'

'Funnily enough,' Drew said, 'last night while Lila and I were dancing, she said she thought there must be a market for wilderness trekking on Dara Island. Said she'd love to cross Dara herself one day.'

Tally couldn't believe her ears. 'You *told* her about our trip?'

'Not a word. She brought it up all by herself. *Dara has so much more to offer than island hostesses*, that was how she broached the topic.'

'Lila knows.'

'You think?'

'That was her telling you she'd figured out what we're up to! If Lila guessed, who *else* did?' If Mack knew, how swiftly would he marshal his crew and come after them? Tally's neck spasmed with foreboding.

Their first night was to be spent at Zara Falls. Tally had not been expecting much of a remote, jungle waterfall, but arriving now, filthy and exhausted, it was an oasis.

The falls ran from an upper pool over a steep cliff face, into a lower pool greener even than the bush around it. Tally splashed straight into the water, still fully dressed, dropping only her backpack. It was immensely satisfying, though she soon realised her error when she joined Drew for the final hundred-foot climb up the rock face to make camp. She could hardly move for tightly clinging clothes and wet, squelching shoes.

'Impetuousness always has been my downfall,' she remarked to Drew, struggling to gain purchase on the final rim.

'No down-falling, please,' he said, hoisting her up.

They emerged on the rock table above Zara Falls. Here, the creek formed a deep, higher pool, with an infinity edge atop the falls. The view was panoramic: a majestic sweep of island and sea, the sun setting over the mainland to their west. On the east horizon, monsoon clouds were bathed glowingly in orange, a sunset rainbow made lurid by storm and sunlight.

'If only the guide book told us the top pool was better.' Tally laughed, shucking off her wet clothing to dry upon a branch. 'I might not have jumped the gun.'

In only her bikini now, she waded into the pool and swam to the infinity edge to lean her elbows over the rock lip. 'Now *that's* a view,' she sighed, her legs floating behind her. 'Come and see.'

'I was going to make you dinner first.'

'Get in here, Huxley.'

Drew undressed and swam towards her, hooking his elbows over the edge alongside hers. Their drifting legs bumped lightly in the cool current.

'I just need a cocktail,' she said. 'Then I'm never leaving this swim-up bar.'

'Can I interest you in a cup of sardine brine, instead?'

'You didn't sneak a single flask of rum into that colossal backpack of yours?'

'I wasn't quite expecting a rugged trek to feel so much like a holiday.'

A romantic holiday, she amended, enjoying the inadvertent nudge of his hip against hers.

'You *are* enjoying our adventure,' she declared.

'I *am*.'

'Despite my complaining?'

'Even your complaining is entertaining, Tally.'

'Entertaining generally, or to you specifically? Because I'm not sure how much of it to include in my story.'

'Oh no, don't include any of your complaining in the story,' he said. 'Make yourself sound stoic and silent.' His crow's feet crinkled.

She laughed, splashing his face, lightly.

The setting sun flared in his fair curls and burnished his bare chest. 'I already told you, Miss Forster – I'm a huge fan of your piquant tone.'

Her insides gave a thrilling jelly wobble. She turned her body fully to face his, blue eyes wide under wet lashes. 'Like piquant women, do you?'

'No, I like piquant writing,' he said. 'Women, I prefer meek and dull.'

'You do *not*,' she huffed.

'No, I certainly don't,' he said, reaching out underwater to pull her to him. She wrapped her arms and legs languorously around him.

Up close, his eyes were as brown and inviting as a puppy's. He looked between her eyes and lips. 'Do you kiss as well as you write?'

'I'll kiss *you* very well,' she said, and lowered her lips to his.

The last of the day's light softened over them, the water flowed coolly around them, and his lips and arms and waist were warm against her.

It was a very fine first kiss.

Drew and Tally were seated cross-legged together before the evening's fire, dry and changed, tin bowls left to wash, watching lightning strobe silver and bright on the east horizon. His arm was slung casually around her lower back.

Goodness knows how they would manage walking two abreast for the next two days, but she sure didn't want him to remove his arm from her ever again. He had been the first to gently disentangle himself in the pool, and to suggest they set up camp before the light was gone.

Tally wondered if his steady calm eventually would rub off on her. Of course, that might require rubbing *her* volatile self all over him …

She unfolded her legs to stretch them out before her, inadvertently disturbing his arm. She was most gratified, however, when he moved it to lightly rest on her leg.

'You do know,' she said, 'this whole trek was just a ruse to get you alone in the wilderness. There *is* no plane.'

'You needn't have gone to so much effort finding a map, then. I'd have come into the wilderness with you on the strength of a rumour.' His thumb traced a lazy circle on her knee.

Tally flexed her feet, happily, and felt this motion catch Drew's attention. He leaned forward to capture the top of her left foot, sliding his large thumb gently up her webbed toes.

Against her will, her cheeks heated. 'Still got your fetish for mermaids?'

'*This* mermaid, anyway,' he said, sitting back so his hand could return to her thigh. 'I met my first mer*man* a few months ago.'

'Oh yes, ha-ha.'

'I'm not teasing you.'

Maybe not with words, but that hand could burn a hole in her thigh.

'He had toes just like yours – second and third, webbed, on both feet.'

'Just go around peering at strangers' feet like a weirdo, do you?'

'In my line of work, I see almost as many bare feet as a podiatrist.'

'Where did you meet this fellow? He might be my *sole* mate …' She grinned.

'No, he was too old for you.'

'Says who?'

'Me.' He squeezed her thigh. 'I met him in Airlie Beach. Told him about your toes, hope you don't mind. I didn't mention your name, just that you were from Dara. He was very interested.'

'*I'd* say! I mean, what are the chances?'

'Pretty good, in his case. He said his webbed toes were a family trait, going on three generations, from his great-grandfather down.'

'Yeah well, I'm a first edition,' Tally said. 'What was his name?'

'Flynn something – sorry, I remember how important last names are to you. I can tell you the name of his boat, though – the *Bluebird*.'

She shrugged. 'What good is that to me?'

PART THREE

The world rolls round,—mistrust it not,—
Befalls again what once befell;
All things return, both sphere and mote,
And I shall hear my bluebird's note

Ralph Waldo Emerson

CHAPTER 26

NIGHT SAILING

Forster's Shack, Dara Island, 1946

And they are gone: aye, ages long ago
These lovers fled away into the storm.

John Keats

There was an art to disentangling oneself from a small child's sleeping embrace that Nerissa had not yet mastered. Delila was as tactile in sleep as the seaweed clinging to rocks outside Papa's cottage.

In the darkness, she had eased herself so far towards the double mattress edge that only a small, dimpled hand still held onto her shoulder. Persistent little minx, she might try clinging to Irene, for once. Nerissa plucked each finger one by one from her shoulder, so that the tiny hand fell to the mattress with a tinkling of the shell charms Nerissa had tied so tenderly around her wrist only yesterday. How was she to know that same bracelet might be her undoing only hours later?

She froze where she hunched, listening to Delila's softly complaining sigh as she rolled over to Irene's side of the mattress. Once Delila had settled, Nerissa resumed her slide over the edge. There was no drop, the mattress being directly on the floor. Nerissa rolled a foot away, across the palm-leaf woven mat, before rising to her hands and knees and beginning the crawl towards the door of their single-room shack.

A voice cut through the darkness. 'Where do you think you're going?'

Nerissa stilled. 'Just to the toilet, *shh* – go back to sleep.'

'Will tonight's bowel motion take three hours again?'

Nerissa's mouth opened and closed in the darkness. *You were dead to the world when I left, I even pinched you to make sure!*

'Sometimes, I just like to sit a while under the stars.'

'Uh-huh.' Nerissa could read Irene's acid look even in the pitch blackness. 'The stars aren't going anywhere. Why don't you get your beauty sleep tonight and see your stars another night?'

'Because I want to see them now.'

'You never *can* see past what you want in the here and now, Nerissa – *that's* what's wrong with you.'

'I don't think there's anything *wrong* with me.' It was more defiant than she meant to sound, but there was nothing keeping her in this shack, this night – not when it might be her last chance, ever.

'You don't know if Richard may return tomorrow, and you're so close to a proposal now. Why would you risk that? You haven't a *care* for our future!'

Nerissa pushed to her feet. No need any longer to crawl, though coming back would be another story. 'In fact,' she said coolly, 'I'm indebted now to think of nothing else.'

She went on her way, pausing only at the door. 'I know what I'm doing, okay? I'll see you in a sec.'

'Don't forget the shovel,' Irene hissed, 'since you're determined to dig yourself even deeper into it.'

Nerissa stepped out into the dark grove of palms, frowning in annoyance. She knew she would get the silent treatment from Irene all day tomorrow, and poor Delila would be made miserable and fretful by it. And then, knowing her luck, Richard would choose tomorrow to come back again, and the women's united front would be blown.

But dread of tomorrow had no place in this evening's adventure. The stars were out, and so was she.

She tiptoed barefoot onto the beach, smiling at the tiny coral avalanches under each footfall towards the languidly lapping sea. She skipped down the little dock to sit upon its end, legs dangling in the balmy water.

First, a prayer of a kind to Papa – wherever he was. Tears shimmered in her eyes as she raised them to the evening sky.

Thank you, Papa, for planting me on this island. We'll be all right without you, don't worry. I know you're looking after us, now and forevermore. I'll make the right choices for all of us – for Irene and Delila, and especially for Dara. She's safe with us both, I promise.

In the distance, there was a soft burr. Nerissa finished her prayer and turned to look towards the horizon, where the full, rising moon illuminated a billowing cloud range. There was a dark speck coming steadily across the silvered sea from the archipelago beyond Dara.

The corner of her mouth deepened into a divot. So, he hadn't gone, after all. She knew he wouldn't, she *knew* it! One more chance to change his mind and make him stay.

Nerissa stood, dropping her slip to reveal the swimsuit she'd worn to bed, and dived pertly into the sea. She settled onto her back, letting water fill her ears so that she could hear nothing but her own heart and the undersea world.

Let him come, then. But never let it be said I called him over. She was only here to float in the starry heavens with Papa.

How long she drifted there she would never know, for she did not wear a watch – did not even own one. She knew he would anchor a way off, but still she could not help the thrill of fear that his dinghy might run right over her as it so nearly had the first time they'd met.

He materialised in the water beside her at a slow stroke.

'Fancy bumping into you here,' he said.

'Why, hello,' she replied. 'It's you again.'

They might have been swimmers passing in a municipal lido's lanes, except that he had five oceans in which to sail his boat, and he'd chosen this sea, the shallows of her island.

She was treading water here, though he was tall enough to stand. She could just make out his grey eyes, glinting in the moonshine.

Flynn.

'I hear *you* have a big meeting coming up soon,' he said.

'Where did you hear that?'

'Made a trip to the mainland for last-minute supplies. The whole beach is abuzz with the news.'

'Just what news would that be?' she asked warily.

'You're selling to Richard Ramsey, after all.'

'You heard wrong. I'm not selling Dara to him.'

He was silent. Disappointed for himself? Or proud of her, for holding out?

She kicked underwater. 'I hate that everyone is over there talking about it like a done deal. I've sent him away more times than anyone can count. Why should this time be any different?'

'Richard himself is telling everyone this time is different. He's sure he's got Dara now.'

'He can be as sure as he likes,' she said. 'It doesn't make my mind up for me.'

They bobbed together. He watched her across the inky swell, saying nothing. She felt a flush climb her body from waist to crown, and was glad for the cover of night.

Finally, he said, 'Will you let *me* try, Nerissa?'

'Try what?' she breathed.

'To make your mind up for you.'

She lowered in the water so that her smiling mouth was concealed. *Yes, that was exactly what she wanted tonight, why she had come in the first place, hoping he would attempt one more time to convince her.*

She lifted her face from the water. 'A woman's mind is her *own*.'

'I guess I'll have to work on something other than your mind, then.'

She laughed, warmth suffusing her. 'What makes you think that will do it?'

'Because it's my last shot,' he said, quite in earnest.

Her face fell, her voice with it. 'You really are leaving, then?'

'I had every intention of setting sail today, as I swore I would.'

'Why didn't you?' *I watched the horizon all day expecting to see you leaving. I prayed for any glimpse of you, even as I dreaded the slightest cloud shadow might shape itself into your sails.*

He set his gaze on her, meaningfully.

'In that case,' she said, 'I think it would only be fair to hear what you have to say …'

'Come away with me.'

She shook her head. 'I see this is to be a repeat of every other night. What a pity, because I've heard it all before: sail the seven seas with me, open my spinach cans, become my galley slave, et cetera.'

It was his turn to laugh, and she smiled to hear it again. He'd become increasingly more serious over the last few nights as her refusal to leave with him had strengthened – at least, to *his* knowledge. If only he had an inkling how much she had weakened during these heady, all-consuming weeks. She was almost ready to throw Dara to the circling sharks – one, in particular.

He moved closer. 'I meant, come away on a little adventure tonight.'

There was a heating coil, low and tight in her belly. She knew what she wanted, and she didn't see why she had to go anywhere else to finally have it.

'Come where?' She'd decided in an instant: if he said merely *to the Hat*, she would spurn him, after all. She wanted more.

'I want to show you something magical.'

He had taken her first to his waiting sailboat, and then through the archipelago and well out beyond it. From her cushion on deck, warmly towel-wrapped, she watched those dark behemoths go sliding by, left behind as Flynn charted their secret course into infinity bestarred. She had never been so far out. Was he taking her to the outer reef? Or further still, to a place she could never return from?

Exhilaration fanned her spirits towards full euphoria.

Flynn dropped anchor in the middle of nowhere, or so it seemed at first to Nerissa. Only the hanging pressure lantern provided any light.

'Where are we?' she said, unable to keep the disappointment from her voice.

'Don't you see it?' He had come up next to her on the starboard side.

She followed his gaze eastward, expecting to see something on the horizon – the regal lights of a distant cruise ship, perhaps. She saw nothing.

'Look closer,' he said, leaning near to point at the water before them.

She removed her attention, with some effort, from his warm breath stirring the damp skin of her neck, and focused on the moon-tipped ripples of the sea.

She saw it first as an absence of waves – a flat oval around which the sea flowed – and then the pale white shine.

'A sand cay,' Nerissa whispered, as though she might disturb the sediment that had taken several thousand years to accumulate upon the reef, forming an isolated isle, a hundred feet wide, surrounded by coral gardens.

'My map tells me this one is unnamed, which seemed rather cruel when I first saw how beautiful it was.'

'I'll have to take your word for it. There isn't much to see at the present time.'

'Will you stay the night with me?'

She turned to look at him. His face was only inches from her own, and smiling down on her. 'I want you to come and see the sunrise from the sand cay.'

'Why?' Half breath, half utterance.

He lifted her chin, leaving his hand to gently cradle her jaw. 'Because it'll change your mind.'

She wet her lips. 'A sunrise will do that?'

'No,' he said, bending his face so that his lips pressed hotly against hers. 'I will.'

A million stars were spread above his head, and she below him, in the powder-soft sand. Tears were in her eyes now as she turned into his neck.

Flynn drew back to look at her. 'You're sad.'

She shook her head, still trying to hide her tears. 'I'm not.'

He held her face between two hands until her gaze reluctantly met his. There was concern, tender and unswerving, in his grey eyes. He stroked hair back from her forehead. 'Tell me to stop,' he said.

'Please, don't stop.'

'You're crying.'

'You make me feel how … empty I've been.' Her eyes shut, sealing her tears.

He kissed her closed eyelids, his arms in the sand a close embrace around her head. 'I don't want to hurt you.'

'You won't hurt me,' she whispered. 'It isn't my first time.'

'Tell me to keep going, then.'

She sighed and opened her eyes to his, full of longing and assent.

His thumbs were at her temples, stroking. Her breath caught at her throat as he began, with unbearable gradualness, to slide into her.

For a moment he stayed there – encompassed and still – letting her settle around him, waiting for her legs to enclose him, too. There was a wry glint now to his desire. 'Still empty, Riss?'

'Not as long as you stay with me forever.'

Salmon hues were rippling across the sky when Nerissa awoke on that tiny isle. Her hand had fallen out of Flynn's, but his arm lay gently over her waist, the sea lapping quietly at their feet.

Nerissa rolled onto her side to look at Flynn, careful not to roll his arm off her. His face was somehow more handsome in sleep, all the chiselled olive lines at rest; the blush of dawn on his bare chest and arms.

Her movement had disturbed him. Flynn's eyes flickered and opened, the first expression to hit them one of pleased remembrance. His arm tightened over her. 'You're still here.'

'I couldn't exactly get away from you on a sand cay.'

They stared at each other. Behind Flynn's smiling face, a candle of gold glowed.

'Here's this sunrise you promised me,' she said, trying to gulp away the ache in her throat. She shouldn't have stayed the night – it was madness. She had to go home! Delila would be awake; Irene would be stalking the shore, already irate. And somewhere on the distant mainland, a yacht – the finest one on the beach – might be powering up to make its crossing.

His smile faltered. 'You're sad again.'

She didn't deny it, her eyes glimmering hotly.

'I couldn't change your mind, then.'

'You made a valiant effort.'

'But you won't come with me.'

'I can't leave my father all alone. He won't let me.'

'He won't even know it.'

'I made him promises.'

'Such as?'

'I – I can't tell you.' Nerissa sat up, watching the *Bluebird* bobbing without a care on the tranquil sea, as though it wasn't an entirely different future she might choose for herself.

He sat up beside her. 'Try.'

'I *can't* leave Delila and Irene.'

'It surely wouldn't be easy, but you could do it. And we'd come back often enough.'

'*How* often?'

She saw that he wouldn't lie, even to win her. 'It might be a couple of years between.'

'No, I won't do that.' She let the boat go on bobbing without her, turning her face to the spreading sunglow. 'And I have Dara. I promised Papa that I'd keep his island safe, come what may.'

'How can you tie yourself down to a piece of land like that? It's a beautiful island, I don't deny it, Riss … but there are so *many* beautiful places to see in the world. Come with me and I'll show you as many as I can possibly fit into one lifetime …'

Her heart – oh how it *ached* to hear him offer such things.

'Why must *I* be convinced to go? Why won't you stay with *me*?' She hated the sulky ring to her voice. She had heard his answer rehashed a dozen times, already, and she no more wanted him to justify his need to wander than hers to stay. The truth was, she wanted to be chosen over a whole world of adventures, in the same way he wanted her to give up Dara for him. 'No, please don't answer that,' she said, waving away his new attempt to explain his own dream, much less impending work schedules in distant seas.

They had reached their impasse quickly this time.

She looked around her now, understanding why he had brought her here to see the dawn. They were marooned in an all-suffusing gold light, a world so boundless they might have been the last two living beings – or the first.

'I'm just glad,' she said, trying to smile, 'that you came back one more time to see me. It hurts my heart to think that if you hadn't put down anchor by my island, I might never have met you at all. We wouldn't have had this ...'

He reached for her, hands cradling her face as he drew her lips to his.

Pushing him back onto the sand, she climbed astride his body. The tide lapped in, running up to caress her calves, foaming at his waist, before dragging back into the sea. The sun was a warm parcel at her back, rays catching in her hair of spun honey and lighting his storm-grey eyes.

With his hands mooring her hips, she moved on him like the sea.

Nerissa came ashore at Dara when the sun already was climbing towards mid-morning heights. There was no sign of Irene, nor yet any mainlanders with fat pocketbooks. A tiny girl was sitting on the sand beside Nerissa's discarded slip, squinting into the glare.

Delila.

As Nerissa waded through the shallows to the shore, Delila leaped up, running to the very edge of the tide to meet her, holding out her slip. 'You fordot dis!' Nerissa accepted this damp and sandy gift with a sad smile.

Behind her, Flynn's boat thrummed into life, once more. Nerissa turned slowly to face him. They had been silent the whole way back – no longer touching, nor looking at one another. Her eyes had been set on the dense green peaks of Dara, her thoughts a vain pitch-and-toss.

He was standing now, a lonely figure under white sails, right hand raised in farewell. Only an hour ago, he had been as close as her own heart's throbbing. From this moment on, he would only grow smaller and smaller, until he was a speck on the distant horizon, vanishing altogether into the silver-blue splendour.

Would she *ever* see him again? He'd made no promises, as she'd made none of her own. He was a stranger to her only weeks ago, and he'd become a stranger now again. Her future was with Dara.

A soft, chubby hand slipped into hers. Nerissa glanced down at the kitten-sweet face peering up at her so worshipfully, green eyes just like her own.

'Who's dat?'

Nerissa lifted her head to look at Flynn one last time, but he was burring away already, back set against her, his wake sending out wavelets that would never reach her shore. Her lungs seemed to deflate further with every yard lengthening between them.

She bent, swinging Delila up onto her hip. 'Oh, darling girl,' she murmured, lips against that tiny brow. 'He was only a mermaid's dream.'

Together they went up over the coral to their bungalow waiting beneath bending palms.

CHAPTER 27

MOUNT TEASDALE

1968

Four hours into the second day of their story-chasing, father-vanquishing expedition, Tally was no longer complaining – not a word.

A solid day's hiking had caught up with her overnight, and every muscle rebuked her, at every step. She was sorry she had wasted so many complaints yesterday when she mistakenly thought the going was tough, remembering that gradient now with the bittersweet nostalgia of one jaded.

She didn't even have the memory of a night well spent to keep her mind off her miserable, good-for-nothing muscles. The tent, as it turned out, had been set up just for her. Alone. Drew had strung up a hammock for himself between two trees, replete with a specially fitted mosquito net.

Tally hadn't anticipated the legs that would nearly collapse under her as she stepped out of her tent for breakfast. Every step since had felt like a feat of determination.

And yet, she was still doing better than Drew.

He had rolled his ankle on a moss-slick rock less than an hour after they had set off for the day, and from the grim set of his lips, and his dogged insistence that he was fine, Tally could tell that he was certainly not. They had since paused to pick a sturdy walking stick each, but Tally was afraid it was too little too late. Apart from Drew's chuckle when she reminded him that she *had* warned him about those nefarious rocks, he had been mostly subdued; concentrating, she thought, on *his* every step.

Tally had since taken the lead, mostly to force a slower pace. She feared Drew would drag himself to the top, commando style, for her quest, and she would call the whole thing off before she ever let him do that.

Tally shot another glance over her shoulder, catching Drew in a wince that was quickly swallowed up by a smile. 'I'm good,' he said. 'Just a stitch.'

She looked smoothly away, a new weight in her chest. Every step now, her heart would reproach her, too. How many more hours would she make him suffer for her sake? *Another four?*

My poor love . . .

It was almost another *six* hours till they were able to make camp, thanks to Tally's deliberately slow pace and the diversions she took from their mapped path to avoid dodgy-looking obstacles. She blamed her sore muscles for her caution, saying nothing of her heart.

'At least there'll be less clambering over boulders tomorrow,' she told Drew, helping him pull off his right boot, which seemed to have shrunk around his ankle. 'We're travelling along a ridge for much of it.'

There was no sunset at their crest to reward them this time, graphite-dark monsoon clouds having moved in over the island. Neither was there an infinity-edge waterfall in which to kiss and canoodle, only a rushing spring in a narrow hollow, enough flowing water to shower under and fill up their canisters. The view was as magnificent as every stop before it, though. Even more of Dara's verdant, jungled curves rolled out below them, Mount Teasdale looming above.

One more day of walking – seven hours, at least – then they would reach the summit and at last, the *Lady Lily*.

Making camp near a mass grave wouldn't be ideal, but Tally wanted as much time as possible to photograph and document the evidence in the cool of evening and morning, before they began the descent the following day.

Tally took a washer to the spring to make a cool compress for Drew's ankle, and dug out another aspirin from their first-aid kit. Then while he rested, elevating his foot, she went to wash and change.

He did not resist her taking control of the camp set-up, nor the cooking of dinner. This, frankly, concerned her more than the grave set of his lips.

'I'm sorry,' she said, as they sat, nursing their bowls in front of the fire she had built.

'Why should *you* be sorry?'

'I make you come with me on this trek, and then my stupid island twists your ankle.'

'You didn't twist my *arm* to make me come with you, though, and I wouldn't have missed it for all the world.' He scooted over closer, gathering her tightly against his side.

'*Hey*,' he soothed, as she looked miserably up at him. 'I'll be all right, Tally.'

'What if you're not? The further we go, the further we are from help. I think you should wait here while I go on tomorrow. I can be back in two days, tops, while you recuperate, ready for the return trek.'

'Yes,' he said dryly. 'I can see your headline already: Star Journalist Discovers Missing Wreck All by Herself with No Help from Anyone Else.'

'More like: Treasure Hunter Comes So Close but Alas So Far.'

'*Alas*,' Drew said, bringing his lips to her cheek, then lower, breathing warmly, to her neck. 'But it was fun coming so close.'

Tally tipped her neck, shivering as he buried kisses beneath the damp up-twist of her hair. In this swoon of pleasure, her unfocused gaze drifted from the slatey roof of the world, down over the deepening shadows and darkening island furrows …

She started with an abrupt cry, straining away from Drew. 'Do you see that? Is that – smoke?'

Drew broke from his caresses, instantly alert. 'Where?'

'There – there! It *is* smoke!'

She heard Drew's sharp intake of breath. Halfway back down the undulating contours of the island, a long pillar of smoke rose to meet the dense sky.

A campfire, atop the previous ridge. Another party coming up the island after them.

Mack and his skeleton crew.

Tally rose, taking her water bottle, and quickly extinguished their own fire. 'Too late now, I suppose,' she said. 'If we saw theirs, they no doubt saw us …' Her teeth minced a lip. 'How far behind us do you think they are?'

Drew was quiet. Too quiet. She turned back to him, keeping her eyes averted from his elevated leg.

'They're at the top of Zara Falls,' he said. 'A day's walk.'

Less, he did not add, *if their ankles are holding up …*

'I don't get it,' she stormed. 'I heard Mack say in the lodge that they were waiting until *after* the monsoon.' She threw her hands towards the blue-black clouds. 'What the hell are they doing coming now? It's going to piss down, why wouldn't they just *wait*?!'

Drew hauled himself up, coming to stand beside Tally. 'You did say that they indicated they were "running out of time".'

She frowned. 'But when they were skulking around Mermaid Bay yesterday morning, he said something about "go time" being after Richard made his final offer to "that bitch" – I was supposed to meet my father yesterday at nine o'clock, so I can only assume he meant me.' She turned to Drew, stark fear in her eyes. 'Standing him up must have tipped them off. It was thoughtless of me – *stupid*!'

Drew took her shoulders in firm hands. 'Stood up or not, your father had no idea you were onto the *Lady Lily*. How could he?'

Too easily. He probably discovered his nineteen forty-six ledger book and treasure map gone. He'd have known immediately who'd been poking around in his office. Maybe that's why he'd ordered their meeting – for which she hadn't shown. Then, to top it off, she and Drew had been sending up smoke signals from Zara Falls last night, marking their progress for all to see.

Drew listened patiently to this tirade. 'It's also possible that they have no idea we're ahead of them. If we can keep our lead tomorrow, we'll get your evidence and be gone before they ever arrive. Then we'll take the longer way back, down the side of Mount Teasdale and around the circumference of the island. We won't run into them. Let's get some shut-eye and we can be gone before dawn.' He pulled her into a bear hug. 'It'll work out,' he said, lips against her hair, 'you'll see.'

Tally nodded, wanting to believe him, but even in Drew's reassuring hold, her insides were hollow with anxiety. It was a *race* now to the top of Mount Teasdale, and her partner was injured already and going slower. What chance had they of keeping ahead?

Drew seemed to be thinking the very same thing. 'My ankle will be fine by morning,' he said. 'I know it.'

Within the hour, a wall of rain engulfed their peak. Tally insisted Drew stay in the tent with her. He did stay, lying down beside her. *Close* beside her, thanks to the backpacks dragged hastily in from the thunderous torrent.

Tally had set her watch for four o'clock in the morning. But what if the party coming after them didn't actually stop to sleep? What if they pushed on through the rain? They'd be on Tally and Drew by morning.

'They've trekked all day, too, they're just as tired as we are,' Drew assured her.

She had her doubts. And unlike Drew and Tally, those blokes knew this route – all its surprises and shortcuts. Tally thought she should be ashamed to call herself the heiress of Dara, knowing so little of this island.

As she lay there in the darkness, both of them silent under the rain's assault, her mind ran to a thousand scenarios, returning always to one: would her *father* be with them, and if so, how far was *he* willing to go to protect his secret?

Some hours later, Drew found her in her bedroll. At her initial drowsy stirring, she thought he was dreaming, only sleep-groping. His movements were too languid and roaming. Awakened fully now by her body's response, she realised the topography behind her had changed.

That was no back pushed insistently against her bottom ...

She rolled over with a groan of longing swallowed by the rain, and the mouth urgently seeking hers.

With nothing to illuminate their discovery of one another, it was all touch, all sensation, all pleasure. She had first met him on a pitch-black verandah, his voice alone guiding her, and now she loved him in darkness, with only the guttural melody of desire to conduct them.

The rainstorm could have washed them into the sea, forty thieves could have come upon them then, and still Tally would have been uninterruptable.

'Oh, my *love* …'

They had survived the night together – barely, if Tally was counting one particular moment there – and they were already well on their way up the long ridge before green slowly shaded in the grey lines of the world.

There was no sunrise.

The rain, diminished but far from defeated, drizzled on and on. Breakfast was no more than jerky strips shared between them. She'd have thought their strenuous nocturnal activities would have given them both leonine appetites.

Anxiety drove them on. Drew was in even more pain – she'd glimpsed the empurpled bulk of his ankle this morning by torch light – and yet, here he was at the lead, pushing relentlessly forward.

This made her more fearful than anything he might have communicated with words. *His* determination said it all. As had the fervent embrace in which she had been awakened. Drew did not merely hold her as a new lover, but as someone he dreaded letting go of.

CHAPTER 28

THE BID

Coral Beach, 1946

The moon was a slender shell chip on the morning Richard finally returned to make an offer that Nerissa could no longer afford to refuse.

He strode ashore at their quiet bay, with his yacht, *Polaris*, at proud anchor, and all the vaunting confidence that had so attracted her those many months ago when he had come asking Papa for her island, rather than her hand.

He nearly had both won now, and she accepted it. His asking and her assent as inevitable as the moon's pull upon the sea.

She and Irene could not hold this island much longer on their own. They lacked the ability and finances to do little more than sustain themselves. Indeed, they had nothing between them but a little girl, and a lie. As much as she pitied herself for admitting it, Dara needed a property baron's acumen. She no longer wanted to live in poverty, among falling sheets of iron and a vanishing colony of chickens.

Would the pythons take her or Irene when they were done with the poultry? At night, Nerissa lay awake imagining a python wending away into the jungle with a bulbous wedge in the shape of a tiny, kitten-nosed girl.

Had Flynn *stayed*, instead of being several weeks already gone, this would be a very different day indeed, marking an ending with Richard, rather than a beginning. Not an unfeeling refusal, for Richard Ramsey had become very dear to her in his own way, and she would have quietly wept to see him go.

When Papa died, it was Richard who had come to her immediate aid with food, supplies and kindness. Who had helped her make arrangements for the funeral, had paid for Papa's coffin, had even joined the other pallbearers to carry that fine coffin up the steep jungled rise to his eternal resting place.

Not for one moment had Nerissa thought Richard acted out of mere benevolence, for of course he'd always had Dara at the forefront of his vision. But even if he had come to her in her grief for ulterior motives, at least he had met her there in the midst of it, when no one else would.

Richard might have been her papa's foe, it was true, but he had been her friend at a time of deepest need. She had come to believe Bertie Forster would have been a fool to refuse his daughter's hand to a man possessed of such dogged perseverance, promising *such things* for Dara and for her.

Flynn had made no such promises. He had confessed openly to wanting his wanderer's life more than her island home, to needing freedom and adventure more than family and security. He had offered naught but love and his own body that had pleasured her so well.

She would have been a sucker to choose love – much less the folly of desire – over a secure future for all of them. It was one thing to dream of a mermaid's life upon the sea: endless days of glimmering blue, sun-warm, salted skin moving upon skin, with only the stars to guide them and the far horizon fastening them to the earth. It was another thing entirely to sail away, perhaps forever, from the only home she'd ever known or wanted, and the last two people left to her in the world after Papa's passing.

Dara and Nerissa were a package deal. Irene and Delila were part of that bundle, and today she needed to ensure, first and foremost, that Richard would honour her commitments before she would ever agree to his.

She had decided to tell Richard the truth – the *whole* truth, from her rebellious adolescent forays to the Hat, to her starlit dalliances with Flynn. Then see how deep ran his determination to have Nerissa and Dara both. There was something more to tell him, too. Something Irene had guessed almost as soon as Nerissa, for they had shared the timing of their monthly cycle almost to the hour since Papa's death – collective grief and vulnerability playing strange tricks on whatever enigmatic rhythm moved the symphony of blood. Irene and Nerissa had parted ways in the most profound manner possible, and no amount of pawpaw had this time brought on the flow.

Best to tell Richard outright, Nerissa reasoned. What did she have to lose?

Everything, Irene had seethed. *Tell him at your peril, and ours.*

Here were her choices, then: tell him, and perhaps be left to raise this baby in paradise as a pauper. Or fiddle, here and there, with some dates, and in the end keep everything: this new baby, Delila, her island, the man who had supported her through grief, and at last, all her far-fetched dreams for Dara's future.

This time, Richard had not come alone. Joining him was a lean, deeply tanned man wearing a palm-woven hat, just like the ones they used to make in the Artists' Colony, with a cigarette drooping from his lips.

Wading ashore to stand beside Richard, he doffed his hat and grinned, a too-wide grin she would recognise anywhere.

'Nerissa,' Richard said, 'I'd like you to meet my friend Mack.'

'The island girl our Dick cannot stop talking about,' Mack said. 'But we already know each other, don't we?'

Nerissa's face did not give the merest hint of discomposure, though she surely felt it. 'A little. You were based a while in the Artists' Colony, I think?'

'That's it, you've got it.' He stuck out a hand.

Nerissa shook it, already turning her attention to Richard, who beamed.

Coming down the beach, hand in hand, were Irene and Delila. Part of their strategy today, and a clear message: *We come together. You cannot have one without the others.*

The tiny girl ran ahead, melding into Nerissa's shadow. Richard bent to offer her a roll of candies he had been keeping in his pocket for just this moment. Usually, he hid the roll in one curled fist, making her guess between right and left hands. Nerissa knew he did it to soften her, more than Delila, and she tallied it each visit on her 'pros' list.

Irene walked boldly up to Richard and offered a cheek to be kissed. A candy of her own, so to speak. Richard might have brought Mack along for support today, but he truly had no greater ally in his gamble for girl and island than Irene Threadwell. Long into many a night had the two women talked through today's game plan. Irene's instructions were explicit: do not let him leave Dara again without sealing the deal *completely*.

Irene extended to Mack the mere cursory nod of a stranger. Why were they pretending not to know one another? Nerissa quelled a shudder of unease. What, precisely, was Mack's intended role today?

'And who is this?' Mack bent his head to look at the girl affixed now to Nerissa's side.

Irene reached to lift the girl onto her hip. 'This is my Lila.'

Nerissa's eyes flickered to Irene. *Lila?* It had been Papa's idea to name her Delila, and Irene had no business changing it.

There was a strange, hollow ache in her tummy – something more lost to this unstoppable course. Some nights, she woke from a terrible dream where she stood on the balcony of a mammoth ocean liner, watching a small, bobbing head left behind in its vast wake, a lifebuoy flung too short.

Richard reached to tousle Delila's hair. Mack still had not taken his eyes off the small girl. Cold terror began to track through Nerissa's veins.

Drawing close to Richard, she laid a small hand upon his arm, allowing him to feel the tremble in her. 'I made a picnic for you and me,' she said, with just a touch of huskiness. 'I'd hoped we might take a walk together, up to Lookout Point.' *At last alone*, she did not need to spell out.

His eyes fell heavily upon her, full of long-thwarted need and churning frustration. And a question …

In answer, she smiled up shy assent: *Not much longer now, dear man.*

Then she paused, without removing her touch from Richard, to glance briefly at Mack, grinning bawdily. 'But I'm afraid,' she said, with the smallest pout, 'I only made enough for two today. I didn't know you were bringing a friend.'

From across the circle, she felt Irene's pride in this performance.

'Mack here,' Richard said, with an emphatic nod in the man's direction, 'is off for a spot of exploring. Aren't you?'

'Sure,' Mack replied easily. Under his hat, his eyes were crisscrossed by woven shadows. 'You needn't see me for hours.'

'And Lila and I have lessons today, don't we, darling? So, we can't join you, either,' Irene said.

Richard took Nerissa's hand in his. 'Looks like you and I will make a go of it together, then.'

It was all too easy; the deal sealed for her.

CHAPTER 29

LADY LILY

1968

They had been climbing Mount Teasdale for the better part of the day. The rain had eased, but the dense cover showed no sign of lifting. At over three thousand feet above sea level, they were in a cloudland now, soaked to the bone, set upon by mosquitoes and leeches, and further slowed by the slippery gradient and the myriad rivulets springing forth.

Apprehension of the tailing crew was a chill wind whispering at their necks, causing each of them to hike with one eye thrown ever backwards over their shoulder. Despite injury and inclement weather, however, they were still on track to reach the rock face marked on Richard's map by mid-afternoon.

They had no warning of the staggeringly deep ravine suddenly springing up between them and their final push to the summit. Tally pulled out her map to glare at it. Nope, definitely not on it. With no bridge across, they would have to go the long way around it.

The detour took them steeply down through a narrow bottleneck, past the excrement-daubed bottom of the ravine. Here, they were met with a stench so noxious, Tally's eyes watered.

Bats, they wondered, or snakes? Snakes *eating* bats, as they soon discovered. Near a grove of fig trees heavily hung with the black-shrouded pods of a bat colony, a whopping carpet python, dangling long, was expertly swallowing one of the creatures.

'*The horror! The horror!*' Tally said.

Drew gave her a dry look. 'Bet you've been hanging out to use that quote for days.'

She beamed. 'You're beginning to understand my *heart of darkness*.'

'I can see there'll be a lot of groaning in my future.'

'You have no *idea* how much groaning,' she said, in just the tone of voice to turn his face back to hers with a roguish grin.

Now *that* thought buoyed her immensely for the next uphill section.

The stink of reptile and bat shit followed them on the other side of the ravine, like something dead and reeking from a hidden quarter. *Smells like we're getting close to a gravesite,* Tally thought but did not say. It was inappropriate, even for her.

This rerouting had added another hour and a half to their trek. By the time they began the final push under the mist-swathed cliff face of Mount Teasdale, they were starting to lose what meagre light they still had. Tally would have to photograph quickly, so they could get clear of the site before Mack's skeleton crew arrived.

It was possible from this vantage point to hear the roar of the waterfall on Teasdale's east side. Tally tried to keep her imagination on scenarios other than being swept off the top of this mountain, sent plummeting into the sea.

How, she prodded her imagination, would a plane wreck look after more than two decades, exposed to the elements, eaten up by jungle? Would there be human remains still visible, or had Mack and her father interfered with those, too? Any personal artefacts left? What should she try to capture of the plane as identification?

She and Drew had discussed the plane's probable condition at length over the course of this hike. The underwater realm, he'd explained, colonised a plane or ship in a highly effective manner; a new coral reef forming on the wreck, teeming with colour and life, attracting diverse plants and fish species seeking safety from predators. A jungle needed to act in much the same way upon a wreck – after the human predators had come first to strip it.

They traversed the last stretch in heavy mist and reverent silence.

Any minute now, we might discover it.

When they did finally stumble upon the first identifiable trace of the *Lady Lily* – a single motor not quite concealed in the wet heath – Tally realised at once how wrong she had been to have imagined the wreck as some solid, hulking thing, still distinctly airplane shaped, albeit draped with green vegetation.

In reality, the wreck was more akin to an overgrown scrap-metal yard. In the soupy white fog, among bent, grey tree trunks, it was a spectral sight.

On the dark and stormy night that the *Lady Lily* had ploughed into the west-facing peak of Mount Teasdale, the aircraft had exploded on impact, the resulting wreckage strewn over hundreds of feet. There had been eleven souls onboard, Drew told her. No one could have survived such a thing.

Tally crouched down before the motor, dizzied as much by hunger and fatigue as the awe of discovery. After so many years replicating that X on her Dara map doodles, *here she was* – and how utterly surreal it felt.

Her hands were shaking as she took out her camera, and after a silent plea for forgiveness from whatever ghosts might still be lurking, began to snap.

Through the mist and drizzle, they discovered what remained of the fuselage another few hundred feet up the rise, on a stony plateau. A twisted hunk of metal was embedded in the rock face, choked by vines, gripped by the trees that long since had grown around it. The name and registration number were still discernible on the metal crumpled around the escarpment like a crushed sardine tin.

Tally and Drew stood together in a winded sort of quiet, absorbing the scene.

'You were *right*,' Drew marvelled.

Tally shot him an exasperated smile. '*You* were the one who solved my lifelong puzzle.'

'It was *your* map.'

'And *your* knowledge of local wartime wrecks.'

'How about we couldn't have done it except together?'

Tally tipped her head against his shoulder. 'Deal.'

They divided here, both lost to their own examinations. Tally's camera was the only sound in the eerie hush. Even the army of mosquitoes swarming hungrily upon them in the fast-fading light feasted in silence.

Tally thought she would be eaten alive before she was done.

'I think I've got almost everything I need,' Tally called to Drew from her position kneeling beside the fuselage. *Almost*, because she wished she had an entire day at the wreckage site gathering powerful imagery for her piece.

What she hadn't found, in the last hour of frantic documenting, were personal effects. Except, and how very strange it was, a woman's red stiletto. Just the one, mouldering away deep in the heath. There were no women onboard, according to Drew's research. Had it been a serviceman's intended gift for his wife?

Whatever other artefacts might have survived the fiery crash and the harsh years that followed – watches and dog tags, suitcases and reading glasses, not to mention hundreds of thousands of dollars – had been pilfered long ago from the site. How many times had they stripped the site? And what had they done with their ghoulish souvenirs?

Drew came to stand beside her. 'Salvage of the main wreckage won't be feasible.'

'No,' Tally agreed, not looking up from her viewfinder. 'I suppose they mean just to bury or destroy the identifying pieces – the name and numbers – try to make it look less like a plane.'

'But why would your father order a cover-up *now*, after all this time?'

At this, Tally's finger paused on the shutter button. 'Isn't it *obvious*? He knows he's losing Dara.'

'How should that be obvious to me?'

'From the moment my father realised Ma had left him, he knew his time on Dara was limited. He had to destroy as much of the evidence as he could before she came back asking for a divorce and division of assets, and ultimately, for his removal from her island.'

'You don't think she knew about the *Lady Lily*, then?'

'No, she never knew.' Tally believed this to her very core. 'The hatred Mack harbours for my mother proves it. She's always been an impediment to their plans, not a collaborator. They've had to keep it hidden from her for over twenty years.'

Tally pushed up from her haunches, holding her camera against her cheek, thinking hard. 'Mack lived on the Hat, and he was active round the archipelago during the war. I think he was the one who first spotted or discovered the *Lady Lily*. He told my father about it, and after he married my mother, they had as much time as they wanted to find and strip the wreck.'

'How do you think Mack knew it was here?'

'I'll *show* you,' she said, taking him by the hand to stand by the steep edge of the plateau, peering seaward. There, below: Dara's smaller isle.

'The *Lady Lily* was just visible from the Hat.'

Drew looked sceptical. 'It's pretty thickly vegetated, and if it was so visible, other planes and boats would have sighted it, too.'

'When the sun sets over the mainland, the last rays hit Mount Teasdale in such a way to make this rock face almost glow, but the effect is only seen when you're standing on the Hat. A metal object, like a fuselage, might give off a strange glint, even if only for a few minutes per day.'

Drew nodded. 'Do you think he was the only one to see it?'

'No one else was supposedly on the Hat in forty-two. Most of them moved back to the mainland, after the Artists' Colony disbanded. Fell apart, more accurately, after Mack tried to take over the whole commune.' She tipped her head with a sudden realisation. 'Wait, Irene Threadwell might have still been living over on the Hat in nineteen forty-two as well.'

Irene. Always there, lurking at the edge of every story.

Irene, Grandpapa's mistress, who bore a secret heir to Dara, and who alone was with him when he died.

Irene, *still* here, more than two decades later, while Ma was not.

Tally pulled on her backpack, tugging the straps firmly, needing to feel the weight of her bag. Inside, Grandpapa's will-in-a-bottle: safe from Irene and her father.

Drew was hoisting up his own backpack. 'You right to go?'

'Just one or two more shots I want to get,' Tally said, 'then I'm ready to skedaddle.'

But they were out of time.

From far below them, came a distant but resounding echo – stone on stone, and timber cracking – something heavy was toppling from a great height, taking trees with it.

Tally looked to Drew in mute distress.

'Displaced boulder, I'd say – in the ravine we circumvented.'

'Knocked down by one of the others coming up after us.'

'Perhaps. We'll need to go *now* if we want to avoid them.'

There was no perhaps about it; Mack and his crew were less than two hours behind them.

Time to get themselves the hell away from this wreckage.

Later, Tally would come to torture herself with if-onlys.

If only they'd left the wreckage of the *Lady Lily* a half-hour earlier, when they still had a little light and some time to hide. If only they'd moved faster, pushed harder, gone in another direction; any other than the one they'd chosen. If only Drew had not twisted his ankle, if only she'd made him turn back, gone on without him; if only she'd never asked him in the first place …

It might have made the difference between life and death.

CHAPTER 30

MERMAID OUT OF WATER

Eyrie, 1946

Nerissa dreamed she was on the *Bluebird*, once more, carving through a glassy sea: the sun scorching bright on her skin, white plumes scudding across the horizon.

She lay flat on her belly upon the foredeck, a hand flung out over clear water, blue rippled shadows on white sand. She was watching a green sea turtle drift alongside, refracted light strobing its large shell. Ever so gently it floated to the surface, face upraised to the light, large black eyes eternally wise.

The *Bluebird* took a sudden lurching turn. She felt the shift through her whole torso, from pelvis to breast, adrenaline charging her limbs. A dark cloud had covered the sun. Her skin, suddenly damp, was chilled and goose-fleshed under a fast-rising wind from the west. Clouds raced towards the gathering tempest, a ferocious indigo.

The turtle had disappeared beneath the boat. Nerissa pushed up on her forearms, peering for her turtle, crying out in alarm. The boat was breaking up beneath her. There was a wrenching twist in her abdomen, as though she was splintering with it.

She was splitting, falling. Someone was calling her name, over and over, dragging her into a fast-moving rip, taking her far from the satin sea, the sand cay, the *Bluebird*.

'Nerissa,' Richard was shaking her shoulders. 'Wake up! You've wet the bed!'

'It'll be hours yet,' Irene soothed, her hand on Richard's shoulder. 'There's still plenty of time to make it there and back.'

Nerissa, bent over Eyrie's brand-new marble kitchen benchtop, was pushing him away, slapping at his hands, kicking and moaning.

He straightened, despair in his eyes as he turned to face Irene. 'She isn't due for another six weeks! I can't *leave* her, what if something goes wrong?'

Irene was unmoved. 'Then something would go wrong with you standing uselessly by, unable to do a thing. Or are you suddenly a doctor?'

'I won't be back for hours, and that's if I can even find that fool Barry on a Sunday! *Curse it!* I should have put her on bedrest, even if I had to lock her in our room. I let her do too much, Irene. If only she'd just listened to me and gone to Brisbane sooner. The best doctors in the damned state waiting to deliver her, and here she is about to give birth on the floor like some poor village girl!'

Irene snatched his hand from where it covered his eyes, forcing him to take in her drilling gaze. 'Listen to me, right now. Labour will go on for hours, yet. You've got time if you leave immediately. You're wasting your chance arguing with me. Dr Shand goes to church every Sunday – it's not so hard to find him, if you go *now* ...'

'That doddering old fool,' he said, fists clenched. 'I didn't want him anywhere near Nerissa. And now I'm forced to rely on him?'

'Every minute you stand here, you could be another one closer to the mainland. You go and find Dr Shand, and you bring him back to Dara. We'll still be right here, labouring away.'

'She'll be alone!'

'She has *me*.'

At this, Nerissa launched into another moan, already cresting a new wave.

'All right, he's gone,' Irene said, coming into Papa's cottage, where Nerissa had insisted on being carried by Richard before he departed.

'It makes no sense,' he'd protested. 'You've got every modern convenience a woman could ask for up here at Eyrie – why would you go to an old shack?'

'Because it's my *home*,' Nerissa had said, lips drawn back from her teeth. She'd made the turn to full-throated feral cries. It had been little more than an hour, but she knew: it would not be long. This baby was determined to be born, and she needed Richard far away from her, first.

'Eyrie *is* your home now,' he had insisted, with more pleading than Nerissa had ever heard from him. But to his credit, he'd mounted no further opposition, carrying her to Papa's shack without so much as a stumble. Had it not been a Sunday, there would have been construction crews swarming everywhere, working on Richard's new resort. Even Mack, Richard's right-hand man, was missing from his beach hut.

Pain split through her. She felt Irene draw near to her side, busily spreading out a medical kit. There was a smaller shape hovering at her side.

Delila.

Nerissa groaned, reaching back for the little girl, feeling the warm, satiny flesh of her small hand, before it was whipped away by Irene.

'You go and play outside now.'

'I can help, I'm a big helper.'

'You mustn't get in the way, off you go.'

'I want to help!'

Crashing once more into a winded heap, Nerissa panted, 'Please, let Delila stay. I want her with me. It's only right that she should see her –'

'*Lila*,' Irene barked. 'Go outside and play.'

When Delila had trudged down the front stoop, Irene's hand locked vice-like around Nerissa's wrist, her voice every bit as tight and unrelenting. 'You stop this right now, you little idiot. Do you understand me?'

'Please, Irene,' Nerissa whispered. 'It's not too late to speak up, I'm sure of it. Richard loves me, he would understand why I had to conceal the truth …'

'Lila is *my* daughter. That's what we all agreed. It was Bertie's wish, as much as yours then. You're just letting your new maternal feelings overpower you. You wanted no part of motherhood, and I've raised her as my own in name and deed. You won't be taking her back off me now to play happy families with Richard. And if you think he's just going to accept a secret bastard as his stepdaughter, you've got another think coming.'

'I could at least *try*!'

'You could, and when he loses that unholy temper of his and sends Lila and me away out of spite and jealousy – what will you do then?'

'I'll never let either of you be sent away. All of us will stay together. I promised Papa, I promised *you*.'

'Then shut your damned mouth and keep your promise to the both of us!'

A new howl lifted Nerissa up onto her knees.

Surfacing from a fresh, dumping wave of pain, Nerissa realised Irene had disappeared. Where had she gone? *I can't* do *this alone …*

Delila.

Nerissa stood and staggered to the door, calling out into the grove of coconuts. 'Irene! Delila, where are you? I need you …'

No answer.

She waddled slowly down the front steps, one hand on the banister, the other poised near her groin, ready to catch the great, aching weight bearing down. A pressure irresistible.

'It's … coming …' A garbled sob.

There's no stopping this baby.

She went into the blinding light beyond the palms, towards the small, twirling figure backlit by glittering turquoise.

Her bare feet, long hardened to Coral Beach, did not even baulk as she lurched heavily towards Delila. Pain had delivered her into madness: if she could get to Delila in time, if she could only reclaim her, this agony would stop …

'Delila,' she gasped, reaching for the little girl standing at the shoreline.

Behind her, she heard Irene's aghast cry, hastening after her. 'Nerissa! What the hell are you doing?'

Too late, too late, too late …

Nerissa dropped to her knees as the immense insistence of life bore down upon her.

She had whited out with pain and blinding sun-glare. And now there was a baby screaming, somewhere near her feet, where warm water rushed in, tinkling.

Nerissa had collapsed backwards onto the towel laid hastily down, coral moulding to her spine, moving beneath her. Irene was crouched below her waist, fussing and swearing, her head only partly blocking the sun so that light cut Nerissa's vision intermittently. 'For Chrissake, of all the bloody stupid things for anyone to ever do … pushing a baby out into the sea! If your husband finds out what you've done, he'll call you unfit to be a mother – he'll have the baby taken away from you!'

Nerissa struggled up onto her elbows, desperate to see the new creature wailing in their midst. What was Irene *doing*? The baby would be drowned or swept away!

'Lie still,' Irene commanded, 'I've got to cut the cord. Lila, run and get more towels, quickly, *go*!'

Nerissa fell back, whimpering now with need. *Let me see my baby – please!*

She'd never known such yearning the first time. Irene had taken that baby directly, as instructed, and never once had asked Nerissa to fulfil a single biological duty. Dara's own goat's milk, diluted and sugared, had sustained the child, while Nerissa had kept her glad distance, waiting for all the sore and swollen parts of her to recede. The baby's mild squawks did not stir her at nights, nor draw her close in the sun-drenched days.

This baby's cry, harshly demanding, seemed to seize and twist a vital part of her, somewhere behind the centre of her breastbone. She ached to answer it, to fulfil her purpose.

At last, the baby was brought up to her chest. 'It's another girl,' Irene huffed. 'And you know he wanted a boy.'

Nerissa strained to take in the squalling face below her chin; dark blue eyes, inch-long tufts of brown hair. 'Oh, her hair is like Richard's.'

'Yes, she'll pass,' Irene clucked. 'Got a temper like his, too, by the sound of her.'

The baby was attempting a crawl, rooting and snuffling against her chest. Nerissa gave a hiccupping laugh, realising what she was after, nudging her towards the nipple. 'No goat's milk for this one,' she proudly declared, and did not miss Irene's sourpuss face. Was this the start of some strange envy?

Lila crunched down the coral, with towels brandished high. 'See, I'm a big help!'

'That you are,' Irene said, flapping open the towels to clean and cover mother and baby. 'Now I have to help Nerissa with this last part.'

Nerissa was aware of Irene's ministrations only in periphery, her commands to push obeyed distractedly. All her focus was on the baby nodding open-mouthed at her nipple.

Lila had come to sit by her head, and was gently stroking the baby's hair away from the tiny, curled shell of her ear.

'Is it a girl?'

'Yes.'

'Is she my sister?'

Nerissa squinted up at Delila's face, trying to read her expression. Had she guessed all by herself?

Irene answered this, quick and firm. 'She's not your sister, Lila. You're not even related. She's Nerissa's baby, and you are mine.'

'What's her name?'

'Well, I have yet to choose a name. Would you like to help me?'

'She looks like a turtle but she doesn't have a shell.'

Nerissa laughed. 'She does indeed. But I don't think Turtle is her name. What about Thalia?'

Delila and Thalia. The perfect sister set, though they'll never know it.

Delila nodded sagely. 'I like it.' She bent closer to examine the baby, delighting as her finger was gripped. She peeled back the towel to peek, grimacing at the fleshy protuberance of the baby's umbilicus.

Gently, she lifted Thalia's foot in the palm of her hand, and Nerissa smiled at her rapt wonder.

'She's a mermaid,' Delila marvelled.

'She was almost forced to swim,' Irene sniped.

'Her toes, Mum,' Delila said, pointing.

Irene leaned over Delila's head to see, holding the baby's two feet together and looking between them with dismay. 'She's only got eight toes. Her second and third toes are joined, on both feet.'

Nerissa tried to raise herself again, already knowing what she would find there – for she had seen it before. She took in the sight of those webbed toes, a tiny, perfect miniature of her father's feet, and eased back against the sand, unable to hear Irene's comment for the blood roaring in her ears.

So, there would be no chance of self-deception, no way she could pretend that this daughter was her legal husband's child, simply born early. She had to go on now, *knowing* and always fearing that Richard might come to know, too.

Irene's words cut through mercilessly: 'This won't pass muster. How do you intend to explain this?'

Nerissa lifted Thalia's feet from her hands and laid them tenderly against the soft, rolling flesh of her own belly. 'It's just a little birth defect, nothing more. Perhaps I took too much sun during the pregnancy . . .'

'I see,' Irene said, 'just like that, then.'

Nerissa was reinstalled already at Eyrie, propped up in the fresh, white sheets of her marital bed, by the time Richard and Dr Shand came burring back over the sea.

The expectant father had been gone less than two hours.

Irene turned away from the window to face her, and Nerissa did not miss the marionette pull of lines around her mouth. 'He'll be here in ten minutes.'

'You're *afraid*,' Nerissa breathed, not meaning to say this aloud.

'And *you* should be too.' Irene's small, pale eyes drilled into hers.

'Afraid of my own husband?' She broke eye contact, gazing down instead at the babe now slumbering in her arms after a period of such peering alertness it had made Nerissa giggle with wonder. 'She looks like she's trying to learn the secrets of the world in the first half-hour.'

Irene's reply had dashed the giggle from her: 'Better get used to it. You've got a lifetime ahead of you hiding secrets from that child.'

Irene came to fuss over her sheets. 'Have you got your story straight?'

Nerissa lifted her chin. 'I don't have a *story*. I just have a baby girl who came a little early and is already taking her brunette beauty from Richard.'

'And has deformed feet to delight her cuckolded father, too.'

Cuckolded? Was that what her husband was now? A shivering grimace passed through her.

'Have you decided on her name? Or will you let Richard have some small part of creating this girl?'

'Her name is Thalia Bluebird.'

A hiss of outrage close behind her head. 'Don't be *ridiculous*! I know you're not that stupid, Nerissa, though I'm starting to think you *are* that reckless.'

Nerissa shifted her warm bundle away. 'It's just a *middle* name, what does it matter?'

'You'd better smarten up quick, girl. You've made your choice, and you've got a long road left ahead of you. Our island depends upon your ability to stay the course.'

'Naming my daughter is jeopardising Dara now?'

'No, Dara will always be ours, but your marriage is the difference between a wood shack and a white palace, and you know it.'

Sometimes she hated Irene. Despised her so much, she could tear Papa's will to shreds, bake it into a cake for Irene and then watch her eat it unaware.

Nerissa heaved a mulish shrug, unwilling to concede. 'Her name will be Thalia Blue, then.'

Today, Nerissa had planned a prison breakout. For two weeks she'd been cooped up in her bedroom, going mad from her husband's doting attention, Irene's dogmatic directives, even the new housemaid's fiddling and faffing. Why did she need a housemaid anyway? They'd managed quite well all this time without one, so why should some silly mainland girl need to be brought over to meddle in Nerissa's domestic affairs? She made a mental note to talk to Richard again about it. She was no invalid, not even the slightest bit grazed from Thalia's birth, and she needed no looking after, much less this level of pandering. She intuited that Richard was overcompensating for having mistimed her removal to the southern doctors and then missing the birth itself. He was trying to redeem himself as a husband and new father, she understood that, but it didn't make the house arrest any easier.

If only Dr Shand hadn't come toting antiquated ideas, Richard might have been persuaded not to wrap mother and baby in cotton wool. And what could she have said in her defence? *I didn't spend a day in my bed after the birth of my illegitimate baby. I was out in the fresh air and sunshine straightaway, free as a bird ...*

Thalia was asleep, and while she slept, Nerissa intended to go for a wander along the beach. Only, was it all right to leave her baby behind at Eyrie? Richard would hear Thalia cry if she were to wake, and surely he would not ignore it? He'd already proved himself quite infatuated with the tiny girl who had his brown hair. He would make a loving and attentive father for their daughter, indeed for all their children to come; she was sure of it. Yes, she decided, it was safe to leave Thalia with her father nearby, but how funny to be grappling with these questions that she'd never needed to think about with Delila.

She made it as far as the hallway, before second-guessing the choice she'd made and turning back at a run. By the time she reached Thalia's bassinet, she was convinced she had committed some catastrophic breach of maternal duty, revealing her fundamental inadequacy. How *could* she leave her own baby behind like that, all alone in the world?

At least Thalia seemed unaware of it. With heated cheeks, Nerissa picked up her sleeping baby and nestled her into the crook of an arm. They would go together to the beach.

On the ground floor, there was no sign of Richard, not even in his office. And to think she'd nearly trusted him to watch her daughter! Guilt quickened her steps out of Eyrie.

And whom should she meet on her way down the hill, through the warren of treehouses under busy construction, but Mack. The man seemed to have come with her marriage, like an unwanted wedding gift; impossible to send back. He was hardly absent from Richard's side, constantly advising him on some thing or other behind the office door that was always closed to her. He crawled all over her island – even the furthermost reaches of Dara's wilderness – without anyone to check him. All too well, she remembered how he'd tried to take over the Artists' Colony, and how the community had scattered altogether after the vote to evict him had failed.

But there was only one person now on Dara who wanted Mack gone, and no one was listening to her. Even Irene, who should have been on Nerissa's side, agreed wholly with Richard that Mack was indispensable for the future.

'Mack is vital to our plans for Mermaid Bay,' Richard would say whenever Nerissa made her timid intimations.

But vital *how*? Nerissa had more than enough ideas to contribute of her own, nearly all of them shot down or shelved to some future date she hadn't much faith in. And just whose island was it?

It doesn't matter, she would soothe herself, *I'm keeping my promise to Papa. That's the important thing. Mack won't be here forever . . .*

At the sight of her coming down the path, Mack stopped, blocking her way forward.

'Well, well, if it isn't the little lady and her happy bundle. Congratulations, Nerissa, on the birth of your daughter.'

'Thank you,' she said with a half-hoisted smile. 'We're very happy.'

'I *bet* you are,' he said, eyes dropping to the baby in her arms. She shifted Thalia ever so slightly in her muslin wrap, putting her tiny upturned nose out of his sight. This man should have nothing ever to do with her daughter.

'It must be good luck,' he went on, 'to bless a marriage so quickly with a child.'

'We think so,' she said calmly. 'Richard was as impatient to be married and begin work on Dara, as I was to be a mother.'

Mack nodded slowly, his eyes now set on hers. 'And I hear you've nabbed naming rights for our resort, too.'

'I suggested the name, yes.' *Mermaid Bay*, for the small mermaid born on Dara's shore. Richard had loved it straightaway. He had been nursing Thalia when she brought it up, and there could be no pretending such delight as his. 'Once Richard heard it, no other name would suffice.' *Especially not that ghastly 'Treasure Island' you petitioned for.*

She watched the top edge of his lip curl – just enough to leave her in no doubt of his contempt for her. 'You've got him exactly where you want him, haven't you?'

Nerissa laughed, masking the hard swallow. 'It's a bride's right, isn't it, to have sway over her husband?'

'It won't last,' he said.

'No, probably not,' she agreed. 'But I'll enjoy it while it does.'

Mack began to move past her, stopping just as he was within a hair's breadth of her so that she could feel the heat of his body, and smell it, too. He looked down at her and Thalia.

'You always did enjoy it, though, didn't you? We didn't call you the Whore of Dara for nothing.'

Nerissa glared at him with cold disdain. She was the wife of *Richard Ramsey*; Murphy McLeod had no power to hurt her, no right to threaten her.

Be bold, you must not falter.

'You should be careful, saying such things in front of my husband – he'll wipe that smug look off your face. You'll be evicted from Dara like that –' She clicked her fingers. 'Don't forget, you're on *my* island.'

Mack smiled at her, a perverse glint in his eyes. 'Richard is indebted to me, much more than he'll ever need you. And should something ever happen to you, this island becomes *his*…' Mack leaned forward, peering hard and close at Thalia.

'Fortunate for you,' he said, 'that this one looks like Richard.'

CHAPTER 31

SKELETON CREW

Mount Teasdale, 1968

Almost as soon as they left the plateau, nightfall covered the jungle, completely. They were scrambling fast down the steep escarpment now, in fog and darkness, with Drew in the lead. They kept their torches sweeping low and short on the ground ahead of them. Going downhill was even worse on an injured ankle, as Tally soon deduced from the sharp hiss of Drew's breath. She wondered how he was managing to hobble at all, even with his walking stick.

They were veering ever to the right, having agreed to take the longer, circuitous route around the west cliffs to Mermaid Bay. They needed a safe place to rest as soon as possible, but if they didn't get far enough away from this peak before the other crew came up the ridge in front of them, they'd run smack bang into one another.

And how were they meant to guess which direction Mack would take around the ravine? They knew now that the others were travelling at a far superior speed, as they had caught them up in less than a day. Tally's worst suspicions had been proven right: while she and Drew had been chasing sleep and other pleasures, Mack's crew had been pressing on through the night.

Drew pulled up abruptly in front of her with a cry of shock and pain: 'Watch out!'

Tally dug her heels in, just managing to avoid walloping into his back. Her first thought was that his ankle had given out entirely. Her torch beam went to meet his, finding the sudden, plummeting mountain drop-off, three feet ahead of where he stood, concealed by heath. He had so very nearly taken them both over the edge.

'Are we back at the ravine, already?'

'Nope, another drop-off.' In daylight, they would have seen it coming – and how many more cliffs and escarpments lay just ahead of them?

'Tally, we have to stop,' Drew said. 'We're thumping around making noise, risking falls. We could get lost.'

'We should have left the crash site earlier,' Tally seethed. 'I got too greedy!'

There was no chance of finding a place to make full camp now, they would have to make the best of whatever cover they could find. The area below this cliff overhang was as good a shelter as any from the ceaseless drizzle, not to mention the others coming uphill.

They clambered down the slippery slope to the small concavity beneath the outcrop. Here, they crouched in the dripping, pungent dark, sodden to the bone, each sore and sorry for the other.

Tally ran her torch and gentle touch over Drew, seeing every insect welt and leech blood stain, all his cuts and bruises. She wanted to strip him down and tend to each abrasion. The most he'd let her help remove, though, was his right boot. She chewed her lip to prevent a gasp of pity at the sight of such ugly bruising and swelling, even in the darkness.

Drew was more interested in seeing Tally fed and watered. 'You've got to eat,' he pleaded. 'You've been surviving on nothing but nuts all day.'

Tally was too exhausted to muster hunger pangs.

They spread out their wet clothes to dry on a boulder, made a token effort to eat and drink, cleaned up the best they could with washcloths, then took to their bedroll, together. There was no question of anything more than sleep tonight. And not even that for Tally. She lay on her side with Drew curled protectively around her, awake long after he had fallen asleep. His steady breath stirred the hair at her neck, as wind rolled across the canopy like surf. Somewhere nearby, a stream flowed, promising a shower and canister refill in the morning.

One thought ran over and over through her mind: *I have to get my evidence safely back to Mermaid Bay. They cannot catch us first.*

Tally awoke in the pale light preceding dawn, missing the warm cocoon of Drew's embrace. She sat up, straining to see him, hoping to hear his voice.

He was gone.

She struggled urgently out of their nest of blankets, kicking the sleeping bag away. Standing up brought a sharp intake of breath, every muscle in her lower limbs aching. Wincing, she moved out of their small cave, whispering his name. 'Drew, Drew – please, where are you?'

'Tally,' came his low reply. 'Over here.'

She followed the direction of his voice, to find him seated on a log, towelling off beside a small spring.

'Damn,' she said, smiling. 'I missed the show. You should have woken me. I'd have liked to join you.'

He returned no smile, however. Indeed, his face looked very, very serious.

'What's wrong?' she asked, instantly alert.

Drew's eyes dropped to his ankle and foot – grotesquely swollen and blackened.

'Oh, Drew.' She hurried to his side, kneeling before him to examine the foot. 'How bad is it?'

He took a long moment before replying. She knew then that there would be no more stoicism, only truth.

'It's bad. I can't even hobble. I had to drag myself over here. I thought an aspirin and a cold shower might shock some numbness into it, but I'm afraid I'm done.' He steeled himself. 'Tally, you're going to have to go without me. I can't get down this mountain without help.'

'No,' she said, quite calmly. 'If you're staying, I'm staying with you. I won't leave you here alone.'

'I'll be perfectly fine alone for a few days. I've got ample water here, you see. And I have enough food, if I'm careful. Shelter, too.'

'Why can't I stay?'

'You need to get yourself and your evidence safely down, then go straight to the police.'

'Won't it be better by tomorrow, if we just rest here for a day? We'll go slow.'

He took her hand, making her look properly at him. 'Tally, I think I've got a serious injury and it's not going to right itself overnight. With rest and medical aid and crutches, I could get along a nice flat path, but I can't manage this terrain.'

'We can stay two more nights, then. Wait for a passing ship and then signal like crazy.'

'*Tally.*'

'Fine, I'll build a stretcher and carry you down.'

'All by yourself?' At last, a shadow of a smile.

Tally felt her lips droop. 'We're safer together.'

'I wouldn't push you to go back alone,' he said, 'if I didn't think you could do it. Without me, you can move fast and stay out of sight. You're going downhill, so you'll have a much easier run. Half the time it took to come up.'

'In my note to Lila, I told her to call the police if we weren't back in a week. If we just sit tight, help will eventually arrive.'

'You told Lila we were trekking up to Mount Teasdale?'

'*No*,' Tally admitted, letting her misery show. 'I didn't even leave a clue where we were going.'

'Well, then.'

She stared at him, beginning to notice more than just the firm insistence of his expression – the tired glaze of his eyes, rosy flush of his cheeks. She reached up, laying the back of her hand against his forehead, as Ma would always do for her. His skin burned.

'You have a fever,' she accused. The real reason he'd dragged himself to the cold spring. She saw he was sorry she'd guessed it. 'Why do you have a fever?'

'It's not too bad,' he said, and his return to stoicism frightened her more than anything else.

She stood up, knowing exactly what she needed to do next. There was a third option neither of them had mentioned.

'Okay,' she said. 'I'll go and get help.'

She did not say from whom.

A fuchsia band was expanding over the sea by the time Tally got away. After helping Drew back to the outcrop, she made a show of setting him up for the next few days until help arrived.

Leaving Drew behind would have been too difficult to bear if she didn't have her plan already in mind. They would be apart no more than a few hours, she swore.

'Stay here,' she said in parting. 'I'll be back in a jiffy.' Then she covered his weak smile with a fierce kiss.

Now, she had to walk into a den of thieves and ask for help.

How? her mind boggled. *Hello, fellas, would you mind breaking off this criminal cover-up to rescue my lover? He's been helping me expose your federal crimes, but now we're in a spot of bother, just need your help getting off this mountain. I'll repay your assistance, if you don't kill us both, by taking my evidence straight to the police …*

Tucked under the belt of her shorts was Drew's machete, pressed upon her with as much doggedness as she had forced the last of her tinned fish and beef jerky onto him. Her bag was lightly packed, keeping the bare minimum for her speed and safety.

As she jogged down the heavily wooded slope towards the ravine, on a path straight for the crew who'd been pursuing them for days, she wondered if she'd given away her sanity right along with her heart.

Within an hour, she had located Mack's crew, following the smell of woodsmoke. Evidently, they were not concerned about revealing their own position.

They were encamped on a quiet outcrop above the ravine, close to the edge. The stone-ringed campfire around which they sat showed this was a well-used campsite. Here they had a sweeping, open view of the forest chamber below, including the bottleneck that she needed to pass through. Tally grasped, heart sinking, that there was never any way she could have snuck by without being seen.

That was always the crew's plan, wasn't it? Wait them out. She and Drew had been under siege without even knowing it. Though, it was hardly a crew – only Mack, Angus and *surprise, surprise*, her father. He was so desperate to contain the secret, he'd come himself.

She saw that he experienced no such astonishment at the sight of her, sliding quietly into their midst. '*Tah-li-ah*,' rolled off his tongue as arrogantly as ever. 'How nice of you to finally join us.'

'Oh, was I invited?' she said. 'I thought this was a cover-up.'

Tally felt her shoulders square, fists ball, chin thrust out to meet his look. How old would she be before she outgrew this feeling?

She looked at the other men, but found she could not hold Mack's unnerving scrutiny. Angus was much easier to glower at, although he did not quail under her stare.

All too late she realised that she was still in possession of her camera and notebook full of incriminating evidence, and Ma's ship-in-a-bottle. Fear traversed the nape of her neck with a ghoul's stroking touch. If they searched her, if they confiscated her backpack, she stood to lose her story and her inheritance.

But there was one person more important than all of it, and she would do anything not to lose him – even supplicate herself before her father now.

'Where's your little friend?' Mack said, cutting to the chase.

She opened her mouth to begin her petition to their humanity. Then closed it – *knowing*, with the searing instinct she'd always prided herself on, that there was no way she should admit to Drew's condition, nor his whereabouts.

Mack the knife, she'd intuited, the first moment she'd laid eyes on him.

She twisted her lips into a scornful smile, at odds with the fear clanging behind her breastbone. 'We went our separate ways,' she said, 'divide and conquer, you might say.'

'Bullshit,' her father dismissed. 'That's her lying face.'

Tally shrugged, smile still twisting. 'He left at sundown, and is already twelve hours down the mountain. You'll never catch him now.'

'He didn't, we would've seen him,' Angus cried, with a conviction that made her think he had been assigned the night watch.

'You're right, he *didn't* come this way,' Tally said. 'He's taking the track down the west slope. It might be slower and harder, but he's got a significant head start on *you*.'

'What west slope track?' scoffed her father. 'You're still bullshitting.'

'Ma didn't tell you *everything* about my island, did she?'

She observed the twitch of his left eye, even as his jaw hardened.

Her father signalled to Angus. 'Search her.'

Angus rose and moved towards her. Her old bully, doing the Bullshark's bidding – it was almost poetic.

Tally stepped back, a hand on the machete at her waist. 'Don't *touch* me.'

Angus stopped in front of her, his back to the men, and put out a hand. 'Give it over.' His voice was firm, but in his eyes she spied anxiety. He was well and truly in over his head.

Exploit that …

She fixed her eyes on him. 'They're *using* you,' she said, fast and low. 'You think they're ever going to let you leave this island now, knowing what you do?'

'Shut your mouth.' Her father's deep refrain; she'd heard it a thousand times before.

'No.' She didn't even look at him. Her focus was set on Angus.

'They're the ones who robbed the *Lily*,' she told Angus. '*You* still have the chance to walk away from this. They'll never be able to hide what they've done now. Drew is on his way to the police with our evidence, as we speak. They're done and they know it. Every moment longer you stay with these desperate men, the more you risk your own life.'

Behind Angus, Mack stood. Despite her resolve, her eyes flicked over Angus's shoulder. The unhurried menace of Mack's smile and posture made her stomach plunge and contract. Every word of what she'd just told Angus, she'd meant to embolden herself. For the next critical few minutes, she needed to imagine Drew fit, strong and healthy, and well on his own way to safety.

Mack came over to the pair at a stroll that was anything but leisurely. Dread climbed the walls of Tally's chest. She swung her Bunsen-burner look now on her father. 'You've finally lost your damned mind, haven't you? So blinded by possessiveness of Dara that you're willing to see your own daughter manhandled by a pair of goons. You sick, sad man.'

She saw this arrow land.

He hasn't lost all humanity – yet. Keep going, say more like that . . .

But it was Mack who cut in. 'Dick doesn't *have* a daughter.'

Tally's eyes flew to Mack, her mind racing to understand what he meant. 'Is that supposed to be a threat?' Her laugh was as hollow as she felt. 'You can't get rid of me any more than you can the *Lady Lily*. Multiple people know where I am and what I'm doing, including my editor.'

If only *that were true. If I hadn't let determination do away with my common sense, for once in my bloody life . . .*

Mack cocked his head at her father. 'Tell her, Dick. What are you waiting for? *Tell* her why she doesn't mean anything to you, why she never has. Let this *whore's* daughter know exactly how unimportant she is to you.'

Tally looked to her father, but Richard's eyes were on the ground. She perceived the heaviness of his broad chest, the way it slumped his shoulders – and knew.

He isn't my father.

Richard Ramsey is not *my father.*

And he's *always known it.*

'Oh my God,' she said, unable to keep the emotion from her voice. 'Is that why you've hated me all my life?'

He did not reply, would not look up.

In her periphery, she saw Mack's grin spread wide.

She stepped around Angus, past Mack, keeping her backpack safely turned away from these men, her eyes locked on Richard.

'That's why you sent me away from my island,' she said. 'And why you hounded me whenever I was here. It explains why you never wanted me to manage your resort. You didn't want me to inherit Dara after Ma, because I'm not *your* daughter ...' Her voice rose with every realisation won, each step nearer.

Richard's face lifted now to stare at Mack shifting slowly in on his left side. Countering her move. She had advanced to within a yard of Richard.

'That's why you're here, isn't it?' she goaded. 'Because you hate me.'

On the other side of Richard, Mack hawked a spit. *Oh yes*, Mack thought he was in control here, but he may have underestimated Thalia Ramsey's power to spur on the man who had raised her.

'I suppose you've come to supervise my removal from Dara, *once and for all*. Seems like something you would do, you sad, pathetic man.'

At last, Richard's eyes snapped to hers. She did not find in them the dark rage she was expecting, nay intending to incite. Something, instead, far more vulnerable ...

Sorrow.

'I am pathetic,' he said. 'I spent over twenty years trying to win a woman who would never love me back, pretending to myself all the while that I didn't know my only daughter couldn't possibly be my own, and that everything I was building here eventually would be given away to my wife's bastard.'

'No *wonder* you hate me,' she said, taking one last step forward, bringing her closer to him than she had been in many years. Near enough to touch. She could smell the fruity tang of his coffee breath, the spice of his favourite soap.

'I don't hate you, Thalia,' Richard said. 'From the moment I first held you, I swore to love you like a real father.'

'Guess *that* didn't last long.'

'I've always tried. You and I were never suited to one another.'

'The problem, old man, is that we are too much alike. I might not be of your blood, but I got my determination from you all the same.'

Mack's laughter rang out, hard and cruel. 'You finished with this pretty little family moment?'

From the corner of her vision, she checked the gloating in his eyes, comprehending this: Richard was as disposable to Mack as she was. If she did not make her move now, there might be *no more* Ramseys left on this island.

She braced herself. 'If there's any part of you that still cares for me as a father, you'll let me walk away, right now.'

Mack issued a hard snarl. 'You think we're going to let you run home and tell on Daddy?'

Tally kept her eyes locked with Richard's, refusing to let them drift to Mack's implacable fury. 'Let me go,' she said. 'Your lie is finished. You've already lost Dara. Harming me won't save it for you now.'

Richard went on staring at her. Behind those brown eyes were machinations she would never fully understand, not as long as she lived. Rallying the fierce determination at the core of her, she said, 'I'm going to leave now, and you're going to make sure, come what may, that these two men don't harm me.'

There was a fast, drawing-out motion from Mack. Her eyes flicked for one second to the right. And there it was, as she had foreseen: *Mack the Knife*.

The large blade was levelled at Richard, a scarlet-scarred bicep taut above it. 'You try to let her go, Dick, and you're *both* dead.'

Tally's heart spasmed under her ribs. Richard's eyes did not leave hers. Only his lips moved. A single word, mouthed.

Go.

Tally did not pause to second-guess this instruction – the first and last command she would ever obey, unhesitatingly, from her father.

She sprang to the left, out of the blade's reach, as Richard swung right, towards Mack and the ravine, with an almighty roar.

'*Ruuuuuuun!*'

She ran.

CHAPTER 32

FREEFALL

Tally was running for her life. Adrenaline had sharpened her senses to a supreme awareness, seeing each branch and rock and root and turn before her with acute clarity. She could not afford to stumble, nor lose direction. All her thoughts and vision were now on forward motion, on staying upright, on survival. Everything depended on putting as much distance between herself and those men as possible, no matter what happened on that ravine behind her.

She crashed down and around the bottom of the ravine on momentum alone, but it was fear and determination that carried her scrambling up the other side, out of sight.

Tally had not been caught by the time she reached the top of the ridge, so she pushed right on, tracking the path by sheer instinct rather than memory. She gave no heed to the noise her progress made. Speed was everything.

Travelling downhill was, as Drew had promised, infinitely quicker than slogging it uphill. But now she felt it was more controlled falling than running. At the bottom of this long ridge, she knew she needed to find the next creek as fast as possible.

Only exhaustion could halt her, and that was a long way off.

Tally did not stop moving until darkness slid over the island, the risk of injury or misdirection proving greater than her determination, which would not wane while ever Drew was stuck on a mountain with murderers.

She was heartened to have covered such a distance, and had seen and heard no sign of pursuers. The creeks were running after the recent rain, and her water canister was never empty.

She made camp just off the creek, laying out the bare essentials for nutrition and sleep. She lit no fire for herself. She had taken only Drew's hammock and insect cover, and she luxuriated in the smell of him, buried deep in the fibres. It was no embrace, but it would hold her through the night all the same.

One more night, she soothed herself on repeat; a desperate lullaby by which to sink into a dreamless void.

By the end of the second day, she was back at Zara Falls. She had sighted the bay below, and knew it was within reach by the end of the following day. Her adrenaline had waned enough that a million other fears had come to torment her, instead.

As she settled into her humble campsite, freshly bathed in the infinity pool, myriad bites and wounds, stings and bruises now made their presence known. Misery, too.

Zara Falls was no longer the oasis she remembered. Without Drew here, the place held no charm. She felt like she was marooned on the last island on earth.

Long after she had eaten her protein, she lay wide awake in Drew's hammock staring up at the impervious, turning stars. Even the moon had set its face coldly against her.

Please, God, let Drew be still alive up there, beholding the same sky.

She swung out of the hammock with a morose sigh and went to sit on the log seat. From her backpack, she took the torch and impossible bottle, and occupied herself with a perusal of the ship and Ma's tender repairs. The torch beam made all new shapes and grooves of the vessel within.

She saw the name, immediately. How could she have missed it the last time? Etched new on the sailboat's starboard side, in glossy, carved letters...

Bluebird.

Tally mouthed this name silently, over and over again. It was enormously important for some reason she already knew but couldn't quite seize. Some story her mother had told her, once? No, that wasn't it. Some clever play on Tally's middle name?

Tally felt Drew's shoulder nudging against her own, saw again the comforting fire blaze before them. They were sitting together, right here, when he said...

I can tell you the name of his boat – the Bluebird.

Whose boat? she demanded of the warm memory seated beside her.

Flynn something.

Right, and why was that guy important again?

He said his webbed toes were a family trait, going on three generations, from his great-grandfather down.

The bottle dropped into her lap as Tally lurched forward to grip her toes.

The Bluebird's *skipper, Flynn, is my real father.*

Oh, Ma.

Discovering the truth of her paternity while her legal father might be lying dead in a stinking, bat-shitted gorge – *because of her* – felt cruel beyond measure.

No wonder Tally had been so healthy despite being born six weeks early. She wasn't really early at all. Ma had tried to pass her off as Richard's, and he'd seen through it.

But he'd wanted Nerissa, and Dara, too much to admit it. And *there* was the great lie hidden beneath the Ramseys' marriage, and Tally's whole life, like a vast ship languishing on the deepest sea bottom.

Tally sagged forward, covering her face with her hands. The impossible bottle, lolling in her lap, tipped off and rolled along the ground to stop, tinkling, against a rock.

Far be it from Tally to read a bottle's mind, but this one was screaming out to be smashed open.

With her teeth gritted around her torch, Tally walloped the bottle against the rocky ground. The sound ricocheted around the top of the falls, yielding nothing. She thwacked it again, mightily, determined to have her answer.

The bottle shattered, and the ship that had been always just out of her reach, a promise tantalisingly close, was beached upon the rocks.

Without a second's delay, Tally flicked open her Swiss army knife and sliced the ship, bow to stern. It was a vicious stroke, and she felt no remorse for it. She peeled it open, shadows bumping with the shake of her hands. Would she find a hull as empty as her mother's word?

Within the belly of the ship, lay a scroll much yellowed and furled with age.

She smoothed it out and fixed her eyes on the bold handwriting inside, so unlike her mother's delicate penmanship. Her grandpapa's last will and testament ...

I entail my island, Dara, to my only daughter,
Nerissa, and her daughter, Delila.

CHAPTER 33

BLUEBIRD

Dara Island, September 1967

In the dark observatory, footsteps sounded overhead. A booming voice, unmistakable. 'Nerissa? Nerissa! Where are you?'

Her husband's heavy step approached the stairwell, her lover's heart still thudding against hers ...

Flynn pulled out of her and away from her so suddenly, the loss felt part of Nerissa's innermost being. Then he was gone, the cold void engulfing her as she slid down the wall and into a ball. She heard Flynn taking the stairs two at a time.

He's going to intercept Richard. For my *sake.*

She cowered in the blackness as her heartbeat tripled. The smell of her was surely all over Flynn; Richard would clock him where he stood!

Her ears strained.

'She's not here, Richard. Only me. Checking I hadn't left my snorkelling gear in the storage cupboard.' Flynn stood at the top of the stairwell, blocking her husband from coming any further down into the darkness. Lying on her behalf, sparing her the most traumatic of confrontations.

But could Flynn really prevent Richard from barrelling past him? Not likely.

The profound blackness undersea was a cloak of safety. Nevertheless, she shrank back hard against the wall, expecting at any moment his descent. And then how long would it take him to hunt her out in the darkness? She imagined his great hands reaching for her face, her neck ...

'Where the *hell* is she, then? Irene said she came down to the jetty!'

Nerissa's mouth hinged open with a silent cry of betrayal. *She would rather throw me to the Bullshark than let me be happy?*

Flynn's reply was unrattled, his position unyielding. 'Can't help you, Richard. I'm not your manager anymore – it appears you'll have to find someone else to keep a check on your wife in future. And now, if you'll excuse me –'

'Don't you *fucking* walk away from me!' Richard's response was thunder in such a small space. 'I'm going to check your boat!'

'You're afraid your own wife is stowing away on my *Bluebird*? If she was that determined to leave you, why wouldn't she tell you to your face?'

It was a message for Nerissa. An entreaty.

Come upstairs now and end it. I'll take you away from all of this, but you must be brave enough to come up those stairs yourself.

She ought to have charged the staircase. *To hell with Dara, to hell with Papa's wishes, to hell with Tally's hopes ... just go, now! End every lie. Take the chance you should have taken the first time ...*

'If she's not on your boat,' Richard snarled, 'then you won't have a problem with me going onboard ... will you?'

'Be my guest,' Flynn said. 'Says a lot about your marriage, doesn't it, mate?' Just goading enough to drive Richard out the door.

Nerissa followed heavy footfalls across the ceiling. One set, only.

Flynn remained near the head of the stairs for a protracted moment.

Waiting for what? Richard to be at a safe distance up the jetty, so that she could make her escape? Or for Nerissa to take hold of her courage and emerge to stand beside him.

The latter, she knew.

Knew it and stayed just where she was, silent and frozen still, while Flynn's footsteps moved slowly across the ceiling overhead. She heard him turn the lock inside her door before he shut it after himself, enclosing her safely inside.

She stayed long after Flynn's footsteps went down the jetty to the *Bluebird*, long after Richard stampeded back up the jetty towards Mermaid Bay, no marital stowaways found, straight past the dark, locked observatory.

She stayed until she heard a sailboat's motor, stayed until she no longer heard it. Stayed until it was sleep rather than cowardice that kept her below.

For the second time, her *Bluebird* had sailed without her.

And then what?

Nothing.

Not a thing to bring her a mite of joy or any hope for the future. A nothingness that seemed to consume her from the inside out. Her regret like a crown of thorns starfish: many-spined and envenomed.

Small and cowardly she had remained, hidden in a grotto of despair, for month after month …

Until one day, there was a knock at Eyrie's front door and a timid Lila standing on her front step, with a polite request to be reassigned accommodation.

It was an excuse, of course it was. Lila might have been tired of living with Irene, but she never would have dared go against her mother's wishes unless she thought it might help the woman she had idolised from afar for so many years. Lila had braved Richard's censure just to check on his fast-fading wife.

More than that; to *reinvigorate* her.

Nerissa thought that she could never have broken free from such spellbinding despair, had it not been for Lila's courage. And courageous it was. Lila was risking her job on Dara to even approach Eyrie, asking after Mrs Ramsey. Richard had never been more vindictive or cruel to his staff, any hint of critique or disapproval of his rule, much less his manager's, squashed as quickly as a midge's bite. People might whisper about Mrs Ramsey's melancholy – she'd caught wind of it – but they lived and worked under the dark bluster and malicious retaliation of Mr Ramsey's gloom.

In this way, Nerissa understood she was making not only her husband, but the whole island sick by her unhappiness.

As she and Lila worked together over the weeks that followed, turning that disused chapel back into a home, they had grown close again for the first time in over twenty years. It was *Lila* who, unknowingly, had helped her to see: by releasing herself from Dara, she would be freeing all of them.

In Lila, Nerissa had caught a tiny, precious glimpse of her own young self, when she still had believed in the dream of Dara. In Lila now, Nerissa saw Dara's future. The way it was always meant to be.

Nerissa knew Tally would never understand, not the way Lila instinctively seemed to, and she made no attempt to write and explain it to her. No good could come from bringing Tally Ho charging home.

Nerissa needed a chance to make her plans for escape. And she couldn't afford to give those plans away to anyone – not *even* Lila, though she had more right to them than anyone. It was too risky. Should Irene catch wind of Nerissa's intentions, there was nothing that woman wouldn't do to protect her twenty-six-year investment – she had proven it before.

Lila was steady enough to guide the ship after Nerissa was gone – as long as she was given just enough to hold the course when Tally inevitably barrelled in, looking to blow it all open, starting with that ship-in-a-bottle.

Between them, she hoped the girls would muddle it out.

She was convinced: for Dara to flourish, Nerissa had to leave. For *Nerissa* to thrive, she had to chase down Flynn …

It was, like so many times before, as though Irene had read her mind. Had smelled the flaming courage and resolve in her, and determined to extinguish it.

Early one afternoon, Irene appeared on the steps of Lila's new home.

'Lila isn't here,' Nerissa said uncomfortably. She oughtn't have been there herself. Despite having officially handed the keys over, there was always some little thing or other she found to do for the cottage, and for Lila. Today, it had been washing and ironing a new cloth for Lila's table.

'I'm not after Lila.' Irene planted herself on the bottom step with her unnerving stare, blocking Nerissa's exit. There never *was* any getting past her. 'I came to pin *you* down.' Her jaw was set dangerously. 'I know what you're up to …'

'Oh?' Nerissa summoned up guileless confusion, though she was sure her terror showed plain as day.

'You've been *avoiding* me.'

'Not on purpose,' Nerissa lied. 'I've been very busy, that's all.'

'Busy trying to take *my* daughter away from me.'

On the contrary, Lila is trying to take herself *away from you.*

'Lila approached me for a place of her own, and I couldn't refuse her request.'

'Couldn't you?'

'It's natural for a young woman to want her independence, Irene.'

'Don't talk to me about what's *natural* in a young woman. *I* raised a good and obedient child. The daughter *you* raised is every bit as screwed up as you were!'

Nerissa's lips drew tight. 'I was a lonely, isolated, motherless girl, if that's what you mean, too young to raise a child of my own. Then to lose my father before I was even twenty, and with a sprawling island foisted on me …'

'The same old sob story that always ends with you sitting up there in a white palace, wanting for nothing, with a wealthy, powerful husband pandering to your every need.'

'I'm so lucky. Gave up real love and hope of happiness to live with a tyrant and have him run roughshod over me and my island.'

'*Our* island.' Irene's stare was pitiless.

Nerissa met that piercing look and did not flinch from it. 'I haven't forgotten your claim on me, not for one single day since.' Her voice shook.

'Good,' Irene crowed. 'You can't take back a promise!'

Did she mean Delila or Dara? Both. They're one and the same to Irene Threadwell.

Irene stepped up, far too close now, hard eyes unblinking in their great pouches. 'So, whatever sneaky, selfish thing you're up to now …' Her glare was inescapable. 'You remember: I won't *ever* let you go back on your word.'

Nerissa blinked rapidly, fighting the urge to scream her secret intentions into Irene's face. *I am leaving, and you cannot stop me this time! You can't force Delila to live with you, and you can't steal her inheritance from her. You'll have to try to wield your blackmail elsewhere now and you won't win easily against my Tally Ho …*

Nerissa steeled herself. 'For so many years,' she said, teeth set with quiet fury, 'I thought of you as a sister, mother, friend, all rolled into one. I believed you had cared for me at a time when I had no one left in the world, with only my best interests at heart. But all the while, you've been a *parasite* on Papa and me, and on Dara. You've cared nothing for my misery, so long as it benefits *your* position and stake here. They might call Richard the Bullshark, but *you* are the remora who first attached her suckling self to him and you're not letting go, not for anything!' Her throat ached with the courage it took to say such shocking things. She drew a ragged breath. 'You have manipulated me for long enough. From now on, you just leave me the hell alone!'

She pushed forward, shouldering Irene aside, and went out into the blazing light of the afternoon.

There was no more time to waste.

That very night, she penned two letters: the first, to be left on Dara; the second, a goodbye letter for Tally Ho, to post once safely on the road. She packed a small knapsack of possessions, light and easy to carry, and placed the smallest clue she dared to leave behind in her secret hat-pin pocket. Then, she took her escape out of her bedroom window, across the rooftop and onto the melaleuca bough stretched out to her like a hand of mercy.

The instant her bare feet hit the ground beneath that tree, she was running for her life. Her freedom, her *love* …

Airlie Beach, March 1968

She had been on the road for nearly a fortnight, slowly tracking her way down the Queensland coast by bus and train, calling into every beach town along the way, asking at pubs and yacht clubs, marinas and jetties. Her wanderer's refrain at every stop: *I'm looking for a boat called the* Bluebird.

She trudged into the waterfront pub in the sleepy town of Airlie Beach to ask these locals the same without much expectation. Flynn had been gone for six months; he might be anywhere in the world by now. Unless he was deliberately dragging his heels, waiting for a day he thought would never come, why should he still be in Queensland waters?

'I'm looking for a boat called the *Bluebird*,' she told the bronzed, broad-shouldered publican behind the main bar, near empty on a Tuesday mid-morning.

'Are ya now? Flynn Barrett?'

'Yes ... yes,' she managed to squeeze out in the crush of winded lungs.

'Flynny not happy enough taking all the pretty girls in our town, ay? Now he's bringing them in from other towns, too.'

She didn't need to process this point right now. If Flynn had been dallying with women from Bellen Beach to Airlie, what right did she have to feel betrayed?

'I'm Nerissa,' she said. 'It's very important that I find him.'

The publican considered her. 'Lucky Flynny,' he said. 'Let me ask some of the fellas when they start coming in this arvo. But the last time I saw him was over a week ago, heading back out to sea. He hasn't been in here since.'

She wasn't sure whether to be dismayed or delighted. *He was here only a week ago ... he's already a week gone!*

'I'd be so very grateful,' she said. 'I have urgent news.'

'Righto,' he said. 'I'll do my best for you. He did stay briefly at the caravan park while his boat underwent some maintenance. You could ask after him there.'

She had gone directly to the caravan park, where she drew on her ever-dwindling funds to secure a night's accommodation – and a lead on Flynn.

Yes, that's right, the caravan park owner confirmed, Flynn Barrett had stayed a couple of nights on land, but he'd since moved on to the Whitsunday Islands. Left a tip, which was more than you could say for most. No, he couldn't tell her *which* island – the bloke had a sailboat, didn't she hear him say? He could be anywhere!

So now, to wait.

Nerissa had settled into her single-room unit with wild hope and humble expectation. Why should she ever deserve to find him again? She had allowed him to sail away not once, but twice.

Three days after their first encounter, the publican himself wandered up to find her in the campground's open-air kitchen. 'Got a tip for you,' he declared, standing over her picnic table.

Her spoon, stirring a mug of tea, trembled to a stop.

'Some fellas saw the *Bluebird* off Stockyard the other day. If you're quick, you might still catch him.'

An electric current coursed through her. 'Pardon me, but what is *Stockyard*?' It was barely more than a whisper.

'Stockyard Beach, on the western side of Haslewood Island.'

'Is that ... far from here?'

'Not too far, a day's outing. You got a boat?'

'No.'

'Plannin' to swim after him?'

'Something like that.' Her throat ached to cry.

'You want a lift, then?'

She let go of her spoon. 'With *you*?'

The publican looked impatiently at her. 'See anyone else offering to help you?' He stuck out a hand. 'Name's Michael. If you want me to take you out, we've got to go right now.'

Nerissa stood, pushing back her teacup, and shook his hand. 'Yes,' she said. 'Please.'

Michael's boat was a motor vessel named the *Katana* that had seen some better days – according to Michael, the best days any man could have. They seemed in agreement that the *Katana* was no less than a winged chariot today.

Michael had grown more garrulous with every mile they went. She realised he was shouting over the engine for her sake, though she wished he wouldn't. His kindness required her to keep nodding and smiling, when all she really wanted to do was to stand and scream into the buffeting wind …

Flynn!

She only knew they approached Haslewood Island when Michael started jabbering on about sheep once having grazed on it. *Sheep* on a tropical island? It made no sense, but then neither had much of his prattle.

Nerissa distinguished the chalky-white line of a deserted beach, the indigo shadows of abundant coral fringing the island. And then, the silhouette that had haunted her dreams not just for the last six months, but the two decades before it.

The *Bluebird*, rocking gently at anchor.

She didn't think Michael could possibly hear her exhalation over the boat, but somehow, he knew to turn his head to her at that very moment, catching her in that moment of sagging astonishment. 'That's the birdy you're after?'

Her look was answer enough.

He nodded, gratified. 'There you go, then.'

She waited for Flynn to emerge from the cabin, if not with some psychic sense of her arrival, then at least the sound of another vessel approaching.

Nothing, and no one, stirred on deck.

The engine slowed to a putter, as Michael drew them right alongside. Still no sign of life onboard. She spied Flynn's trusty red dinghy; he was surely there, so why did he not come bounding up? Her eyes scanned the beach in case he had swum to shore.

The devil whispered in her ear: *What if he's below deck right now with some new woman? One too smart to ever let Flynn Barrett sail away.*

Cutting the engine, Michael was beginning to mirror her uncertainty. He gave her a nudging nod towards the *Bluebird*.

She opened her mouth, but her crumpled face did the talking.

I can't. I can't. I can't. The silent mermaid, fixed and frozen in her glass cage.

His brows came down heavily, and she registered Michael's irritation in the way she'd always marked Papa's frustration – and quaked beneath it.

Papa.

He who'd carted his daughter to a faraway, deserted isle, but had neither the wherewithal nor stamina to foster her flourishing upon it. Papa had bought Dara seeking escape from the arduousness of work and his crushing mental fatigue, but had discovered his own nerves ultimately inescapable. The same man who had struggled to modulate his moods and emotions in the city found himself again on that island. He was capable of as much cold neglect in a warm land, and this time Nerissa had no other adults from whom she might draw succour – no teachers or housekeepers, not even any friends her own age.

She had sought whatever comfort and company she might from those folks on the Hat, her only companions for so many years. In time, she'd found puppy love there, too, with dear Walter.

Idyllic, Tally would come to describe her mother's childhood, refusing to hear of her emotional floundering, her loneliness and her most hidden desire: a life beyond the insular world prescribed her.

Nerissa had not been first trapped on Dara by Richard Ramsey. It was Bertie Forster who had brought her to that sea-ringed prison and locked her in it. With what? Nothing more than a promise: *I'll keep Dara for you, come what may.*

She might have left at any time. She'd come within a sliver of freedom, once, when Flynn had sailed into Dara's waters and had asked her to leave with him. She'd nearly given her father's island away to Irene Threadwell, just to escape Papa's will and her promise to him.

What took her so long to realise she could free *herself*?

Michael was done with her strange silence. She saw him make a move and thought he would restart the motor, take her away again without her ever opening her damned mouth.

Instead, he was calling out on her behalf. '*Ahoy there*, Flynny – you in?'

Water burbled around the hull. No answer.

He lifted his chin to shout again, but Nerissa reached out a hand to stop him. Then took two fingers to her lips and let out a shrill whistle.

Once, twice, a third time.

There was a single splash on the starboard side of the *Bluebird*, then an answering call. Michael and Nerissa both raised a hand to their eyes, straining to make out the figure in the sun-sparkled water, stroking around the stern of the boat.

Flynn.

He stopped, treading water, pulling a face mask up onto his forehead to reveal his bewilderment.

Her cupping hands dropped from her eyes, revealing her own face, framed by loose honey waves.

'*Riss?*' His eyes went to Michael behind her. '*Mick?*' Back to her again. 'What are you doing here?'

'I want to go *with* you.'

'What about Dara?'

'Dara can't hold me anymore.'

His smile was one of disbelieving wonder, as was hers.

'But what about Tally?'

'What *about* her?'

'Were you ever going to tell me that marvellous girl was *my* daughter?'

Her heart plunged. 'How – how did you know?'

'I met a young wreck diver here in the Whitsundays who couldn't stop talking about Tally Forster from Dara Island. He told me about her toes, just like mine.' A shadow of pain passed over his bright-lit face. 'Why didn't you *tell* me, Riss?'

'You had long sailed on from our archipelago by the time I guessed.'

'I haven't been able to move on from this one since I found out.'

Nerissa stood up. 'I'm coming with you.' The boat rocked beneath her as she clambered up onto the bench seat.

Come what may.

She was glass breaking, a bottle opening, a scroll unfurling.

She leaped, limbs starfish-splayed, skirt billowing wide, out into the blue.

He must have stroked towards her even as she flew, because he was right there when she surfaced.

They met in a clashing of lips and legs and cleaving arms that surely seemed, to their bemused onlooker, like a drowning embrace.

CHAPTER 34

HEIRESS FOUND

Dara Island, 1968

Tally had gone up Mount Teasdale a star journalist, chasing the biggest story of her life, but she was limping back down sans a father, an inheritance and a lover.

The *pursued*.

The sun rising over the Coral Sea in cloud-piercing resplendence of gold and lilac lit upon a forlorn figure struggling down the last, long ridge. She had been walking already for hours, unable to sleep a minute on that plateau of broken bottles and dreams.

She moved unseeingly over the creek bed, unthinkingly through each jungle tangle. Fatigue was all she knew now; a blizzard wiping out everything else.

Even determination failed her. Only the basic animal instinct for survival, the weakest of homing signals, drew her step by step, closer to home.

It wasn't even her home anymore.

With her mother vanished, this island belonged to her secret older sister, the real mistress of Dara ...

Delila.

They caught her close to Table Rock. Too late she heard them coming, trampling and slashing through the rainforest. She'd run across this whole island, only to be captured an hour from Mermaid Bay. Now, she needed to hide for her life.

Tally cast her eyes around this dense corridor of forest, terror thudding in her breast.

Hide me, hide me, hide me.

There –

On her right, a few yards off the creek bed, a mouldering, fallen log, long enough to encompass her whole body. Once a rainforest giant, the tree had lain here for so many years that it had been rotted out by microbes, fungi and insects to form a hollow centre.

Get inside.

She scrambled over rocks to the log, throwing her backpack under some nearby heath. Feet first, she squirmed and squeezed herself down into the tree. It was only just wide enough; she felt every inch of bare skin pulling and scraping against the wet, decaying wood. For a heart-stopping moment, her head and chest still sticking out of the log, with the sound of male voices almost upon her, she met resistance at her feet.

She kicked and stomped, pushing all her body weight until the obstruction gave way – *thank Christ!* – then she wriggled down until she was hidden, right up to her hands cradling her brow. Hidden, yes, but trapped too. Should they find her here, there was no way of escape.

The men entered the clearing, sticks cracking heavily underfoot. Tally tried to slow and space her breathing, but she was gagging on the smell of decay, suffocatingly thick, and the crawling of her skin, as if a thousand worms moved against her.

If this was how it felt to lie in a grave and decompose, no wonder Grandpapa was forever trying to climb out of his.

Tally lay entombed, breathless as a corpse, and waited for them to pass her by.

But soon after they had passed, they came again, rocks rolling under feet, deep voices at a murmur.

They know I'm here. They can see my bag in the undergrowth. I must have dropped something on my way through. They can hear my heart ...

They stomped right by her tree, no break in stride, going straight on. Then returned, almost as quickly.

Tally's mouth opened to release a silent scream of frustration. What were they doing on this infernal loop? Tormenting her before capturing her?

A third time the footsteps crunched by, at a faster clip, their voices louder – and unfamiliar.

Through fear-spent cognition, she finally comprehended: it was not two men hunting her around a grove, but rather a column of men walking by her unawares. And they weren't coming down the rise, they were going up.

More of them arrived, stomping after the last, conversing with fresh energy and purpose. This party had to be a dozen strong ...

Rescue.

From within the tree, one voice stood out among the others, blessedly familiar: soft and lilting, sensible and kind. A voice Tally had known from inside Ma's womb and recognised as that of her sister, even before the concept had a form.

My sister, Delila.

Tally began to struggle again, this time forward. Grunting and pushing and wriggling to free herself, beginning to cry out – a sound muffled by the log walls. She was desperate to flail and punch, shocked that the log didn't somehow break open under the force of her determination.

Finally, her head was through, but her hips had rotated; like a cork, she was wedged in tight.

She kicked with fury, hollering, 'Lila! I'm here!' convinced the party had gone too far to hear her. 'Lila, come back! Please, help me!'

'*Tally?*' Footsteps crunching, branches scraped back, and there she was, leaning around in front of the hollow tree, green eyes agog.

Lila's face cracked open in a smile of blazing relief. Her words, however, were wonderfully wry. 'Didn't you think to take a tent?' She reached for Tally, beginning to pull.

Dragged out, Tally collapsed on the ground to lie in a heap.

Lila began to shout, 'I've got her – I've got Tally!' She traced her fingers over Tally's bruised and battered body with such tender concern in her eyes, it brought an answering ache in Tally's throat.

An ache that grew to her jaw, spread to her chest, sent a burning heat rushing up behind her eyes and nose. A curious seizure had taken hold of Tally's torso, making her heave and shudder, uttering choking gasps.

The commotion had drawn a crowd, strange faces peering, their number growing. A walkie-talkie squawked and crackled, emitting a tinny voice. Through the blur of backpacks, walking poles, boots and machetes, she picked out police uniforms, volunteers from the Bellen Beach Lifesavers Club, even Shep.

Lila had brought in the cavalry.

Tally tasted salt. She lifted her hands to her cheeks to feel the warm wetness running freely from her eyes.

She was weeping.

CHAPTER 35

LILA SPEAKS

'How could you possibly know where to find me?'

Lila's laugh lifted to the ceiling of Eyrie's grand verandah. 'You're not the only one who can solve mysteries, Tally. Besides, you bumbled around dropping all sorts of clues.'

'Name just *one*,' Tally cried, half sitting up. '*Owww –*' She fell back onto the rattan couch to a dry look from the doctor suturing a cut on her thigh.

Bellen Beach had a brand-new lady doctor now, and if that wasn't outrageous enough, Dr Liz Chappel was young and modern, with a blonde bob and warm brown eyes. Dr Liz had been attending to Tally's many abrasions, cuts and contusions for almost an hour – after Tally first prescribed herself a mostly medicinal brandy – proving herself frank and unflappable in the face of Tally's frustration.

Tally had tried in vain to foist herself on Drew's rescue party. It was a preposterous idea. In her state, she would be the worst kind of hindrance, but still she'd battled.

They had taken her detailed instructions and a hastily sketched mud map, and Shep had gone on in her stead, promising to bring Drew back. Then, once again, Lila had chaperoned her home.

Tally refused to admit any other scenario into her mind but Drew's safe retrieval and their reunion. The women had been back at Eyrie for a few hours, and though Tally knew it would be days yet until she saw Drew, she already had one eye trained on the garden terrace for his appearance.

Not just him.

What about Mack? Could he still come after her, even here?

A lone police officer was waiting on standby down at Mermaid Bay to take Tally's report, just as soon as she was done with Dr Liz, but would he be protection enough against a man who could fight off both a box jellyfish and a Bullshark?

She could not shake the fear that crouched on her shoulders, dark and taloned, whispering, *Run, run …*

Surely, her father – Richard – would walk up the pathway at any minute. She didn't know how to turn off the ear so long tuned for his gait on the cobblestones.

Ironically, she might have been glad of Richard's guard birds this time, but the cage lay empty, the door hanging open. In his last act before departing for Mount Teasdale, Richard had released those demon birds, along with Olga.

Tally felt sorry for the birds. They'd known nothing but captivity, and how would they survive outside it?

How will any of us?

She winced at the needle doing its work. She would have quite a few scars after this. Probably no more beauty pageants for her.

Forcing her attention away from her thigh, she said, 'Walk me through these so-called clues I left.' *The nerve of her.*

'Righto.' Lila smiled. 'Well, first, your editor showed up.'

'*What?*' Tally clenched nails into palms to stop herself from leaping up. 'My editor came *here*? *Jonathon?!*'

'Mr Tremblay said he'd been expecting a call from you, and that you're nothing but punctual – sorry, pushy,' Lila teased. 'He was sitting on some tremendous information for you, and a *warning* about one Murphy McLeod, a person of interest in a murder case in Western Australia dating back ten years. He didn't want to give me the gruesome details. When Mr Tremblay didn't hear from you, he figured you'd gone and thrust yourself into the story again –'

'Rude.'

'His words. Anyway, he thought he'd better get down here and see if he still had a Girl Reporter, or if he had to find another intrepid woman to run rings around the rest of his newsroom.'

'You're quite the mimic, aren't you?'

'He's had us in stitches at happy hour. I've grown fond of Mr Tremblay.'

'He's married, Lila, and far too –' She boggled. 'He's still *here*?'

'We put him up in one of our best treehouses. He said he was overdue an island holiday. The man *is* awfully pale …'

Tally balled her fists again, longing to run and see him. Just *wait* until Jonathon heard the story that she had for him! She would start writing it the very instant she got out of this makeshift hospital bed. Her mind already was leaping ahead to compose her stunning lead, but Lila was going on again …

That's right – the clues.

'After Jonathan arrived, I was all fired up. I knew something must have gone awry, but I had to first figure out what. Things started falling into place pretty quickly. From your note, I knew you were with Drew and how long you expected to be. From the Bellen Beach Yacht Club, I learned Drew's boat was in the marina and he was planning to be on land for a week at least, confirming you were both still on Dara. Drew and I had talked about trekking Dara Island while we were dancing the other night, and he was *awfully* uncomfortable discussing the idea, so I guessed *that* was what you must be doing together. But the *why* took a bit more work.

'I figured Mack's return to Dara after so many years, right when Mrs Ramsey had disappeared, could be no coincidence. She lived in terror of Mack ever coming back. She thought he had some diabolical hold over Richard. Her, too, if you ask me, indeed everyone on this island. But how funny, I thought, that my mum had no such fear of the man. An anomaly. Why would she of all people be immune? I went to the source to find out.'

The source? *God help us, Lila's been moonlighting.*

'It was like my mum had been … *waiting* for me to finally figure it out.'

'I got the same feeling when I spoke to her,' Tally said.

'Stop me if I'm covering old ground.'

'You might answer my last questions.'

'Yes, well, as it turns out, my mother and Mack go a very long way back.'

'To the Artists' Colony on the Hat. I'm aware.'

'Indeed, they were lovers over there, decades ago, but then it seems there were a lot of lovers on that island, if you catch my drift.'

'Yes, even my ma had a young lover in the colony.'

'Lucky for *me*, I suppose,' Lila said, her face deadpan.

Tally could scarcely believe what she'd heard. She shook her head to clear the stolid, cloudy feeling between her ears.

Lila took pity on her bafflement. 'Oh, surely you know this part.'

'I do, but *you're* not supposed to. I was waiting for *my* big reveal and now you've gone and spoiled it.'

'It seems I scooped you.'

'Does sound like the sort of thing an older sister would do.'

Lila leaned forward, her brow knitting, green eyes earnest. 'Do you mind, Tally?'

'When I was tiny,' Tally said, 'I thought you were like the sister I'd always wanted. I only mind that we didn't get to grow up in full knowledge of it.'

Lila's reply came by way of a crushing embrace. With what little air was left to her, Tally said, 'I have a photo of your father here, if you'd care to release me.'

Lila drew back, boggling at her.

'I stole it from Mad Ginger.' Tally opened the backpack close by her side; she had not once allowed herself to be separated from it. Her hand bypassed the scroll inside with a tiny tremble of anticipation. *Soon.*

She proffered the photograph. 'The young man standing right next to Ma – his name was Walter Isaac. Last seen heading off to war, to escape our grandpapa's vengeance.'

Lila held the photograph close to her face, eyes poring over young Nerissa and Walter. Tally let her have the moment.

'No wonder I'm not very tall,' Lila allowed finally. She looked up with a smile, eyes brimming. 'Thank you, Tally. This means the world to me.'

'I have a far bigger revelation for you, but first you have to finish your story.'

Lila nodded. 'So, between them, Mack and my ...' She looked uncertain.

'Irene,' Tally affirmed.

'Irene,' Lila repeated, 'shared a dream of taking Dara one day.'

'Whoa, what? Skipping ahead, aren't you?'

'Not at all. Life in the colony, on that tiny isle, wasn't grand enough for either of them. Lot of free love before it was in style, but no real money, comfort or property rights. And there they were, staring at the vast island of Dara, day in and day out, uninhabited, except for an old man and his strange, lonely daughter.

'There had to be a way to get a share of it, and they both circled around, trying to find a way in. Mack assisted Bertie with physical labour, trying to make himself indispensable, while Irene struck up a friendship with Bertie's daughter, vying for something more intimate with Bertie. Neither of them would have succeeded in their plans. Bertie was notorious for his possessiveness, over both daughter and island. He wasn't letting either go, come what may.

'Bertie hadn't reckoned on me showing up, though. A big old problem growing by the day. Mrs ... Nerissa was determined to go to the mainland to have me, then give me up for adoption. She didn't want a bar of motherhood, or me.

'It's all right,' Lila added, seeing Tally's face. 'We're sisters, but we were born to very different mothers. Anyway, Bertie was dead-set *against* Nerissa going over. He must have feared she'd get a taste of life outside their isolated home and stay there. Meet some mainlander and settle away from him for good. Here, Irene spied her chance. She offered to take and raise the baby herself, so long as Bertie provided a roof over her head and an island under her feet. Easiest solution, Nerissa thought, in her naivety, and she agreed to the bargain. Wasn't Bertie chuffed! No chance of Dara ever going out of his hands, even after death ...

'I was born, and Irene claimed me as her own. More accurately, claimed her share in an inheritance. For a couple of years there, she really thought she was home and free. Bertie even brought in Mack, his friend – and hers – to survey a plot for a house of her own, just down the beach. As soon as the war was over, Bertie said, they'd get right onto it.

'About this time, a property baron by the name of Richard Ramsey arrived, with his eye on Irene's prize. Richard was the biggest threat she'd faced yet, but she saw him turned away time and time again by

Bertie. She watched Richard fall in love with Bertie's daughter, and a new idea, an even longer plan, began to form.

'It was Nerissa herself who would prove the impetus. She was beginning to talk about stretching her wings, wanting to experience some of the world outside this insular place. She wanted to escape *me*, more than anything – seeing me trapped here, like she was, a mini-Nerissa in the making. Bertie understood this very clearly, the wily old coot, and he started making noises about Irene moving back to the mainland *with* the baby. If it came to choosing, he was keeping his *daughter* with him.'

Here, Lila stopped to gather her thoughts, looking thoroughly parched. If there were any maids left in Eyrie, Tally would have rung at this juncture for tea.

When Lila began again, she slowly enunciated every word. 'It was lucky for Irene, then, that Bertie Forster passed so suddenly, and shockingly, before she was ever forced to leave. Lucky his death put the three of us left on Dara in such dire straits that another plan, already well thought out, should provide the perfect answer.' She stopped now and stared at Tally.

'Good lord,' Dr Liz put in, without looking up from her work. 'What kind of town have I moved into?'

Tally couldn't help herself; she sprayed laughter. All that tear-letting she'd done earlier seemed to have opened some dark and inappropriate hold.

Control regained, she said, 'I came to understand the luck of Irene Threadwell after I beheld her fine collection of shells.'

'She's a psychopath, I think.' This, from the girl Irene had raised. The hair on Tally's arms spiked up hotly.

'With Bertie Forster out of the way,' Lila went on, 'the island was now Nerissa's and Irene's – or at least, *she* thought. But what could they do with it all on their own? They had no real money to put in it, no vision for infrastructure. The main island might have been bigger than the Hat, but it was still deserted. They needed to attract investors.

'With perfect timing, Richard comes sailing over again – with his good mate, Mack, in tow. Just as Irene had planned. Nerissa and Richard were each under pressure to make the deal – the union, I should say. Irene and Mack had been working the same long game from opposite angles. It was a marriage of convenience for four parties, with an unholy alliance behind it. Mack knew *exactly* how far Irene would go to get Dara, just as she knew how he planned to safeguard the island for Richard and himself.'

'The *Lady Lily*,' Tally said. 'Mack showed it to Richard and was blackmailing him with it.'

'But once he'd made his wealth through Dara, Mack didn't care to stay on the island. He had a talent and hunger for wreck-stripping – though he'd call it salvage work. Before Mack departed, he left a souvenir for Irene. Insurance, should Richard ever try to throw her off Dara.'

Lila put her hand in her pocket, then held out something.

In her palm, a steel tag, with letters and numbers stamped onto it. The cotton tape, once securing the tag, long since rotted away in the jungle.

Tally strained forward to see. 'It's an American soldier's identification tag.'

'A dog tag, I believe they call them.' Lila placed it in Tally's hand.

She turned it over, reading the soldier's name and serial number, his blood type, a home address many seas away, and the next of kin who had waited decades for their questions to finally be answered.

Her eyes brimmed again, ducts flowing freely after years of dereliction.

Lila was not done yet, reaching into her pocket for something else. 'Mack gave Irene this trinket, too.' She held out a man's watch, the glass shattered, leather strap burnt and degraded, two hands stopped at the moment of impact.

The time: eleven minutes past nine.

The moment the *Lady Lily* went down.

Minor surgery finished, the women were settled back together now on the lounger, Tally's feet propped up on a stool. They had made their own tea. Dr Liz, apparently loath to go, was still making extensive medical notes on the rattan chair opposite.

It was time for Tally's denouement. She inhaled deeply. 'Ma used Richard, too, in her own way. It's just lucky for *me* that he did want to marry her, given Ma's preference for sending her illegitimate babies to the mainland for adoption ...'

She searched Lila's face for astonishment at this, and did not find it.

'Flynn Barrett,' Lila said simply.

Tally shook her head. 'Irene had known *that*, too. What *power* she's held over Ma ...'

'Irene seemed to think so.'

'How Ma must have *felt*, with my secret father walking around right under Richard's nose. No wonder she wanted me far away from Dara, why she never tried to bring me back again.'

'Richard must have guessed eventually, because he sent Flynn away in disgrace six months ago.'

'Right when Ma's letters turned so morbid.'

'The saddest thing,' Lila said, 'is that it took Nerissa so many months to go after him.'

'She'd already spent a lifetime trapped on this island with her own father, trapped with Irene, trapped by a baby, trapped in a marriage, trapped by a will, trapped by her promise to *me* ...' Tally inclined her head, the scales falling – *finally* – from her eyes.

'The bottled-up mermaid.'

She reached into her backpack for the scroll – and Lila's inheritance. She handed it over to Lila with an immense exhalation.

'And now, she's free.'

CHAPTER 36

HAPPY HOUR

Eyrie, five days later ...

Tally thought she might go crazy before the rescue party finally returned. It was late afternoon, and they were only hours out now, according to the lone runner sent well ahead of the party.

He had come barrelling into the lodge's makeshift command centre that morning, sweating and panting, declaring to the large contingent already gathered that there was one body, two prisoners and an injured patient coming down the mountain behind him with the police and volunteers.

Tally was thankful to be standing behind the reception desk when this declaration was made, for her knees had buckled.

'*Who's* dead?' she cried, gripping the desk as though her life depended on it. 'Tell me! *Who?*'

It was Mr Ramsey. They had found him at the bottom of that steep ravine, with catastrophic knife wounds. Neither fall nor stabbing would have been survivable on their own, much less together.

It might so easily have been Tally, if not for him. Richard Ramsey *had* given her life, in the end. When numb shock passed, she would weep for him as the only father she had ever known.

For now, her thoughts were on just one man. Though she had wrung every drop of information she could get out of the forerunner about Drew, she still would not allow her heart to accept that he was safe until she felt his pulse with her own hand.

The day after Tally's rescue, an additional team with more medical aid had followed. Tally had been unable to insert herself in that one, either, even though they could see she was completely recovered; she'd even had half a night's sleep. Ridiculous.

There was nothing Tally could do to bring him more quickly down that mountain.

Knowing Drew was close had slowed the hands of the ship's-wheel clock to such an interminable pace, she had begun to shout obscenities at it. The more colourful the better.

'Your *mouth* would make a parrot blush,' chastised Lila.

Lila was growing more confidently into her big-sister role as every hour dragged by, especially since Irene had vanished from Dara four nights ago, taking only what she could carry onto a dinghy. The daughters of Dara were now motherless together in every sense.

'How else can I make the time pass quicker?' Tally despaired. 'I've run out of ways to occupy myself.'

'Go and clean a treehouse,' Lila said. God knew they needed every fresh room they could get, what with the ever-growing crowd of volunteers converging on Dara.

No, the treehouses were too far away from the action. Tally had been encamped in the lodge every day of her vigil.

She had tried to keep herself busy with her work. The story of the *Lady Lily* and its cover-up would be the biggest one she'd ever written for the *Cairns Ledger*. And the last, at least for a while ...

After this, she and Lila had much work to do remaking Mermaid Bay Resort in their mother's image. It should be *all* about the ambience, they'd already agreed to that.

Tally had raised a few rum cocktails with Jonathon before he'd departed, in commiseration for the career she was putting on hold, indefinitely.

'You can always come back to work for me,' Jonathon had assured her, throwing back liquid melancholy as quickly as she. 'And in the meantime, I'll take any stories you can find down here.'

She was grateful for the open door, for every possibility straining to unfurl. Tally thought she might even like to work for herself one day. She'd had the wicked idea of starting a community magazine in Bellen Beach. Wouldn't be a patch on the *Cairns Ledger*, and she would always miss the pace and variety of a big-city newspaper, but she thought she could sniff out stories no matter where she was. Take those jokers, for instance, who thought they could mine *her* reef.

Maisie was the thing Tally would miss most about her life in Cairns – top of the list. Her dear friend had come all the way to Dara to hand-deliver a letter from Ma that had arrived at their Freshwater cottage only days ago.

Ma's letter, dated the night before her disappearance but posted after it, was still in Tally's pocket, read a hundred times already. It was the goodbye letter she had wanted; the cool hand laid on the back of her neck...

My Tally Ho,
When you get this, I will be well on my way
to a place I do not yet know. You will be very
angry with me, and hurt, but in time I hope
you'll begin to understand. Please do not come
charging after me. I am safe, prepared and
determined.
Tally, I have escaped Dara.

For almost four decades, I have been bound to this island. Beholden to my papa's selfish whims, my husband's control and my daughter's right to inheritance. But trapped, most of all, by my own lies and cowardice.

Twice now, I have let the man I love sail away from me.

It is not too late for me to go after him.

You will storm home to fight your father for Dara; I cannot see any way around it. I never could. For a lifetime, Tally, you have believed yourself the sole future custodian of Dara. I'm sorry that I could never tell you the truth: there was another little girl, before you, who rightfully deserves Dara. A girl who never knew me as her true mother, but who might in time come to accept her birthright.

You will find her in Papa's chapel. She has everything that you, and Dara, need to tide you over.

You asked my forgiveness once, for seeking your freedom.

I can only ask the same of you.

I have to find my Bluebird . . .

Ma

Maisie had stayed on after delivering this missive, and was by Tally's side now, holding a ladder for her against the wall of reception.

Death-staring the ship's-wheel clock had reminded Tally that Richard's ghastly turtle shells hung alongside should come down as a matter of urgency. They were obscene, and not at all in keeping with the new Mermaid Bay.

Lila approved this activity with a pleased nod. 'That ought to keep you busy for at least a few minutes.'

It was certainly giving Tally, atop her ladder, more reasons to swear and gripe.

She didn't hear the commotion outside the lodge door over the sound of her own raging. Missed the noisy hiccup before a communal intake of breath, a sudden falling quiet. Did not catch the looks passing between Lila and Maisie at the bottom of her ladder.

It was *his* voice that stopped the torrent of foul words at her lips …

'A downpipe still seems more your style.'

She spun around, hammer dropping.

Drew was standing below her, though he *couldn't* be.

Her eyes roamed madly over him, crying *truth*.

There were two men standing on either side of him, with the readiness of bodyguards poised to catch him if he fell. But with the help of wooden crutches, he *was* standing; his whole foot strapped and wrapped in some complicated way. He was sunburnt, wind-chapped, sling-bound, rumpled and dishevelled, daubed with all kinds of lotions and bandages.

Tally felt the burning upswell preceding a sob, and knew it was going to be a washout when she let go of this one.

She nodded at his leg. 'I see you're well on your way to a peg leg.'

'*You're* the pirate.' There was a quaver in his voice.

She hurried down the ladder to stand before him. There didn't seem to be one unblemished inch of him. She looked helplessly at him through tears, wanting to plead if she might touch him and how, but her throat had closed.

'Oh, cat-burglar, my cat-burglar,' Drew said, 'our fearful trip is done.'

EPILOGUE

Eyrie, one year later …

Drew's sleeping embrace was a warm ocean Tally was, as ever, loath to leave. She disentangled herself with the stoicism of one who knew she had the same to return to that night, and every night after it. She patted Drew's nice sleeping face, and his nice sleeping bottom, and rose to dress for the day.

Swimsuit and shorts, aviators propped on her head, fraying shell bracelet at her tanned wrist, bare feet.

The hallway was quiet as she slipped out of their bedroom and went towards the stairs. Lila's door lay wide open, her suite within impeccably clean, and Lila herself long gone from it. Mermaid Bay's steadfast owner-manager was down at her post by sunbreak each day.

Tally did not tarry for breakfast; she would share her usual late brunch with Lila, after the morning rush was done.

She hurried through the clean-swept, cobbled pathways of the treehouses, over the twinkling suspension bridge, past the staff village turn-off and down to the lodge.

Through the wide windows at reception, she glimpsed Lila's golden-brown head bent earnestly over the day's manifest. Not an *i* would be left undotted, nor a *t* uncrossed. They might be joint proprietors, but

Lila was the manageress Tally could never be; Lila's plans for Mermaid Bay, and Dara, more wonderful than Tally and Ma had ever dreamed up together.

Behind Lila's head at reception, was a colourful display of pinned postcards, featuring islands upon islands and Ma's delicate penmanship on the back. Each postcard addressed in just the same way ...

Delila and Thalia, my dearest girls.

Tally paused now for her habitual moment of gratitude: for the rightness of Dara's lost heiress found; the joy of a *sister* gained; the happiness of a mother freed.

Thank you, for this life.

With an ache in her chest, she went on towards Coral Beach, passing under the 'welcome' arch, thoughts moving ahead to her own office at the very end of the jetty in Ma's observatory. Tally had never written so well in all her life as she did over water. Just ask Jonathon, who, true to his word, had kept a regular weekly column for his beloved Island Girl Reporter.

Tally would begin work as she did each day, eagerly snaffling the newspapers from the skipper of the Dara Island ferry, to devour with two strong cups of coffee at Ma's desk. She couldn't wait to read today's *Ledger* and her latest exposé.

As Tally came out onto the jetty into the gold-lit and lustrous morning, she realised the ferry was docked already, a half-hour too early.

Only that couldn't be so – it wasn't the right shape, size or colour for the ferry, and there was no crowd disembarking, just two coming up the gangplank together: a petite woman, one arm crooked high, holding a hat to her head, and with her a very tall man.

Coral rolled and tinkled below the jetty as Tally stood motionless and stared, trying to make sense of it.

The cry splintered from Tally's mouth in the same instant she realised her feet were moving beneath her. She was thundering down the jetty, driftwood hair streaming behind her, arms flung wide …

'*Bluebird!*'

ACKNOWLEDGEMENTS

Dara Island, although a fictious island, is based on the magnificent tropical islands of Far North Queensland, including Green Island, Fitzroy Island, Dunk Island, Bedarra Island, Michaelmas Cay, Low Isles, Pelorus Island, Hinchinbrook Island, and Double Island and neighbouring Scout Hat.

Thanks to my family's tourism work, I spent so much of my childhood on these idyllic islands and the Great Barrier Reef. How *lucky* I was to have had such a paradise for my weekend playground. I was only a girl, snorkelling on Green Island, when I first decided to write about a trapped mermaid and her underwater observatory. A tiny idea that spawned a whole novel as I grew up.

To my beloved mum and dad, thank you for planting us in gorgeous Cairns, gateway to the Great Barrier Reef, and for raising us as tourism industry brats.

My huge, heartfelt gratitude to my fabulous agent, Selwa Anthony, for championing my novels. You always see through the weeds and reeds of my early drafts to the story I'm *really* trying to tell – and help me write my way back to it. Thank you, Selwa (and Linda!) for supporting me every step, and word, of the way.

A trillion thank-yous to the amazing team of Echo Publishing – Juliet Rogers, Diana Hill, Emily Banyard, Cherie Baird and Kaarina Allen – for bringing my stories to their best and then to bookshelves, with such care, kindness and belief in me. My deepest thanks to Bonnier Books UK for taking my novels to the world.

My brilliant editor, Alexandra Nahlous, it has been a dream come true to work with you again on *Mistress*. Thank you for bringing your absolute magic to my manuscript.

I have the most sublime covers, thanks to the astonishing talent and vision of Louisa Maggio.

I first started writing Tally when I was only nineteen years old myself, and as I wrote her again in 2022–23, I often felt I was raising a third teenage daughter. Growing Tally up – and getting this book *out* of me – cost many tears, tantrums (mine, as much as Tally's) and sleepless nights, and I simply couldn't have managed it without my very dearest cheerleader and Bossiest Beta Reader, Kate DiGiuseppe.

Big hugs to Karen Trenorden and Ally Thurstans for beta reading my manuscript at short notice, and for being treasured friends and fellow booklovers.

To my precious friend Paula, who always reads the last pages first, thank you for the many debriefs over long coffee/op-shopping dates.

Thank you to Lucy, for saving my sanity every second Tuesday, and for serendipitously arriving to talk about the Hinchinbrook Island trek on the very day I sat down to start writing it.

I'm so grateful to my fantastic in-laws for their splendid stories of growing up in Cairns. I owe the pet emu in Freshwater and the plucky under-bridge swims to Vicki Kenny, and I was greatly inspired by Des Kenny's stories of his time in the Ellis Beach Surf Life Saving Club as a young man. The club's colourful past is extensively documented in

Carol Libke's book *Ellis Beach, Our Club*: *The History of Ellis Beach Surf Life Saving Club 1957–2007*.

Thank you, Cara and Adam Kenny, for taking us bareboating through the Whitsunday Islands; for pina coladas with a dance, and a safe mooring in strong winds.

My heart bursts with gratitude for my readers all across the world. Your messages, reviews, posts and letters mean everything to me. Thank you for sharing your love for my novels.

Can I thank a beach? I'm going to thank a beach. Mission Beach, the most beautiful of all – thank you for being *our* happy place.

And above all, thank you Team Kenny – Liam, Dash, Aurora, Eleanor and Teddy. Special thanks, my intrepid family, for testing out various plot points for me: kayaking to Scout's Hat; escaping flooded campsites in the dark night; helicoptering to Dunk Island; finding secret, romantic waterfalls; hiking mountains and running marathons; spearfishing delectable crayfish for our dinner; exploring cyclone-ravaged, deserted islands; spotting manta rays and crocodiles in the wild; twisting ankles, and surviving stinging trees and mango allergies and snake encounters and tropical infections. Life with you six is definitely stranger, and infinitely more wonderful, than fiction …

x Averil

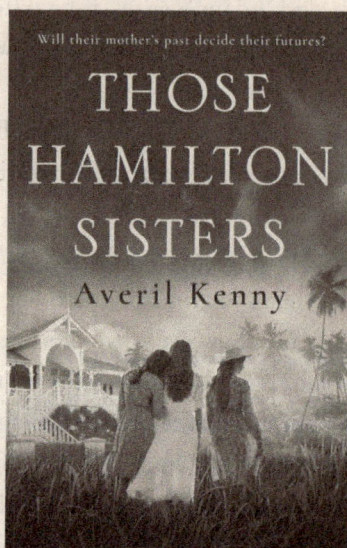

And her sweeping historical story of family,
secrets and small town mystery . . .

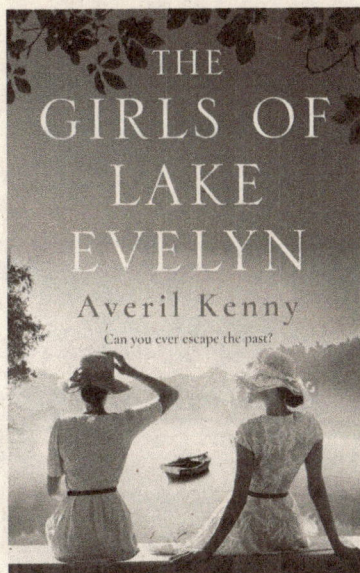

THE
GIRLS OF
LAKE
EVELYN

Averil Kenny

Can you ever escape the past?

1958. When it-girl Vivienne George flees on the eve of her wedding she seeks
refuge in a scheduled lodge surrounded by the lush rainforest of tropical North
Queensland. There, she is relieved to find that the small farming town couldn't
be further from the high society she's left behind.

Now, Vivienne spends her days swimming in beautiful Lake Evelyn
where she befriends the larger-than-life Josie. But all is not as it seems
in this quiet, close-knit community.

Vivienne soon learns that over a decade earlier, Celeste Starr, a beautiful actress,
died tragically in the lake's dark waters, spawning a curse that has plagued the
girls of the town ever since.

Fascinated by Celeste's tale, Josie decides to stage a play about her death,
with Vivienne in the lead role, setting off a chain of disturbing events . . .

Available now